A FAR JUSTICE

A FAR JUSTICE

A novel

RICHARD HERMAN

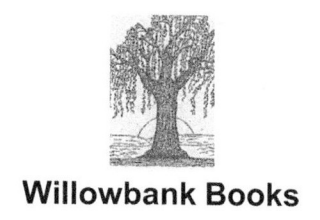

Willowbank Books

SECOND EDITION
2024

Originally published by
Willowbank Books

A FAR JUSTICE. Copyright © 2010 by Richard Herman, Jr. All rights reserved. No part of this book may be reproduced, stored in a retrieval system, or transmitted by any means without the written permission of the author except in the case of brief quotations embodied in critical articles and reviews.

This is a work of fiction and all characters, incidents, and dialogues are a product of the author's imagination and are used fictitiously. Any resemblance to actual persons, living or dead, places, or events, is entirely coincidental.

Published as an original eBook by Lume Books.
Cover art and design by Maria O'Neil Consulting.

Also by
Richard Herman

The Price of Mercy
(writing as Dick Herman)
The China Sea
The Trash Haulers
The Peacemakers
Caly's Island
(writing as Dick Herman)
The Last Phoenix
The Trojan Sea
Edge of Honor
Against All Enemies
Power Curve
Iron Gate
Dark Wing
Call to Duty
Firebreak
Force of Eagles
The Warbirds

In memoriam
Janice Hayes Perkinson
whose friendship and wisdom
made this possible.

"Law stands mute in the midst of arms."
                                                Cicero

Prologue

Saudi Arabia

Gus Tyler stood in the dark and took a deep drag on the cigarette, ratcheting up the flood of nicotine and caffeine coursing through his body. A line from Shakespeare came to him. "O! withered is the garland of war." It seemed the right thing to say.

Where had he first heard it? *Oh, yeah,* he thought. *That time Clare sweet-talked me into seeing 'As You Like It' at the Shakespeare Festival in Ashland.* He had been a fan of Old Will ever since. He couldn't remember what came next so he fast-forwarded a few lines. "And there is nothing left remarkable beneath the visiting moon." On cue, an almost full moon filled a break in the overcast. He reached out and held it in his hand, only to slowly crunch it in his fist, willing it into darkness. He opened his hand and it was still there, hanging in the cloudy night sky.

The war was exactly forty hours old.

A sergeant bounced out of the bunkered entrance into the command post. "Sir, Colonel Cannon is looking for you."

Gus Tyler stubbed out his cigarette. *These things are going to kill you.* He marched back into the command post, leaving the moon to watch over the airbase at Al Kharj.

The wing commander, Colonel Jim Cannon, was on the secure line in the glassed-in mission control cab, and waved Gus to come inside. At thirty-one years of age, Captain August "Gus" Tyler was the best of Cannon's pilots, a true combat leader and at the top of his game. He was lean and stood exactly six feet tall. He had a full head of dark hair cut short, and his brown eyes were close-set. He had the required straight teeth and crooked grin required of all fighter pilots, and could have served as a poster boy for the tactical Air Force. Women considered him very attractive but he had no trouble refusing the not infrequent offers for a few innings of extramarital sport that came his way. He was on the promotion list for early promotion to major but hadn't pinned on his bronze oak leaves yet, which to his way of thinking was a good thing. Field grade officers flew desks, not jets. Gus Tyler was a happily married man doing exactly what he wanted to do – flying the F-15E Strike Eagle.

Cannon mouthed the words "Black Hole" as he listened on the phone. The Black Hole was the name given to the Special Planning Group in Riyadh that directed the air campaign to help drive the Iraqis out of Kuwait. "How many jets?" Cannon asked. He listened for a moment. "You got it." He punched off the connection.

"Gus, Saddam's trying to extract his army and they don't want the bastards to regroup north of the Euphrates. The Iraqis have got the mother of all convoys moving north out of Kuwait City. We told the Saddamites that anyone movin' in a military formation is a legitimate target, and only deserters on foot would be safe. But they don't seem to believe us."

"Their brains haven't kicked in or they're slow learners," Gus said.

"Both," Cannon replied. "Latest count shows over a thousand vehicles beating feet north out of Kuwait City. The Black Hole wants us to bomb the livin' hell out of the bastards. You want it?"

"That's why we're here."

"Just remember what they did to a lot of innocent women and children in Kuwait. That should put some hate in your heart. Who you want on your wing?"

"Skid, with Woody in his backseat."

"You got 'em. And in your pit?"

"Toby."

"Who else? He hates flying with Armiston and will wet himself at the thought of doing something productive. I think he's in mission planning. You and Skid launch ASAP and bottle 'em up while I get jets coming your way." Cannon's eyes followed Gus as he walked quickly out of the command post. He took a deep breath and looked at the master clock on the wall. It was exactly 22:04 hours, February 25, 1991.

"Shit oh dear, Gus," he murmured. "Do it right. This is gonna be a biggy."

A Far Justice

Mutlah Ridge, Kuwait

The Belgian's knuckles turned white as he clenched the truck's steering wheel and stared into the dark. He strained to see the tank carrier they were following, and desperately wanted to turn on the headlights to avoid another rear-end collision with the huge, low-bed vehicle transporting a T-72 main battle tank. But the Iraqi sergeant had made it very clear what would happen if he did that, or delayed the convoy because of another accident. "How much farther, Hassan?"

The young Palestinian sitting next to him clicked on his penlight to check the odometer and study the map. "Six kilometers to the border." Hassan held the map for the Belgian to see. The Belgian's heart raced. Six kilometers – just under four miles to the promise of a new, and very rich life. Not that Hassan knew what was in the truck. For some reason, that was important to the European. They were almost there.

The Belgian reached out and held Hassan's hand near the instrument panel, directing the penlight onto the temperature gauge. It was almost pegged, all because of the collision. The radiator had been pushed back onto the electrical cooling fan, creating a horrendous scraping noise. Luckily, the radiator was still intact but he had to disconnect the fan before it did further damage. As long as they kept moving at a decent pace, they didn't need it. He listened with a trained ear to the diesel engine of the big truck and gave silent thanks it was a Caterpillar. No one made better diesels than the Americans.

The tank carrier loomed up in front of them and the Belgian stomped on the brakes, dragging the heavily loaded truck to a grinding halt inches short of the stopped vehicle. "What now?" the Belgian muttered. Hassan switched on the hand-held radio the sergeant had stolen from the Kuwaitis. Arabic filled the cab. "I didn't understand that," the Belgian said.

"There's an airplane in the area," Hassan explained. They waited.

Panic ripped at the European. "Go!" he shouted at the huge truck in front of them, pounding the steering wheel in frustration. He knew the temperature gauge was off the scale. In front of them, the tank's auxiliary motor hummed as the turret slewed around, pointing the 125mm cannon to the southeast and to their deep right.

"There!" Hassan shouted. Well to the east, the distinctive rocket plumes of two surface-to-air missiles reached up and streaked towards an unseen aircraft. Two explosions marked their target. "Allah be praised!" Hassan shouted, his voice filled with triumph. "They got the kafir." The tank carrier started to move, but the tank's cannon didn't return to the aft travel position. Instead, it swung around and pointed in the direction they were going, to the north and safety. The Belgian eased the shift lever forward and slowly let out the clutch. The cannon fired and the tank carrier rocked from the recoil as the radio exploded with shouting voices.

"What are they firing at!" the Belgian shouted.

"The plane!" Hassan shrieked. "They keep missing!" More tracers cut the dark sky. Suddenly, three explosions at the head of the miles long convoy ripped the night apart. Then a fourth, much larger explosion pounded at them. Again, the tank carrier slammed to a stop, and again, the Belgian was barely able to stop in time. Now the tank was firing a round every 10 seconds. "There it is!" Hassan screamed. "There! There!" He pointed to their left at a low-flying shadow. Then it was gone, hiding in the night. Seconds later, the rear of the convoy erupted in a red cloud closely followed by three rolling explosions. The Belgian's head twisted around and he caught the distinctive shape of a jet fighter as it pulled off its bomb run. Tracers from the convoy reached out but crossed far behind the jet. More voices were yelling over the radio.

"What are they saying?" the Belgian demanded.

"The kafir bombed both ends of the convoy!" Hassan shouted, his panic matching that on the radio. "We're trapped!"

"Get out!" the Belgian ordered. He kicked his door open and the dome light came on. He bailed out of the cab.

The sergeant was there, waving his AK47. "Get back inside!" There was no doubt he was going to pull the trigger and the European scrambled back into the cab. The Iraqi stared at the two men, not sure what to do with the Belgian. However, the Palestinian was not a problem. He hurried around to Hassan's side of the truck and jerked the door open. With a few well-practiced moves, he strapped Hassan's right wrist to the handgrip mounted on the dashboard with a plastic tie-tab. "If you want him to live, stay in the truck and drive."

A Far Justice

"Oh no," Hassan sobbed. He pointed to the head of the convoy with his free hand. Burning trucks highlighted the jet fighter as it rolled in for a bomb run, coming straight down the road and directly at them.

Panic ripped through the Belgian, and he threw a pocketknife at Hassan to cut the plastic tie-tab. "Get out!" He jumped out of the truck and rolled on the ground as the fighter roared directly overhead, two hundred feet above the ground and leaving a trail of bright flashing sparks in its wake. "Hurry!" he yelled at Hassan who was still fumbling with the knife, trying to open the closed blade. The Belgian scrambled on all fours and fell into a shallow depression as the twinkling, popping lights reached him. The flashing sparks were exploding grenade-size bomblets and the Belgian threw his arms over his head as a man-made hell washed over him. He felt a sharp pain as shrapnel cut his forearm. Then it was over. He raised his head. His truck was in engulfed in flames and he could see Hassan jerking at the plastic tie-tab, still trapped in the truck. It wasn't in an effort to escape but involuntary spasms as he slowly cooked. The tank fired a round at the jet and the Belgian's eyes followed the tracer into the sky. He saw the twin plumes of the fighter's engines as it climbed safely into the night.

"You fucking bastard!" he screamed. A killing rage coursed through his body and soul, and, for the first time in his life he truly hated.

1

Schiphol Airport, the Netherlands

Gus Tyler stood in the main concourse of Holland's international airport, a rock in the mainstream splitting the flow of humanity surging past him. He looked for the familiar face of his son, but Jason wasn't there.

An attractive young woman bumped into him and dropped her bag. "I'm so sorry," she said. Her breast brushed against his arm as he bent over to pick up her carry-on bag. "We were on the same plane," she murmured, obviously attracted to the tall and lanky American. At fifty years of age, Gus Tyler was still fit and possessed a full head of dark hair that was only now turning gray at the temples. He hadn't lost the straight teeth and crooked grin so characteristic of his generation of fighter pilots, and he could easily pass for forty.

He returned the smile, his eyes alive with amusement as he handed her the bag. He was being hit on and it was a welcomed ego stroke. "Right. You reminded me of my daughter at first." She blushed at the gentle brush-off and pushed past him. He picked up his old green Air Force B4 bag and followed her, still looking for Jason.

A pretty young woman, heavy-set with short blonde hair and big blue eyes, was holding a sign with his name. "Colonel Tyler?" she called. He waved and pushed through the crowd. She was not the type Jason usually dated, much less proposed to, and he was anxious to meet the woman who would soon be his daughter-in-law. "I'm Aly van der Nord," she said, extending her hand. "Jason had to work this evening. How was the flight?"

He dropped his bag and took her hand. Her grip was firm and strong, not the least bit feminine, and he liked her serious nature. "You would not believe." His flight out of Sacramento on Monday afternoon had been cancelled and he had been endlessly delayed by weather and more flight cancellations. He had finally reached JFK in New York where a helpful ticket agent suggested he fly into Holland rather than Belgium. KLM had done the rest and even booked him on the train from Schiphol to Brussels. "It's very kind of you to meet me."

She picked up his bag with an easy motion. "When you were delayed, Jason couldn't make it. He has to lead the honor guard for a ceremony with the general." His son was a technical sergeant assigned to the Air Force Security Forces detachment at SHAPE, Supreme Headquarters Allied Powers Europe, in Belgium, and the general was SACEUR, the Supreme Allied Commander Europe. "So I jumped at the chance." She led the way down the main concourse. "If you want, you can stay with us tonight and Jason will drive up tomorrow. He's scheduled for a week's leave. Or I can drive you down to Casteau tonight. It's about a three-hour drive, depending on the traffic."

Gus did the math. It would be after midnight when they arrived. "I am pooped," he admitted.

Aly smiled and Gus felt much better. "Good. It will be a chance to meet my parents and they want to show you our farm. How is Mrs. Tyler doing?"

"Not too good, I'm afraid. The quacks thought it was multiple sclerosis at first, but now think it is a rare form of lupus."

"Jason told me," was all she said.

For some reason, Gus completely trusted the young Dutchwoman. "Did he tell you about Michelle?" Michelle was their oldest child and had never married. It took time to explain how happy she was and what two great twin boys she was raising.

"Jason is very proud of his sister." She gave him an easy smile. "Things like that don't matter anymore."

Jason has a winner here, Gus thought.

Outside, a cold North Sea wind whipped at them as they hurried to her car. Suddenly, Aly stopped. "This is embarrassing," she said in a low voice.

For a moment, Gus didn't understand and only saw three people huddled together against the cold, blocking the sidewalk. Then he saw the banner. "I don't read Dutch, but it looks like they've got the beak about the US."

"The beak?"

"It's an old slang expression for when someone is angry."

Aly laughed. "I like that. Don't worry about them, they're harmless." She walked straight toward the small group without fear. They politely stepped aside and cleared a path.

Then he saw the man holding a poster. His face was a mass of burn scars and his ears and lips were gone. Plastic surgery had reconstructed part of his nose but the fingers on his right hand were stumps. Only his eyes were normal. The two men stared at one another as if they had met long ago but couldn't remember where or when. *This guy is straight out of hell,* Gus thought. The man held the poster up. The words

U.S. WAR CRIMES IN IRAQ - 1991

were written in black and splattered with red paint drops to represent blood. The man saw Gus's reaction and spun the poster around.

HIGHWAY OF DEATH

was printed in bold letters over the famous photo of the charred head of a dead Iraq soldier staring at the cameraman. Slowly, the man brought the poster next to his face. In the half-light of the street the two merged, and the poster became a dark mirror into the past. Gus froze, unable to move as the ghosts of war surged out of their walled niche, demanding their freedom. Silence bound the two men. "You were there?" Gus finally asked.

The man's mouth cracked into an open slit. "Yes, I was there." His words were soft and sad.

Gus didn't believe him. "Was it bombers?"

There was no anger or hurt in the apparition's words, only a melancholy echo. "I don't think so. It was night and I couldn't tell. At first, there was only one airplane. It flew very low and bombed the trucks in front. Then it maneuvered very quickly to bomb the rear of the convoy and trapped us. It came back one more time and flew down the highway, dropping its death. More planes came later. I tried to run away but couldn't hide in the desert. I dug a hole but they found me."

"Come," Aly said, taking charge and bringing Gus back to the present.

"Have a nice day," the man said as they walked away.

"You mustn't let it upset you," Aly said. "They all claim to be victims to get money from the state. He has told the lie so often he believes it himself."

Gus stared straight ahead. "He was there."

Paris, France

Henri Scullanois sat at his desk in Le salon de la rotonde, his office in the Quai d'Orsay, the high temple of French foreign policy. His face was expressionless but he was pleased with the thick, elegantly bound document on his desk. The title said it all.

An Investigation into
United States War Crimes In Iraq,
March 19, 2003 to January 20, 2009

The name was underneath the title in smaller type.

Denise Du Milan
Prosecutor
International Criminal Court

France's investment in the United Nation's International Criminal Court in the Hague had finally paid dividends, and Denise Du Milan, the court's newly appointed prosecutor, had accomplished a near miracle. Somehow, she had triggered an investigation and overcame the inherent prejudices of the court's Pre-Trial Division. The presiding judge hated women, another judge detested the French, and the third disliked people in general. But she had made a compelling case for the "reasonable basis" required by the Rome Statute that had created the International Criminal Court. He sensed the hand of Denise's husband, Chrestien Du Milan, at work in the background, busily pulling strings and calling in past favors.

He considered Chrestien Du Milan a fool, a dilettante who still played the old-fashioned game of sex and politics. But as Scullanois's wife, Renée, had cautioned, Chrestien Du Milan was a force in French politics that could not be ignored and that a political liaison was in order. That was her shorthand way of telling Scullanois she was sleeping with Du Milan. His intercom buzzed. "Minister," his secretary said, "Madam Prosecutor Du Milan is here."

"Please show her right in," Scullanois said. He stood in front of his desk and the historical grandeur of the room engulfed him. Sunlight streamed through the large bay windows at his back, backlighting the Minister of Foreign Affairs with a halo. His secretary escorted Denise Du Milan through the massive double doors and quickly withdrew. As always, Scullanois tried to stand more erect when he saw Denise. She was tall and thin with a wild mane of dark auburn hair gathered at the back of her neck. At thirty-six, she was considered one of the most beautiful women in France and fashion magazines were acutely interested in whatever she was wearing. It was an expense Chrestien Du Milan gladly bore.

They ritually bussed each other's cheeks, and Scullanois motioned to the two exquisite antique chairs by the bay windows "The court's approval of your petition for investigation has astounded us all. And someday, you must tell me how you deal with the Dutch. They are so, ah, so boringly bored."

She gave him a ravishing smile. "The Dutch can be a bit provincial. Thank God the court is more cosmopolitan. Fortunately, everyone on the court fully understands the need to bring the Americans to justice, especially after the wretched Iraqi affair."

Scullanois carefully considered his next words and relied on Renée's advice. "I have tried to seek a common ground and return them to the community of nations, but I have not been successful. They are so full of themselves – and dismissive of all others as they blunder through the world. They cannot ignore us as if we were small, willful children."

Denise arched an eyebrow. Chrestien had said the same thing the evening before, and although she hadn't asked, she suspected that he had been with Scullanois's wife. The coincidence was too much and she was certain that Scullanois was also playing the old game of sex and politics. While she accepted that as part of life, something deep inside rebelled and demanded a little payback. But that would have to wait. "They are a culture of the moment, and now they use globalization as a weapon. Truly, it is the new American colonialism, and they are incapable of thinking beyond the next quarterly balance sheet." Her voice rang with the same clarity that made her a force in the courtroom. But more importantly, the very inflection of her tone captured the genetic codes buried deep in the language that defined the French psyche.

"Your investigation could not have come at a more opportune moment," the foreign minister said. He waited to see if she understood the political ramifications of her investigation.

She did. "You are, of course, referring to the United States' feeble efforts in the United Nations to stop the Chinese from re-establishing their sovereignty over Taiwan."

"Chinese patience is at an end," Scullanois said. "They are preparing to use military force if necessary. Their preparations should be complete by the first of the year. Of course, the United States is trying to use the UN to constrain China. We are ready to support the United States in the Security Council, if they become a member of the International Criminal Court."

"Which will never happen," Denise added. "They claim it would subject their military to our jurisdiction in any conflict beyond their borders." She allowed a tight smile. "Which it would."

Scullanois came to the heart of the matter. "If you can bring an American to trial for war crimes, it will offer us an opportunity to establish an alliance with China. It will convince the Chinese that their interests are our interests. How better to do this than by embarrassing the United States in the court of world opinion and allowing China to regain Taiwan? We can change the orientation of China away from the United States and towards France. This can open economic windows that we can build into a greater Franco-Sino axis."

"But all this would be in violation of the constitution of the EU," Denise said, touching on a subject best avoided by mere mortals. But they were above those constraints.

Scullanois answered in a low voice. "Then the European Union must not learn of it. Unfortunately, the minister of justice tells me there are, ah, other 'legal' difficulties with your inves- tigation."

"There is a jurisdictional problem," she replied. "We can only try an individual from a country that is a member of the court."

"A major difficulty as the United States is not a member," he allowed.

"The Americans allow this foolishness called 'dual citizenship.' We must find an American soldier who was born in a country that recognizes this dual citizenship and is also a member of the court. Of course, he must have fought in the Iraqi war and killed at least one civilian."

Scullanois thought for a moment. "But considering the American position on the court, imprisoning one of their citizens is politically unthinkable."

A whisper of a smile flickered across her lips. She believed that the current president of the United States was a fool and she was more than willing to challenge him. "We have a narrow win- dow to act while the United States is occupied by the Taiwan crisis. As long as the Americans need Europe's support in the United Nations, they will not risk our anger by challenging the court's jurisdiction. We can extend that window by delaying in the United Nations."

Scullanois thought for a moment. "Can the court act fast enough?"

"With the proper help, it can." She stressed the word "help."

"Brilliant," Scullanois said. He wanted to ask her about Chrestien's role in all this but thought better of it. There might be some hidden costs he had not considered. However, he was confident Renée would find out and tell him. The image of a naked Denise waiting in a bed flashed in his mind's eye. He considered making an offer, but dropped it. "I'm quite sure our bureaus can identify at least a dozen or so names and, ah, provide all the required 'help' the court will require. Of course, our role in all this must remain secret to avoid complications with the EU." He thought for a moment. "But taking one of these people into custody may be a problem."

"Americans love to travel," she replied. "I'm quite sure something will present itself."

"I will speak to the prime minister this morning."

Denise leaned forward. "I can move forward on a moment's notice."

NATO Headquarters, Belgium

Aly held onto Gus's arm as they walked down the quiet halls of NATO's headquarters, and she was proud to be part of his family.

Gus and Jason had spent five wonderful days on her family's farm and the two big Americans had done yeoman labor helping her father build a new barn to breed and raise pigs. Her mother had repeatedly commented on how they looked more like brothers than father and son, and Aly suspected that her mother had a crush on the elder Tyler. But who could blame her? Now Gus was wearing his new uniform and was going to administer the oath to Jason so he could re-enlist. Aly van der Nord overcame the no-nonsense part of her Dutch nature and decided she loved her future father-in-law.

The man waiting for them was a younger, but much bigger and more muscular version of Gus. "We're doing it in SACEUR's conference room," Jason told them. "The general is going to be there." He held the door and led them down the hall. "I believe you know General Hammerly." General Douglas Hammerly, US Army, was the new Supreme Allied Commander Europe.

"I met Doug during the Persian Gulf war in Saudi Arabia when he was an up-and-coming major. They called him 'the Hammer' then."

"We still do," Jason admitted. "What the general wants, the general gets. We've got a videophone so Mom and Michelle can watch."

"That's super," Gus said, feeling not quite so guilty. He had been away far too long and it was time he returned home. They entered the conference room where the video camera was set up and six other security cops were waiting. An airman dialed Sacramento and Michelle's voice came over the loudspeaker. "We're all here," Gus's daughter said, "and Mom can hear and see you all."

"Hi, Hon," Gus said. "I'm catching a flight out of Schiphol tonight and should be home tomorrow."

"Mom says she'll be here," Michelle replied.

General Hammerly came through the side door that led to his office and extended his hand. "Gus Tyler. It has been a while."

"1991," Gus said, recalling the time they had first met.

Hammerly smiled at Jason. "Well, shall we do it?"

Jason nodded and stood in front of the American flag while the airman handed Gus the enlistment oath to read. Gus joined his son and they raised their right hands. Gus started to read. "I, Jason Tyler, do solemnly swear that I will support and defend the Constitution of the United States against all enemies, foreign and domestic . . ."

Aly listened as Jason repeated the oath. She chanced a glance at the general and saw the resolve in his eyes, the set of his jaw.

Gus's voice swelled. "That I will bear true faith and allegiance to the same . . ."

Aly studied the men and understood. They were a band of brothers.

Schipol Airport

Aly guided her small car to the curb outside the departure terminal. "Right on time." She leaned over and kissed his cheek. She felt an overpowering urge to say "I love you," but her Dutch sensibility squashed that urge with a more formal, "Give my regards to your family."

"Thank your folks again for me. It's been great, and I can hardly wait for the wedding."

Then he was gone, walking into the terminal. A security guard motioned her to leave, but she hesitated, unable to take her eyes off his back. She blinked twice when two men wearing uniforms closed in on Gus and grabbed his arms, forcing him to drop his suitcase. One quickly slapped handcuffs on his wrists as three more men wearing dark overcoats surrounded him. Aly jumped out of the car and ran into the terminal. "What are you doing?" she shouted in Dutch. "Who are you?" Aly van der Nord was a big woman and she charged into the group, pushing one of the civilians aside. She folded her arms and planted her feet, blocking the way. "Answer my question!" One of the uniformed men jerked an aerosol canister from his belt and sprayed her in the face while one of the men wearing an overcoat kicked at the back of her left knee. Pain ripped up her leg as she fell to the floor choking and crying. "Who are you?" she coughed as the men hustled Gus out the door and into a waiting van. She tried to stand, but her knee collapsed under her weight and she sat on the floor. A woman rushed up to her. "Are you all right?"

Aly rubbed her knee and grimaced with pain. "I don't know." She took two deep breaths as she sat on the floor. "Do you have a cell phone I may use?" The woman fumbled in her handbag and fished out a phone. Aly's blunt fingers punched at the buttons, dialing Jason's number. It seemed an eternity before he answered. "Jason, your father was arrested." She paused to catch her breath. "We're at the airport." Another pause. "No, I don't know who it was."

The woman standing over her said, "The uniforms. I think it was the Maréchausée."

Aly relayed the information. "It was our constabulary." She listened for a moment. "Yes, that's right, the Maréchausée. Do you know them?" Her eyes opened wide as Jason explained the powers of the Maréchausée. "No, he didn't resist. I did."

2

Georgetown, Washington D.C.

Reporters circled the sidewalk outside the elegant townhouse like vultures and hungrily noted the guests flowing into the cocktail party. Without exception, the arriving glitterati were the guiding lights, the lodestars of the capital; however, the denizens of the media went into an absolute feeding frenzy when Maximilian Westcot and his young and beautiful wife arrived. Westcot was acknowledged as the most rapacious financier and investor west of New York City, and one of the wealthiest men in the United States. It was rumored that not even his accountants, nor the IRS, knew exactly what he was worth.

Westcot was a bear of a man, short, stocky, and barrel-chested, all topped with heavy black hair. He also had the disposition of Grizzly and the reporters gave him a wide berth, focusing instead on his young wife. But not one was brave enough to label Suzanne a 'trophy wife.' Strange things happened to reporters who crossed Westcot, and no one wanted to be in the financier's crosshairs.

Inside, each guest went through the required rituals and established his, or her, own orbit in the ever-changing constellation of Washington's power elite. However, Max Westcot was content to stand back and be the impartial observer as orbits collided. In his own way, he was a very practical scientist and delighted in measuring the interplay of forces. When he applied his private calculus, for it was not a rational universe, he suppressed a laugh. Much to his satisfaction, the brightest star in the evening's sky was his wife, Suzanne, and the spectacular dress she was wearing. It had cost him twelve thousand dollars and was worth every cent.

The dress was a study in graceful simplicity and decorum. It was a classic off-the-shoulder floor-length gown that was not revealing in the least. Yet the material seemed to shimmer and take on a life of its own as it caressed her body. A substantial majority of men in the room, an exact quantity he had yet to determine, hoped there was nothing between it and Suzanne. Every woman in the room was certain of it. True to Westcot's principle of attract- tion, attention circled her like stray asteroids captured by the gravity of a sun, which was exactly what Westcot wanted. While he was at the party, he was not part of it. He was a comet, free to roam the evening sky.

A dark-suited young man smiled at him. "Sir, I'm Mr. James Weaver's personal assistant." Westcot arched a bushy eyebrow. He only knew James Weaver by reputation but in the galaxy of Washington politics, Weaver was the super nova of political operatives. He was rumored to be the President's political hit man and, under normal circumstances, only allowed out of his cage for elections. "Could you spare a moment?" Westcot nodded and followed him through the elegant rooms and up a back staircase that led to a study where an over-weight, nondescript middle-aged man with thinning dark hair was waiting. Only his bright blue eyes gave life to a placid exterior.

"Jim Weaver," the man said, extending his hand. They shook hands as Westcot took his measure. They exchanged pleasantries. Then, "The boys picked up some interesting message traffic. We thought you might be interested." He handed Westcot a mini CD player. Westcot sat down and plugged in the earpiece. His eyes narrowed and his face turned to granite as he listened. The "boys" were the National Security Agency and the message traffic was a series of intercepted phone calls between Henri Scullanois and his Chinese counterpart in Beijing. The conversations had been scrambled for transmission, but NSA had penetrated that particular system years before. "I'd say you are about to be rogered by the French."

"That will be a cold day in hell. Do you know how much I've invested in the Sudan?"

"Counting bribes and payoffs, we estimate over a billion dollars."

Westcot was not impressed with the accuracy of their intelligence. "That's in the Block Five oil concession alone."

"And the Chinese were your silent partner," Weaver added. "You bribe the rebels for protection, develop the oil independent of the government in Khartoum, ship it out through the port at Djibouti, and sell it to the Chinese."

"Why not? Khartoum takes eighty percent right off the top. The rebels are willing to settle for thirty percent."

"Our options are limited if the French close Djibouti on you. That would put the Frogs in the driver's seat with the rebels, or they could kiss and make up with Khartoum."

Westcot thought for a moment. "You may not have any options, but I do."

Weaver was certain of it. But would Westcot use them? He pushed a little harder to encourage him. "Regardless, the French definitely have their fingers in the pie."

Westcot's voice was low and hard. "Which I will cut off at the elbow." He returned the mini CD player. "May I keep this?"

Weaver nodded. He ejected the disk and handed it to Westcot. "It's been sanitized. Don't reveal the source." Westcot waited for the quid pro quo. "The President has a problem and would like your help. An old friend of yours, August Tyler, was arrested by the International Criminal Court."

Westcot arched an eyebrow. "Gus? I hadn't heard. We were roommates at the Air Force Academy."

"Happened yesterday evening in Holland. The details are sketchy but they're charging him Friday with war crimes committed during the Persian Gulf War in 1991."

"I assume the situation with China, Taiwan, and the UN is unchanged," Westcot said. Weaver nodded in answer. "So, the President can't do squat all about it."

Weaver put the best spin on it he could. "The President is not without options, and the State Department is pursuing Tyler's release through diplomatic channels."

"Right," Westcot scoffed. "But if he pushes too hard for Gus's release, he'll piss off our European allies something fierce, which will have a backlash in the UN when it comes to containing the Chinese."

"That's a fair assessment," Weaver conceded.

"So Gus gets hung out to dry," Westcot muttered. "Gus is one of the good guys. He doesn't deserve that. So what does the President want me to do?"

"Do whatever it takes to free him, short of starting a war."

"I thought you'd never ask."

Richard Herman

The Hague, the Netherlands

Denise looked up from her notes when the TV crew arrived. She nodded at the director and went back to work as they hooked up microphones in the recently completed main courtroom of the Palace of International Criminal Justice. Technically, the court was located a few kilometers north of The Hague in Scheveningen, a seaside resort. She could overlook that connection with fun in the sun but preferred not to think about the court's permanent home on the Alexanderkazerne, an old Dutch army base with its image of military tribunals. However, she thoroughly approved of the building's modern architecture, which she saw as a statement of the new world order and universal justice.

She spoke to the director to insure the cameras were all sighted on her. While the court proceedings would not be televised live, the tapes would be edited and available on the Internet soon after the session was concluded. She uncapped her OMAS fountain pen to sign the confinement order that would keep Gus in a cell during the trial. Deciding that would be premature, she recapped the pen.

Without thinking, her fingers absentmindedly wrapped around the pen and moved in a gentle stroking motion. She loved the elegant featherweight pen, with its faceted shape, deep burgundy color, and gold and platinum nib that was broken in to her handwriting. Chrestien had given her the pen when she had graduated from the Sorbonne fourteen years ago. But that was before they were married, and when he was simply an old friend of the family.

Two guards escorted Gus into the courtroom. Although she had reviewed his dossier and studied his photograph, this was the first time she had seen him in person and was struck by his rugged good looks. He was wearing a dark suit with a light blue shirt and striped tie that did not quite match. That bothered the Parisian in her soul. She watched as he stood in the dock and surveyed the courtroom. "You may sit down," she said. He glanced at her but remained standing. Instinctively, she compared him to the other men in the courtroom. He overshadowed the clerks and lawyers who inhabited the ICC. She smiled to herself. Isolation and confinement would soon change that.

She tried to listen when he spoke to his guards. Both smiled and one cast a glance in her direction. The grin on the guard's face quickly disappeared when he realized she was looking at him. She decided Tyler had made a crude male remark. It angered her that the guards obviously liked him. She made a mental note to have them replaced.

Unconsciously, she tossed her hair into place and adjusted the white bib court protocol required her to wear over her black robe. Alex Melwin, the court-appointed defense counsel, hurried into the room, his black robe flapping about his long skinny legs. She dismissed Melwin as a foolish Irishman. She strained to hear Gus's voice, to gauge its impact. Melwin spoke a few words in a low tone she could not understand.

"Get lost," Gus said to Melwin.

The black-robed clerk came to her feet. "Please stand for the entrance of the judges and remain standing silently until the judges are seated." Denise glanced at Gus, taking his measure. He was taller than everyone else in the room. She made a mental note to wear shoes with higher heels.

The three blue-robed judges conducting the pre-trial hearing entered through the door behind the bench and took their places. "The International Criminal Court is now in session," the clerk intoned.

The presiding judge, Sir John Landis, was a brilliant dyed-in-the-wool English eccentric and spoke in slow, measured tones. "This confirmation hearing into the charges levied against August William Tyler is now in order. Please be seated." Denise sat down and automatically donned her headset. Although the official languages of the court were Arabic, Chinese, English, French, Russian, and Spanish, the working languages were English and French. Because Gus, the accused, spoke English, the trial would be conducted in that language. She listened to the French channel to insure the translator was correctly interpreting the proceedings. Satisfied, she removed her headset and brushed her hair back into place.

After confirming that all parties were present, Landis asked if there were any objections, observations, or petitions for the Pre-Trial Chamber's consideration. Both Denise and Melwin said there were none. Landis turned to Gus. "Have you received a copy of the document containing the charges brought against you?"

"Yes, your Honor, I have," Gus replied.

"Do you understand these charges?" Landis asked.

"Yes, sir, I do. But there's a problem."

"Which is?"

"When I asked the registrar of the court to contact the American Embassy for legal counsel, I was told that I had to select my defense counsel from a pre-approved list of lawyers. I thought I had the right to choose my own lawyers."

Denise came to her feet. "Your Honor, if I may. The accused indeed has that right under Article Sixty-seven of the Rome Statute. However, Rule Twenty-two of the Rules of Procedure and Evidence requires that the counsel for the defense shall have an established competence in international law and procedure. To that end, and in conjunction with Rule Twenty-one, the registrar must create and maintain a list of counsel who meet the criteria of Rule Twenty-two. It is from that list that the accused must select his defense counsel. As the defendant rejected all the names on the list, the presidency of the court assigned Mr. Melwin as his defense counsel."

Gus shook his head at the flow of numbers. "Are we playing Bingo here?" Fortunately, the judges did not hear it. Gus raised his voice, full of command. "I am not represented by Mr. Melwin." Denise sucked in her breath, totally caught off guard by the force of his voice.

"May I ask why you object to Mr. Melwin?" Landis asked.

"He's a fool," Gus said. Denise came alert, quickly revising her estimate of Gus. He had correctly pigeonholed Melwin and effectively dismissed him before he could compromise his defense. "As soon as I'm allowed to contact the American Embassy or my family, I'll arrange for my own counsel."

"Your Honor," Denise said, "Mr. Tyler is charged as a Panamanian citizen. The United States Embassy has no interest in this matter." Gus looked at her thoughtfully.

The three judges conferred briefly before Landis spoke. "The registrar will review Mr. Tyler's request for change of counsel and allow him to contact the American Embassy, if the registrar so deems. Mr. Tyler, as you are not aware of the court's procedure I will, at this point, indulge you to a degree. This court draws on both the Romano-Germanic tradition of accusatory law and the adversarial approach of common law, with which you are familiar. For the time being, Mr. Melwin will remain the defense counsel of record. I suggest you listen to him. Do you understand all that I have said?"

A Far Justice

"Yes, your Honor, I do." Nothing in his voice indicated that his surroundings or the judge cowed him. "However," Gus said, "I have another question."

Landis blinked twice, obviously irritated. "Which is?"

"Why am I here? I am a citizen of the United States and my country does not recognize the court."

Denise came to her feet. "Your Honor, if I may?"

Landis seemed relieved to hear from her. "Proceed."

"Mr. Tyler is . . ."

Gus interrupted her. "It's Colonel Tyler."

"The court decides its own protocols," Denise said. "You will be referred to as Mr. Tyler."

"May I ask why?" Gus asked.

"The court will not cover your crimes with the respectability of a military title," Denise answered.

"Yet, I'm here because I fought a war, acted under orders, and was wearing the uniform of my country at the time."

Again, Landis conferred with the other two judges. "As the defendant is retired and no longer on active duty, the court will refer to him as Mr. Tyler."

Denise nailed Gus with a cold stare, fixing her first triumph. She waited for the cameras to swing onto her. "To answer your original question, Mr. Tyler, the court has jurisdiction over you because you are a citizen of Panama."

"My father was a sergeant in the United States Army and stationed in the Canal Zone at the time of my birth. I am an American citizen who happened to be born in Panama. I left there when I was eleven months old and haven't been back."

Denise's lips compressed into a tight smile. "Panama recognizes dual citizenship. Therefore, you are also a citizen of Panama. As Panama is a signatory to the Rome Statute forming the International Criminal Court, *ratione personae* is established." She tilted her head and looked at Gus as though that explained everything. He mouthed a few words and both guards smiled. One had to place his hand over his mouth and look away.

"May I ask what is so funny?" Denise demanded, now fully aware the cameras were fixed on Gus and not her.

"I said, 'I love it when she talks dirty like that.'"

23

Landis tapped his pen and a camera swung in his direction. "Mr. Tyler, do not insult this court or make light of its authority."

"I apologize, your Honor. It won't happen again."

"Mr. Tyler, our purpose today is four fold. First, to establish if you understand the charges lodged against you. Second, to inform you of the evidence against you. Third, to hear your plea to the charges, and, lastly, to consider any request for your interim release. To satisfy the court in the first matter, can you explain the charges in your own words?"

"I am charged with the war crimes of committing murder on the night of 25-26 February, 1991, on Mutlah Ridge in Iraq, and using prohibited weapons."

"The first charge," Landis explained, satisfied that he was back in control of his court, "is the war crime of willful killing one or more persons protected under The Geneva Conventions of 1949. The second charge is the war crime of using weapons prohibited under the same conventions. How do you plead to the charges?"

Gus's voice boomed in answer, again full of command. "Not guilty."

Landis made a note. "Madam Prosecutor, you may present the evidence against the defendant."

Denise picked up a thick document and placed it on the clerk's desk. "If it pleases the court, I will summarize the evidence proving Mr. Tyler's guilt."

"The court concurs," Landis said.

She adjusted her reading glasses and started to read. "The defendant was in command of an F-15E fighter-bomber on the night of February 25 to 26, 1991, and that he did attack an unarmed convoy comprised of many civilians in the vicinity of the Iraqi-Kuwaiti border known as Mutlah Ridge. Further, witnesses confirm he knew civilians were traveling in the convoy in civilian vehicles, were not taking a direct part in hostilities, and that he did bomb such vehicles carrying innocent civilians." Denise continued to read in a monotone, surprising Gus by the depth of operational and technical detail in her summary. After each point, her assistant passed a folder of documents to the court clerk, piling up a visible mountain of evidence for the TV cameras. The visual effect was damning. For Gus, it was an eternity before she ended.

Landis cleared his throat. "We have reviewed the evidence against Mr. Tyler in enough detail and find it sufficient and admissible. Therefore the defendant will be bound over to trial commencing on a date to be determined." Landis jotted down a note. "We have one last issue to resolve. Should the defendant be released from custody prior to trial? Mr. Tyler, do you have anything to say in this regard?"

"Your Honor, my wife suffers from a severe degenerative disease and is dying. I should be with her. I give my word that I will return for the trial."

Denise scoffed loudly as she stood. She waited until all three cameras were on her. "While I do not doubt the intentions of the honorable gentleman, I seriously doubt the United States government will allow him to return for trial. Therefore, we recommend that he remains in confinement."

Landis tapped his pen, and glanced at the other two judges. Both nodded. "The court agrees. Mr. Tyler will remain in confinement in the Netherlands."

"Your Honor," Gus said, "will I now have access to competent counsel and be allowed visitors?"

Landis gave him a studied look. "The court has already ruled that the registrar will review your request for counsel. For your information, outside counsel is allowed as a second chair, subject to certain restrictions. The issue of visitors is between the prosecutor and the incarcerating authority, which is the Kingdom of the Netherlands. This hearing is adjourned." He stood.

The clerk popped to her feet. "Please stand." The room was silent as Landis and the other two judges hurried out of the room. Immediately, a clutch of reporters rushed at Denise.

"Signora Du Milan," a reporter asked in Italian, "is this the first time you've seen Tyler?"

"That is correct," Denise answered in the same language.

Another reporter asked in Spanish, "What do you make of him?"

Denise gathered up her notes and stuffed her briefcase, forgetting to sign the confinement order. "He's another arrogant American cowboy," she said in Spanish. "It is time we brought them to the bar of civilization, don't you agree?" Nods all around. "Please remember that this man, no matter how charming and handsome he may appear, slaughtered thousands of innocent civilians in a few seconds. He must be held accountable."

She glanced at Gus who was staring at her, his face passive, his eyes fixed and unblinking. A jolt of fear rocked her when she realized it was the look of a hunter and she was in his sights. She reached into her briefcase and extracted the confinement order. She uncapped her OMAS and signed it with a flourish.

San Francisco, California

The old VW minivan belched smoke as it lumbered up the westbound approach to the new Oakland Bay Bridge, slowing the Friday afternoon rush hour traffic. "I haven't seen one of those in years," Hank Sutherland said to himself as he fell in behind. He made a mental note to stop talking to himself.

Henry "Hank" Sutherland was not an imposing man, and at forty-seven years old, he tended to blend into the background. He stood a shade over five feet ten inches tall, had a boyish face with freckles, all topped with a full head of barely controlled sandy-brown hair. Unfortunately, he had been spending too much time in the classroom – he taught law at the University of California, Berkeley – and was out of shape and putting on weight. For reasons totally beyond him, women found him attractive and men trusted him. But behind his friendly hazel eyes lurked a soaring intellect and the tenacity of a pit bull.

The minivan slowed as it pulled onto the recently completed suspension span leading to Yerba Buena Island in the middle of the Bay. Traffic piled up behind him. Hank closed the outside air vent and resigned himself to the usual stop-and-go Friday rush hour traffic. He turned on the radio and hit the button for his favorite news station. Unfortunately, nothing had changed and he listened as the commentator fixated on the same subject. "According to an Associated Press news flash from The Hague in the Netherlands, the International Criminal Court has identified the pilot accused of war crimes as August William Tyler, a retired United States Air Force colonel."

Directly in front of him, a convoy of four vans and an old school bus loaded with people coalesced around the old VW minivan and slowed even more, effectively blocking any traffic from passing. The blockade slowed and let the old VW minivan set the pace. The lanes in front of the convoy rapidly opened as frustrated drivers leaned on their horns.

The horns grew louder as the convoy halted in mid span, well short of Yerba Buena Island. "What the hell," Hank said. Men and women streamed off the bus and unfurled a large banner. On cue, a TV crew drove up on motorcycles to record the demonstration. More signs appeared, all condemning the United States for committing war crimes. Two men, one on each side of the bridge shinnied up the suspension cables. Both were carrying the end of a long line attached to the banner. The lines were quickly attached, and the men slid down, hoisting the banner above the stopped traffic.

STOP AMERICAN WAR CRIMES AGAINST THE WORLD

Horns blared behind him. "Don't do this!" Hank shouted. Then he saw it. A woman was holding a poster with a man's photo and the word

KILLER

scrawled in red across it. Another woman climbed up a small ladder clutching a bullhorn.

"Oh no," Hank moaned. It was one of his students at the University of California at Berkeley. "The ditzy one." Hank taught at Boalt Hall, Berkeley's law school, but he had been shanghaied to conduct a graduate level seminar on international law, his specialty, for the political science department. It was a decision he had regretted from day one. He couldn't remember the young woman's name, and while she was intelligent, he despaired of her critical thinking skills and feared for the legal profession should she pursue a law degree. "Madison," he mumbled, finally recalling her name. He set the parking brake and got out to hear.

"We need the TV cameras over there," Madison ordered, pointing to the clear traffic lanes. "I want the stopped cars as background." The TV reporters dutifully obliged and moved to their appointed location.

An attractive young woman got out of a car two lanes to Hank's left. "I've got to catch a flight!"

Madison turned her bullhorn on the woman. "This is more important than you catching an airplane, lady."

"My job depends on it!"

Madison blasted her with "If you're not part of the solution, you're part of the problem."

The loud bass of truck air horns echoed over them. Hank stood on his car's doorsill in order to see. Six truck drivers were out of their trucks and headed his way, picking up angry drivers as they came. "Now it gets interesting." He reached for his cell phone and dialed 9-1-1. He quickly described the situation. "You got a riot about to start. And it's gonna get very ugly very fast." He broke the connection. He looked skyward and spread his arms. "Why me?"

"Here come the rednecks," Madison announced over her bullhorn.

"Now that really helped," Hank muttered. He opened the sunroof to his car and stood on the driver's seat. His eyes narrowed as he surveyed the combatants. He calculated there were at least eighty demonstrators, about half women. He counted the men surging past his car. Seventeen. But more irate motorists were joining them by the second.

One of the truck drivers pointed at Madison who was still standing on the ladder orchestrating the demonstration. "Get her!" The battle was joined as a dozen or so of the demonstrators formed a defensive line.

"We come in peace!" a young woman shouted as the demonstrators locked arms.

"Peace my ass!" the same truck driver yelled. He barreled into the line, his muscular arms pumping with short, hard jabs. More men piled in behind him, giving weight to the attack. The line split apart and the men headed straight for Madison. "Grab the fuckin' bitch!" the truck driver shouted.

Another shout echoed from the rear. "Over the side!"

The mob picked it up it as a war cry. "Over the side! Over the side!"

Madison dropped her bullhorn and jumped from the ladder. But she was too slow in reacting to the threat and two men grabbed her.

A Far Justice

The chant grew louder as the men carried her to the nearside of the bridge. More demonstrators joined in trying to save Madison.

Hank climbed out through the sunroof and slid down onto the hood of his car as a man banged a baseball bat against his car's fender. He glared at Hank, his eyes filled with hate. "Hey man!" Hank yelled. "You got the wrong car." He pointed at the old VW van directly in front. "Nail that one!" He slid off the hood and gave him an encouraging look. "Let's get the bastards." Again, he pointed at the VW van.

The man yelled an obscenity at Hank and lunged at him. It was the wrong move. Hank pushed him aside and pounded him with four, blindingly fast rabbit punches. The man went down as Hank grabbed the baseball bat out of his hands. "Crazy bastard," Hank said. "Get out of here." The man scrambled for safety. Hank used the bat as a battering ram and bulldozed his way straight for the kicking and screaming Madison. He held the baseball bat low to keep it hidden and reached the girl just as the men started to heave her over the side. He brought the tip of the bat up in a sharp upward motion into the elbow of the man holding her feet. He collapsed in a spasm of pain, dropping Madison's legs. Hank encircled her waist with his left arm, holding her tight.

"Not her," Hank shouted, now holding the bat high, ready to swing. "The van! Get the van!" A man grabbed him from the rear. Hank bent his knees and went into a crouch as he jerked his body sideways. At the same time, he twisted into his assailant and drove the butt of the bat into his stomach. The man went down spewing vomit over Madison. "Throw the goddamn van over the side!" Hank shouted.

A voice picked up his order. "The van, the van!" It became a chorus and the mob turned toward the van, momentarily diverted. But it was only a temporary reprieve.

Hank scooped up Madison in a fireman's carry. "Play dead," he told her. She played the role and her arms and head dangled lifelessly. He angled through the crowd that was pushing the van towards the bridge railing. The lane in front of his car was now open. He reached the back of his car and lifted the trunk lid. He dumped Madison in and slammed the lid.

"What the hell you doin'?" a voice shouted behind him.

"Taking her to the morgue," Hank shouted back. "Let's get the hell out of here." Ahead of him the men had pushed the van against the railing and were rocking it back and forth. Hank jumped in behind the wheel and started the engine. Sirens blared from Yerba Buena Island as police and emergency vehicles approached, coming towards him in the clear lanes. He accelerated straight ahead as the van went over the railing and the police cars arrived. A line of traffic shot the gap he had opened, adding to the confusion.

* * * * *

Hank sipped at his tea while his wife, Catherine, gently cleaned a nasty abrasion on Madison's left knee. Catherine was a big woman often described as statuesque, and towered over the waif-like Madison. "There now," Catherine said, "you should be okay. You were lucky. The fall would have killed you."

"They're all bastards," Madison announced.

Catherine was an accomplished lawyer in her own right but had given up practicing law to raise a family. But she fully understood the deadly mix of anger and opportunity. "Men can get that way, especially when you make them angry. You lost situational awareness."

"What exactly does that mean?" Madison asked.

"Your perception of the situation did not match reality," Hank explained. "Besides, always know how to get out of Dodge when the situation turns to crap – like today."

The phone rang and Catherine picked it up. She listened for a moment. "Hank, it's Marci Lennox, the reporter from CNC-TV." She pulled a face and covered the mouthpiece. "She recognized you and wants to interview you for the evening news."

"No way," Hank replied. "Tell her to go away."

Catherine took a deep breath. "I don't think the media will be going away soon. Apparently, you're some sort of hero for saving Madison."

"Lovely. Absolutely lovely."

"Another call," Catherine said. She punched the call-waiting button and listened. "Hank, I think you should take this one. It's the attorney general." She handed him the phone with a worried look.

A Far Justice

He took the phone and glanced at the waiting image on the small screen. "I think I'm in trouble."

3

Washington, D.C.

Hank's cell phone vibrated as he followed the young woman through the marbled halls of the Department of Justice. He glanced at the message on the offending instrument and arched an eyebrow. Max Westcot wanted to speak to him soonest. Hank reread the message as the lawyer in his soul sounded alarms. First, the attorney general, and now the modern-day equivalent of a robber baron wanted to speak to him.

"I must apologize," his attractive guide said, "but the attorney general has been called to the White House." She checked with the assistant attorney general's receptionist and led him through.

"Thank you," Hank murmured, still groggy from the Friday night's redeye flight from San Francisco. His alarm signals went ballistic and he was jolted awake when he saw the man waiting with the assistant attorney general.

The assistant AG stood and extended his hand. "Hank, thanks for coming so quickly. I don't believe you know Mr. Weaver."

Hank was well aware of James Weaver's reputation, and he went into a deep defensive crouch. This was a meeting that never happened, which explained the attorney general's absence. They men shook hands all around and Hank sat down. "So, what can I do for you?"

The assistant AG leaned forwarded, his 'I only want to help' look in place. "Mr. Weaver asked if we would solicit your help in the Tyler case." He waited for a response from Hank. There wasn't one so he shifted into his 'we really need your help' approach. "Specifically, we want you to defend Colonel Tyler before the ICC."

There was no doubt in Hank's mind that the 'we' was the president of the United States. "As an official of the United States defending one of its citizens?" Hank asked.

The assistant AG shifted in his chair, not liking the way Hank was going. "No. That would be de facto recognition of the court by the US, which we certainly do not want. You would have to go as a private individual."

The 'we' was still in play and Hank understood it was a request that he couldn't refuse. "So, I'd be on my own?"

"Let me be candid," Weaver said. "We asked the attorney general to approach you because you are, without reservation, our country's leading expert on the ICC, and one fine lawyer. Colonel Tyler's trial is going to be a three-ring circus, a soap opera that will dominate the nightly news. But given the current crisis over China and Taiwan, we cannot risk angering our European allies and can't intervene, at least for now. The State Department is involved but our best option is to provide Colonel Tyler with a topnotch defense. That's you. But our role in this must not be revealed."

"As the US has no status with the court," the assistant AG added, "we need someone who is lacking, shall we say, an official stamp of approval, and has a good reputation with the European media. Which you do, thanks to what you did on the bridge yesterday."

"So I defend Colonel Tyler while you pursue other means to gain his release."

"The President does have wide-ranging powers under the American Service-Members' Protection Act," Weaver said.

"To use all means necessary to free any service-member detained or imprisoned by the ICC," Hank added, paraphrasing the congressional act. A hard silence came down in the room as Hank considered the offer. What he didn't know worried him. Finally, "I need to think about it. Do you have a file on Tyler?"

The assistant AG shoved a thin folder across his desk. "Here's all we have, plus the transcript from his arraignment hearing this morning in The Hague."

"The ICC calls it a confirmation hearing," Hank said.

"The court appointed an Irishman to defend Tyler," Weaver said. "The guy is a real bozo and a drunk to boot, but Tyler did a creditable job defending himself. He challenged the court's jurisdiction and ended up looking pretty good. But we need you there as soon as possible to minimize the damage."

"How soon may we expect an answer?" the assistant AG asked.

Hank glanced at his watch. It was just after nine in the morning. "I'll let you know this afternoon." He stood, dropped Tyler's file into his briefcase and left.

The assistant AG watched Hank close the door and took a deep breath. "Will he do it?"

"I imagine so," Weaver answered. "He's only lost a handful of cases in his career and this is a challenge he can't refuse."

"Do you think he can win this one?"

Weaver shook his head. "No way in hell."

Riverview, Maryland

Hank pressed the doorbell of the colonial style house and waited. For some reason, he had assumed that Max Westcot would never be caught dead in anything approaching normality. He pressed the bell again as he took in the beautiful garden and wide expanse of grass that sloped down to the Potomac River. In the far distance, on the other side of the river, he could see the trees surrounding Mount Vernon, George Washington's estate with its never-ending throngs of tourists. Westcot opened the door and welcomed him inside. Westcot was shorter than Hank expected, no more than five feet eight inches, and built like a fireplug topped with heavy dark hair. "Thanks for coming. How did the meeting go?"

Rather than ask how Westcot knew about the meeting, Hank only nodded and said, "They want me to defend Colonel Tyler."

Westcot led him into the study that had an even better view of the Potomac. He stood by the French windows. "Please, have a seat. Are you?"

Hank sat down. "May I ask why you're interested in the colonel?"

"We were friends and classmates at the Air Force Academy. I got into some trouble and he went to bat for me. It was a pretty rough patch but he got me through it. He's a good friend."

"Forgive me, Mr. Westcot, but I suspect there's more to it than friendship."

"I do have other interests that are involved."

"Is oil one of them?" Westcot stared at him and didn't answer. Hank's instincts warned him to level with the financier. "To answer your question, I am thinking about defending the colonel but haven't made a final decision."

Westcot gazed out the window towards Mt. Vernon. "Sometimes I wonder how George Washington managed to get along with the French."

"Do you think they're behind this?" Hank asked.

Westcot snorted. "Their pecker tracks are all over it."

Hank heard the anger in his voice. "So Tyler is a sacrificial pawn caught in a geopolitical pissing contest."

"To put it mildly. The French go at each other with gusto, and God only knows who is doing what to who over there. But basically, the French are the French and play their own game."

"And you're a player in the pissing contest. Or have I got it wrong?"

Westcot studied Hank for a moment. "No." Silence. Then, "If you decide to defend Gus, I'll be in your corner."

"In what way?"

"Obviously out of sight but in any way I can; money, information, contacts, a top notch legal team, you name it. But you'll be a free agent."

It all came together for the lawyer. Westcot was the cutout between him and the government, but if anything went wrong, he would be hung out to dry. He made a decision. "I'll do it."

Westcot handed Hank a wireless phone in a black case approximately three by five inches in size and a half-inch thick. "This looks like a mobile phone but we call it a percom, short for personal communicator." He didn't tell Hank that one of his companies had developed it for the CIA. "Open the lid to turn it on. It's got a touch screen but it's also voice activated and will only respond to your voice. Just tell it what you want and it does the rest." He handed Hank an in-canal hearing aid. "Listen with this. Your contact is Cassandra. She's your link to my people who will back you up to the max."

"Pun intended?" Hank quipped.

Max Westcot did not have a sense of humor and stared at the lawyer for a moment. "Cassandra will provide you with whatever information you need. The percom also functions as a computer, a GPS, and a video cell phone. You can even play games. The battery is good for seventy-two hours of continuous use. To recharge, simply place it next to any power source like a battery or electrical outlet, even a high-voltage power line will do if you're within a hundred feet, and it will recharge in about twenty minutes."

Hank inserted the earpiece and opened the case. The top half was an LED touch screen and the bottom half had a small microphone grate. The screen flicked to life and the image of a pleasant-looking middle-aged woman appeared. Her dark hair was streaked with gray and pulled back and tied in a loose bundle at the back of her neck. She was wearing a white, classical Greek gown. It was an image that could have been lifted from an ancient Grecian urn he had admired in a museum. He heard a voice in his ear. "Good afternoon, Professor Sutherland. Or do you prefer to be called Hank?"

He gave Westcot a quizzical look who only nodded in encouragement. "Ah, good afternoon, Cassandra. Hank will be fine."

"What can I do for you?"

"I'm just learning how this works," he told the image.

"I can give you a description or answer questions you might have. But based on past experience, it's easiest to learn as we go along. If you don't mind, from time to time I'll suggest things for you to consider."

"Sounds good. Talk to you later." Hank closed the lid to the percom.

Cassandra was still there. "If you want privacy, tell me to terminate the connection. But I do have a watchdog feature you might find useful. We establish a half mile secure zone around your location and monitor all telephone, radio, and computer transmissions within that zone."

"I'll settle for privacy right now," he replied. Suddenly, he sensed he was alone. "I'll be damned."

Westcot allowed a tight smile. "You'll get used to it." He handed Hank a credit card. "No limit." The meeting was over and he walked Hank to his car. They shook hands and Westcot stood in the drive as Hank drove away.

Hank drove about a mile before curiosity got the better of him. He parked and opened the percom's lid to turn it on. "Cassandra, are you there?"

The image appeared on the screen and the voice in his earpiece was back. "Good afternoon, Hank."

Hank closed the lid and dropped the percom into his shirt pocket. "Are you a real person?"

"I like to think I am. The image you see and my voice are computer generated. Basically, I'm a data information program programmed for voice recognition. However, I am monitored and controlled by a very real person. I'm allowed to give you some technical details of how the system works, if you'd like."

"I'm a lawyer. I wouldn't understand a word you said. By the way, can you see me?"

"I have a built-in camera. Point the red infrared lens on the side of the case at whatever you want me to see."

"Do you have a dossier on me?"

"Of course. It's quite extensive. I can extract some highlights." Without waiting, the voice recited the basics of Hank's life, including the exact amount in his checking account. "Oh," Cassandra said, "this is very naughty. Apparently, you had a brief affair with Marci Lennox, the TV reporter . . ." Her voice trailed off. Hank whipped out the percom and opened it. Cassandra was on the screen reading from a long scroll, a bright blush on her face. She glanced up at him. "Well, I did say it was naughty. Was she really that skilled in bed?"

"That is none of your business."

The image became serious. "Certainly," Cassandra answered. "I won't reference it again."

"Why the cutesy imaging about being shocked and embarrassed?" Hank asked.

"Your profile suggested it was a way to add a personal touch to increase interaction."

"And increase my dependence on you . . ." He stopped, waiting for her reaction.

"Which could lead to control," Cassandra said, completing the thought for him.

"You guys are good," Hank said, now certain the CIA was in the loop.

"Thank you. Shall I go on?"

"Tell me about Tyler."

"Shall I read parts of it or do you want a printout?"

"How do I get a printout?"

A Far Justice

"Find any copy machine or computer printer. Place the percom so it's touching and tell me what you want to print out. I'll do the rest."

Hank started the car and headed for Washington D.C. "Please give me the abridged version on Tyler." He listened as he drove.

"August William Tyler was born in 1960 in the Panama Canal Zone, graduated from the Air Force Academy in 1982, and married Clare Leeson four days later. They have two children, Michelle and Jason, and twin grandsons by their daughter. Women consider him very attractive and he's received many offers for extra- curricular activities. But he has always refused those. Career-wise, he flew F-15 fighters, fought in the 1991 Gulf war, commanded a fighter squadron when he was a lieutenant colonel, and the First Fighter Wing as a colonel. He was earmarked for general but retired in 2006 when he was forty-six years old to care for his wife." Her voice grew sad. "She's dying from complications resulting from lupus."

"He sounds like a nice guy," Hank said.

"By all reports, he is," she replied.

"Can you call the assistant attorney general for me?"

"Of course. Would you like to make it a conference call with Mr. Weaver?"

"You know about our meeting this morning?"

"Of course," Cassandra replied. "We don't know what was said but we did make some logical assumptions."

"Contacting Weaver will be sporting."

"Do I sense a test?" Cassandra asked. She made the connections and had both men on the line in less than a minute. "I'll do better next time."

"Gentlemen," Hank said, "I've decided to represent Colonel Tyler. So how do I proceed from here?"

"A plane will be waiting at Reagan International to fly you to the Netherlands," the assistant attorney general answered. "Our embassy there will make the necessary arrangements."

"We do appreciate your sacrifice," Weaver said.

Hank broke the connection. "Cassandra, I need directions to the airport."

"Of course. Turn left at the next stoplight. I'll change it to green and stop the oncoming traffic. Hank, may I venture an observation?"

"Certainly."

"I do wish Mr. Weaver had not said 'your sacrifice.'"
"Yeah, I caught that. Can I trust them?"
"Hank," Cassandra admonished, "this is Washington."

4

The Hague

"I am sorry," Alex Melwin said, "that you have such a low opinion of my efforts on your behalf." The Irish lawyer's thick accent was almost incomprehensible and Gus strained to understand all he was saying. "I assure you, I have correctly followed the court's procedures. Further, I seriously doubt that another lawyer will be able to do better, considering the case the prosecutor has forged."

Gus wanted to beat Melwin senseless and looked around his cell for any tool that would do the job. By US standards, the cell was very spacious, comfortable, and private. It was complete with a TV, a wall-mounted telephone, private bathroom and a kitchen- ette. Still, it was a jail cell. When things go wrong get aggressive, he thought. It was a credo he lived by when flying combat. "Alex, you are one cheerful, absolutely worthless son of a bitch. Now go find me a real lawyer and crawl back under the Blarney Stone." Melwin stared at him in shock. "You look like a constipated beagle."

"I do not share your expertise on the bowel movements of beagles," the lawyer finally said.

Gus laughed. "That's funny. Okay, indulge me for a moment. How strong is this so-called 'case' against me?"

"The war crimes you are charged with under Article Eight have very specific elements, which Madam Du Milan, based on the evidence I have seen, will have no trouble establishing that you factually committed."

"That I 'factually committed,'" Gus repeated. "Now how is she going to prove that? Besides, what happened to the presumption of innocence?"

"Of course you are assumed innocent, that's why the prosecutor must present the facts to the court."

"Melwin, I know a kangaroo court when I see one."

"I assure you, we are not a kangaroo court."

"Does the term 'bullshit' have meaning around here?

"It's obvious you don't understand our system of law."

"You are absolutely right about that. By the way, do I have attorney-client privilege under your system?"

"Please remember that I am a member of the court, and have certain obligations to the court that override attorney-client privilege as you Americans understand it."

I'm going to wring your scrawny neck, Gus promised himself. "So what brings you here today?"

"Madam Du Milan is going to meet with us and offer what you Americans call a deal."

"A plea bargain," Gus corrected.

"For admitting your guilt to the court, she will recommend a sentence of 12 to 25 years which means you will be eligible for parole in eight years."

"Eight years doesn't sound like a bargain to me. I'll take my chances."

"An unwise choice. She is due here at any moment and you should listen to her."

"Must I?" Melwin shook his head and stared at the floor. Gus leaned back in his chair and waited in silence as he plotted what to do with the Irishman's body.

The door lock clicked and Denise entered the cell unannounced. Both men stood and Melwin offered her his chair. She sat and crossed her legs. "I assume Alex has explained why I'm here." Gus nodded but said nothing. "Considering the circumstances, I believe it is a very generous offer."

Gus's fingers drummed a tattoo on the table as he framed an answer explaining exactly what she could do with her "generous offer." He decided it was anatomically impossible but certainly worth a try. "Excuse me if I don't bounce off the walls with joy, but eight years sucks."

"Please remember who you're talking to," Melwin cautioned. "Madam Prosecutor, I must apologize for my client's . . ."

Gus interrupted him. "I'm not your anything, Melwin. So shut up and get the hell out of here."

"Your hostile attitude is counter-productive," Denise said.

"Hostile? Madam Prosecutor, you haven't seen hostile." He came to his feet. "First, I have done nothing wrong. Second, I'm not sure if Melwin here is my prosecutor or executioner. Third, my wife is terminally ill and she's the most important thing in my life. I should be with her."

"Monsieur Tyler," Denise said, "you are a war criminal who wantonly massacred thousands of innocent people. You are exactly where you should be."

"Those 'innocent people' were doing their damndest to kill me, and it was only a couple hundred." Gus and Denise stared at each other, locked in a contest of wills. The phone on the wall rang breaking the hard silence. Gus picked it up. "Yeah?" He listened for a moment. "Send them in." He banged the phone down. "I've got visitors."

"You are only allowed visitors with my approval," she replied. She stood and took a step toward the phone.

Gus stared at her. "Really? They're from the American Embassy."

"They have no status here," Denise said.

"Justice Landis is concerned about visitation privileges," Melwin said. It was enough to make her hesitate. "And the registrar did approve contacting the US Embassy." Denise gave the Irishman a look of total contempt.

"Alex," Gus said, "you just might make a lawyer yet."

The door lock clicked and a guard opened the door. A fussy, potbellied, immaculately dressed little man walked in carrying a slim black briefcase. Hank Sutherland followed immediately behind. The man reached into his breast coat pocket and whipped out his identification. "Winslow James, United States Embassy." He held up a gold embossed black leather ID holder for examination.

Denise didn't bother with it. "You are?"

"The deputy charge of mission, Madam Prosecutor."

Denise quickly re-evaluated the situation. After the ambassador, the elegant little man was the most important US diplomat in the Netherlands. He was definitely not someone to trifle with and chance angering the ICC's Dutch hosts. But something about him suggested he could be manipulated. "Monsieur James, while the court acknowledges your country's interest in this criminal, you are lacking jurisdiction."

James lived up to her suspicions. "Madam Du Milan, we are fully aware of the court's position; however, we beg your indulgence . . ."

Hank interrupted him. "The same statement is true for the court. It has an interest, but no jurisdiction."

Denise and Melwin turned as one towards Hank. "You are?" she asked.

"May I present Professor Henry Sutherland," James said, trying to defuse the tension. "Professor Sutherland is Professor of International Law at Boalt Hall, the University of California."

"Professor Sutherland, I'm honored," Melwin said. He extended his hand and was relieved when Hank shook it. He turned to Denise. "Professor Sutherland is the United States' preeminent authority on the court."

"I'm aware of his reputation," Denise said. "Your purpose here?"

"To represent Colonel Tyler," Hank replied. "If he so desires."

"He so desires," Gus said.

"But the court does not recognize Monsieur Sutherland as being qualified," Denise said. "Further, the president of the court has reviewed Mr. Tyler's petition for a change in counsel and has rejected it. That decision is final and Monsieur Melwin will remain the attorney of record."

"As I understand the court's procedures," Hank replied, "my counsel may be assisted by others, including professors of law with relevant experience. No certification is required and Melwin here only has to file a letter of notification with the registrar. Or has that changed in the last twenty minutes?" Denise stared at Melwin. The Irishman got the message and gulped. "I . . . ah . . . at this point in time . . . I have no need of assistance." Denise smiled at him.

"Well then," James said. "As I am satisfied as to Mr. Tyler's well-being . . ."

Hank interrupted. "It's Colonel Tyler."

"Of course," James replied. "We have no further business here." He buzzed for security central to open the door. The lock clicked and the door swung open. James minced out, but Hank didn't move.

"You're excused, Monsieur Sutherland," Denise said. Hank hesitated for a moment and considered his options. He nodded and followed James. "Monsieur Tyler," Denise said as she stood, "may I suggest you listen to your attorney?" She cocked her head and gave him an inquisitive look. She turned and left, closing the door behind her.

"Well," Melwin said. "We do need to talk."

"Get the hell out of here before I give you a drowning lesson in the toilet."

"I am acting in your best interests, Mr. Tyler." Gus stared at him, his eyes hard and unblinking. "Ah, I mean Colonel Tyler," Melwin said.

"You finally got that one right," Gus said. He reached across the table for Melwin who darted for the door.

"I'll report this to the guards!" Melwin shouted as he jabbed at the buzzer. The door opened and he darted to safety.

"Do that!" Gus shouted down the corridor. Two guards rushed in and Gus held up his hands in surrender. "Sorry, just exercising a little attorney-client privilege."

The first guard shook his head. "Please Gus," he said in impeccable English. "We cannot allow you to hurt him."

"Melwin's a manlike object, not a him."

The second guard snorted. "True enough."

"I give you my word that it won't happen again," Gus promised.

The two guards looked at each other, nodded, and left, slamming the door. Gus took a deep breath, sat down, and buried his face in his hands. *Ah, shit,* he moaned to himself.

* * * * *

The scantily clad girl walked Melwin to the door and helped him with his coat. She stood on her tiptoes and kissed him on the cheek. The proprietress caught it and pulled a long face. It was obvious the two were very fond of each other, and who knew what the besotted Irishman would do? Marriage was not unheard of and she didn't want to lose one of her top producers. She decided to increase the girl's price the next time Melwin called for an appointment. "Same time next week?" the girl murmured.

"As always," Melwin said.

He gave her a little squeeze and stepped into the night. The door closed quickly behind him. He stood for a moment under the light that illuminated the discrete sign that announced Anabella Haus, the best bordello in Holland outside of Amsterdam, and carefully buttoned his coat against the rain. He hurried down the walk toward his car. A shadow split off from a tree and materialized into a man who stood almost six and a half feet tall. His muscular frame blocked the path. "Mr. Melwin, may we talk?"

Melwin pushed by the man. "And you are?"

"Jason Tyler. I'm Colonel Tyler's son. You haven't returned any of my calls."

"This is an inappropriate conversation," Melwin said, walking even faster.

"Guess again," Jason answered in slow measured tones. Melwin heard the steel in his voice and half-ran to his car as he fumbled for the remote control. He jabbed at a button and was relieved when the car lights blinked and the locks clicked open. Melwin jumped inside and slammed the door, making sure he was locked safely inside. He fumbled with the key as Jason knocked on the passenger-side window. "Please, sir. This will only take a moment." Panic ripped through Melwin and he dropped his keys. Jason wrenched the passenger door open as Melwin found the keys and jammed them into the ignition.

The engine roared to life as Jason shoehorned his body into the passenger seat. He seemed to fill his side of the car and handed Melwin the car's door handle. "You need to get this fixed. Cheap German crap."

Melwin's jaw started to quiver. "Please don't hurt me."

"If I wanted to do that, I'd have nailed you the moment you stepped out of that whorehouse. We just need to talk for a moment." Melwin jammed the car in gear and mashed the accelerator, barely missing the car parked in front of him. The car careened down the street, its path a perfect reflection of the panic twisting inside the Irishman. "Why don't you park over there before you kill us both."

Melwin did as commanded and pulled to the curb. Ahead of him he saw the distinctive shape of a *Rijkspolitie* patrol car and breathed easier. "Get out of my car."

"My, my, a little backbone. Now here I thought I was going to have to assemble one and jam it up your ass. Or do you Irish say 'arse' like the Blokes?"

"What do you want?"

"The Dutch won't let anyone visit Dad. I want him to have regular visiting privileges and an American lawyer."

"Both are beyond my control."

Jason opened the door. "Then resign and get someone who can make it happen." He got out of the car.

Melwin's eyes were locked on the patrol car. "Threaten me again and I'll have you up on a charge."

"That was merely a friendly piece of advice, not a threat." He stepped back, waiting for Melwin to leave. "But I do have your address if we need to talk some more." Melwin gunned the engine and sped past the still motionless patrol car as Jason watched. He walked past the patrol car and the two policemen who were sound asleep.

* * * * *

The guard glanced at the untouched food on Gus's tray. "Is it that bad?"

Gus shook his head. "I'm just not hungry." The wall phone rang and Gus picked it up. He listened and acknowledged the call before hanging up. He sat down and attacked the food, feeling much better.

"Good news?" the guard asked.

"My so-called lawyer is here with Professor Sutherland, the man I want to represent me."

"That is good news," the guard conceded. "May I join you?" Without waiting for an answer, the guard sat down and spoke in a low voice. "Madam Du Milan is in Paris until Monday and the prison superintendent has granted you normal visiting privileges."

"I'm most appreciative," Gus answered. "Please thank Superintendent Blier."

The guard stood. "My government supports the court, but all this is not right." He left, leaving the door open as Gus attacked the food.

He was on his second cup of coffee when Hank arrived. "Where's Ichabod Crane?"

Hank closed the door and sat down. "Melwin signed me in and left." He placed his personal communicator on the table and opened the lid. "He's drafting a notification letter to the registrar that I'll be assisting him. Du Milan will have a fit when she sees it."

Cassandra appeared on the screen and he heard her voice in his ear. "The room is bugged. Do you want me to jam it?" Hank turned the percom's ruby lens on himself and nodded.

"Why did Melwin change his mind?" Gus asked.

"Apparently, your son spoke to him," Hank said, smiling. "You might say Melwin had a religious experience. I am looking forward to meeting him."

"You'll like him. I really appreciate what you're doing, Professor Sutherland."

"I prefer to be called Hank. By the way, you did a great job at the confirmation hearing on the jurisdiction issue."

"I heard some guy give a talk about the ICC at a Rotary Club luncheon. What the hell is going on here?"

Hank chose his words carefully. "The court is still staking out its territory and is desperate to justify its existence and cost. Unfortunately, the court is turning into a monstrosity with a bad case of legal creep. They're investigating areas like environmental pollution, drug trafficking, and crimes against human dignity, which is all far beyond its original charter. While they deny it, the court's ultimate goal is to expand its jurisdiction over non-member states. They call it 'universal jurisdiction' and your case is one of the stepping stones in that process."

The way Gus paced the floor reminded Hank of a caged tiger he had seen in a zoo. The animal had ranged back and forth in her cage, her muscles rippling beneath her skin, glaring at the world in defiance. "You know my wife is terminally ill. I've got to get back to her."

"I know. But the court doesn't move fast and follows a process that takes time. For some reason, they've fast-tracked your indictment, which is not like them at all. I could challenge them on it, but I don't think it would do any good."

Gus made a decision. "Keep things moving as fast as you can. So what happens next?"

"You'll be tried by a three-judge chamber from the trial division. There's no jury and they can convict with two votes."

"Whatever happened to trial by jury and a unanimous decision?"

"You have none of our constitutional protections here. I'll press ahead, but we'll be lucky to get a court date within a year."

Gus was shocked. "What?"

"It's the process I mentioned. All the concerned countries that are members of the court have to be notified and given time to respond."

"What about the evidence? The prosecutor, what's her name, had a pile of it."

"Denise Du Milan. As for the rules of evidence, it can get shaky. Hearsay is routinely allowed. The judges only have to consider it truthful, relevant, and necessary. So far, the prosecutor has not released any of the evidence she cited in your confirmation hearing. Her staff says it will be released at the 'proper time.' The good news is that her staff is mediocre when they're having a good day. Make that a very good day and very mediocre."

Gus sat on the edge of his bunk and stared at the floor. "Ah, shit. I'll never get out of here. Do you know that I can't even call my family?" He snorted. "Local calls only and I have to pay for them. Ninety dollars a call."

"Does your family have a videophone?" Gus nodded in answer. "Good." Hank handed Gus a cell phone and gave him an encouraging look.

Gus punched in his home number and his daughter's image came on the small screen. "Oh, Daddy!" she cried. Hank stepped outside and closed the door to give them privacy.

5

The Hague

The elevator doors on the fourth floor of the Palace of International Justice swooshed back and Denise stormed out. It was just after ten A.M. on Saturday morning and her hard leather heels resonated on the Italian marble floor, echoing down the wide corridor of the severely modern building and announcing her presence to her waiting staff. In many ways it was a first, for the ICC never worked on Fridays, Saturdays, Sundays, holidays, or for six weeks in mid-summer. With one exception, her staff of nineteen was contemplating filing a mass grievance for the gross inconvenience of being called in on a weekend. They took little consolation in being paid triple time for their efforts.

The double-glass doors leading into the prosecutor's offices divided with a will of their own, and the waiting staff imitated the parting of the Red Sea, forming a corridor leading to her office. One look at her face was ample warning that filing a work grievance would have amounted to professional self-immolation of a most gruesome nature. Images of widows throwing themselves on funeral pyres hovered in their minds. They would have to settle for the triple time.

"Good morning, Madam Prosecutor," the assistant prosecutor said. Denise considered the man a non-entity and didn't even look at him. She sloughed off her leather topcoat, letting it fall to the floor. A secretary scrambled to pick it up.

"Coffee," she snapped. She had made the 280-mile drive from Paris in a little over three hours and was in desperate need of a caffeine jolt. She threw the end of her scarf over her shoulder and peeled off her driving gloves. She gave the assistant prosecutor a look of contempt and dropped the gloves on the floor. "Get Melwin. Now. And the prison superintendent."

"Monsieur Melwin is in reception," came the answer. "With another gentlemen."

"Who is?" she snapped.

Being braver than the average, the assistant prosecutor answered. "Sutherland. Melwin's second chair."

"I am aware of that development," she said icily. She paused for a moment, containing the fury that threatened to consume her. She took three deep breaths, as Chrestien had taught her, tossed her hair into place and entered her private suite. "Ah, bonjour, Alex," she sang. "And Monsieur Sutherland. So good to see you again. Please come in." She led them into her corner office with its panoramic view of The Hague, the beach at Scheveningen, and the North Sea. She offered them chairs and sat behind her huge black-lacquered desk. Assuming that Hank did not speak French, she reverted to that language. "One word from me, Melwin, and we will crush you like a grape." Then, in English, "As your country is not a member of the court, Monsieur Sutherland, your serving on the defense is quite impossible."

The last of Melwin's backbone crumbled. "It was all a misunderstanding," he said.

"What misunderstanding?" Hank asked. "The registrar was officially notified Friday, per the rules of the court. By the way, where's the evidence?"

"It will be released at the proper time," Denise replied. "As for the registrar, Alex has merely to file a letter of removal."

"Of course," Melwin said. "The first thing Monday morning."

Hank sighed and stood to leave. "Melwin, you have the backbone of an amoeba. Madam Prosecutor, you are making a big mistake."

Denise came out of her chair. "Do not threaten a member of this court. I'll have you declared a *persona non grata* and removed from the country."

"Offering advice is not making a threat," Hank replied. "See you in court."

"That will not happen," Denise called to his back as he left.

Hank closed the door gently behind him and stood for a moment, taking stock of her assembled staff. Judging from the expressions on their faces, they had heard every word. He smiled at them. He had read five of their opinions and briefs and was not impressed. For all its faults, the American legal system did have a way of pigeonholing the weak and incompetent, and he knew pigeons when they were roosting, or in this case, molting. They were in for some rough times. A man who looked totally out of place came through the glass doors and spoke to the receptionist. Hank pulled the percom out of his pocket and held it casually in his left hand so the ruby lens pointed to the newcomer.

"That," Cassandra's voice said in his ear, "is Superintendent Hans Blier of the Hugo de Groot prison where Colonel Tyler is being held." Hank shook his head at the irony of the prison being named after Grotius, the founder of international law. Or maybe the Dutch did have a sense of humor. He pushed his way through Denise's staff and headed for the elevator.

"Cassandra," he said aloud, "I'm striking out here. It's time for Plan B."

"Which is?" she asked.

"It's time to go to the media."

"I can arrange it. I assume you intend to burn some bridges."

"They're already in ashes," Hank replied. "I intend to build new ones. According to Gus's file, his son is stationed in Belgium. I need to get him involved."

"I'll put you in contact," Cassandra replied.

* * * * *

As one, Denise's staff watched Hank as he disappeared down the hall. They were amused by the way he talked to himself. The intercom buzzed. "Will all department heads and Superintendent Blier please come to the conference room immediately." Blier, the assistant prosecutor, and six department heads obediently filed into the conference room. Melwin stood in the corner, a very chastened schoolboy.

"Please remain standing," Denise told them. "This won't take long." She paced the floor. "We haven't seen the last of Sutherland. Given the high level of media interest, I expect to see him next on television. We're going to take the initiative and make him respond to us, not the other way around. Therefore, we're going to trial as soon as possible, not later than Wednesday, December first."

"Five weeks!" the assistant prosecutor protested. "We need at least a year."

"Then don't let things get out of hand," she replied sweetly. Her voice hardened. "I set the agenda and drive events, not . . ." She almost called Sutherland a *trou du col*, asshole, but settled for "that *cochon*." Pig. "I want a full media blitz starting tomorrow."

The assistant prosecutor gasped, his face wracked with shock. "Tomorrow is Sunday!" Being called in on a Saturday was bad enough, but working on a Sunday was outrageous, a gross violation of all human decency.

"Sunday is a very slow news day," she explained. "By announcing on Sunday, we will dominate the Monday news." It was a trick that Chrestien had learned from the Americans. "Further, all leaks will be approved by my office." She turned to Melwin. "In the future, I want close coordination on Tyler's defense and no more surprises. Superintendent Blier, I want no one, and I mean no one, visiting Tyler without my approval. Have I made myself clear?"

"Very clear, Madam Prosecutor," Blier replied. She missed the Dutch stubbornness in his voice.

"Does everyone understand what I want?" she demanded. She was answered with total silence. As one, her entire staff decided to call in sick on Sunday. The media blitz would have to wait until Monday.

Hoevelaken, the Netherlands

Cassandra played the guide to perfection. "Turn right off the Autoweg and follow the signs into town." Hank relayed her instructions to the taxi driver and guided him through the small town. It was Monday afternoon and children streamed across the road, making their way home after school. He smiled at their fresh-scrubbed looks and bulging book bags. "You're on Ooesterdorpstraat," Cassandra continued. "The van der Nord's farm is just ahead of you."

"I'm still in town," Hank protested.

"Dutch farms in this area are very narrow," she replied, "maybe a hundred feet wide, and run back from the road."

He closed the privacy window between the front and rear seats. "I've read the file you gave me on Melwin and want to out him."

"When?"

"Today."

"Consider it done. Here you are."

The driver saw the address and turned into the driveway of a traditional Dutch farmhouse with brightly painted shutters. Hank could see a modern barn in the rear and a narrow field that stretched back over two hundred meters. A young, very pretty, and heavyset girl was waiting for him. "I'm Aly van der Nord."

"She's twenty-two years old," Cassandra said in his ear. "Jason Tyler is waiting inside." Hank paid off the driver and followed Aly inside. He blinked twice when he saw Jason and immediately thought of a professional football player on steroids. "He doesn't use steroids," Cassandra told him.

"You guys are good," Hank murmured, fully aware that Cassandra and the computers were honing his personality profile to a fine edge. Not only did they anticipate his question about Aly's age, they gauged his reaction to Jason.

"Thank you," Cassandra replied. "That was the first thing I thought when I saw him."

"Professor Sutherland," Jason Tyler said, extending his right hand. "We really appreciate all you're doing."

They shook hands. "It is a pleasure to finally meet you," Hank said. He tried to keep a straight face. "Especially as Alex Melwin speaks so highly of you. By the way, I prefer to go by Hank."

"The Air Force will do whatever it can to help," Jason said. "For obvious reasons, it has to be very unofficial. If you need anything, just tell me or Aly." He handed Hank a thick envelope. Hank looked in the envelope and was surprised to see a thick wad of hundred dollar bills along with another credit card. "For expenses. The credit card is for an unlimited amount. Use it as you see fit. And you'll need this."

Jason handed him a small 22-caliber Beretta semi-automatic pistol that fit his hand perfectly. Hank handed it back. "No way," he said. "The ICC is death on any weapons inside the palace. Not even their bailiffs or security guards are armed."

Jason filed that information away and pocketed the automatic without a word. "I'm scheduled for an interview on TV this evening at Hilversum," Hank explained. "I'd like you and Aly to be there. Just hold hands and look very worried."

"It's not far from here," Jason said. "We can drive you there."

"Hilversum is the home of our national radio and TV," Aly added. "That's where the major studios are. It may be late before we're finished, so why don't you stay with us tonight?"

"I'd be delighted," Hank said.

* * * * *

Hank sat in Aly's car while she opened the garage doors. Cassandra was back, her voice low and matter-of-fact. "You'll be interviewed by Harm de Rijn, Holland's most popular newscaster. He's intelligent, sophisticated, and is highly critical of our foreign policy. We suspect he'll concentrate his questions on why Americans are against the court and why you were removed as Melwin's assistant. We fed him the information about Melwin, but don't know if he'll use it. You might have to lead the discussion that way. Hold on, here's something new that was just released. Alphonse Relieu, the court's senior president, announced the trial will start on December first."

Hank sat upright. "Son of a bitch! That's five weeks away."

"Wrong response," Cassandra counseled. "Play on the rush to judgment and the lack of independent defense counsel. Refer to it as Star Chamber proceedings that totally violate the spirit and intent of the court."

"Justice run amok."

"Exactly," Cassandra replied as Aly climbed in behind the wheel.

"Pardon?" Aly asked.

"Just talking to myself," Hank answered. "I do it all the time."

A Far Justice

The Hague

Gus cycled through the four TV channels he was allowed to watch. He checked his clock. It was nine o'clock Monday evening and the Dutch news was buzzing with the breaking news on his trial and the delayed interview with Hank Sutherland. *Why the delay?* he wondered. Finally, Harm de Rijn's reassuring countenance ap- peared on the screen. He was sitting in a news studio with Hank seated across a small table sipping the ever-present cup of coffee. Jason and Aly were sitting next to him and looking very worried as de Rijn introduced them. *The family angle is a nice touch.* It was obvious why de Rijn inspired trust and confidence in the Dutch. He was the gold standard for the modern Dutch burgher – fifty-something, handsome, with a mass of carefully styled gray hair, bright blue eyes, and an honest and open, but very serious face. Gus turned up the volume of his TV to catch every word of the interview. *Come on Hank,* he thought. *We need a homerun.*

"As you no doubt have heard," de Rijn said, looking intently into the camera and speaking in Dutch as sub-captions in English crawled along the bottom of the screen, "the International Criminal Court announced late today that the war criminal Tyler's trial will start in five weeks and that our guest, professor of law Doctor Henry Sutherland, has been removed from the defense team by the defense counsel, Alex Melwin." He turned to Hank and spoke in English as the sub-captions changed to Dutch. "Thank you for being here and I apologize for the delay in starting this interview. But given the intense interest in this case, we did want to broadcast live at a time most of our viewers would be watching."

Gus banged his hand on the table, finally understanding. *You delayed the interview until all the players coordinated the spin.*

A quick smile played at the corners of Hank's mouth. "Thank you for the excellent dinner while we waited. One of the pleasant surprises I've discovered is that Dutch cuisine is truly world class."

De Rijn took the compliment graciously and keyed off it. "It was the least we could do. As you have also probably discovered, we Dutch are much more attuned to world events than Americans."

"Now that's a true statement if I ever heard one," Hank conceded. "Everyone over here seems to know about the International

Criminal Court and the arrest of Colonel Tyler. Personally, I think it's a matter of geography. In the United States, we're just too spread out and too far away to feel physically involved. Distance does lessen the impact."

Gus's laugh filled his cell. Hank had taken the issue away from de Rijn. *That's not the answer you wanted, was it?*

"Perhaps," de Rijn continued, "we could start by asking why Americans are so hostile to the court?"

Don't ask the question if you can't stand the answer, Gus thought.

"It's not a question of hostility," Hank replied, "but of a fundamental conflict that goes to the very heart of the International Criminal Court. Our constitution guarantees every US citizen the right to a trial by an impartial jury of his peers. There is no trial by jury under the ICC."

Gus read the expression on de Rijn's face. *You didn't like that answer either, did you?*

The door of his cell swung open and a guard he had never seen before, a hulking brute of a man, rushed in. He turned off the TV, quickly disconnected it, and jerked it off the shelf. "It is not allowed," he said with a heavy guttural accent. "The prosecutor's orders." He walked out, kicking the door shut. This time, Hank heard the lock click shut. The lights went out.

So why are they turning up the pressure? Gus wondered. He stretched out on his narrow bunk, folded his hands behind his head, and thought about it.

* * * * *

Denise tried to relax into her office chair, as her elegant OMAS pen twiddled in her fingers like a miniature baton. But nothing helped as she focused on the TV screen that retracted into the center of her black-lacquered desk. The TV camera zoomed in on de Rijn as he made a show of consulting his notes. She raged to herself as her anger broke over the seawall that contained it. Less than an hour ago, de Rijn's producer had assured her they would crucify Tyler in the court of Dutch public opinion. But that wasn't happening, and Sutherland had captured the interview.

De Rijn looked into the camera. "Professor Sutherland, you have gone on record as saying the court is the logical outgrowth of the Nuremberg Trial at the end of World War II."

"I never used the word 'logical.' While the ICC is seen as an outgrowth of Nuremberg, the comparison does not hold up under close scrutiny."

"Nonsense. Of course it does."

Hank shook his head. "Nuremberg was held after the unconditional surrender of Germany to the Allied Powers. The trial was convened by the Allied Powers who, because of Germany's unconditional surrender, were the sovereign authority in Germany, and held jurisdiction. The defendants were Germans, and the trial was held in the heart of Germany for crimes committed in Germany or German occupied lands. No one has ever explained how we got from that situation to the International Criminal Court."

De Rijn dropped that line of questioning. "Is that your only objection to the court?"

"The court claims that it has jurisdiction over states that are not parties to the Statute of Rome," Hank replied.

De Rijn smiled, now on firmer ground. "It's called the doctrine of universal jurisdiction. The civilized world believes it is an idea whose time has come."

"Yet the Statute of Rome specifically limits the jurisdiction of the court to states that are parties to the statute."

De Rijn smiled patronizingly. "Nonsense."

"This is a matter of public record," Hank said. "The jurisdiction of the court is clearly stated in the preamble and Article Four of the Statute. The court simply does not have jurisdiction over Colonel Tyler. He is a citizen of the United States and is not subject to the court's jurisdiction."

"But he is also a citizen of Panama, which is a signatory to the Rome Statute establishing the court."

"Not exactly," Hank replied. "Colonel Tyler can apply for Panamanian citizenship based on the location of his birth. But he has never done so. In fact, his parents filed a notification of his birth as a native United States citizen with both the State Depart- ment and the Immigration and Naturalization Service. Therefore, by both international and United States law, he is a citizen of the United States, which has not waived jurisdiction to the court in this matter."

Denise gripped the OMAS tightly in her hand. "Monsieur Sutherland," she murmured to the TV, "the world has changed and the court can interpret international law as it applies in this situation." She hoped it was a true statement but her Gallic sense of logic warned her it was not. She tapped the pen lightly on her desk.

De Rijn looked into the camera and said, "Professor Sutherland, why did Mijnheer Melwin remove you from the defense team?" Denise's eyes narrowed and the pen's tattoo picked up a beat. Hank touched his right ear as if he were adjusting a hearing aid.

"I can only speculate at this point," Hank said. "I was on the defense team at the request of Colonel Tyler. But I was proving to be a deep embarrassment for Mr. Melwin."

"That is a very serious charge," de Rijn said, "that demands an explanation."

"This is not the time or place to discuss Mr. Melwin. Let's say he is not suitable for the defense and leave it at that."

Denise gripped the pen and squeezed until her fingers turned numb. She dropped the pen and hit the phone's speed dial to call her husband.

"You are, of course, referring to Melwin's sexual proclivities," de Rijn said.

Hank looked shocked. "It's rumored that he has a drinking problem, but this is the first I've heard of that."

"You've never heard of the Anabella Haus?"

"The name means nothing to me."

"The Anabella Haus," de Rijn continues, "is a bordello a short walk from the court that is frequented by Mijnheer Melwin, usually on a Monday night."

"Well," Hank replied, "as it is Monday, that is certainly convenient."

Denise heard the phone ring but there was no answer. She hung up, frustrated. On the TV, de Rijn struggled to suppress a smile. He finally managed a condescending look. "You appear to be very upset with the court."

The camera focused on Hank and his face filled the screen. "I'm upset about many things. The court is making too many decisions in secret, and I keep asking to see the evidence. But so far, the prosecutor has not turned over a single item to Colonel Tyler's defense team. I suspect that a competent lawyer will shred whatever she has. And why the rush to judgment?"

De Rijn's head jerked up. "Are you suggesting the court is rushing Tyler's trial knowing the United States will not react for fear of losing Europe's support in the United Nations in its feeble attempts to punish the Chinese?"

"Wow. That's saying a lot in a single sentence. But those are your conclusions, not mine. By the way, his proper title is Colonel Tyler. Further, the United States is not trying to 'punish' the Chinese but trying to keep them from invading Taiwan."

Denise hit the speed dial to call Chrestien on his cell phone, raging with frustration. He answered on the sixth ring. "Are you watching Sutherland's interview on Dutch TV?" she asked.

Chrestien's voice was heavy and labored. "Of course."

"Who are you with?"

"No one."

She knew he was lying. "Sutherland is making us look like a Star Chamber! He's done everything but say it."

"Stop worrying," Chrestien replied. "I'll take care of Sutherland." He broke the connection.

* * * * *

The paparazzi were the first to arrive outside the Anabella Haus. Within minutes, seventeen men and women were milling about, searching for the most advantageous camera angle. Two TV camera crews arrived next and parked their vans on the opposite side of the street. Roof-mounted digital TV cameras on telescopic standards extended like all-seeing eyes, and zoomed onto the front door. A Dutch TV crew was the last to arrive and couldn't find a place to park. Frustrated, they drove around to the back. They all settled down, sensing a story about to break.

Three hours later, a weather front moved in off the North Sea and pelted the throng with rain and a blustery wind. One of the more enterprising members of the BBC TV crew decided a reconnaissance run was in order, and biting the bullet for the good of his assembled brethren, took up a collection to avail himself of the services inside. He was back within forty-five minutes and announced that Alex Melwin was indeed there and refused to come out. "The girls seem to like him," the Brit said, earning a fifteen second sound bite on European TV.

Unfortunately, or fortunately, depending on one's viewpoint, it immediately went on the air and the proprietress of the Anabella Haus, who was glued to the TV, panicked. She promptly ordered Melwin to vacate the premises. He refused but her 'social director' had the muscle to enforce her wishes. He escorted the hapless lawyer to the rear door and ejected him into the driving rain. Melwin ran for his car, chased by a TV cameraman and three paparazzi.

The pursuit team had grown to nine when Melwin reached his BMW. He scrambled inside, and locked the doors as he twisted the ignition key. The engine over revved as it came to life. Melwin slammed the car into gear. The car rocketed out into the street and skidded on the wet brick surface. In his panic, Melwin kept his foot buried on the accelerator and cranked the steering wheel the wrong way. The car did exactly what it was told to do and went into a spin, carving what was later described as "perfect whifferdills down the street" before it crashed into the two parked TV vans.

Fortunately, no own was hurt as Melwin had the presence of mind to fasten his seat belt, and as paparazzi are experts in making death-defying leaps to safety. Unfortunately, Melwin was trapped in the crushed car and it took over an hour to extract him with the Jaws of Life, all of which was recorded on TV along with a most revealing interview of the proprietress of Anabella Haus.

Later, Melwin would claim he was the victim of a slow news day. But based on the ratings, it was a very good day for the morning news.

6

Near Utrecht, the Netherlands

"The traffic is heavy for a Tuesday morning," Aly said as she turned onto the autoweg taking them past Utrecht and leading to The Hague. As usual, the bumper-to-bumper traffic was moving at over ninety MPH on the Dutch freeway.

Hank took a deep breath and tried not to think what would happen if a driver made even the slightest error. "I appreciate the ride. But I could have taken the train."

"Why?" she asked. "Besides, how often do I get someone to read an English newspaper to me?" She made a quick lane change. "What else does it say?"

Gus's trial was turning into a three-ring circus and even the London Times was giving it front-page coverage. "It keeps getting better and better," Hank said. "Listen to this. 'Mr. Melwin maintains he was interviewing a prospective witness at the house of prostitution on Monday night. However, he refused to comment on the proprietress's statement that he is a regular patron with very special needs.'"

"Well, that explains it. He had to be sure the witness doesn't blow it." She gave Hank a hopeful look. "I hope that's a joke in English." Hank laughed, liking her more and more. "He must think we're turnips," she said. "He should resign and let you defend Gus."

"He'll probably resign but I seriously doubt the court will let me defend Gus."

Aly made another quick lane change, this time cutting off a huge Volvo truck. The truck driver leaned on his horn. "We're being followed," she told him. "Third car back, a blue Mercedes."

Hank fought the urge to turn and look. He checked the side view mirror and found the car. "Are you sure?"

"Fairly sure," she answered. She made another lane change and barely made the next interchange. The Mercedes shot past, not able to turn with her. "I'm probably paranoid. But nothing has been the same since Gus was arrested." She slowed to make the sharp bend leading onto the next autoweg.

"Things will never be the same," he predicted. "Life's like that when something this big hits you."

"Hold on!" Aly shouted. A sharp jolt and loud bang sent the car skidding sideways. Hank was vaguely aware of a silver car careening along beside them. The cars collided again, rolling Aly's car into the merging traffic. A bus clipped the rear of her car causing them to spin as they rolled. The shoulder harness on Hank's seatbelt broke and his head banged off the dashboard, knocking him out. But Aly was still very conscious. She reached out and grabbed Hank's shirt. By any standard, she was a strong young woman, and she held on with a death grip, pinning him back in his seat, and keeping him from further injury.

The car flipped off the road, bounced into the air, and came to rest right side up in a narrow canal. Dirty, fertilizer-rich water cascaded through the shattered window on Hank's side of the car. A rush of adrenaline coursed through Aly but she never panicked. She released her seatbelt and then reached across to free his. With one hand, she held Hank's chin above the rising water while gripping the door handle on her side of the car. She waited. Less than two inches of air was trapped against the roof when the water pressure equalized enough for Aly to shove the door open. She pulled Hank out after her and immediately broke the surface. The car was barely submerged and she heaved the still unconscious Hank onto the roof. She scrambled onto the hood, and, lying on the windshield, gave him mouth-to-mouth resuscitation. He coughed and sputtered. Then he rolled over and threw up.

The Hague

Gus stretched out on his bunk and folded his hands behind his head, tuning out the usual afternoon hubbub outside his cell. He closed his eyes and let the memory take him back.

A Far Justice

"Mom, Dad," Michelle said, "we need to talk." Gus heard the worry in her voice and nodded. He gave Clare 'the look.' Michelle was in her sophomore year in college and they hadn't been in their circle of confidents for quite a while. "Problems in school?" Gus asked. Michelle shook her head and he saw the tears in her eyes. "I'm pregnant," she blurted. A long silence captured them. "Kevin," Gus said, naming her boyfriend from Berkeley. Michelle nodded. "Are you getting married?" Clare asked. Michelle shook her head. "He wants to go into politics after his father," she replied. "Do you want to keep the child?" Clare asked. Michelle nodded. "We've got plenty of room here," Gus told her.

A knock at the cell door drew Gus back to the moment. A much-chastened Melwin was standing there. "What do you want?" Gus demanded.

"Only a moment of your time," Melwin said. "I'm resigning from the court."

"Bully for you."

"I've withdrawn the letter of rescission to the registrar and restored Professor Sutherland as an advisor to your defense counsel. I've also recommended that he be certified to appear before the court."

"Why the sudden change of heart?"

Melwin's voice shook. "My life is under threat. Colonel Tyler, please tell your people that I've acted properly in this matter."

"I don't know who the hell 'my people' are. But I certainly know who my enemies are and you made that list." He unleashed the anger and frustration that had been building like a cancer and threatening to consume him. "I've done nothing wrong, which seems to mean nothing to you or this fucking monstrosity you call justice." He took a deep breath and reined in his emotions.

"Please, Colonel Tyler, I'm not your enemy." He motioned at the still opened cell door and a guard carried in a small TV set. "All your privileges have been restored."

"Why?"

"The Dutch are very sensitive to criticism," Melwin explained, "and they are being blitzed by the press, all thanks to Sutherland."

"I hadn't heard," Gus replied.

"You don't understand our system of justice."

Gus's anger was back. "If this is your idea of justice, then I pity you."

Melwin backed towards the door, anxious to escape. "Professor Sutherland should be out of hospital tomorrow morning. He'll bring you up to date."

"Hank is in the hospital?"

"He was in an auto accident," Melwin replied. Gus fixed him with a cold stare. Melwin panicked, certain that Gus was going to hit him. He darted out of the cell.

Utrecht

Aly was waiting for Hank when he checked out of the hospital the next morning. They walked in silence to a car where Jason was waiting. Other than a few words of greeting, they were silent until they were well clear of the hospital. "The court's registrar certified you as qualified to appear before the court," Aly said. "Dad was officially notified this morning and he appointed you as lead counsel. So I guess you're in – finally."

Jason handed Hank his percom. "I think it's okay."

Hank fitted the earpiece and opened the lid to turn it on. Cassandra was waiting for him. "Are you okay?" she asked. Hank nodded in answer. He would tell her later that he only suffered a slight concussion. "That's a relief. I realize you can't talk now but we are fairly certain it was a genuine accident. We can't be absolutely sure, so to be safe, use my watchdog feature. If there is a threat out there, we should be able to pick it up."

"Will do," he told her.

"Say again," Jason said.

"Just talking to my computer to be sure it still works," Hank replied. "Aly, I'll need an assistant. How are your office skills?"

"I studied office management in high school. But I'm rusty."

"Excellent. Jason, can you take some leave and help?"

"Can do."

"Good," Hank said. "Let's go to work."

Cassandra was back. "You're being followed." Hank twisted around but only saw a line of trucks behind them.

A Far Justice

The Hague

Denise stood at her office window and looked down on the milling throng of reporters, cameramen, and the curious crowding into the forecourt of the Palace of International Criminal Justice. Her knuckles turned white as she clenched the phone to her left ear. "I can't control it, Chrestien. Melwin has resigned, and the registrar certified Sutherland this morning. He's now the counsel for the defense."

"Don't worry about Sutherland," her husband said. "We are making excellent progress with the Chinese. We only need to maintain the crisis in the United Nations until the first of the year. Just let events unfold."

"The court is coming under heavy public pressure and Relieu is worried about the accusations that this is a rush to justice."

"Two can play Sutherland's game. Release the photos of Mutlah Ridge that I sent you."

"But they're so terrible, so gruesome."

Chrestien took a deep breath, a sure sign that he was irritated with her. "Which is exactly why they haven't been released before. Point to them and claim that justice has been denied too long." He mouthed a few words of support and broke the connection.

She sat down and dropped the phone in her lap. She tried to relax and let the wonderful chair do its magic but a niggling suspicion that she had made a mistake kept eating at her. The more she thought, the more certain she became that she had to delay the trial, appease the media, develop the case against Tyler, and most of all, get a sense of Hank Sutherland. She made a note to have the assistant prosecutor compile a dossier on Sutherland. She considered the man an idiot, but he should be able to do that. The intercom buzzed and she picked up the phone. Sutherland was waiting in the outer office with his staff. "He has a staff?" she wondered aloud. "Send them in."

Denise bisected Aly the moment she entered the office and dismissed her as being too heavy, too plain, and too Dutch. There was no doubt that the huge man was Gus's son with the same rangy good looks and ambling gait. Instinctively, she sensed that Hank was going on the attack. She buzzed for the assistant prosecutor and his deputy, feeling the need for reinforcements. "What may I do for you?" she asked. The two men who served as her assistant prosecutors entered unannounced and stood against the rear wall. "Do you need a delay to prepare?" She glanced at her deputies who both nodded. They obviously shared her doubts.

"Not at this time," Hank replied. "But we do need to see the evidence and your witness list. I also need Melwin's files."

Denise's niggling suspicions mushroomed into panic. Why wasn't he demanding time to prepare, and insisting the court follow its normal process with months of built-in delay? Her need to read his dossier grew more intense. "We will deliver everything we have to your offices." Her two deputies made notes and looked very uncomfortable.

"Unfortunately," Hank said, "I don't have an office."

"The registrar will make space available for you," the assistant prosecutor said.

Denise gave the man a withering look. "But the rent is quite high," she added. "Five thousand dollars a day." She ignored the shocked look on her deputies' faces.

"Is Visa a problem?" Hank asked.

"Speak to the registrar," Denise replied icily. "The prosecutor does not deal with financial matters."

* * * * *

Jason carried in two file boxes and sat them down on the big conference table in their new offices. "Melwin's files," he said. "There are two more outside."

Hank peeled off the file index taped to the top box and studied it for a moment. "Interesting." He opened the first box and rifled through it. "Where's Aly?"

"She's badgering the prosecutor's staff about the evidence and witness list as we speak."

Hank allowed a tight smile. "I image they're enjoying that." He pulled a folder out of the box and sat down. "Security around here is nonexistent. Can you fix it?"

"No problemo. I'll have the place swept for bugs, and get a couple of office safes. Anything else?"

Hank nodded. "I need to see everything the Air Force has on Gus – his personnel file, his records from the Academy, training records, medical file, Officer Efficiency Reports, you name it."

A Far Justice

"You got it," Jason promised. He gave Hank a worried look. "We've only got a month. Is that enough time?"

Hank thought for a moment. "Normally, no. But this case will not be tried in the courtroom. It's all politics and the media is the judge and the public the jury."

"So Dad's already convicted."

"Far from it. Send Aly in the moment she gets back." Hank kicked back, propped his feet on the table, and started to read. After a few moments, he sat up and opened a second file. "Melwin," he murmured, "you are full of surprises."

Hank was standing over the table and arranging Melwin's files when Aly stormed into his office. "They gave us twelve boxes of evidence." She slammed a thick folder down on the table. "This is their witness list! There's over two thousand names on it."

"It's a game lawyers play to swamp the opposition with misleads and needless work." Aly grumped a few words in Dutch and left. Hank picked up the prosecution's witness list and read the first name. "Interesting," he mumbled to himself. "The Secretary General of the United Nations. Two can play at that. Cassandra, are there any former members of Saddam Hussein's regime living in Europe?"

"There's Muhammed Saeed al-Sahaf, the minister of information better known as Baghdad Bob, five in all."

"I'll put them all on our witness list. I also need the names of weapons experts and professors of international law who can help us, preferably European. Also, can you research the prosecution's witness list?"

"Will do," Cassandra promised.

Hank glanced at the second name on the prosecution's list. "Who in the world is Uwe Reiss?" He scanned the list, quickly ticking off the easy ones. A name buried in the middle caught his attention. He pulled out one of Melwin's files and his eyes opened wide as he read. "Son of a bitch!" He buzzed Aly on the intercom. "I've got to talk to Gus. Can you cross-reference Melwin's files with everything the prosecutor gave us?" Aly said she'd get right on it.

* * * * *

It was after the evening meal when Hank reached Gus. "How's it going?" the lawyer asked. He sat down, opened his briefcase, and made sure his percom was on.

"Things got better after your interview on TV," Gus said. There was a gaunt look in his eyes.

Hank sensed Gus was fighting off a major bout of depression. Being locked up did that to a sane person. "The Dutch are very sensitive to public criticism. Hopefully, I can make them even more responsive."

"You're being monitored," Cassandra said. "Shall I scramble it?"

Hank nodded at the percom. "Gus, as you know, the trial is scheduled to start in a little over a month. I can request a delay, it's up to you."

"Look, I want out of here so bad my eyes are crossed. But isn't that rushing things? Can you be ready by then?"

Hank took a deep breath. "If this were the States, no way. But this isn't the States and . . ." His voice trailed off.

"And the verdict's already in. I'm going down, aren't I?"

Hank had anticipated this moment. Long experience had taught him that the prosecution's case always looked strongest at the beginning and that it took time and work to break it down. He was afraid a truthful explanation would drive Gus deeper into depression, and he wanted a vigorous, upbeat, morally outraged August Tyler for the world to see and judge. "Well, Du Milan thinks you are," Hank replied. "I haven't found the right hammers yet. Don't worry, I'll find them."

Cassandra's voice spoke in his ear. "I'm using up a lot of power and need to recharge. Place me against an electrical outlet." Hank did as Cassandra asked and leaned the percom against a wall plug. "Ooh," she purred. "That feels better."

"Am I going down?" Gus repeated.

"Get that out of your head. Nothing here is a done deal. From the evidence I've seen so far, they haven't got much of a case. My plan is to go for maximum media exposure and once we're in the courtroom . . . well, let's just say I'll make it very interesting for them." Gus did not look convinced.

A Far Justice

"The court doesn't have juries," Hank continued. "Well, I'm going to use the media and make the public the jury. I'm going to take the verdict away from the judges."

"Can you do that?"

Hank cracked a tight smile. They were making progress and Gus was coming around. "Well, you saw what happened after one interview on TV. It's a media circus out there and no one wants to be caught in the spotlight. Look at poor Melwin."

"I'm supposed to feel sorry for him?"

Hank shook his head. "No, not at all. What I'm trying to say is that a guilty verdict is not a done deal. Don't let Du Milan get inside your head. That's why she isolated you, to break you down and make you vulnerable."

"So what do I do now?"

"Tell me about the Reverend Tobias Person."

7

The Hague

Gus paced the floor. "Toby Person. He was a backseater in Strike Eagles, that's the F-15E. We were in the same squadron. He looked all of eighteen years old, a little pudgy, and maybe five feet six inches tall. His hair flopped down over his forehead like a sheepdog, and he spent a lot of time gazing into space, seeing a world no one else saw. Not a figure to inspire confidence, but he was the best damn WSO – weapons systems officer – to ever strap on the jet. When there was serious work, Toby was the man." Gus shook his head in wonder. "Toby Person. Who would've ever thought?"

Hank nodded in agreement. The Reverend Tobias Person was a living legend in Africa, a missionary in the Southern Sudan. "You said you were in the same squadron."

"Yeah. I was chief of training and didn't have a regular WSO, so I hijacked him for the Mutlah Ridge mission to fly in my backseat. Jim Cannon, our wing commander, had teamed him with a pilot who couldn't fly worth diddly squat." He snorted. "Davis Armiston. What a prick."

Hank's head came up. "The General Davis Armiston?"

"One and the same," Gus replied. "He was a captain then and totally lacking in situational awareness." He drew into himself, going back in time. "Toby learned Arabic over there." He gave a little laugh. "We gave him a bad time about it at first, but he just pressed ahead. We stopped laughing when the Saudi Air Force liaison officers attached to the Wing started to ask for his help in explaining things. Toby was different. After the Mutlah Ridge mission I found him in the chapel. It was a small room set aside for the chaplains to use. He was just sitting there, staring at the table they used for an altar, like he was seeing what wasn't there. I never thought he was overly religious but I'll never forget what he said. 'I guess we did good out there.' It was the way he said it. Not painful, just sad."

"What did you say?" Hank asked.

"I told him we were just doing our job. It wasn't bad, it wasn't good. Then he asked, 'Why do we do this?' Hell, what was I supposed to say? I asked myself that same question every time one of our buddies bought it. Do you know how many memorial services and funerals I've been to?" Gus drew into himself. "I quit counting at fifty."

"What did you tell him?"

Gus shook his head, still not satisfied that he had found an answer. "'There's an obligation to serve that we must honor.'"

Hank sensed he was seeing a part of Gus Tyler that very few would be privileged to experience. "Even at the risk of your own lives," he added.

Gus looked up and his wry grin was back. "Yeah, but we don't talk about that. Doesn't go with the image."

"We're going to have to go over the mission in detail," Hank said. "But it can wait for now."

"There's a videotape of the mission," Gus told him. "Recorded through the HUD, that's the heads-up-display. It's got the audio and all the symbology; airspeed, altitude, weapons settings."

"What happened to it?"

Again, Gus shook his head. "I have no idea. Jim Cannon, the wing commander, had it sealed and me certify it. The last I heard it was sent to Headquarters CENTCOM."

"We'll find it," Hank said, continuing to take notes. "So what happened after the attack on Mutlah Ridge?"

"The war was over in a few days and we rotated back to the States. Toby resigned his commission, got out, and we lost contact. I sort'a followed his career. He fast tracked a medical degree in Florida then went to Mission Awana in the Sudan, near Malakal on the White Nile. He was in the news big time two years ago when the Sudanese Army attacked the mission."

"Right," Hank said. "The Air Force had a detachment of C-130s at Awana flying relief and peacekeeping missions for the U.N. They were almost wiped out and the commander wounded."

Gus shook his head. "Dave Alston, an old buddy from the Air Force. He was seriously injured but he made it."

A Far Justice

"Cathy and I heard the Reverend Person talk at a fund raiser," Hank said. "Powerful. You wouldn't recognize him now. Skinny, balding, burnt by the sun, hands like claws. He's made a difference in the Sudan."

"Why all the interest in Toby?" Gus asked.

"I apologize for doing it this way, but I had to get your unbiased reaction. The Reverend Tobias Person is on the prosecutor's witness list. According to Melwin's notes, Person made a sworn statement that claims you and he knowingly bombed civilians on Mutlah Ridge."

Gus stared at the lawyer. "No way he'd say that. You don't know Toby. Make that no fucking way."

"That's good to hear. I haven't seen the statement yet, but there is no way they'll get it in."

* * * * *

The Palace of the ICC was deserted when Hank returned and a sleepy security guard let him in. "Use the rear entrance at night," the guard grumbled. The motion-activated lights followed Hank's progress across the entrance rotunda and down the main hallway. He stopped outside the main courtroom where Gus's case would be heard and tested the big double doors carved from African mahogany. He felt them give and he pushed his way inside. The lights automatically came on.

Although the décor was austere and modern, the floor plan was much the same as any courtroom. But the differences were telling. Hank sat down at the defense counsel's table and sank back in the leather chair. Like a good soldier, his eyes scanned the battleground where he would engage the enemy. The prosecutor's table was to his immediate right and a small reading lectern was centered between the tables and facing the judge's bench, which was constructed of the same rare wood as the doors. "How many trees died for this?" he asked in a low voice. On the left side of the bench, the dock, the small enclosure where Gus would sit during the trial, replaced the jury box. The witness box was on the right side of the bench. The long clerk's table was in front of the bench, between the lectern and the judges. Over a hundred seats for spectators filled the back half of the room, and a TV control room overlooked the courtroom from high above the big entrance doors at the rear.

Cassandra's voice was low and urgent. "Hank, don't say a thing. I monitored a signal. The room is bugged. Tap your fingers on the table." He did as she asked. "The bug is underneath," she told him. He sank back into the chair, thinking. Reluctant to give up the comfortable chair, he pulled himself to his feet and headed for the stairs. Again, the lights marked his progress. "Smile," Cassandra said. "You're on Candid Camera."

"Very original."

"Well," she replied in a huff, "I'm *only* a computer, not a comedienne."

Aly was alone in their new offices still feeding documents into a scanner so the computer could automatically cross-reference Melwin's files with the prosecutor's evidence package. "How's it going?" he asked.

"I'm almost done," she answered.

"Can you search for Tobias Person and a Colonel James, or Jim Cannon?"

"Of course." She typed a command into the computer. "There are six references for Person but so far there is nothing on Cannon."

"Let me know if something turns up." He keyed the computer and searched for Toby's statement. He found the file number and dug it out only to discover it was in French. "Aly," he called. "How's your French?"

"Not bad," she answered. "It was my third language in high school."

"Can you translate this for me?" She did and Hank gave silent thanks for the Dutch educational system. When she finished, he kicked back in his chair. "Damn," he muttered. "We're going to need an official translation." She promised it by the end of the next day and went back to work.

Hank closed his eyes, relaxed, and let his mind wander. It was a technique he had developed years before when he was still a deputy district attorney, and the strangest ideas and connections would often emerge. Sooner or later, something worthwhile would pop out and capture his attention. He drifted off as a hodge-podge of images cycled out of his subconscious. He fell asleep.

A Far Justice

Hank's eyes snapped open. Early morning light streamed through the windows and he was alone. He smiled. "Folks," he murmured, "things just got interesting." Aly had left a note for him. She had finished and had found three more references on Tobias Person but nothing on a James Cannon. She'd be back around noon, and Jason should return with the office safes sometime that day.

"Cassandra, I need to locate James Cannon, a retired Air Force colonel who was Gus's commander in the Gulf War at Al Kharj Air Base. Also, we need the videotape of Gus's mission over Mutlah Ridge. It was recorded through the HUD of his F-15. It was sent to Central Command in 1991."

"If it still exists," she answered, "we'll find it. Searching for Cannon now." Then, "Most unusual. Please wait a moment."

Hank played with the computer and called up the new references on Toby. "What's the current situation in the southern Sudan?"

"There's a very nasty civil war going on down there. Islamic fundamentalists captured the government in Khartoum, and control all the oil revenues. The southern Sudan tribes, mostly Dinka and Nuer, are fighting for their independence."

Another thought came to Hank. "Can you search the court's data base for Person and Cannon without them knowing?"

She made small talk while doing it. "All of the registrar's records are part of the public record and are on the Internet. But the prosecutor's files are protected by a firewall and a sophisticated entry protocol."

"Can you get past it?"

"Ooh, you are wicked. Hold on, this may take a few moments while I break in. This is more difficult than I thought. Here we go. There's nothing in their computer on Cannon and they gave you everything they've got on Tobias Person."

"At least everything that is in their computer," Hank corrected. "Have you found anything on Cannon yet?"

"Nothing," she replied. "Apparently he's been secured."

"What does that mean?"

"He works for either the CIA or the National Security Agency. I can't go there."

"Lovely. I need to call Melwin."

"His cell phone is off, but he's at the Anabella Haus."

"What's he doing there at this hour?"

"He's trapped again. Three paparazzi are waiting outside."

* * * * * *

The paparazzi were sitting in their cars outside the Anabella Haus when Hank drove up. Knowing there was no way he could avoid them, he knocked on one's car window and asked if Melwin was inside. "Been in there all night, mate," the photographer replied.

"Got any photos yet?" the Englishman shook his head. "I've got to talk to him," Hank explained. He walked up to the front door; fully aware he was being photographed. He rang and a beautiful girl opened the door a crack. "Tell Melwin to call me on my cell phone." He jotted a number down on his card and handed it to her. He pointed to the waiting paparazzi. "They won't go away until he comes out." The girl nodded and closed the door. Hank waved at the photographers and retreated back to his car. His percom buzzed before he got there. "I'll take it," he told Cas- sandra.

"What do you want?" Melwin asked.

"I want you back on the team," Hank told him.

"Colonel Tyler won't approve."

"He will after I tell him why. Alex, I read four of your opinions and was impressed. You also know how the court works and I think you want to help Gus. Besides, what do you have to lose?"

"Did you set me up?"

Hank lied. "No. Du Milan was using you, and you set yourself up. I'll be in my office all day." Hank broke the connection and laughed. For the first time since arriving in Europe, he was thoroughly enjoying himself. He headed for his hotel to shower and change. It was going to be a long day.

* * * * * *

It was late afternoon when Jason, still wearing his uniform, wheeled in two five-drawer office safes. It amazed Hank the way Jason easily moved the heavy safes around, and he understood Melwin's fear. "I'll need to reset the combinations," Jason said.

"Can you sweep the office for bugs first?" Hank asked. Jason pulled a small black wand out of his heavy attaché-style briefcase and went to work. Within moments, he had found three microdot monitors not much larger than the head of a pin.

"This is good stuff," Jason told him. "I've never seen anything this small."

"Get rid of 'em."

"You're not going to register a complaint?" Jason asked.

"Nope. But sweep the office every morning." Hank thought for a moment. "Jason, we need to find a Colonel Jim Cannon, Gus's commander during the Gulf War. Apparently, he's got some sort of hush-hush job with the CIA, or whatever the spook du jour organization is these days. Maybe one of your sergeant buddies knows something, or someone."

"The NCO Good-Old Boy and Kick Ass Society is alive and well," Jason replied. "I'll shake the tree and see what falls out."

The percom was on and Cassandra's laugh filled Hank's ear. "Do I sense a little competition here?" Hank fought the urge to answer her. "Actually," she conceded, "he might be able to backdoor Cannon's whereabouts. Good thinking."

"Hank," Aly called from the window overlooking the forecourt. "You need to see this." Hank hurried over and was stunned by the size of the crowd flowing into the forecourt two floors below them. A huge banner was unfurled against one wall.

STOP AMERICAN WAR CRIMES NOW

Hank glanced at the TV on the far wall and then back to the crowd below him. It was a strange sensation. He had a bird's-eye view of the entire scene while focusing on the details as seen by the cameraman. Unfortunately, he had no idea what the Dutch commentator was saying but a gut instinct warned him that it did not match reality from his vantage point. He heard Aly gasp and turned around. She was staring at the TV.

"The photographs," she whispered. The cameraman had focused on the huge photographs a group of demonstrators were holding above their heads. "They're horrible."

Hank's stomach turned as highly detailed images of the six photographs cycled across the TV screen. "What are they saying?" he asked.

Aly translated. "This is the carnage from the Highway of Death. This is what Tyler did when he dropped prohibited weapons on innocent civilians. This is why the world is outraged." She pointed at the photo that depicted a desert landscape littered with dismembered and incinerated bodies and burnt-out vehicles. "What did that? Napalm?"

"CBUs," Jason said. "Cluster bomb units, not napalm. They're explosive, not incendiary. The fires were caused by gas tanks the CBUs set off."

"Oh, dear God," she whispered. The image of the inside of a tank filled the screen. The interior was coated with what looked like a thick tomato soup mixed with large chunks of beef and bones.

"Dad didn't do that," Jason said. "Most likely a thirty-millimeter round with a depleted uranium warhead from an A-10 hit the tank. The projectile is so dense and hits the outside of the armor with so much velocity that a massive shock wave travels through the armor and is reflected off the inside surface that flakes off bits of metal. That's the result."

They all winced when the next photo cycled on the screen. Dismembered bodies littered the ground around a destroyed vehicle. "Most likely a direct hit by a 500-pound Mark-82 on a personnel carrier," Jason explained.

A bitter, coppery taste flooded Hank's mouth. "Gus?"

"Possible," Jason conceded.

"I can't believe Dad could do something like that," Aly said.

Hank walked over to the window and stared down on the crowd. "Yeah, he probably did," he finally said.

Aly joined Jason and held his hand. "What kind of world do we live in where good, decent men do things like that?" she asked.

"Gus didn't do it by choice," Hank explained. Below him, the crowd was growing larger by the minute.

"Oh," Aly said, still looking at the TV. She ran to the window where Hank was standing. "Over there, next to the wall." She pointed to a lone demonstrator holding a placard next to his face. "I saw him at the airport when I picked up Gus. He claimed he was there."

Hank's eyes drew into narrow squints as he studied the man below him. Even at a distance, he could see his horribly scared face. "Aly, can you get his name?" She hurried out of the room with Jason. Hank watched from the window as Jason emerged from the building

A Far Justice

and bulldozed his way through the crowd with Aly in his wake. They reached the demonstrator and Aly spoke to him. It was obvious the man recognized her. She handed him a business card and Jason escorted her to safety. They were back in the office within minutes.

"His name is Uwe Reiss," she told them. "He's from Belgium."

"Tallyho the fox," Hank said. "You're looking at the second witness for the prosecution."

Aly changed the TV channel to BBC World News. Scenes of similar demonstrations from every capital in Europe but Warsaw and Prague cycled across the screen. A woman newsreader announced that the recently released photos of "The true destruction on the Highway of Death has outraged Europe, and the demonstrations demanding justice have even reached the United States." A scene of a large demonstration in San Francisco flashed on the screen.

"The Bezerkelies are at it again," Hank said. The scene on the TV changed to a bigger demonstration in Washington D.C. "This is not good," he murmured. "Okay troops, it's late and time to knock off for the day. Jason, why don't you and Aly go see your dad and keep him company? Maybe call home?"

* * * * *

Jason stared at his cell phone. "Sorry, Dad. No one's home and Michelle isn't answering her cell phone. Hopefully, she'll call back while we're still here."

Gus paced the floor of his cell, five paces up, five back. "She's probably out shopping." But they knew that was not true. Michelle never left Clare alone and a nurse, or one of her boys, would have answered the phone. "How's it going?"

"It's too soon to be sure," Aly told him. "But Hank seems very confident."

"How are they treating you?" Jason asked, deliberately changing the subject.

"The Dutch? No complaints. They leave the cell door open all the time and I've got the run of the halls. I've met most of the guards. Nice guys." He perked up. "One of them has a brother who flew F-16s for the Dutch Luftwaffe. He's one of the Dutch pilots who shot down those Serbian fighters in 1999."

81

Aly was shocked. "The war in Kosovo? I knew we were there with NATO, but we didn't shoot down any of their airplanes."

"Yeah, you did," Gus replied. His tone was relaxed and upbeat. "Two of them."

"Why didn't we hear about it?"

"I don't know. But I'd be very proud of what they did."

The cell phone rang and Jason punched it up. Michelle's face appeared on the screen. "I just got your message. I had to take Mom to the emergency room and they don't allow cell phones inside."

Jason handed the phone to Gus. "What's going on, Pump-kin?"

"Oh, Dad, Mom's really bad. I don't know . . ." Her voice trailed off.

"It's okay, darlin'. Just do what you have to. Tell her that I love her and will get home as soon as I can."

"I've got to get back inside. I'll call as soon as I learn anything."

"I love you, Pumpkin." Gus punched off the call and resumed his pacing. "I've got to get out of here."

8

The Hague

Hank looked up from his desk Friday morning when a very sober and rigid Melwin presented himself for inspection. Hank waved the Irishman to a chair. "Come on in."

"Professor Sutherland, I don't know how to thank you."

Hank smiled. "Don't even bother." He sank back into his chair. "I prefer Hank. Okay if I call you Alex?" Melwin nodded in answer. "Alex, you can help us in a very specific way. Once the trial starts, I want you to raise every legal issue in the book and question everything. If someone even breathes 'universal jurisdiction'. . ." Hank deliberately let his voice trail off to see how the Irishman would respond.

"Ah," Melwin said, *"quasi delicta juris gentium."*

"I believe the correct term is *ratione bullshitus*."

Melwin tried to smile, but couldn't manage it. "That is not a legal term I am familiar with. But universal jurisdiction is certainly the court's strangest excursion into unknown legal territory, and, I might add, totally beyond its charter." His voice grew sad. "Crimes against humanity, war crimes, genocide – the curse of our civilization. And we can't seem to stop any of it. But for the first time, the court offers a chance to prosecute those responsible."

Hank urged him on. "And?"

"While it denies it, the court is determined to impose its jurisdiction on states that are not parties to the Rome Statute. Such an over-reach of authority will cause a reaction. At what cost to the court, I don't know, but I do fear for its very survival. And, as you have learned, the court is easily manipulated by the prosecutor, which only compounds the problem."

"Alex, we're going to get on fine." He tossed Melwin the official translation of Toby's statement. "What do you make of this?"

"I am familiar with this. It is what you Yanks call 'the smoking gun,' and will prove to the court's satisfaction that Colonel Tyler knew there were civilians in the convoy when he bombed it. Now all the prosecutor has to prove is that his bombs killed one civilian."

"It will never see the light of day in this court," Hank promised.

"Unfortunately, there's a good chance it will. There's an overlooked provision buried in Article Sixty-eight of the Rome Statute that states evidence can be presented by electronic or other special means in order to protect victims or witnesses."

"Lovely," Hank muttered. "The good Reverend is caught up in a nasty little civil war in the Sudan. Does that mean if he can't get out, the prosecution can enter his statement as evidence?"

"It has never been tested in court, but it would appear so."

"Son of a bitch!" Hank roared. "What happened to the defendant's right to examine the witnesses against him in court? There's no way they could get away with that in the States."

"Pesky thing, your Constitution," Melwin murmured.

"Gus swears that Person would never say anything like that." Hank paced the floor. "But he knew Person twenty years ago. Who knows where he's coming from these days. Maybe he believes they really did know there were civilians in the convoy."

"Maybe they did know," Melwin said, playing devil's advocate. "The court is required to produce the witnesses, if it can. But it has no power to subpoena them, and as the prosecutor has Person's sworn statement, there may be a certain lack of urgency."

"And if we also call Person as a witness?"

"Ah," Melwin replied, "that might increase their sense of urgency. But if Person appears and verifies his earlier statement, it would become his word against Colonel Tyler's. The question then becomes, which witness would play better with the court?"

"I'd rather take my chances getting the statement excluded."

"It is a conundrum," Melwin said.

"Think about it," Hank said. "Anyway, here's the game plan. We're going to question every aspect of the court that we can. I want to hear the judges' sphincter muscles snapping shut every time you stand up. The court is on trial, not Gus."

"And if we destroy the court in the process?" Melwin asked

A Far Justice

"Then it would have happened anyway. All we did was speed it up."

A knock at the door interrupted them. Aly entered carrying a heavy file box and a letter. "The prosecutor sent these down," she told them. "Its Gus's Air Force records."

Hank quickly thumbed through the file box. "How in hell did she get these?"

"More germane," Melwin replied, "is why did she send them down now? She's had these for weeks. I had assumed all this had been forwarded to you."

Instinctively, Hank knew the answer. The firewall on the prosecutor's computer had alarmed when it was penetrated but if Cassandra's masters were half as good as he suspected, no one at the ICC would ever backtrack the intruder. However, Denise had assumed, correctly, that Hank was the guilty culprit. She was playing cover-up in case he had discovered a reference to Gus's personnel files. "So what else does she have?"

"I need to go through it in detail," Melwin said, "but I believe this is all."

Aly handed Hank the letter. "They've added two more names to their witness list."

Hank read the letter. "I'll be damned. She's calling General Davis Armiston." Hank's fingers drummed a tattoo on his desk. The implications of a retired United States Air Force four-star general testifying for the prosecution were staggering. "The other one, Nativadad Gomez, I've never heard of."

Cassandra's voice was there, filling his ear. "Nativadad Gomez is a naturalized American citizen who works for the Air Force in the Personnel Center at Randolph Air Force Base." She paused. "By the way, we think the prosecutor turned over Colonel Tyler's personnel files because they know their computers were penetrated." There was an embarrassed silence. "We're working on that one."

Hank considered his next move. "Aly, please notify the prosecutor that we're adding another name to our witness list; James Cannon, Colonel, United States Air Force, Retired. If we can find him. Don't tell them that last bit."

* * * * *

Aly and Hank waited in the corridor outside the cell to give Gus some privacy while he called home on Hank's cell phone. Aly leaned against the wall and closed her eyes. "It's wearing him down," she said. "Every day, he's more and more like a caged animal."

"At least he can call home," Hank said.

Her eyes opened, full of tears. "It's not helping."

Gus came to the door and handed Hank his cell phone. "The doctors want to keep her in the hospital for now."

"Are you up to talking?" Hank asked.

Gus checked his watch. "I've got an appointment with the prison shrink in a few minutes. I can't put her off any longer."

They went inside and Hank closed the door. "We need to talk about Melwin. I've brought him on as second chair." Gus's head jerked and his eyes flared with anger. Hank held up a hand, holding the pilot's anger in check. "I read a few of his opinions and went through his notes. His analysis of the prosecutor's case and strategy was brilliant."

"A lot of help that was," Gus snapped.

"He was stymied by the system," Hank replied. "But he knows how the ICC really works; who swings the big bat, who pisses on who, and how deals are cut behind chamber doors. But here's the real kicker – the ICC is hanging its hat on the doctrine of universal jurisdiction. They see that as its future and it's the only way they can justify the expense of maintaining the court. Apparently, Melwin is the only person on the ICC who openly questions the validity of universal jurisdiction."

"So why didn't he resign?" Aly asked.

"Because the ICC pays his salary," Hank replied. "A damn good one, by the way. A gut feeling tells me that Alex is unemployable any place else."

"Like most of the clowns there," Gus said. "He'll sell us out in a heartbeat."

"I don't think he will," Hank said. "Never underestimate Du Milan. She figured out our strategy days ago so it doesn't matter what Melwin might tell her."

Gus checked his watch. "I've got to go."

"We'll talk later," Hank said. "For now, write down everything you can remember about Jim Cannon and Davis Armiston."

Gus's anger flashed. "Armiston! He couldn't fly the jet worth beans and only survived the Gulf War in '91 because Toby was in his backseat. The Armiston I knew was infinite confidence and zero competence. He was all politics and the youngest general since World War II. He pinned on his fourth star the week he became SACEUR. Rumor had it he was a total bust."

"Du Milan is calling him as a witness," Hank said.

"Oh, no," Gus moaned. "He hates my guts."

"Don't go falling on your sword and doing pushups yet," Hank cautioned. "Don't be late for your appointment. We'll talk tomorrow." Aly hugged him and they left.

Gus sat for a few moments and forced his anger away. "Fuckin' Armiston." He stood up, stretched, and headed for his appointment with the prison's psychiatrist. Hank's interview on Dutch TV with Harm de Rijn had changed everything and he now had free access around the prison during the day. The only thing he couldn't do was walk out the main gate. He found the office in the administration block and knocked. The door opened and he sucked in his breath. The young woman standing there was six inches shorter than him, with dark blonde, carelessly cut hair, and a trim figure. She was very attractive in an unconventional way and rippled with an undercurrent of sexuality.

"Please come in," she said. "I'm Doctor Therese Derwent." They shook hands in the formal European manner and she motioned at the two easy chairs arranged in a comfortable corner of the office. They sat down and she crossed her ankles as she picked up his case file. "I have been monitoring your progress here."

"Progress?" he asked. "What human being makes progress caged like an animal?"

"Please forgive me, that was a poor choice of words. I am concerned with how you are adjusting to your confinement."

"I'm adjusting to my confinement just fine."

"Are you?" She picked up the remote control for the DVD. The TV came to life. "These are not in chronological order," she explained. "But they do make more sense arranged this way." A series of scenes showed Gus wandering the corridors gazing aimlessly at his surroundings. Then he was pacing his cell. From time to time, he paused and carefully examined an item. Nothing escaped his scrutiny. She flicked off the DVD and leaned forward to study his face for a few moments. "You're planning to escape," she announced. It wasn't a question but a statement of fact. "Please don't."

"Now why would I want to do that?"

"I understand your wife is quite ill and in hospital."

"I'm surprised you're the least bit concerned."

"May I see your right hand?" she asked. She took his hand with both of hers, and her touch was warm and soft. "Most of the residents here enjoy conjugal privileges. I know the tensions can build and become quite unbearable."

"Are you offering yourself up for the cause?"

"Please, don't be rude. But certain accommodations can be made."

* * * * *

It was late that same afternoon and Hank was listening to the BCC when he first heard the announcement. The President of the ICC had named Gaston Bouchard, a Belgian, as the presiding judge for Gus's trial. The other two judges would be announced at a later date. "What's the bad news here?" he asked Cassandra.

"Gaston Bouchard is Belgium's former ambassador to the UN and the leading proponent of the doctrine of universal jurisdiction. He is also rabidly anti-American."

"Rabidly?" Hank asked.

"Like in junkyard dog," Cassandra replied. "I have a very detailed file on him."

Hank sat his percom on top of a printer and a lengthy file started to spit out. "Cassandra, I need a profile on the Reverend Tobias Person. The prosecution has a statement he made claiming that he and Gus knew there were civilians at Mutlah Ridge. Gus says he would never make such a claim but I want to know where Person is coming from." He picked up the file on Bouchard. It was not good reading and he was still mulling over the implications when Aly buzzed him on the intercom. Bouchard had commanded his immediate presence in his offices on the top floor.

"Take the elevator to the seventh floor," she told him, "and cross the fly bridge to the East Tower." Based on what he had just read, Hank knew better than to delay and hurried for the elevator.

A Far Justice

Bouchard's outer office was a complete counterpoint to the rest of the ICC's palace and reminded Hank of an antechamber he had seen at Versailles, Louis XIV's palace outside Paris. As expected, he had to cool his heels for thirty minutes, allowing Bouchard to establish his preeminence. It was a game Hank could play but for now, respectful humility was the order of the day. "Nice tapestries," he said to the receptionist. She responded with an icy stare and ignored him. He shrugged and tried to make himself comfortable in a chair not built for normal humans. He chalked it all up to 'the treatment.' He stood when Denise entered, certain the imperious Bouchard would immediately receive them. He was almost right.

"Leave all electrical devices with me," the receptionist ordered.

Hank laid his percom on her desk. "Wonderful hospitality," he said. The receptionist opened the massive double doors to Bouchard's inner sanctum and ushered them in.

The man waiting for them was an overweight bureaucrat who fancied himself an intellectual and was impressed with his importance as a judge. As a young man, he was considered handsome, but forty years, 125 pounds, and a choleric disposition had changed him into a cantankerous old man who could not understand why people avoided him. Although Bouchard was fluent in English, he spoke in French. "Madame Prosecutor, please translate my instructions. I have called you both here to make clear what I expect."

Denise translated his words. "Professor Sutherland is very knowledgeable about court procedures and protocols, and I would prefer we speak in English." Hank arched an eyebrow, surprised that she was standing up to Bouchard.

Bouchard pointed at Hank and continued in French. "You are, above all else, a member of the court and have an obligation to justice that transcends your duties to the accused. Therefore, there will be none of the courtroom tricks you Americans are so fond of." He waited while Denise translated. "I am instituting what you call a gag order. You will not speak to the press, any individual, or appear on TV until a judgment has been achieved. Further, there will be none of your Perry Mason surprises in my court. All evidence and witnesses will be properly presented well in advance. I expect all substantive questions to be presented in writing before raised in open session."

Hank listened as Denise explained Bouchard's rules. "Substantive?"

Bouchard drummed his fingers on his desk, obviously irritated at Hank's questioning of anything he might say. "Questions with substance, meaning they are essential or fundamental." The beat increased. "This is exactly what I will not tolerate in open session. Do you understand?"

"Yes, your Honor. I fully understand."

"That is all," Bouchard said. "You are excused."

Denise led the way outside and waited while Hank retrieved his percom. "I don't like him either," she confided. "Perhaps we should discuss ways to resolve any conflicts?"

"Sounds like collaborating with the enemy."

Denise gave him a look he could not decipher. "As officers of the court, we are not enemies and must work together."

"Perhaps it would be better if only our staffs conferred at this point."

"Of course." She turned and walked away.

He ambled across the fly bridge and paused at mid span, taking in the view. The forecourt seven floors below him was still crowded with demonstrators who had taken up permanent residence. He spoke in a low voice. "Okay, Cassandra, what's going on with Du Milan?"

He gazed at the misty horizon on the North Sea as he listened. "We monitored a phone call between Madam Du Milan and her husband, Chrestien. He wants her to establish a more personal relationship to curb your uncivilized tendencies."

"*Moi*? Uncivilized?"

"Yes, you, Monsieur Barbarian. They've seen how you exploit the media and want to rein you in. By the way, pressure is building in the United States for the President to free Colonel Tyler."

"I don't think the President is quite ready to invade The Hague. What's the story with Natividad Gomez and General Davis Armiston as witnesses?"

"Gomez is the one who gave them Colonel Tyler's personnel records. They need her to establish the source, and the validity of the files. Armiston can testify that Colonel Tyler was there and did fly the mission."

"So Gomez is a spy."

"More of an exploited lover. As for Armiston, he needs the publicity to make a run for the presidency."

"Why would any sane person want that job?" Hank muttered. "Anything on Person yet."

"Nothing about the statement he made. The bad news is that the missionary society financing the mission is strongly pacifist. Our profilers say we're dealing with an unknown quantity."

"I need to talk to the Reverend."

"Hold on," Cassandra replied, "I'll see what I can do." She made small talk. "What did you think of Bouchard?"

"You guys don't miss much, do you? He lived up to expectations."

"Sorry, Hank. I can't get through to the Sudan. All normal lines are down, the satellite channels are blocked, and there's strong interference on the radios. It might be jamming. The supply line to the mission has been cut, and it appears to be surrounded by the Sudanese Army and Islamic militias."

"What does your legal team think about Person testifying?"

"They don't recommend it."

* * * * *

The images on the screen smoothly transitioned as the assistant prosecutor recapped his Power Point briefing on one Henry Michael Sutherland. The final image zoomed in on Hank sitting at a table in his hotel's sidewalk café as he read that morning's edition of the London Times. It was a subtle way of saying their information was current. He ended with the traditional, "Are there any questions I can answer, Madam Prosecutor?" Denise smiled graciously and shook her head. He handed her the thick confidential dossier. "Many of the details are fascinating," he said. "My colleagues say he has a suppressed Rambo complex, but I think that is a gross simplification of a very complex and intelligent man. He has an aggressive trait that is contained and focused by the scholarly and mild side of his personality."

"So which is the real Sutherland?" she asked.

"It depends on the situation, Madam Prosecutor. As I mentioned earlier, he did challenge a mob and save a demonstrator from being thrown over the side of the Oakland Bay Bridge. He clubbed one man with a baseball bat rather unmercifully." He suspected that would get her attention and it did.

"I would like to compare photos of Tyler and Sutherland." The assistant typed in a command and the computer responded. The large screen split and images of Gus and Hank appeared. "Leave it on," she said, dismissing him.

"Do not underestimate this man, Madam Prosecutor." He bowed and left her alone, pleased that she had allowed her the last word.

Denise thumbed through the dossier. She leaned forward in her chair and studied the photographs of Gus and Hank. Thanks to the large, high-definition screen, they were almost life-sized. The lean and rugged, good looking Gus was a total contrast to the pleasant and buoyant Hank. There was no doubt that half the women following the trial would be attracted to Gus. Fortunately, the senior president of the ICC had assured her that the three judges hearing the case would all be men, which she could play to her advantage.

She worked her way through the thick document, occasionally looking up at the screen. She finished and sank back in her chair, the still opened dossier on her lap, her eyes locked on the screen. She let her emotions run free. There was no doubt that Gus was very appealing.

* * * * *

The Dutch were well known for their frugality when it came to heating and Gus wondered why his cell was so warm so late in the evening. Rather than complain, he opened the door for cross-ventilation, stripped down to his shorts, and got comfortable on his narrow bunk. He turned on his nightlight to read, taking advantage of the few short evening hours before the lights went out. But he couldn't focus on the words as he slipped back into the past.

It was a short drive from the Officer's Club to their quarters in family housing. Clare sat quietly but he knew something was bothering her. He cast back, trying to remember anything from the promotion party all the new captains had thrown that evening. He could only think of one thing. Clare hit him on arm. Hard. "What was that all about?" he asked. Her voice was matter-of-fact. "She was throwing herself at you." He shook his head. "Who? I must've missed that." He braced himself for the answer. "Miss Tits, that's who. Captain what's-his-name's date. And you didn't miss it. In fact, you were rather enjoying it." He heard that certain tone in her voice and relaxed. "Give me a break. They're engaged and she was just buttering up the boss." He waited for her answer. "Well, she certainly wanted to do more than spread a little butter, especially if she got you alone." Gus sighed, fully knowing what was coming. "I wouldn't know what to do." Clare released her seatbelt and cuddled against him. "Then I better teach you so you'll be prepared when it happens." This was a variation he hadn't seen before. "You know I'm a slow learner." Her hand played with the buttons on his shirt. "We'll work at it until you get it right."

"May I come in?" Therese Derwent said, breaking his reverie. She was standing in the doorway and holding two books in the crook of her arm. She had changed in her office for an evening out and was gorgeous.

Hank swung his legs over the side of the bunk and sat up. "Please." He motioned to one of the two chairs in his cell. She placed the books down on the table and shrugged off her coat. Her simple dress shimmered in the light but what interested him was the identification card dangling from a thin black lanyard around her neck. It was the first time he had seen one in the prison.

"I thought you might find these interesting reading," she said. "One is the history of the court and the other a critique of the doctrine of universal jurisdiction by Alex Melwin."

Gus came even more alert at the mention of Melwin. "Thanks," he said, wondering why the psychiatrist had picked late Friday evening to drop them off.

"Today was not a good beginning," she said, "and I'm afraid you might have misunderstood. Language is always a barrier but we are worried about you. I was hoping we might talk again. Perhaps Monday?"

He made a show of considering it. He gave a little nod. "It's my wife, you know."

"I know," she said. She stood up. "I must go."

He hurried over to help her with her coat. "Hold on for a second. I'll walk with you." He pulled on a pair of warm-up pants and a T-shirt. He slipped into his sandals and followed her into the corridor.

"I can't really complain about the way I'm treated here," he told her. "Still, I get so damned depressed."

"We see our prisons as places of rehabilitation, not punishment. We can work on the depression." They reached the end of his cellblock where the gate was closed, sealing the inmates in for the night. She slid her identification card through the electronic lock. The gate slid back and he saw the guard in the glassed-in control booth on the other side. He was stretched out on a bunk watching TV and the lights were down low. The guard never looked up or checked the TV monitors. "This is as far as you can go at night," she told him.

They shook hands and, again, the warmth of her touch surprised him. "Thanks for the books. I'll read them over the weekend." He watched her as she walked down the corridor and through the next gate. He ambled back to his cell, deep in thought.

9

The Hague

Gus stepped out of the cubicle shower after his routine Monday morning exercise, dried off, and carefully examined his beard, thankful there was very little gray. But was it too long? He strongly suspected the psychiatrist keyed on small behavioral traits. So how would she react to a three-day growth of beard? Would she see it as a sign of growing depression, perhaps vulnerability, or find it attractive as Europeans often did, or a little of all three? *What if she sees right through it?* he thought. He quickly shaved and pulled on a clean pair of warm-up pants and a loose sweatshirt. He slipped on his running shoes and checked the mirror. For better or worse, he was going for the clean athletic look.

    He walked down the corridor, carefully checking for the identification cards he had seen Friday night. The guards were only wearing their normal badges and the gates were all open. He made the connection. *Gates close and ID cards come out. So the cards are also access control keys they only use at night.* He needed to work on it. The door to Derwent's office was open and he wandered in. She smiled. "Right on time." He closed the door and she motioned him to the easy chairs in the far corner. They sat down and she bent forward. He caught a slight fragrance of expensive perfume. "Tea? How was your weekend?"

    "Thanks for the books. I'm not a lawyer but I'm thankful we didn't join the ICC."

    "Please explain."

    For a moment, he considered faking an answer. *Go for the truth.* "Based on what I read, I am a war criminal."

    "Is that true?" she asked.

He deliberately fidgeted. "The way I read the Rome Statute creating the court, if a fighter jock like me, kills a single civilian in combat, he's committed murder."

"You disagree with that?"

"Of course I do. We don't go out there to deliberately kill civilians."

"But it does happen," she said. "Shouldn't someone be held accountable?"

"That's why we have the UCMJ – the Universal Code of Military Justice – for when it happens deliberately. Look at William Calley and the Mai Lai massacre in Vietnam. We court-martialed him."

She leaned forward and touched the back of his hand. "I think you're feeling persecuted and have convinced yourself that you're a scapegoat for political reasons."

"Are you suggesting it's anything else?"

She didn't answer. Instead, "How are you handling the tension?"

"I could handle this if my wife was okay." He rose and paced the floor. "We were married right after I graduated from the Air Force Academy in 1982." He stopped and looked at her. *But you know all that, don't you?* "Since then . . . well . . . Clare's my life." He stared at the window. "I remember when Michelle was born, she's our oldest, and when I first saw her Clare was nursing her in bed. I just stood there, not able to take my eyes off them." He pulled into himself, remembering. Then, "Now Clare's dying and I'm not there." He whirled on her. "I'm not a war criminal."

Her voice was barely audible. "I know that."

He came up short, surprised by the tears in her eyes. He sat back down, his elbows on his knees, hands clasped, head bent low. "I'm having trouble sleeping at night. This place seems to moan at me."

"But it is quiet at night," she said. "Not like your prisons."

"It's still a prison and I'm here, looking out, caged in." He fell silent for a moment to let his anguish show. "Do you know what it's like to takeoff on a cruddy overcast day like this and punch through a cloud deck?" He stared at his hands; his voice low and charged with memory as he took her with him. "Suddenly, you break out on top of the clouds and all the grays, browns, and muck of the earth are all behind you. I can't remember how many times I leveled off and skimmed the tops of the clouds. The sky hangs over you like a crystal crown. Then you snap roll and the world spins, yours for the sorting out. You brush the top of the clouds and then you're pulling on the stick, climbing like a homesick angel, and reaching for the sky. For a few brief moments, all the trivial problems of this silly world are behind you."

Derwent's eyes glowed with understanding. "It must be like riding the whirlwind."

Gus looked at her. "Hell, I don't know how to explain it except you're truly free." He paused for effect. "All I know now is that I can't sleep at night."

She jotted down a note in her folder. "You surprised me today, Gus. I expected you to be needing a shave and perhaps come on to me." He gave her his lopsided fighter pilot grin and she closed the folder before standing up. The session was over. "I can help with your sleeping problem."

They shook hands and Gus ambled back to his cell. *There may be something here.*

Amsterdam

Late that same afternoon, a tour boat nosed out of a narrow canal and turned into the much larger Amstel River. The tour guide pointed to the luxury hotel. "The Amstel Intercontinental. Its restaurant, La Rive, is one of the best in the world."

Hank scanned the hotel's terrace that overlooked the river as they approached and worked to hide his nervousness. The boat nudged against the hotel dock and Hank stepped ashore. He scanned the dock area, wondering if he was recognized. He climbed the stairs to the terrace where a dark-suited young woman was waiting.

"This way, Professor Sutherland," the young woman said, leading him to a side entrance.

"Why all the secrecy?" he asked.

"Because Mr. Westcot prefers it."

Hank grew even more worried. It was the second time Westcot had summoned him and he didn't like being on the financier's radarscope. Hank followed her to a service elevator and they rode in silence to the top floor of the hotel. The elevator door opened onto a luxurious suite. She stayed behind and the door closed, leaving him alone.

"Over here, Hank," Westcot said. The financier was seated in an overstuffed wing chair by the fireplace smoking a cigar. He stood and they shook hands. Westcot pointed him to a seat and paced the floor. "How's it going?"

"They announced the presiding judge, Gaston Bouchard."

Westcot humphed. "Met him once. A pompous ass. He possesses the perspective of a horse – a very intelligent horse, but still a horse. How's Cassandra working out?"

"She's been a wonderful help. I couldn't do it without her."

"Excellent. We've backed her up with a top-notch legal team. Use them." More pacing. "The President tried to get the court to release Gus but it isn't going to happen." He shook his head. "The idiots got the bit in their teeth and are out of control."

"What the hell is going on?" Hank asked. "I feel like the proverbial mushroom here; totally in the dark and fed bullshit."

Westcot decided to level with him. "It's pure power politics and the French are into it up to their eyeballs. They've managed to link the trial to what's going on in the UN. It's a chance for them to make political hay by prosecuting an American for war crimes before the ICC. Some crap about universal jurisdiction."

The lawyer in Hank keyed on the anger lurking behind Westcot's words when he mentioned the French. "The court is trying to extend its authority over non-member nations. Gus's trial is a waypoint in that process."

"That is not going to happen," Westcot predicted. "But they've got the President walking a tightrope, keeping the hawks in Congress under control while not pissing off said European allies, who happen to adore the court."

"And Gus gets hung out to dry," Hank said.

"Exactly," Westcot replied. "It also gives the French an opportunity to play kissy-face with the Chinese and strike a deal that could make them the economic powerhouse of Europe."

The anger was back and Hank suspected Westcot was involved because a deal between the Chinese and the French would cost the financier mega dollars. Had he known, the actual figure would have astounded him. "What the French are doing goes against the EU."

Westcot snorted. "Indeed it does. It will piss off the rest of Europe something mightily when they figure it out."

"Is it take-off-the-gloves time?"

"When the time is right," Westcot replied. "Right now, it would take the UN option off the table in regards to China. The President's options at this point are very limited, which leaves Gus swinging in the wind."

Hank thought for a moment. "Maybe not. I think I can win this one." Westcot's head snapped up. "But I need some help. They've called General Davis Armiston as a witness and I'll need to discredit him if he takes the stand. Also, I need to find Gus's old wing commander when he was in Saudi Arabia at Al Kharj."

Westcot puffed on his cigar and billowed smoke. "Armiston is a worthless piece of shit and wants the White House. He'll do whatever it takes to win it." He allowed a tight smile that frightened the lawyer. Like so many things, it had all came together for the financier in a rush. Now it was only a matter of playing it out. "Call Henri Scullanois, the French foreign minister, as a witness. Scullanois dealt with Armiston when he was SACEUR. No love lost there. Use Scullanois to discredit Armiston."

"And?" Hank asked, knowing there was more.

Westcot didn't answer. Instead, "As for Cannon, I can't help you there."

Hank had not mentioned Cannon's name and hoped his face did not betray what he was thinking. "Well," Westcot said, fully aware that he had made a faux pas by naming Cannon and that damage control was in order, "how about dinner? La Rive is an experience not to be missed."

"Do we want to be seen together in public?" Hank asked.

"Good point," Westcot conceded. He reached for the phone, "Well, if we can't go to La Rive, La Rive will come to us." He gave Hank a knowing look, still playing damage control. "Perhaps some companionship for later this evening?"

"Can I take a rain check?" Hank asked. It was time to get out of Dodge without burning a very important bridge. "I really have to get back to The Hague."

The Hague

They had warned him and Gus knew the news was bad. "Dad," Jason said, "you need to talk to Michelle." He handed Gus his cell phone, his eyes full of worry. Aly stood in the open door to the cell, her worry matching Jason's. But for some reason, she felt better with Gus involved.

Gus nodded and took the phone. "We can't run away from it," he said. His jaw tightened as he hit the speed dial to call his daughter. He waited for the connection. "Damn, I should be there."

Michelle's pretty face came on the screen. There were tears in her eyes. "Thank God. I was afraid they wouldn't let you call."

"Jason and Aly told me. How bad is she?"

"The doctors said they can make her comfortable, that's all. Is there any chance you can come home?"

"None at all. The bastards here have a lot to answer for."

"There's something else," Michelle told him. "Max Westcot called and offered to transfer Mom to the Mayo Clinic. He said he'd cover all expenses. Mom's doctors are all behind it."

"I hate relying on the charity of others," Gus said.

Behind him Jason said, "Max Westcot has got more money than a herd of horses have hair. Make that a huge herd of horses. It won't even show on his radar screen."

Michelle heard him. "It is the Mayo, Dad."

"But that would mean leaving her alone in a strange hospital," Gus said.

"Me and the boys will be there," Michelle promised.

Gus made the decision. "Okay, do it."

"I think it's the best thing to do," Michelle said.

They said good-by and Gus ended the call. "It shouldn't end this way," he said to no one. The lights in the ceiling and corridor blinked. "Lights-out in fifteen minutes," he told them. Aly kissed him on the cheek and she and Jason disappeared out the still open door. He stood in the doorway and watched them go through the gate at the end of the corridor as Therese Derwent passed them. He retreated back into the cell and sat on the bunk to wait for the psychiatrist.

"May I come in?" she asked.

"Certainly," he replied.

Derwent walked over to the built-in buffet and drew a cup of water before sitting next to him on the bunk. She handed him a small aluminum foil packet. "Take this. It will help you sleep." He ripped it open and popped the capsule into his mouth. She handed him the cup and placed two fingers on his throat. "You must swallow," she said. He gulped and she smiled. "Lie down." She moved out of the way while he stretched out. He deliberately faked sleepiness but Derwent didn't leave. *Too much personal attention,* he thought. *Need to work on it.* He relaxed and breathed deeply.

Derwent sat on the edge of the bunk and touched his wrist to be sure he was asleep. She monitored his pulse for a moment. "Clare is most fortunate to have you," she murmured. She sat there until the lights blinked the last time before rising. She closed the door behind her.

"I'm the lucky one," he said to no one. He fell asleep.

10

The Hague

Hank sat under the umbrella heater in the glassed-in sidewalk café and sipped at the steaming cup of coffee. He waited for the caffeine to jumpstart his brain. Ever so slowly, he came alive. He took another sip as the waiter presented a warm pastry for his breakfast. It smelled delicious. He studied the people hurrying by on their way to work and decided that he liked the Dutch – not that he understood them. But he was certain that if he looked and listened long enough, the Dutch and the Netherlands would make sense. He just wished his wife were with him to share the experience.

He glanced at the Tuesday morning edition of the London Times. With thirty days to go, Gus Tyler's upcoming trial was still making the first page. He read the article with satisfaction. The British were finally acknowledging that Gus was an American citizen, which, sooner or later, would be crucial. He stared across the street as he considered his options. A silver Audi he had seen the day before pulled out of its parking space from across the street. A blue Mercedes immediately pulled in and the driver of the Audi signaled by bending the forefinger on his right hand and raising it to his eye. The driver of the Mercedes replied with the same sign. A jolt of adrenaline coursed through his body. It was the same Mercedes. "Cassandra, I'm having coffee at my hotel's sidewalk café and a blue Mercedes just drove up. Am I being followed?"

"If you are, I'm not monitoring any electronic communications or signals." That explained the hand signals. "Can you get a license number?"

"I'll try." He scribbled his name on the bill and picked up his briefcase. He stayed on the opposite side of the street and walked briskly away from the back of the Mercedes, heading for the Palace of the International Criminal Court. A heavy truck and a streetcar clogged the narrow street, stopping traffic in both directions. He darted across the street and melded into the crowd as he walked back towards the Mercedes.

He saw the driver's hand reach up and adjust the rearview mirror, angling it in his direction. Certain the driver had seen him, he pushed through the crowd as the Mercedes pulled into traffic. He started to run after it as the traffic opened up and started to move. He put on a burst of speed as the Mercedes moved away, quickly outdistancing him. He came to halt. "Damn."

"The first part of the license number was 90-BN," a man said in English.

"Thank you," Hank replied, still looking at the Mercedes. He turned to say more, but the man was gone. He liked the Dutch even more. He reversed course and headed for the Palace.

* * * * *

Aly was waiting when Hank reached his office. "I dropped in and saw Dad this morning." She handed him two sheets of paper. "This is all he could remember on Cannon and Armiston." She followed him into his office with a mug of coffee and the morning mail. As soon as he was alone, he said, "Cassandra, I got a partial license number on the Mercedes, 90-BN. I couldn't make out the last."

"That's interesting," Cassandra said. "90-BN and BN-90 were part of the license numbers the Dutch reserved for American servicemen stationed in The Netherlands. But that was over twenty years ago. Those numbers have been inactive since then."

"Is there a connection?" Hank asked. "I wouldn't be surprised if the front license is different than the rear."

"I'll work on it," Cassandra replied. "My power cell needs charging."

He placed the percom next to an electric outlet and wandered into the outer office. "Aly, I need to speak to Jason when he gets here."

"He's in the canteen eating breakfast," she told him.

Exactly eight minutes later, Jason was in Hank's office. "We've got to find Cannon," Hank told him. "Pull out all the stops."

"I'll ask General Hammerly," Jason promised.

Aly ran into the office. "I just got a call from one of my friends who works downstairs. General Armiston is in the building." Hank arched an eyebrow, pleased that Aly was a member in good standing in the Dutch Secretaries Mutual Protection and Gossip Society.

* * * * *

The double glass doors leading into the prosecutor's offices slide silently back and General Davis Armiston marched in. He stood six feet tall, walked with a military bearing that befitted a man of his experience, had a full head of dark-brown hair streaked with gray, all cleverly orchestrated by his stylist, a square jaw, rugged good looks, and wore an immaculately tailored dark-blue pinstripe suit. Thanks to an excellent speaking voice, deep blue eyes, and a quick smile he was a public relations triumph.

The receptionist buzzed Denise and she hurried out of her office to greet one of her star witnesses. "General Armiston, this is indeed a pleasure," she cooed.

"The pleasure is all mine," he cooed back in French. She escorted him into her office and they sat down. An aid pushed a teacart loaded with the requisite silver service and pastries in after them. They bantered in French while taking mid-morning tea and carefully scouting each other. Then, "Madam Prosecutor, I hope you know how much this upsets me."

"Please, I prefer Denise. I can understand your feelings about testifying against a fellow officer."

"Denise, I hope you know there are many Americans who support and believe in the International Criminal Court."

"It is the wave of the future," she assured him.

"No doubt you are aware that Gus is basically a good man, certainly an excellent pilot, but like so many of his generation, an automaton who never understood the moral ramifications of his actions when flying combat."

"Which is exactly what we must explain to the world," she said.

"I hope you know there are certain things I cannot, and will not say."

A niggling doubt tweaked at her. "Then we must go over your testimony in some detail – to preclude any misunderstanding. But for the moment, we must discuss what you can expect when interviewed by our media."

"The media has never been a problem in the past," he assured her.

"Ah, yes," she replied. "But I think you'll find Harm de Rijn much different than his American counterparts."

Armiston smiled. "And when will this happen?"

"At your convenience," she replied.

Armiston became all business. "I have an opening this afternoon at four."

"Justice Bouchard has issued what you Americans call a gag order. I'm hoping that you will say what I cannot." He gave a tight smile in answer and she picked up her phone to arrange the interview. "Done," she told him. "Four o'clock at your hotel." She handed him a typed list of questions. "Here's what you can expect."

Armiston scanned the list. "I need to speak to my advisors but I see no problem." He stood. "This suit will never do. Denise, I believe that you and I will get along famously."

She shook his hand, not sure of it at all.

* * * * *

"How did you sleep last night?" Derwent asked.

"Like a log," Gus replied. He sat down to the ever-present cup of coffee while she made a note in her folder. "Can I ask what's in there?" He gestured at the folder.

She closed the folder. "I'm participating in an on-going study about personality disorders. My research group has asked me to evaluate men and women who, shall we say, have problems with the law."

"Perhaps," he ventured, "the problem is with the law and not the individual."

She smiled. "Perhaps." What she didn't tell him was that part of the study required her to rate the physical attractiveness and intelligence level of her subjects to determine if there was a correlation. Based on the study's criteria, she rated Gus at the ninety-fifth percentile level on attractiveness and estimated his IQ around 130. But there was something about him she could not identify, and that excited her.

She opened her notebook. "You've told me about flying, but what was it like to fly in combat? Were you afraid?" She couldn't read the look on his face. Was it a smile?

"It's not like anything you can imagine. Of course there's fear. But that's when you're lying in bed waiting for the alarm to go off." He thought for a moment. "It's the routine that gets you through. In Saudi, I flew the nightshift and slept during the day. Thank God our quarters were air-conditioned, but the noise on the flight line would usually wake me up by mid-afternoon. I had a routine and would get up, exercise, and shower and shave. After that, I'd check my mail, hit the dining hall, and go to the squadron. I was chief of training so I'd fly with different backseaters, weapon systems officers, to check them out and see how good they were. I didn't have a regularly assigned WSO but preferred to fly with Toby Person. He was the best."

He slipped into memory. "One night Toby and I were assigned an area in western Iraq to patrol, all part of the great Scud hunt. Scuds were the missiles Saddam was lobbing into Israel, and we were worried that if we didn't stop them, Israel would come into the war. That would have ripped the coalition apart so the pressure was really on. To be honest, we weren't being too successful." He paused while she made notes. "Toby had been talking to a Saudi liaison officer and studying the charts. He wanted to search a different area but the high rollers wouldn't buy it." He scoffed. "They said there was nothing there. So it was the same old routine: listen to whatever Intel was saying, brief the mission, suit up, and step to the jet. I'd preflight the bird and Toby the weapons." He laughed. "Do you know what's the last thing you do before climbing up the boarding ladder and strapping the jet on? You take a leak."

"Where?" she asked.

"Any place that's convenient. Toby and I used to stand in a corner of the revetment and piss on the sandbags. I'd hum the Air Force song." He sang a few words. "Off we go, into the wild blue yonder." He blushed.

"You have a very good voice," Derwent said. "What would Toby do?"

"He'd sing along." He chose his words and images carefully, taking her with him as the mission unfolded. "We'd take a deep breath and climb the ladder. If you've got a good crew chief, the cockpit is all set up for you, the switches, everything. You double check anyway. Then it's crank engines and taxi for the end of the runway to meet up with your wingman for quick check."

"Quick check?" she asked.

"A ground crew from Maintenance gives the jet one last inspection, checking for leaks, cut tires, loose panels, and making sure all the safety pins are pulled. Then you wait to make your takeoff time. The radio call is always the same. 'Pounder One and Two, taxi into position and hold.' Now things happen real fast. 'Pounder One and Two, cleared for takeoff.' You release brakes and stroke the burners, torching the night. Twenty seconds later, your wingman is rolling and you're headed for western Iraq.

"The airborne controller checks you into the area and there is absolutely nothing moving on the ground. So we'd bore holes in the sky until it was time to head for a tanker for an airborne refueling. My wingman always hooked up first but this night, he can't transfer fuel. So I send him home." Derwent noted how Gus kept slipping between the past and the present as he talked. "Then we hooked up to take on 9000 pounds of fuel. The boomer cleared us off and we return to the area single-ship to continue the patrol. It's the same old story, bore holes and turn jet fuel into noise. Then the TSD, the tactical situation display, it's a screen on the instrument panel with a moving map, cycles to an area I've never seen before.

"I asked Toby, 'What the hell is going on?' He said, 'I got another place to look.' Well, his 'other place' was out of our area and operating anywhere else without clearance was a no-no. I wasn't about to do it. You should have heard Toby bitch and moan. He can really be creative at times. So I head for the extreme northwestern part of our patrol area, which gets us fairly close to where Toby wants to look, and still keeps us legal. That's when he finds it on the radar." He stopped to take a sip of coffee.

Derwent was caught up and in the cockpit with him. "Toby finds what?"

"A convoy. The radar has a moving target indicator that only shows what's moving, and Toby has four big targets moving across the desert in a convoy. Then they disappeared."

"Because they stopped moving?" she asked.

"Exactly. I figure they don't have warning gear that could have detected our radar and the odds were they've stopped to launch the missile. So I tell Toby to freeze the last location of the convoy and put the radar in standby so they can't detect us – just in case they do have warning gear. I head for the deck."

"You're going to attack them?"

"No way. I'm going to take a look and report back. I level off at 400 feet, engage the TFR, that's the terrain following radar, and push it up to 500 knots heading for the convoy's last location. It's pretty rough terrain but the TFR is working like a charm. Toby says '400 feet ain't high.' Stalwart fellow, Toby. So down we go another 200 feet. The turbulence is pounding the hell out of us now and I'm sweating like a pig."

"Can you see the ground?" She was breathless, reliving the moment with him.

He shook his head. "Too dark. We pop to crest a ridge and for a split second, we have altitude. The TEWS, our electronic warning gear, is screaming at us. A hostile radar has picked us up, probably a SAM, that's a surface-to-air missile. I roll the bird 135 degrees and slam us back to the deck. While this is going on, good old Toby brings the radar back to life and sweeps the target. They're moving again, and I figure they've detected us and are running for cover. Now I got an image on the FLIR, that's the forward looking infrared, which is like looking at the world through the bottom of a green coke bottle. I see the rocket plume of a SAM at our two o'clock and comin' right at us. I jink like hell, loading the bird with eight Gs. The missile overshoots. A very bad mistake for them."

"How so?"

"You never lose the right of self-defense and I don't need clearance to nail 'em. So sayeth the rules of engagement. Now the FLIR breaks out the target. A truck and a fuel tanker are sandwiching a TEL with a couple more trucks and a bus behind."

"TEL?" she whispered. She wasn't making notes and her eyes were wide and unblinking.

"TEL stands for transporter, erector, launcher," Gus said. "A really big vehicle that carries the missile."

"So you saw the rocket."

"Nope. The TEL was camouflaged. Behind the fuel tanker is a bus and I see a few smaller vehicles flanking the convoy – outriders running escort. A red stream of tracers reaches up from one of those puppies, right at us. Toby's head is buried in the back, working the radar, getting a system lock-on so he doesn't see it. The TEWS is still screaming at us and I turn off the audio."

"Why?"

"So I can concentrate. Toby's got the TEL locked up and the weapons system is doing its magic. All I got to do is get close enough. Two more SAM's are coming at us but I figure they're SA-7s, shoulder-held missiles that aren't much of a threat, not as long as I can keep us on the deck and going like stink. The tracers cut behind us. The bastards can't shoot. We over fly the convoy and I rip six Snake Eyes – I mean I rippled six Mark-82, five hundred-pound bombs. Shack.

"The jet rocks something awful and the lights on the warning panel go crazy. We're headed down and I stroke the 'burners and pull, going for the moon. Behind us, the convoy goes up like the Fourth of July on steroids."

"What happened?" she asked breathlessly.

"The fuel tanker and whatever was on the TEL exploded. The warhead I guess."

"I mean what happened to you?"

"We took a hit. Lost most of our hydraulics and holed the right wing something fierce. We were leaking fuel like a sieve. No way we can make it home so I call for an emergency refueling." He gave a little laugh. "It was a long way back to the tanker. Almost flamed out for fuel starvation. But we got hooked up and the KC-135 dragged us back to Al Kharj, where we landed."

"Did you get a medal?"

"No way. We were out of our area without clearance. Some general at CENTCOM, that's Central Command, wanted to court-martial us. But my wing commander, Jim Cannon, wasn't having any of it since they had shot at us."

She reached out and touched his cheek. Her hand was warm and moist. "You're sweating."

"So are you."

She pulled her hand back and shook her hair. "It must be the thermostat."

* * * * *

A Far Justice

Gus sat on his bunk, his back against the wall as he watched Davis Armiston being interviewed by Harm de Rijn on Dutch TV. The overhead lights blinked, warning him that it was fifteen minutes to lights out. "You're still the same oily son of a bitch," Gus said to no one. *Stop talking to yourself. This place is getting to you.*

The camera zoomed in on Armiston's face. "While most American's are opposed to the ICC," Armiston explained, "there is a substantial, and growing minority who believe we should participate."

Now don't go falling all over yourself with unbridled joy, Harm.

De Rijn did. "That is very encouraging to hear, especially after the cowboyism and amateurism that has characterized Amer- ican foreign policy for the last decade."

"One of my foreign policy goals," Armiston replied "is to reach out to our European allies in a meaningful way and rebuild the ties that are the bulwark of the western alliance."

"Rebuild, my ass," Gus said. He hit the power key on his remote control and the TV went blank. He closed his eyes and sat there, his head against the wall.

"Rebuild what?" Derwent asked from the doorway.

"How long have you been there?"

"Just a few moments. I was listening to your General Armiston. I take it that you don't approve of what he said."

"Armiston is a total asshole. He'll say whatever he thinks will get him elected."

"Do you know him personally?"

"I knew him when he was a captain, later a lieutenant colonel, he hasn't changed a bit."

"So he was a fighter pilot like you."

"Davis Armiston doesn't know the meaning of the term."

Derwent drew a cup of water at the buffet, and handed him a sleeping capsule. Before he could take it, she sat on the bunk next to him, and as before, placed her fingers lightly on his neck to feel him swallow. "We must be very careful with these," she murmured. Her fingers lingered longer than necessary. She rose and walked to the door. "Your story about the Scud missile was most exciting. Sleep well." Then she was gone, closing the door behind her.

Gus heard the lock click and spat the pill into his hand. He waited for the lights to go out. When it was dark, he walked to the buffet, still holding the capsule. He unrolled the paper towels and placed the pill on the last sheet. Then he methodically rolled the towels back up. *We're getting there.*

11

NATO Headquarters

Power is a relative thing and the two men sitting in office of the Supreme Allied Commander Europe, or SACEUR, were a case in point. Maximilian Westcot was one of the wealthiest men in the United States and moved on the world stage with ruthless arrogance. He was also the confidant of the President of the United States, and had direct access to sixteen prime ministers and heads of state. On the other side of the desk, General Douglas Hammerly was an accomplished professional warrior who had commanded units in combat and a brilliant strategist. With one order, he could set thousands of men and women in motion. But more importantly, he was a leader men and women willingly followed into combat.

"The President is walking a tight rope on the Tyler issue," Westcot explained. "Publicly, he's concentrating on the Taiwan crises. Behind the scenes, he's pursuing a two-fold approach to free Gus. He's willing to let the wheels of diplomacy turn to a certain extent to see if the system can correct itself. At the same time, he's asked me to explore more informal avenues, including private appeals to the court and some of my European friends."

Hammerly understood perfectly: the President was using the backdoor to pressure the ICC, and he, as SACEUR, had better get on board. It was part of the world he lived in where informal links were as important as the formal chains of command. The trick was knowing when and how to respond, and as it was Maximilian Westcot, the response had better be positive. "Given the widespread public demonstrations we're seeing over here," Hammerly said, "appealing to their better natures or sense of justice is a waste of time."

"It does look that away. But Hank Sutherland believes he can win, provided that he finds a key witness and gets him on the stand."

"Who is?"

"Colonel James Cannon," Westcot replied. "I know what Cannon does. Unfortunately, I goofed, and Sutherland is aware that I know Cannon."

Hammerly steepled his fingers and studied Westcot, carefully guarding his words. Cannon was a key player in Operation Phoenix, a top-secret special operation that tracked down and killed terrorists. It had been a long struggle and the ranks of the terrorists had been decimated, largely thanks to Cannon who wielded the knife that targeted individuals with small airborne-delivered, precision-guided munitions. Hammerly made a decision. "I'll see what I can do. And if Sutherland fails?"

"Then there will be a rescue mission."

"The CIA?"

Westcot shook his head. "The Director of National Intelligence refuses to get involved. Which, given the current state of our intelligence services, is a very wise move. They would screw it up big time."

The general agreed with him. "I assume you're telling me all this for a reason."

Westcot nodded. "We need Sergeant Tyler's help."

"You've got it. He's already providing covert security for Sutherland. By the way, exactly who is the 'we' in all this?"

"Shall we say a non-governmental organization with a lot of backing?"

"Ah," Hammerly said, his suspicions confirmed, "the dreaded NGO working independently of any established government but certainly supported by a government."

"I couldn't possibly comment on that," Westcot intoned, playing the same game as the general.

The Hague

Alex Melwin sipped at his afternoon tea and eyed the last scone on the teacart as Hank paced the floor. "Why don't you finish it off?" Hank said. "Take a look at this. It came in today." He didn't tell

A Far Justice

Melwin that the mini disk was courtesy of Cassandra and her team. He made a mental note to introduce Melwin to Cassandra at the right time. He hit the start button on the video player and Toby Person materialized on the screen as he guided a BBC reporter through his mission in the southern Sudan.

"This is Mission Awana," Toby said, sweeping the area with a broad wave of his hand. "It's really a plantation in that we're largely self-sufficient. Thanks to the river, we've over 4000 acres under year-round irrigation, and export food, mostly a type of disease-resistant sorghum. We also have some cottage industries that could be commercially successful. Equally important, we have the best schools and the largest medical station in sub-Sahara Africa. Our hospital has three doctors, an operating room, a hundred beds, and a training school for nurses and midwives. Our medical teams vaccinate over 10,000 children a year."

A loud explosion echoed over him. The men ran and the picture twisted and turned as the cameraman followed Toby and the reporter into a bunker. They all piled inside and were soon joined by a hoard of children. A little girl crawled into Toby's lap and sucked her thumb. Toby listened as a second explosion shook the bunker. "That's our daily reminder that we're caught in a civil war." The dull whomp of two outgoing mortar rounds reached them. "That's outgoing counter-battery fire. D'Na is pretty good at discouraging them." They sat in the stifling heat as silence engulfed them.

A heavyset figure, about five-feet eight-inches tall, and dressed in combat fatigues filled the doorway to the bunker. Her hair was cut short, her facial features classical Dinka, and her dark skin glowed with health and vitality. She would never be considered beautiful by western standards but she was a strikingly handsome woman. "It's all clear," she announced. The children burst from the bunker as she laughed.

Hank hit the pause button. "I would not want him as a hostile witness on the stand," he said.

Melwin swallowed the last of the scone. "Agreed. Much better to take our chances and try to exclude his statement."

Hank restarted the video and let it play out. "He is impressive. Any ideas on how to keep it out?"

"A few," Melwin replied. "None good. We could call Person as a witness for the defense, and then press the Victims and Witnesses

Unit to produce him at the trial, which they probably can't do. I'll remind the court that when Person gave the statement, he was not subject to cross examination, and as he is a witness for the defense, the introduction of the statement in his absence is prejudicial to Colonel Tyler's defense."

"Will that work?"

"With Bouchard? I doubt it. But the other two judges might agree."

"Pity we don't know who they are," Hank said.

"There are five other judges in the trial division and they all want to hear this case. I can tell you that none will be sympathetic to Colonel Tyler."

"I didn't need to know that," Hank muttered. He made a mental note to have Cassandra's team profile all five. "Notify the court that we're calling the Reverend as a witness."

* * * * *

Westcot was enjoying himself. He was sitting in the receiving chamber of Alphonse Relieu, the ICC's senior president, and wondering where the other two presidents of the court were hiding. But he was not surprised. He did have a well-deserved reputation, and braver souls had run for cover when Max Westcot sighted down on them. Sir John Landis, the presiding judge at Gus's confirmation hearing, was made of much stronger stuff and was sitting next to Relieu. There was no doubt in Westcot's mind that the meeting was going nowhere, but it was exactly the type of exchange he loved. He made a mental bet that he could send at least one of the two men scurrying for the restroom. He ran his handicapping system and decided Relieu was the odds-on favorite.

The three men stood when Denise entered the ornate chamber. It was the first time Westcot had seen her in person and he sighed, deeply regretting that his marriage license lacked a mileage limitation. Denise bestowed a beautiful smile on him and his regret multiplied substantially. She sat down, crossing her legs, and gestured to the chair next to her. He joined her and she touched the back of his right hand.

"This a pleasure," she murmured. "Chrestien has spoken of you so many times." Her hand lingered on his.

"Madam Prosecutor," Relieu said, "thank you for coming on such short notice. Monsieur Westcot has a most interesting, but very informal, proposal from his President."

Denise arched an eyebrow. She was aware of the power and influence Westcot wielded and doubted that Relieu could stand up to him. "Of course we are most willing to hear whatever your President may offer." She withdrew her hand and the battle was joined.

"If the court," Westcot said, "will release the colonel, my government is prepared to recall him to active duty and charge him with war crimes."

"I am familiar with your Manual for Courts-Martial," Landis said. "Bringing charges does not automatically mean a court-martial."

Westcot was not a lawyer but his percom was on and his legal team, without doubt the best in the world, was feeding him information through his earpiece. "Considering the severity of the charges against Colonel Tyler, I'm confident the officer conducting the pretrial investigation will recommend a court-martial."

Relieu caught the slight shake of Denise's head. "The preamble to the Rome Statute establishing the court clearly states that the court's authority is complementary to national criminal jurisdictions, which hold primacy over our proceedings. We will, of course, defer to Panama should they decide to bring Tyler to trial." His voice shook as he looked at Denise. "The court cannot grant the United States primacy in this matter."

Westcot gave Relieu a long look that asked why he was being so stupid. A European politician could only antagonize the President of the United States up to a point. Anything beyond that had serious consequences. "May I ask why? This is a proposal that satisfies both our needs."

Denise again touched Westcot's hand. "Complementarity only extends to member countries of the court. Now should the United States ratify the Rome Statute and become a party to the court, then perhaps . . ."

"That will never happen, my dear," Westcot told her. She gave him a sad look and withdrew her hand. "But I assure you, our system of military law reflects the law of armed conflict."

Landis chimed in, not the least intimidated by Westcot. "You must think we're simpletons. The law of international armed conflict separates the intended effect of an action from its logically foreseen effect, which the Rome Statute will never do."

Westcot listened to the voice in his earpiece. "So," he replied, "if a pilot bombs a train station to stop a troop movement and kills civilians who just happen to be in the train station, he's guilty of murder."

Denise nodded. "Under every civilized system of law."

Westcot's legal team was way ahead of her. "Under every system of criminal law," he replied, "but not under the law of armed conflict."

"A court-martial," Landis said, "would undoubtedly find Tyler not guilty. That would be a mockery of justice and the court would be forced to declare it a sham trial and have the prosecutor bring charges against him."

"Which is double jeopardy," Westcot said. He came to his feet and fixed the two men with a cold look. "I assure you, you are making a very bad mistake." He turned and stalked out of the room, leaving a heavy silence in his wake.

Relieu ran for his private restroom.

12

The Hague

"You seem in a much better mood this morning," Therese Derwent said.

Gus looked around the psychiatrist's office, searching for a bug. He couldn't find one He settled into a chair and sipped at his coffee. "You know, the one thing I really hate about this place is eating alone."

"Is that important to you?"

"Dinner was the one thing Clare always insisted on. We'd all gather, no matter where we were, camping, on a boat, you name it. Sometimes the food wasn't so good, but the dinner was always great."

Derwent smiled. "Family, sharing, and conversation. Perhaps that defines us as humans."

"And a society," he added, certain he had made a friend.

* * * * *

Hank arrived in Denise's office thirty seconds early. He bestowed his best smile on the receptionist and waited. At exactly 10:30 A.M. on Friday morning, the fifth of November, the receptionist buzzed Denise and announced his presence. Denise dispatched the assistant prosecutor to usher him in, and Hank suspected they were playing one of the games the ICC specialized in. The court was meticulously correct in following its procedures as long as the prosecution's case was not in jeopardy.

Denise rose to greet him with a pleasant smile. He wasn't sure who had designed the business suit she was wearing but the results were a study in judicial restraint, business functionality, exquisite taste, and subdued sexuality. Hank estimated the cost around 2000 euros. He missed it by half. They shook hands and Denise nodded graciously. "May I introduce Natividad Gomez?"

Hank turned to the woman sitting opposite him. She was short, overweight, and on the dowdy side. Like so many heavy women, she had a smooth and lovely face. He estimated her age around forty but like so many things that morning, he was wrong. He smiled at the lawyer sitting next to her. "Hi, Coop. It's been a long time. How's the ambulance chasing business?"

R. Garrison Cooper's bushy eyebrows twitched and he glared at Hank. "Personal injury is a much maligned field." Cooper's gravelly voice betrayed his years of boozing.

"I take it you know each other," Denise said.

"Coop was the defense counsel on a court-martial I prosecuted," Hank explained. "He managed to snatch defeat from the jaws of victory."

"My client," Cooper grumped, "changed his plea to guilty at the last moment. I was winning."

"So what brings you here?" Hank asked.

Cooper cleared his throat. "This is a very unusual case and I've volunteered my services as Miss Gomez's legal adviser."

"Publicity is a wonderful thing," Hank said. Cooper's career was in decline and in desperate need of a boost. Cooper glared at him but didn't take the bait. Hank sat down. "Miss Gomez, thank you for your help. This is a formal deposition" – he nodded at the court recorder – "and the questions are much the same ones you'll hear if you take the stand." He opened his leather folder. "Your full name."

"Natividad Adelina Gomez."

Hank jotted her name down followed by her initials. "Your age?"

"Don't answer that," Cooper said.

Hank sighed audibly. It was going to be one of those days. "Are you married?"

"Don't answer that," Cooper repeated.

"Place of birth?"

"Again, don't answer that," Cooper said.

Hank switched to Spanish and asked if she was a US citizen. Without thinking, she replied in Spanish that she was a naturalized US citizen. "Thank you," Hank said.

"Do that again," Cooper said, "and this deposition is over."

"Please describe where you work," Hank said. Cooper nodded, allowing her to answer.

"I work for the United States Air Force Personnel Center located at Randolph Air Force Base outside San Antonio, Texas. I have been employed for eleven years and I am a clerk in the Records Division."

Hank knew a rehearsed answer when he heard one and gave Cooper high marks for properly preparing his client. "Did you have access to the records of Colonel August William Tyler?"

"Yes, I did."

"Did you remove or make copies of Colonel Tyler's records?"

"I made copies," she answered.

"Were they complete and did you make any changes or omit anything?"

Her English was very stilted and formal. "I copied all the records on Colonel Tyler I could find. I did not make any changes or omit anything."

"Did you provide these copies to another person?"

Cooper whispered in her ear. "Yes, I did," she answered.

"His or her name?"

"Don't answer that," Cooper said.

"I'm trying to determine the authenticity of the records and establish the custodial chain," Hank said. He turned to Natividad. "Have you reviewed the files currently in possession of the court?"

"Yes, I have."

"Are they complete and unaltered?"

"I think so," she replied.

"You think so," Hank said. He closed his folder. "Thank you for your help, Miss Gomez." He stood and nodded at Denise. "Madam Prosecutor." He left the room with Cooper in close trail.

"Hank, we need to talk," the older man said.

Hank stopped. "She's in a world of hurt."

"I know that. I only got involved yesterday. The poor woman did what she thought was the right thing."

"Coop, what she did makes her a spy, and I'll make that point the moment she takes the stand." He wasn't sure how he would handle Gomez on the stand but he let the threat resonate, certain it would get back to Gomez and Denise. "Gomez will be arrested the moment she returns to the States. The court cannot compel a witness to appear, so if you really want to help her, convince her not to take the stand. Contact the DOJ and cut a deal while you still can."

"Believe me, I've tried. I told her that Du Milan only needs the records to prove Tyler was there, and there are other ways to do that." He paused for a moment. "By the way, how's it feel to defend an innocent man when the court is stacked against you?"

Hank lobbed another bombshell to confuse and distract Denise. "Who said he was innocent?"

NATO Headquarters

Jason marched into the General's office and came to attention, waiting to be recognized. Hammerly took in the big man. Technical Sergeant Jason Tyler, USAF, was everything he wanted in a security cop, smart, resourceful, and loyal. He hoped his sons turned out as well. "At ease, Sergeant. Have a seat. How's your dad doing?"

"Confinement is tough, but he's managing."

"I understand your mother has taken a turn for the worse."

"Yes, sir," Jason answered, "she has. She's in the Mayo."

"Any problems with Sutherland?"

"None, sir. We've got a covert security team in place 24/7. Intel is still reporting some threats, but we're not seeing it."

"How's your cover?"

Jason allowed a frown. "Sutherland made one of our teams outside his hotel but thought it was hostile. He doesn't know we're there, and the ICC and the Dutch are clueless. Sir, we need to call Colonel James Cannon as a witness but can't find him."

Hammerly nodded. "I'll see what I can do but you need to keep looking."

The Hague

The TV coverage of Armiston's departure from Schiphol Airport reminded Hank of the send-off given to rock stars and Hollywood celebrities. The general held up two fingers and waved the victory sign. "I shall return," he announced.

A Far Justice

Hank flicked the TV off and threw the remote control down in disgust "You are one piece of work." He leaned back into this chair, closed his eyes and went to work. What to do about Natividad? He fitted his earpiece and opened his percom. "Cassandra, what have you got on Natividad Adelina Gomez?"

"I heard you met her today," Cassandra said.

"You heard right. I felt sorry for her."

"The Department of Justice has issued a warrant for her arrest."

"Any chance of Cooper cutting a deal for her?" Hank asked.

"He's already approached them. They're willing to listen – if she cooperates. There's not much in her file. Thirty-one years old, born in Juarez Mexico, naturalized in 2004, clean record with the police, outstanding job ratings. She does have a boyfriend we haven't identified. Here's an interesting tidbit. Our profilers think she's a virgin."

"In this day and age?"

"It does happen," Cassandra replied.

"What do you have on Henri Scullanois?"

"Volumes."

"What exactly is he up to?"

"I'll have our analysts work on it and get back to you," she said.

Hank broke the connection and buzzed Melwin. "Alex, you got a moment?" The Irishman said he did and Hank ambled into his office. He stretched out in a chair, folded his fingers across his stomach and tried to look serious. "Alex, me lad, here it is Friday afternoon and I want to ruin everyone's weekend."

"That's very sporting of you," Melwin replied. "Exactly how do you plan to do that?"

"I want to call Henri Scullanois as a defense witness." For a moment, he was certain Melwin was suffering labor pains. "Why not?" Hank ventured. "If they can call the UN's Secretary General, why can't we call Scullanois?"

Melwin was finally able to breath. "It's different. Countries do not join the court to have their national policies put on trial. It's an unspoken understanding." Hank waited for him to work it out. "Brilliant," Melwin breathed. "Absolutely brilliant." He reached for the phone and called Bouchard's receptionist. "Please inform the Justice that we are amending our witness list and notification to that effect is on the way." He listened for a moment before he hung up.

"Bouchard is in Brussels and won't be back until Wednesday. But I think you just changed his plans." He buzzed Aly on the intercom and asked her to draft the notification. "Hank wants it delivered to Bouchard's office this afternoon." He turned to Hank. "It will be ready for your signature in a few minutes and she'll deliver it personally. I must say, this is very uncivilized of you."

"I certainly hope so," Hank replied.

Île St-Louis, Paris

Denise cradled the exquisitely cut crystal glass snifter in her hands and savored the aroma. The cognac, like everything around her, was testimony to a wealth and privilege that very few men and women ever experience. She sipped at the pale gold liquid and let its warmth capture her. It was the perfect cap to a perfect dinner. And she loved the elegant surroundings. The Hôtel L'Abord was not the biggest mansion on the island, the Rothschild's Hôtel Lambert held that honor, but it was one of the oldest and dated back to 1629. It was also unique in that it had always been in the possession of the L'Abords, if for no other reason than the family had the knack of picking the winning side of the revolution of the moment. When that failed, they bought their way out of trouble or left the country.

Their hostess, the elderly Comtessa Eugenie L'Abord, was the current occupant of the mansion. The Comtessa was the resident harpy of French politics and could make and break political careers at will. Even Denise's husband, Chrestien, danced attendance on her. On this particular Friday evening, the Comtessa had blended the skills of her chef with an informal atmosphere to create a culinary triumph. The four other guests were witty and cultured; all certified as the brightest and best, not to mention the wealthiest, denizens of French society and politics. Like them, Denise was casually dressed yet perfectly at ease in the regal surroundings.

The elderly Comtessa sat beside Denise. "I was so worried that you couldn't make it back from The Hague."

"I wouldn't have missed this evening for the world," Denise said. "It was a difficult week, and this was just what I needed."

"It must be that wretched American. I can't remember his name."

A Far Justice

Denise laughed and every man turned towards her. "Hank Sutherland. Actually, I quite like him."

The Comtessa was shocked. "*Sacré bleu!*"

Denise smiled at the old-fashioned expression. Her eyes followed the butler as he crossed the room and spoke to her husband. Chrestien stood and followed him out. "Monsieur Sutherland is a very unusual man," Denise said, "and not what he seems. He is very intelligent and quite brave." The countess went into a deeper state of shock. "If you're interested I'll send you his dossier. It is very interesting reading."

"I would not even speak to the likes of him," the Comtessa said, casting Hank into oblivion.

Chrestien was back and joined them. "Comtessa, I must apologize. A most unfortunate message." Cell phones were forbidden in the presence of the Comtessa and the tactful spoke of messages, not phone calls. "There is a matter I must deal with. As always, dinner was magnificent." He glanced at Denise and looked at the door, the signal that she was to come with him. "Thank you for inviting us." Chrestien kissed the old woman lightly on both cheeks and she cooed in pleasure. Denise stood and Chrestien guided her out of the room. The pressure on her elbow was ample indication that he was very upset. The moment they were settled in the privacy of their Rolls Royce, Chrestien glared at her. "Have you lost control?"

She arched an eyebrow. "Not that I'm aware."

"That pig Sutherland has called Scullanois as a witness." His rage was barely under control. She had only seen him this upset once before when a reporter had described him as 'a very rich but very silly human being.'

She considered the implications. "Brilliant," she finally murmured. "He can't refuse to appear if asked."

"I won't allow it," Chrestien announced.

"It will be an embarrassment whether he appears or not. Hank will . . ."

"Hank?" Chrestien said, interrupting her, his anger hard and cold as ice.

All her alarms were in full play. She knew what Chrestien was capable of doing when anger ruled his good judgment, and damage control was in order.

"Everyone calls him Hank as it seems to make him smaller and friendlier, much less of a threat. I mustn't underestimate him again."

"Must I repeat myself? I don't want Scullanois on the stand. I can hear the question, 'Monsieur Scullanois, France identified the defendant to the court and provided the evidence against him. Yet your government never received a formal request from the United Nations or the court to do so. Why the secret involvement?'"

"Your worry matches mine," she said in a low voice. "American lawyers have a much-used phrase, 'Never ask a question unless you know the answer.' I suspect Sutherland can impeach Scullanois' testimony if he hears anything less than the truth."

"That's why he must not testify," Chrestien said, much calmer now. He ran through the lineup of allies. "Of course," he breathed, very relieved. "Bouchard is the presiding judge and will never allow it."

"Sutherland will immediately appeal that decision."

"And the Appeals Division will rule for Bouchard," Chrestien added.

"Sutherland is very persistent," Denise said. "He can appeal that decision to the presidency of the court. I'm not sure how they will rule, but Relieu hates Scullanois."

"Alphonse Relieu is a fool," Chrestien muttered. "Fortunately, he can be manipulated."

"In most cases," Denise replied.

"Are you sleeping with him?" Chrestien asked.

She was shocked. "Of course not!"

"Why aren't you?"

13

The Hague

The telephone call came at exactly nine o'clock Saturday morning. "Professor Sutherland," a woman said, "Justice Bouchard wishes to speak to you and Madam Du Milan at eleven this morning."

Hank recognized the voice. It was Bouchard's icy receptionist and he decided a little payback was in order. "I'm so sorry. I have a previous engagement."

The gasp on the other end of the line was very audible. "Perhaps you don't understand the seriousness of Justice Bouchard's request."

"I assure you I do," Hank replied. "But it would be unthinkable for me to cancel at such a late moment. I'm quite sure Justice Bouchard will understand. Of course, I will be available anytime Monday." He broke the connection and smiled. He was in his hotel room comfortably settled on a couch reading two briefs Melwin had given him. Outside, a cold wind was blowing off the North Sea, driving a spiteful rain. It was no day to be out and about. He sipped at his coffee and the phone rang again.

It was the receptionist. "Please Professor Sutherland, I cannot tell Justice Bouchard that you are not available."

Hank let out a very loud sigh. "I can be there at four this afternoon."

"Please, sir," she pleaded. "You don't know Justice Bouchard."

Hank was now certain she had a serious problem. He did a slow mental count to five. "This will be most inconvenient but I will be there."

The relief in her voice was plain to hear. "Thank you, sir."

* * * * *

Hank presented himself in Bouchard's outer office at exactly eleven o'clock. The receptionist glanced at the surveillance camera mounted high in a corner niche and gave him a hopeful look, willing him to understand that Bouchard demanded a certain level of disrespect on her part. "Please be seated," she said. "Justice Bouchard will be a few moments." Hank glanced at his watch and cocked an eyebrow. "Thank you," she murmured. He definitely had a friend at court. Exactly twenty minutes later, Denise walked in and they were immediately escorted into Bouchard's inner sanctum. Without waiting for permission, Hank sat down. Bouchard glared at him, his face red and puffy.

"What can I do for you?" Hank asked.

The angry jurist threw the witness notification at him. "The court does not call foreign ministers as witnesses. This is unacceptable. Withdraw your request."

Hank pitched his voice low and soft. "No."

The simple word hung in the air, and, for a moment, Hank was sure Bouchard was having a heart attack. "You seem to misunderstand me," Bouchard rasped. "As a matter of principle, the court does not . . ."

Hank interrupted him. "There is no misunderstanding. Scullanois is on our witness list and going to stay there."

"Then I will remove you as defense counsel."

"A very unwise move at this late date," Hank replied. "And I believe that particular prerogative falls to the three judges serving as presidency." He paused to let that sink in. He leaned forward and spoke in a confidential tone. "The patience of my President is not unlimited."

"You will not threaten me!" Bouchard shouted.

Denise played peacemaker. "I had a similar misunderstanding with Professor Sutherland. I can assure you that it was not intended as a threat."

Hank played it straight. "No, of course not." But from the look on Bouchard's face, he had made his point.

"What is the purpose of calling Minister Scullanois?" Bouchard asked.

"Probative value," Hank answered.

"You must be more specific," Bouchard said.

"To what end?" Hank replied. "We both know that you are going to deny my request to call Scullanois."

"That is correct," Bouchard said. He signed the notification's transmittal cover with a flourish and marked it as denied. "Of course, you may appeal my decision."

"Of course," Hank said. "By the way, when will President Relieu name the two other judges hearing the case?"

"That decision has not yet been made," Bouchard replied.

Denise turned and touched his arm. "President Relieu is worried the pressure of publicity could compromise the judges' objectivity."

"Of course," Hank replied, not believing a word of it.

"That will be all," Bouchard said. Hank rose to leave and followed Denise out of the office, leaving Bouchard fuming at his desk.

"I seem to have ruined his weekend," Hank said.

"And mine as well," Denise said. "May we talk?"

Hank grinned. "My place or yours." He paused. "I love that line." They walked in silence to his office where Aly and Melwin were anxiously waiting. Hank motioned for Melwin to join them and asked Aly to make coffee.

Denise came right to the point. "You know Tyler is guilty so what is to be gained by calling Scullanois as a witness?"

Hank notched one up for his side. "I think you know why."

"It will be most revealing," Melwin said, playing the game.

"You've upset Justice Bouchard unnecessarily," she told them.

Hank relaxed into his chair and leveled with her. "This is nothing compared to what's coming when the trial starts. If Bouchard's got heart problems, you'll want his doctor and a defibrillator handy."

"Need I remind you," she said, "that we are all officers of the court and not antagonists."

Hank smiled. "Of course not."

She returned his smile. "Perhaps dinner tonight?"

Hank was amazed that he actually considered it for a moment. "Perhaps after the trial?"

She smiled. "Until then." She swept out of the office, leaving a faint trace of her trademark perfume behind.

"A very wise move," Melwin said.

"I wonder if she can cook," Hank mused. "And she does smell nice."

"She assumes you want to call Scullanois as a witness to discredit Armiston," Melwin said.

"But she can't be sure, which stresses the system. By the way, Bouchard won't allow the court to call Scullanois."

"You can appeal it," Melwin told him. "But the appeals division will uphold Bouchard. Then you can appeal it to the presidency."

"Why? They might override Bouchard and allow us to actually get Scullanois on the stand."

Melwin understood perfectly.

* * * * *

Gus searched his cell looking for a hidden camera. But he couldn't find one. *Okay, there's got to be one. But where?* Frustrated, he gave up and flopped down on his bunk. He grabbed the remote control and cycled through the four channels the prison piped into his TV set.

Then it hit him. *It's the TV!* He chastised himself for being so slow. He stretched out and nodded off to sleep. The phone rang, jolting him awake. He padded across his cell and picked it up. "You have a visitor," a guard told him. "A Mrs. Suzanne Westcot."

Max's wife! he thought. "After visiting hours?" The guard didn't answer and broke the connection. Gus glanced at his watch and frowned. *She's got a lot of clout.*

Gus's favorite guard walked through the open door. He looked very pleased with himself and smiled as a young woman squeezed by him. She was dressed in a warm-up suit, her blonde hair was pulled back in a ponytail, and she looked all of eighteen. "Suzanne Westcot," she announced, extending her right hand.

Gus shook her hand, surprised by the strength in her grip. *It must be the tennis,* he decided. "My pleasure, Mrs. Westcot."

"Please, its Suzanne. Max asked me to drop in and get acquainted. Can we discuss Clare?"

"Of course, but we are being monitored."

Suzanne's face froze and she picked up the phone. "I need to speak to Superintendent Blier. Immediately." She waited, her foot tapping rapidly. "Hans," she sang, "please turn off all your wretched monitoring devices in Colonel Tyler's cell." She gave a curt nod. "Thank you." She hung up. "There now, we should be able to talk in few moments."

"Do you really think he'll do it?" Gus asked.

"Of course." She hesitated for a moment, obviously concerned. "You need to call your daughter." She opened a percom that was a duplicate of Hank's. "Please contact Michelle Tyler. I believe she's at the Mayo Clinic."

"Dialing," a man's voice said. Tyler's daughter answered almost immediately and Suzanne handed the percom to Gus.

"How's it going, Pumpkin?" Gus asked.

"Oh Dad, Mom's taken a turn for the worse. I haven't called because I was hoping she would rally, but she hasn't and the doctors aren't hopeful at all. There's a new procedure developed by Westcot Pharmaceuticals they want to try. But it's very risky."

Gus looked at Suzanne. "What's the procedure?"

"It's a stem cell-based gene replacement regime that's been in development for some time. But it involves a series of operations. Max pulled out all the stops after he talked to you last October, but no one really knows if it will work." She let it sink in. "Or what the side effects are."

"And Clare will be your guinea pig." Suzanne gave a little nod. Gus spoke to his daughter. "How does Clare feel about it?"

"She knows the operations will be painful but wants to do it. Dad, there's nothing left. I think we should try it. They'll need your written permission."

"Okay, let's do it." They spoke for a few more moments before hanging up.

Suzanne stood up. "The Superintendent's staff will help us with the paperwork."

Gus was impressed. "On a Saturday night?"

"Hans has been most helpful." She almost asked Gus if he wanted her to stay the night but thought better of it. It was an answer she wasn't prepared to hear. Again, she extended her hand. "Max says not to worry," she whispered. "If you need anything, call me." She pressed a business card into his hand. "Anytime."

14

The Hague

Aly was waiting with a fresh pot of coffee when Hank arrived at his office Monday morning. She took one look at him and poured a mug to the brim. "Jason is back," she said handing him the coffee.

"I need to speak to him soonest."

She held her bombshell for last. "Dad had a visitor Saturday night. Suzanne Westcot."

The name worked faster than any shot of caffeine. "Max Westcot's wife! What's she doing here?"

"He didn't say."

Hank escaped into his office and tore off the page of the countdown calendar on the wall. The number twenty-four shouted at him as if it were a ticking time bomb ready to explode. He sat down and called up his E-mail. There were over one hundred messages and he was still at it when Jason knocked on the office door. "Any news on Cannon?"

Jason shook his head. Hank motioned Jason to a chair and buzzed for Aly and Melwin to join them. "Okay folks, after meeting with Bouchard on Saturday, I'm willing to bet half my sex life that the verdict's already in."

"From what I hear, that's not much of a wager," Melwin replied.

Hank ignored him. "We've got twenty-four days to find a lever to make the judges change their minds. Otherwise, I'm going to blow the court apart."

Melwin looked very distressed. "I hope that won't be necessary. I'll try to find the lever you need."

Hank didn't look convinced. "How's Gus doing?"

"We spent most of Sunday with him," Jason replied. "He seemed in good enough spirits. Suzanne Westcot told him about an experimental stem cell-based gene replacement regime, and they're going to try it on Mom."

"Hopefully, that will do some good. You and Aly keep his morale up. Also, do whatever you can to find Cannon. He's critical."

"I've talked to General Hammerly about it," Jason replied. "He said he would look into it but didn't sound very encouraging. I'll chase some of my contacts down."

"Twist whatever arms need abusing," Hank said. "Alex, you and I need to talk. Let's go to work, folks." He waited until they were alone.

Hank turned his percom towards the Irishman. "Alex, I want you to take the lead and open the trial."

"You're mad."

"Not at all. Think of me as the bête noir. I'm the pit bull for the defense, the hired killer while you're the brains, the European intellectual, flawed in a way every man can identify with. You're also a recognized supporter of the court while I'm the brash American cowboy. You handle all the legal issues and I'll handle the witnesses. We'll flip for the closing statement."

"You might have told me sooner. It will be devilish hard with only twenty-four days remaining."

Hank placed his percom on his desk and turned it on. "Alex, me lad, it's time you met Cassandra. Cassandra, can you and the boys help Alex here?"

"Most assuredly," Cassandra answered over the percom's loudspeaker.

"I didn't know you had a loudspeaker," Hank said.

"Well, a girl has to have a few secrets, doesn't she?" Her voice had a definite Irish lilt.

* * * * *

"Good evening."

Gus looked up from the book he was reading and saw Therese Derwent standing in the doorway of his cell. She was holding two plastic carrier bags.

"Dinner," was all she said. He jumped up as she sat the bags on the small table. "Superintendent Blier would only allow one bottle of wine." She spread the contents out. "I kept thinking about what you said about sharing dinner with your family."

He almost asked if dinner had anything to do with Suzanne Westcot's visit but thought better of it. The psychiatrist gave him a sweet smile. "And no, this has nothing to do with your Saturday night guest."

"Can you read minds?"

"Not at all, but the entire staff is talking about the way she had Superintendent Blier jumping through hoops."

"Her husband is one of the most influential men in the States."

"Oh, I didn't know. I heard she was very pretty. And very young." She finished arranging the table. "Come. Open the wine." They sat and made small talk as they ate. Much to his surprise, he relaxed and felt the blinding tension ease. Finally, they were finished. "You seem in a much better mood," she said.

"Yeah, I am. I don't know how to thank you."

"Will you need help sleeping tonight?"

"No, I don't think so."

"It amazes me where you find the strength," she said. "Most would crumble under similar circumstances, but you seem to grow stronger."

"I couldn't have done it without you," he lied.

She smiled at him as she cleared the table and packed the bags. "What a lovely compliment." Then she was gone.

Gus closed the door and stretched out on his bunk. *I'm out'a here.* He rolled over and went to sleep.

* * * * *

Hank's countdown calendar showed twelve days to go when R. Garrison Cooper stormed into Denise's office with Natividad Gomez in close tow. He came right to the point. "Madam Prosecutor, you don't really need my client's testimony in court."

Denise spun her chair around and looked at Natividad across the expanse of her black lacquered desk. There were tears in Natividad's eyes and she felt sorry for her.

"I can still save her from going to jail when she returns to the States," the crusty old lawyer said. "But not if she testifies."

135

"Perhaps," Denise ventured, addressing Natividad directly, "it won't be necessary for you to return to the United States. I understand your family still lives in Mexico."

"Outside Guadalajara," Gomez said.

"Could you retire there on, say, fifty thousand euros a year?" Denise asked.

Natividad's face lit up. "Very comfortably."

"I'll need that offer in writing," Cooper said.

"Would a bank account in Switzerland suffice?" Denise asked. She picked up the videophone and hit the button to Hank's office. "Hank," she chimed, smiling into the camera for affect, "Mademoiselle Gomez and Monsieur Cooper are in my office. Would you be willing to accept her sworn statement and not bring her to the stand?" She pursed her lips and pouted prettily at his reply. "Yes, I understand completely. I would want to cross-examine her if I was representing Colonel Tyler. And don't forget about our dinner date." She broke the connection and gave Natividad an encouraging look. "How would you like to go shopping this afternoon?"

* * * * *

Hank tossed the phone in the air and it bounced off the ceiling. He caught it. "No way," he muttered. Allowing Natividad's statement in as evidence would open the gate for Toby's statement, and that would be a disaster. The image of Denise sitting across a small table and smiling at him over a glass of wine tickled his imagination. "Damn." He hit the speed dial on his cell phone to call his wife. Her image appeared on the fourth ring. "Cathy, I really need you here . . . strictly for your legal skills, of course." Her laughter was music to his ears. It was quickly arranged and he buzzed Aly. "My wife is arriving next Friday. Can you reserve a suite at the Amstel Intercontinental?"

"Smart move," Aly told him.

15

The Hague

Melwin stood in front of the big poster boards lining the walls of his office. He gestured at the boards with their ordered boxes connected by arrows and information points. Rows of manila folders were carefully arranged on the conference table, all keyed to the big boards. He had created a masterful legal argument and had brought it all together with one day to go. "That's it," Melwin said. He collapsed into a chair next to Hank. "I still believe the lack of temporal jurisdiction is our most compelling argument for dismissal. We should lead with that rather than saving it for later in the trial."

"I agree it is our best argument," Hank replied, "But, given the court's rather cavalier attitude about jurisdiction, it's all in the timing. Hopefully, by the time we raise the issue we will have given the court other reasons to bail, and they will latch onto *ratione temporis* like a drunken sailor grabbing the last bottle of rum." The American smiled. "Melwin, I got to admit, what you've done is absolutely brilliant."

"Thanks to Cassandra and her team," Melwin said.

"It was a pleasure," Cassandra said with a definite Irish accent. The percom had become permanently attached to Melwin and Hank suspected the Irishman even took it to bed with him.

The intercom buzzed. "I know you said not to disturb you," Aly said. "But Bouchard wants to see you immediately in his office, and you have a visitor, Marci Lennox. She says you know her."

"Ask her if I'm in trouble," Hank said. He heard a familiar, and very wicked laugh in the background. "I'll be right out."

"Is that the Marci Lennox?" Melwin asked. "American TV's weapon of torture for inflicting pain and punishment on the rich and powerful?"

"The one and only," Hank admitted. "A ghost of sins past. Alex, take the rest of the day off and get a good night's rest. You'll need it tomorrow." He went to meet his guest.

The woman waiting with Aly was trim and pretty with an elfin look that suggested a mischievous nature. But there was nothing playful about the way she did business. She rushed up and gave Hank a hug. "You haven't changed a bit," she said as a cameraman recorded it all.

"Marci, you are looking better than ever. I take it you're covering the trial."

"Only the first day or two," she said.

"That's a lifetime commitment in your business." He pulled back to look at her. "I'm sorry, but the court has me under a gag order. I can't talk to the media."

"Not even to verify a few facts?" she asked. She didn't wait for an answer. "I hear Melwin has a drinking problem and his girlfriend is a prostitute. And what about the rumors that women are visiting Tyler late at night in his cell?"

"Still doing the sex and scandal bit?"

"It does help the ratings."

"Sorry, Marci. I can't talk. I've got to go." He beat a hasty retreat, fully aware that he was being videotaped.

The corridors were almost deserted and he stopped on the fly bridge linking the two towers. The forecourt below was packed with people, banners, and TV crews. A long line of trucks with raised satellite antennas stretched down the street as far as he could see. The circus had started.

Bouchard's secretary actually seemed happy to see him. "I must apologize for the short notice," she whispered. "Security told him about the TV reporter in your office." She raised her voice as Denise walked in. "Please go right in."

Bouchard looked at him with an icy calm. "It has come to my attention that you spoke to a reporter a few minutes ago, which you were specifically ordered not to do. I have no choice but to demand that President Relieu remove you as defense counsel."

"Marci Lennox came to my office unannounced, and I honored your request not to speak to the press and refused to answer any questions. If you remove me now, well, just look outside your window."

Denise played the peacemaker. "Monsieur Sutherland cannot stop reporters from approaching him. I see no problem as long as he refuses to answer their questions."

Bouchard grumped as his fingers beat a tattoo on his desk. "Very well. I will overlook it for now. President Relieu has announced that Justices Carla Della Sante and Heinrich Richter will also be sitting with me."

"I was wondering when he would get around to that," Hank murmured.

Bouchard ignored him. "In regards to tomorrow, once the court is called to order, I will make a few opening remarks and then ask for opening business. As I stated earlier, I do not tolerate surprises in my chamber. Are there any petitions, objections, or observations for presentation at that time?"

"There are none," Denise answered. Her answer seemed to satisfy Bouchard.

"Good. The charges against the defendant will then be read and I will ask for Tyler's plea. I assume it will be not guilty. Then I will ask for opening statements and that will conclude the day's activities." He fixed Hank with a hard look. "Do not attempt to make a mockery of these proceedings, Monsieur Sutherland."

"I won't disappoint you," Hank replied.

"See that you don't," Bouchard said, dismissing them.

Hank tried to remain calm as he hurried back to his office. But Aly saw through him the moment he came through the door. "What's happened?"

"Has Alex left yet?"

Aly motioned at the Irishman's office and Hank rushed in. "The other two judges are Della Sante and Richter."

Melwin thought for a moment. "It could be worse. Richter is probably the most intelligent judge on the court. He's very deliberate and logical." A worried look crossed the barrister's face. "But his father was a member of Hitler's German Youth and we don't know how he feels about Americans. As for Della Sante, she is extremely well-connected politically in Italy, and a very opinionated and emotional woman. Do not expect any two days to be the same."

"Lovely," Hank muttered. "Absolutely lovely."

"There is one thing, she's the only judge who didn't want the post. She was pressured by her government to serve on the court."

Hank was hopeful. "It sounds like the Italians know how to select judges." He firmly believed that no one who wanted to be a judge should ever be allowed on the bench.

16

The Hague

Hans Blier, the prison superintendent, walked purposefully down the corridor leading to Gus's cell. Two guards carrying a dark blue suit, white shirt, and a new pair of black oxford shoes followed him. Blier waited while a third guard opened the door. "Colonel Tyler," he said, "the court ordered you to wear a suit, not your uniform. Please change."

"I'm on trial because of what I did as an officer, but can't wear my uniform?"

Blier's face was unreadable. "This is beyond my control." He held up a set of handcuffs and a waist chain. "If you persist in wearing your uniform, I will have to use these." He let it sink in. "I would prefer to have my staff escort you to the courtroom with dignity."

Gus made a decision. "A little privacy, please."

* * * * *

Two prison guards wearing dress uniforms escorted Gus into the holding cell immediately behind the courtroom where the court's chief of security was waiting. "Why are you late?" he demanded. "The trial starts in four minutes, and he should be in the dock." His face flushed with anger. "Where are his handcuffs and waist chain? The prosecutor ordered them on during the trial."

The guard in charge of the detail gave him a disdainful look. "Superintendent Blier never mentioned handcuffs or a waist chain. We will have to send for them."

"There isn't time," the chief of security wailed. He motioned them down the hall, anxious to get his charge into courtroom on time.

"Please thank Superintendent Blier for me," Gus told his guards.

The chief of security held the door to the courtroom and a single guard escorted Gus into the dock, the small enclosure where he would sit for the trial. Hank and Melwin were already seated at the defense table, both wearing the required black robes with white bib. Hank stood and walked to the dock, fully aware the TV cameras were recording his every move. As the microphones were turned off, he assumed the media networks had lip readers trying to pick-up what they were saying.

Gus grinned. "You look real pretty in that outfit."

"Wore one just like it to my prom," Hank said. The two men looked at each other for a moment. "Just like we discussed, okay?"

"You got it," Gus assured him.

Hank returned to his table as Denise entered with her two assistants. There was a slight stir as Jason entered the courtroom with Hank's wife, Catherine. The audience buzzed with interest and heads turned as they found their seats immediately behind the defense table. Jason was wearing his Service Dress uniform, and carried the Security Forces dark-blue beret with the Defensor Fortis patch in his left hand. Hank wanted the father and son team to loom larger than life, to dominate the courtroom with a commanding presence. Half the woman in the audience bisected Catherine Sutherland and gave her high marks for her well-cut and stylish business suit. The other half envied her for having such a handsome escort.

Hank turned to his wife. "The prosecutor is giving you the once over."

"She is beautiful," Catherine allowed, fully aware that there were many kinds of judgment going on in the courtroom. She spoke in a low voice. "It was just announced on the news that the President is pushing the UN for action on China."

"I imagine that will definitely speed things up here," Hank replied.

The head clerk glanced nervously at the audience and the TV cameras. The red light on her desk blinked and she took a deep breath. "Please stand for the entrance of the judges." The spectators in the packed courtroom came to their feet as the three blue-robed judges filed in. Bouchard was his usual lumbering gray self. Carla Della Sante was a petite, bird-like woman in her mid-fifties, with short, obviously dyed, dark blonde hair. Heinrich Richter was a nondescript, balding, heavyset man in his early forties.

A Far Justice

The clerk panicked and couldn't remember what to say next. Denise bent over her microphone and spoke. "Please remain standing silently until the judges are seated." Every commentator in the media booth set high above the audience at the rear commented on Denise's regal beauty and how her commanding sense of presence had averted an embarrassing moment.

Bouchard took his seat, obviously peeved at the awkward beginning. "Please be seated." The audience sank into their seats and the courtroom was absolutely silent.

The red-faced clerk found her voice. "Good morning your Honors. The International Criminal Court is now in session, the prosecutor versus August William Tyler." She bowed to the judges.

This was Bouchard's moment and he swelled with importance. He spoke in English. "Good morning and I welcome all to this chamber. We are a court of international criminal law concerned with crimes common to all of humanity. Many spectators will find our procedures different than their national courts. However, our goal is the same: we seek justice for humanity. As is customary, we begin each day by asking the prosecutor and the defense whether they have any objections, observations, or petitions for the chamber's consideration. Madam Prosecutor, are there any issues to be brought before the court?"

Denise stood. "There are none, your Honor."

Melwin came to his feet. "May it please the court, the defense has a petition for your consideration at this time."

Bouchard's face flushed with anger. But he was painfully aware that the TV cameras were zooming in on him and managed to control his voice. "Please proceed."

Melwin stepped to the podium and opened a manila folder. "Article Twelve of the Rome Statute clearly states that this court only has jurisdiction over individuals who are citizens of States that are parties to the Statute. As Colonel Tyler is a citizen of the United States, which is not a signatory to the Statute, *ratione personae* is not established. Consequently, the court does not have jurisdiction over Colonel Tyler. Therefore, we petition the Court for dismissal." He handed the petition, a blue-covered four-page document, to the clerk.

Denise was on her feet. "I must object to learned counsel's use of the defendant's former military title."

Bouchard spoke quietly with Della Sante and Richter. "That issue," Bouchard announced, "was decided by the pre-trail chamber. The defendant will be referred to as Mr. Tyler."

Della Sante leaned forward and folded her hands. "Signore Melwin, the issue of jurisdiction was also decided by the pre-trial chamber." She leafed through the red-covered bench book in front of her. "Rule 122 states that once such an issue or objection is ruled on in the pre-trial confirmation hearing, it may not be raised again in the trial proceedings."

Melwin bowed respectfully to her. "Your Honor, if I may refer to the transcript of the confirmation hearing." He turned a page. "If you will carefully review those proceedings, you will see that no motion or objection was filed by any officer of the court or the defendant. During the pre-trial proceedings, the defendant merely asked, 'Why am I here?' At that point the prosecutor explained her position on *ratione personae*. The court then continued without a petition or objection ever being placed before it. That issue is now before the court for the first time in the proper and correct form. By its own rules of procedures, the court must rule on a question of jurisdiction before continuing."

Bouchard's face flushed. "We will recess to review defense's petition and will reconvene in one hour."

The clerk bounced to her feet. "Please stand." Bouchard stood and led the other two judges out.

"Well, that was quick," Catherine said.

Hank spun around in his comfortable high-backed chair. "You ain't seen nothin' yet." He leaned close to his wife and lowered his head so the cameras could not focus on his face. She was an accomplished lawyer in her own right and Hank trusted her judgment. "Cathy, I've got a feeling about Della Sante."

"I'll work on it," Catherine promised.

As planned, Melwin walked over to the dock. On cue, the cameras followed him. "Colonel Tyler, I know what you think of me, but I am totally dedicated to your defense."

Gus extended his hand. "Hank was right about you and I apologize." They shook hands, playing to the cameras.

Exactly one hour later, a different clerk entered the courtroom and sat down. Hank glanced at the man. "Well, I guess we know what they were really deciding." The red light on the clerk's desk blinked. This time the clerk got it right and they were back in session.

Bouchard took his seat and looked over his glasses at Melwin. "We have reviewed defense counsel's petition to dismiss. We find that the prosecutor's position during the pre-trial proceedings was correct, and that the defendant is also a citizen of Panama, which is a member of the court. Therefore, the court does have jurisdiction and the petition is denied."

Melwin was on his feet. "May I ask what the court's vote was?"

The request caught Bouchard off guard and he glanced nervously at Della Sante. "The court is in consensus."

Hank leaned into Melwin. "He didn't say 'unanimous.' It looks like we've got a friend at court."

"Indeed," Melwin replied in a low voice.

Bouchard cleared his throat. "The clerk will read the charges to the accused."

The clerk stepped to the center podium. "The defendant is charged with the war crime of willful killing under Article Eight of the Rome Statute and with the war crime of employing prohibited weapons under Article Eight of the Rome Statute." He detailed the specific elements of each crime and sat down.

Bouchard turned to Gus. "Do you understand the nature of the crimes you are charged with?"

Gus stood, and, as Hank had told him, hesitated. It was a deliberate ploy to give the cameras time to fully focus on him. "Yes, your Honor, I do."

"How do you plead to the charges?"

Gus's head came up, his jaw set, his voice firm. "Not guilty." The words echoed over the courtroom.

Bouchard jotted down a note. "Madam Prosecutor, you may present your opening statement."

Denise stepped to the podium and, fully aware that the cameras were on her, fought the urge to toss her hair into place. "Since time immemorial, war has been the curse and the fate of humankind. But for the last thousand years the civilized world has tried to limit and control its destructiveness."

Hank resigned himself to a long speech and split his attention as Denise spoke. It was a skill he had developed as a prosecutor, and he relied on a sixth sense to catch the key words and phrases he called

145

'bullets.' "The law has proven to be our refuge and guide in this quest," Denise said. Hank studied the three judges for their reactions. Nothing. He waited for Denise's first bullet. It came twelve minutes later. "The precedents of Nuremberg and the Tokyo war trials must not be lost." The look on Richter's face was ample evidence that Denise had pushed the wrong button. But Della Sante was different. She had a calm and understanding look but there was something about her neither Hank nor Catherine could read.

Again, Hank waited for the next bullet. Denise did not disappoint him. "International law," she said, "has given us guideposts by distinguishing between civilians and combatants. We must not erase this distinction, we must not allow anyone to cross this line and drag humanity into the depths of unrestricted warfare using weapons that are inherently meant to be indiscriminate and widespread in their effects." A low murmur of approval swept through the audience.

Hank studied Gus's reaction as Denise continued. The pilot was playing it perfectly with just the right mixture of respect and doubt. He glanced at his watch. Denise had been talking for over an hour. He studied the judges and their body language and decided they weren't really listening.

"The Rome Statute," Denise said, playing to her audience, "has been rightfully criticized for its inability to reach into the past and to correct obvious crimes against humanity. Fortunately, our system of justice has grown and matured and we can now correct this fault." Della Sante beamed as she listened. Ten minutes later, Denise reached a conclusion. "The law is not mere theory but an instrument for bringing justice to those who commit crimes against humanity. No state or organization is on trial here, only the individual who committed these crimes, who wantonly killed hundreds of innocent people. Need I remind the court, or the world for that matter, that there is no statute of limitations for murder? As such, the court's jurisdiction is not subject to any statute of limitations. For these reasons I bring you the criminal Tyler. I do this under the authority of the Rome Statute, and in the name of the United Nations, and for all humanity."

A smattering of applause rippled across the room and crescendoed into a roar. Bouchard looked tolerantly at the audience as it died away. "We are in recess for lunch and will reconvene in two hours." The courtroom rapidly emptied as the spectators and judges hurried to the restrooms.

Hank turned to his wife. "Any ideas?"

"A few," she said. "I'll know better after we finish today. I'd suggest Alex keeps it short."

"That's the plan." Hank ambled over to Gus who was still in the dock. "How's your bladder doing?"

"No problem. Why?"

"You need to project an image of a man totally in control of himself, and at ease with who and what you are. When anyone looks at you or Jason, I want them to see who they want to be. When they look at the judges, they'll see who they are."

"And if they look at Du Milan?" Gus asked.

"Hopefully, the women will see a pampered, upper-class Frenchwoman and the men someone they want to take to bed. Get some lunch but keep it very light. We don't need you nodding off."

Hank and Melwin ate a light snack in Hank's office as they edited Melwin's opening statement. All too soon, they were back in court and the clerk called everyone to their feet, starting the afternoon session. Melwin stood and murmured, "Friends, Romans, and countrymen." He had his work cut out for him as he stepped to the podium. "If it pleases the court. We have heard an eloquent opening statement that appeals to the very depths of our civilization. Who can condemn any effort to limit and contain war? But war is a sickness of our civilization and not the individual. We have also heard an invocation to justice based on the unspoken principle of universal jurisdiction under the auspices of the Rome Statute creating this court. However, the idea of universal jurisdiction is little more than a legal chimera, a hopeful wish that is impossible to attain. It is not embodied in the Rome Statute or in the charter of the United Nations. We are convened here, in a court of law, to hear the evidence and judge August William Tyler by the law, and not by a notion that lacks the test of time and experience.

"If I may quote from the Report of the Preparatory Commission for the International Criminal Court, 'The Rome Statute creating the International Criminal Court embodies a three-tiered hierarchy of law. The first tier is the Statute itself. The second tier is the applicable treaties and principles of the rules of international law, including the established principles of the international law of armed conflict. The third tier is pointed towards domestic law.'"

Bouchard leaned forward in his chair. "The court is fully aware of the governing principles of the Rome Statute. Do not waste our time."

"Indeed, your Honor," Melwin replied, totally unfazed by the unprecedented rebuke during an opening statement. "But I must note that these three principles form the very tripod on which the court is created. Ignore the international law of armed conflict and the edifice of the court cannot stand on the remaining two legs. And by the law of international armed conflict and its attendant conventions, August William Tyler has not committed a crime."

He sat down.

Bouchard blinked, surprised by the brevity of Melwin's opening statement. "The court is adjourned until tomorrow morning at ten o'clock."

* * * * *

Marci Lennox's four bodyguards quickly captured a space outside the courtroom doors and held it against all comers. Within moments, she had Jason and Catherine in front of her microphone. "Mrs. Sutherland, you are a lawyer in your own right and have pleaded many cases in court. Were you surprised by the brevity of Melwin's opening statement?"

"Not at all. The defense has simply cut to the heart of the matter."

"Can you explain?"

"It's quite simple," Catherine said, "Mr. Melwin has drawn a line between the international law of armed conflict on one side, and the so-called notion of universal jurisdiction on the other."

"I take it you disagree with the law of universal jurisdiction."

"It's not a law of any type. Further, the idea of universal jurisdiction is the unwanted stepchild of established international law that allows any state to try an offender for crimes such as piracy and slavery that took place where no state had territorial jurisdiction. The men and women who drew up the charter of the United Nations never heard of it, and I assure you, they would have been shocked if they had. The judges will have to make a choice. Are they going to stay on established legal territory or venture into the unknown?"

"Is there any indication of which way they'll go?"

Catherine gave her a thoughtful look. "At this point, no."

* * * * *

Denise stormed past Bouchard's secretary and barged into his office. "Today was a fiasco!"

"We have solved the problem of the clerk," Bouchard replied.

She paced the ornate carpet in front of his desk. "That was only the beginning. I ordered Tyler chained and shackled. That didn't happen."

"I can't change that now."

"There was no need for you to recess to rule on Melwin's petition. You should have taken it under consideration and continued."

"Unfortunately, Melwin was right and we had no choice."

"For God's sake, why did you admit that you were split on your decision?"

"I cannot give Sutherland the opportunity to claim we are operating in secret."

"He's also openly speaking to his wife, challenging your gag order."

Bouchard's face flushed. "I cannot keep him from speaking to his wife."

"And end these petitions."

"I'm trying to."

"Then do it." She strode out of his office

Amsterdam

Catherine stood at the window of their suite in the Amstel Intercontinental as the three men finished eating dinner. "I expected the audience to boo when you finished."

Melwin was surprised. "Really? Any idea why they didn't?"

She turned to them. "It's hard to tell, but I think it was Gus. He's a commanding presence."

"That is the idea," Hank said. "By the way, who do you think was the dissenting vote on the motion?"

"Richter," Jason replied.

Melwin sipped at his wine. "I agree."

"It was Della Sante," Catherine said. The three men looked at her in amazement. "What you see is a very emotional post-menopausal woman. She is an idealist but underneath, she's the most hardheaded judge on the ICC. In the end, she'll go with the law every time."

The Hague

"May I join you?" Derwent asked. Gus clicked off the TV and motioned her into his cell. "By all reports," the psychiatrist said, "you had a very good day in court."

"Hank says it won't last."

"Do you need to talk about it?" she asked.

"Hank told me not to."

She handed him a thin narrow box. "For you," she said. He opened it to reveal a plum-colored silk tie.

"Thank you. It's really nice."

"It will go very well with your dark-blue suit and Della Sante will like it." She hesitated. "Have you called home lately?"

Gus nodded. "About two hours ago. Clare had her first operation yesterday and seems to be resting comfortably."

Derwent considered her next words. "Do you need help sleeping tonight?"

"I'm okay," he replied.

"Well, good luck tomorrow."

He followed her to the door and watched her walk down the corridor to the entry control box. She swiped her ID card and the gate swung open. Gus closed the door to his cell, crawled into his bunk, and turned out the light. Only then did he allow himself the luxury of a "Check six, folks."

17

The Hague

Aly was waiting with the mandatory mug of coffee when Hank arrived at the ICC the next morning. "I had an interesting talk with Bouchard's secretary," she announced. Hank cocked an eyebrow. The when and where of that conversation were two things he didn't need to know. "Marie Doorn is the clerk Bouchard fired yesterday. She and Bouchard's secretary are good friends and Marie needs her job very badly. No one will hire her now. Alex has worked with her in the past and says we can trust her."

Hank thought for a moment. "Could you use an assistant?"

"It would be helpful." Hank picked up the phone, called the Registrar, and quickly arranged it. "Smart move," Aly told him.

Melwin was waiting in Hank's office. "I expect Du Milan will present the evidence today and call her first witness."

"Alex, that ain't going to happen." He explained what he had in mind.

Melwin stared at him in disbelief. "There are times you frighten me."

* * * * *

Gus stood in front of the mirror in the holding cell and adjusted the tie.

"Nice tie," Hank said.

Catherine agreed. "It goes very well with your suit."

"The prison shrink gave it to me. She says Della Sante will like it."

"Gus," Hank began, "we need to talk about today."

"The cell is bugged," Gus replied.

Hank set his percom on the table. "I've taken care of that. What you do today is critical so please listen very carefully to what Catherine says." Gus nodded. "Good. I've got to make sure Melwin is ready." Hank hurried out of the cell.

* * * * *

Catherine sat beside Jason in the same seat as the day before and handed Hank his percom. "Gus is ready," she said.

Hank sat the percom on the defense table and Cassandra spoke in his earpiece. "It's still there and it is on." Hank nodded at the percom's camera as the clerk called the court to order. "Break a leg," she said.

Melwin waited patiently for the opening ritual to unfold and popped to his feet the moment Bouchard asked if there were any matters before the court that had to be heard.

Bouchard pointed his pen at the Irishman. "I will only warn you once, Monsieur Melwin. Do not make a mockery of this court's proceedings by filing frivolous petitions. It will not be tolerated."

Melwin tried to look contrite. His head came up. "If it may please the court. I am obligated to bring to your attention a most disturbing fact. The defense counsel's table has been bugged and I fear all our conversations have been monitored. I have no choice but to demand you declare a mistrial."

Bouchard started to come out of his seat but caught himself in time. "Demand? You demand nothing of this tribunal."

"Tribunal, m'lord?" Melwin asked, laying on his Irish accent. "I thought this was a court of criminal law."

Della Sante tapped the microphone in front of her for attention. "Signore Melwin, please forgive us for the problems of speaking in a foreign tongue. We all understand this is not a tribunal as you understand the word but a court of justice."

"Thank you for the clarification, your Honor. Still, the defendant's right to a fair trial has been seriously compromised, perhaps beyond the ability of the court to correct. Therefore, I must ask for a mistrial and for Colonel, ah, excuse me, Mr. Tyler's immediate release."

Richter cleared his throat. "This is a very serious charge. What evidence do you have?"

Melwin tapped the table. "Here. The listening device is on the underside of the table."

"How was it discovered?" Richter asked.

"I discovered it this morning with this, your Honor." He held up the wand Jason used to sweep their offices.

Bouchard found his voice. "The court is adjourned while we investigate."

Gus came to his feet. "Your Honor." His voice was firm and clear, and resonated with authority. "May I speak?"

Every head in the courtroom turned in his direction, and, for a moment, Bouchard hesitated. "Granted."

"May I suggest that the entire courtroom be swept to see if there are any other monitoring devices?"

Richter cleared his throat. "An excellent suggestion. Thank you, Herr Tyler."

* * * * *

Marci Lennox stood outside the main entrance leading into the forecourt and keyed her microphone. "The court stumbled from one disaster to another today, first when Colonel Tyler's defense team revealed that the defense table was bugged, and then when the presiding judge, Gaston Bouchard, referred to the court as a 'tribunal.' In an interesting twist, Colonel Tyler asked that the entire courtroom be swept for bugs. His demeanor and calm attitude left most observers with a positive impression of a man in full. This is Marci Lennox in The Hague with more to come."

She lowered the microphone when she saw Jason and Catherine. "Sergeant Tyler, Mrs. Sutherland, may we speak?"

"Only off the record," Catherine replied.

Marci turned off her mike. "What do you make of this bombshell that Melwin dropped on the court?"

"Too soon to tell. But it strikes at the very integrity of the court."

* * * * *

Relieu almost choked as he looked at the six microdot monitoring devices removed from the courtroom. "Monsieur Sutherland, as President of the International Criminal Court, I must apologize for this incident. Our chief of security assures me that the monitoring devices were placed solely to insure security inside the courtroom."

"Then you agree that a mistrial and Colonel Tyler's immediate release are the only remedies."

Denise paced the carpet in front of Relieu's huge desk. "As one of the bugs was also found under my table, that would be premature."

"So it's okay as long as we're dealing with an equal opportunity bugger?" Hank asked. "For the record, the microdots were manufactured by the French."

"Not material," Denise snapped. "Besides, your case was no more compromised than mine."

"So let's start over, just to be sure. And in the meantime, release Colonel Tyler."

"Those decisions fall to Justice Bouchard," Relieu said, passing the buck.

* * * * *

Denise curled up on the sofa in her small but very elegant and modern apartment and attacked a large bowl of ice cream. "I love the flavor you Americans call French Vanilla," she told Natividad Gomez.

Natividad nibbled at her ice cream in a much more ladylike way. "I consider myself more Mexican than American."

Denise studied Natividad, approving of what she saw. "That thought will be very helpful when you are on the stand."

"When will I be called?"

"It could be as early as next week. Do you want to go over your testimony again?" Natividad's expression indicated she did. "Sutherland will probably start by asking if you are a spy in the pay of a foreign country." Denise's words pounded at Natividad but she reiterated the answer they had carefully rehearsed. They worked at it for another hour before Denise called it a night and sent Natividad back to her suite in the Des Indes, the palace that had been converted to a luxury hotel.

Denise checked the refrigerator and dished out the last of the ice cream. She liked the soft-spoken and graceful Natividad. Slowly, she paced her apartment, wondering what she was going to do with what remained of Natividad once Hank destroyed her on the stand.

18

The Hague

Hank and Melwin were in their robes and ready to leave for the courtroom on Friday morning when Marie Doorn, their newest assistant, joined them. She was a middle-aged, pleasant looking, and very petite woman that life had passed by. She handed Melwin a folder. "Precedents from the International Court of Justice. The trial division relies on them for guidance during deliberations."

Melwin thumbed through the folder. "Really? I didn't know that."

"The court has not seen the need to make it public knowledge," Doorn said.

Melwin followed Hank to the courtroom, his head down as he carefully read. Hank had to guide him to the defense table. They sat down and Melwin continued to read, beside himself with excitement. "Excellent. Excellent."

"Be sure to thank her," Hank said. Gus entered through the side door and stood in the dock for a moment, inspecting the spectators. The pilot nodded to Hank and sat down. "A man in command," Hank murmured.

The red light on the clerk's desk blinked and everyone stood before the clerk could speak. The judges filed in and Bouchard took his seat. "Please be seated," he intoned, starting the third day of the trial. "The court has investigated the presence of listening devices in the courtroom. The security division of the court installed them for security purposes and no unauthorized disclosure of confidential and privileged conversations occurred. Therefore, the defendant's petition for a mistrial is denied. Madam Prosecutor, are there any other issues for the court's consideration?"

"There are none, your Honor."

Melwin was on his feet. "The defense adds Henri Scullanois to its witness list."

"The court has ruled previously on this issue," Bouchard replied.

Melwin opened the folder Marie Doorn had given him. "There are ample precedents for modifications and additions established by the International Court of Justice." He handed the citation list to the clerk. "Further, in view of the listening devices that were discovered yesterday . . ."

Denise interrupted him. "The calling of Monsieur Scullanois is totally unrelated to the issue of monitoring devices in the courtroom, which, need I remind the court, were placed solely for security reasons."

"But were of French manufacture," Melwin replied. "Is Madam Prosecutor worried that we will discover a connection?"

Della Sante leaned forward. "The prosecutor makes a good point."

Richter cleared his throat. "I find little probative value in calling the foreign . . ."

"Your request to call Monsieur Scullanois is denied," Bouchard quickly said, relieved that both judges were in agreement.

"As I was saying," Richter added, "I find little probative value in calling Herr Scullanois at this time, in this matter."

Bouchard's jaw worked as he chose his next words. "However, the court will consider any request defense counsel may have for additional witnesses who are experts in security procedures and monitoring devices." Satisfied he had defused the issue, he continued. "Madam Prosecutor, you may open your case."

Denise stepped to the podium with a thick notebook. She opened it and carefully uncapped her OMAS pen, deliberately playing to the cameras. She checked off her first point. "If it may please the court, we will prove that the defendant killed one or more persons on the night of February 25, 1991 on Mutlah Ridge in Iraq, in an international armed conflict sanctioned by the United Nations. Further, we will prove that he was aware that such persons were protected under the relevant articles and protocols of the Geneva Convention, and that he was aware of their presence on Mutlah Ridge."

Melwin came to his feet. "Your Honor, the defense will stipulate that any action on Mutlah Ridge that occurred on the night in question took place within the context of an armed conflict sanctioned by the United Nations."

"Is that agreeable to the prosecution?" Bouchard asked.

"It is, your Honor," Denise replied.

Bouchard looked at Della Sante and Richter who both nodded. "The court accepts the stipulation."

"In addition," Denise continued, "we will prove that the defendan Tyler employed weapons that are inherently widespread and indiscriminate, and are in violation of the international law of armed conflict." She spoke for forty more minutes outlining the evidence before capping her pen and closing her notebook.

"Please call your first witness," Bouchard told her.

"The prosecution calls the Secretary General of the United Nations."

An expectant hush fell over the audience as the elegant and dignified Secretary General took the stand. Ziba Katelhong was a tall woman and carried her heritage with pride. Her hair was cut short in the traditional Zulu manner and she was big-hipped and heavy. The clerk handed her the declaration to tell the truth. Ziba Katelhong read with a clipped English accent, the product of the best public schools in England. "I solemnly declare that I will speak the truth, the whole truth, and nothing but the truth." She sat down.

"Now there's an oath with teeth," Hank said in a low voice. He split his attention as Denise led the Secretary General through the standard questions while Cassandra spoke in his ear, outlining the prosecutor's strategy.

"They're more worried about jurisdiction than we thought," Cassandra explained. "Du Milan must link the court's jurisdiction to the authority of the United Nations. This is right up Alex's ally. Let him handle it."

Denise reached the heart of Katelhong's testimony. "Does the crime before this court fall under the jurisdiction of the United Nations?"

"Yes," the Secretary General answered. "All crimes against humanity fall under our jurisdiction. This is embodied as one of our purposes in Article One of our Charter. This was further developed in the Universal Declaration of Human Rights in 1948. As the massacre on Mutlah Ridge occurred in a conflict conducted under our authority, the United Nations has jurisdiction." Again, Hank split his attention while Denise continued to pose questions that were answered by political rhetoric. She ended by thanking the Secretary General and sat down to a polite round of applause.

"Be gentle," Hank told Melwin.

"It will be difficult," Melwin replied. He stepped to the podium and started by asking where Katelhong was on February 25, 1991. He quickly determined that she had been in college in Switzerland, was not a delegate or employee of the United Nations at the time, and had never been to the Middle East prior to that date. "Madam Secretary, is the United Nations a signatory to the Rome Statute creating the International Criminal Court?"

"Don't be ridiculous. The United Nations fathered the court."

"Ah, I see. May I ask who was the bride?" A tickle of laughter worked through the audience. Bouchard banged his gavel, quieting the audience. "Madam Secretary, what is the formal relationship between the United Nations and the court?"

"The court has not been brought into a formal relationship with the United Nations."

"Then whatever jurisdiction the United Nations had at Mutlah Ridge cannot be legally delegated to the court."

Katelhong flared. "The Gulf War was under United Nations mandate and the court is our creation."

Melwin was incredulous. "Are you saying the court is a branch of the United Nations, subject to veto in the Security Council, and not an independent body?"

Denise was on her feet. "Objection. Counsel is engaging the Secretary General in debate."

Bouchard spoke quietly to Della Sante and Richter. "Sustained," he said in a loud voice.

Melwin was unperturbed by the ruling. "Madam Secretary, when did the prosecutor first approach the United Nations about this case?"

She answered in a condescending tone. "I cannot answer your question."

Melwin sensed an opening. "Cannot or will not? Or, Madam Secretary, is the business of the United Nations conducted in secret?"

"I deal with many sensitive issues that cannot be discussed in public."

A Far Justice

"Surely you can give us an approximate date. Was it before or after the charges were filed against Colonel Tyler?"

"Objection," Denise called. "The Secretary General has stated why she cannot answer."

Melwin let his disgust show. "Or are we dealing with political influence that strikes at the prosecutor's impartiality? If the court is to succeed, there must be no tint of partisan or political pressure." Again, Bouchard conferred with the other two judges and sustained Denise's objection.

"Madame Secretary, was Panama a combatant in the Gulf War?" Her answer was a simple no. Melwin looked at her expectantly. "Has Panama prosecuted any of its citizens for fighting in that war?" Again, she answered no. Satisfied, Melwin said, "The defense has no further questions, but reserves the right to recall the witness." Denise had no questions and Ziba Katelhong marched regally out, glad to escape.

Hank leaned into to Melwin. "How do we recall her to the stand?"

"I'll notify the Victims and Witnesses Unit. But we need a date."

Hank thought for a moment. "The first day we start our defense."

"As the court has no power of subpoena, I doubt that she'll appear."

A tight smile played at Hank's mouth. "Whatever way she plays it will be a mistake."

Denise returned to the podium. "The prosecution calls Peter DeGroot."

Hank was worried. While he remembered seeing the name on the witness list, he couldn't recall anything significant from Cassandra's research. He had assumed that the prosecutor had included it with many others as chaff meant to distract and preoccupy his staff. He heard a loud murmur from the spectators when Harm de Rijn came through the side door. "What the hell?" he said, totally surprised.

Cassandra's voice was in his ear. "Du Milan sandbagged us. We assumed she was calling a Dutch politician with the same name. DeGroot is de Rijn's real name. He was a correspondent during the Gulf War and very critical of the war."

"One of Saddam's boys?"

"Unfortunately," Cassandra replied.

159

The clerk stood and handed de Rijn the undertaking as to truthfulness. De Rijn read it aloud majestically. Hank steepled his fingers under his chin and listened as Denise established de Rijn's identity and led him through the pro forma questions placing him on Mutlah Ridge after the attack.

"At this time," Denise said, "the prosecution enters into evidence the videotape the witness recorded during his time on Mutlah Ridge."

Melwin came to his feet to object. "Shouldn't we see it first?"

A chuckle rippled across the courtroom as Bouchard stared at him. Della Sante whispered in the Belgian's ear and he nodded. "Counsel for the defense is correct," Bouchard said, biting his words.

A murmur of anticipation worked across the courtroom as the lights darkened and a screen dropped from the ceiling. An image of destroyed trucks and cars appeared as de Rijn's narration, in Dutch, described the scenes of carnage. An English translation crawled along the bottom of the screen. Key phrases seemed to leap out, the result of clever highlighting and volume control. "Over two thousand trucks and vehicles destroyed . . . the charred and dismembered remains of over three thousand men and women . . . the stench of scorched flesh filled the air." Two women spectators ran from the room. The video ended and the lights came up.

Denise stood at the podium. "Are these scenes that you personally witnessed?"

"That is correct," de Rijn answered. "And I will take them to my grave."

Denise continued to question him, fueling the emotional impact the video had created. Finally, she looked at the judges as tears streaked her face. "We can ask no more of this witness," she said.

Melwin stood to question the video's authenticity.

Cassandra spoke in Hank's ear. "You want it entered as evidence." Hank reached out and touched Melwin's arm, bringing him back to his seat.

Bouchard breathed in relief. "The video by Harm de Rijn" – he corrected himself – "Peter DeGroot is entered as prosecution exhibit one. The court is adjourned until Monday at ten o'clock."

* * * * *

A Far Justice

Marci Lennox's bodyguards were hard pressed to hold an area open as spectators and demonstrators pressed into the forecourt. Her cameraman was forced into a close-up. "Secretary General Katelhong avoided answering hard questions from the defense implying the United Nations exercises undue influence on the court. The court rocked with another shock wave as the Netherlands' premier news commentator, Harm de Rijn, took the stand under his real name, Peter DeGroot. The videotape that he recorded on the Highway of Death drove two women from the courtroom and left the prosecutor in tears, adding to the emotional carnage of this trial."

Her director in New York was on the satellite feed. "Good stuff Marci. Get your tight little butt on a plane and get back here."

"I'd rather cover it from here," she told him. "Wait until you see Sutherland in action. It's going to get very interesting. Can you get Liz to anchor it from your end?" Liz was Elizabeth Gordon, CNC-TV's star anchorwoman.

* * * * *

Marie Doorn was waiting in the office for the post mortem when Hank, Melwin, Catherine, and Jason arrived from the courtroom. "This just came in on the computer," she told them, holding up a miniature CD disk. "I downloaded it."

Cassandra spoke in Hank's ear. "I sent it. This is de Rijn's original video. It was only shown once, late at night on Dutch TV. You really need to see it, and there's more coming."

They watched the video without a word. "My God," Hank whispered when the screen went blank. "They edited it. What were they thinking of?"

"Maybe they thought the original was safely buried," Catherine said.

Melwin shook his head. "Europeans treat evidence much differently than Americans and the English."

"It's going to get very interesting on Monday," Hank replied.

"Be careful," Catherine counseled. "You're stressing the judges."

"That is the idea."

She shook her head. "But you don't want them to prematurely self-destruct."

161

"If NATO is any indication," Jason scoffed, "a Belgian, German, and Italian will do that without any help."

19

Amsterdam

"What a lovely day," Catherine said. She held onto Hank's arm as they browsed their way through the Sunday antique market on Nieuwmarkt Square. Catherine was an inch taller than her husband, and well-proportioned for her height. Her salt and pepper hair was cut in a stylish bob and she drew more than a few appreciative looks. Occasionally, a head would turn, recognizing Hank. But for the most part, they were just two more tourists. "It's hard to believe it's December."

Hank pushed their way through the crowd. "When the sun comes out, the Dutch make the most of it." A church bell pealed and he pointed to their left. "Oude Kerk. There's been a church there since the 1200s."

"Can we go? Is it far?"

"Couple of hundred yards. But it's right through the red light district."

"It can't be busy on a Sunday morning."

"You'd be surprised. The Dutch are very enterprising, not to mention horny." She laughed, enchanting him as always, and he gave in. "Okay, so don't go blaming me later for making you go through there."

"Of course I will." They headed across the square and turned down a narrow street. "Introducing de Rijn's tape was very clever of Du Milan," she told him. "It fixed the horror in everyone's mind."

"There was no way I could keep it out. But they made a mistake. Shouldn't have edited it."

"So what are you going to do?"

He spoke very slowly. "Shove it down de Rijn's throat bit by bit." He held her arm tightly. "Don't turn around. We're being followed." He made sure his percom was on. "Cassandra, are you there? There's a blue Mercedes behind us."

Her voice was in his ear, reassuring and safe. "I'm here. I'm not monitoring anything but I'll notify the police. Turn left at the next street and head for the canal. Cross over the drawbridge and turn right. Keep the canal on your right."

"It's gaining on us."

"Don't panic. Do you see the canal?"

They walked faster. "In sight. Almost there."

"Cross over and I'll raise the bridge."

Hank pressed Catherine's elbow and they hurried over the little drawbridge. It started to rise. The Mercedes stopped, still trapped two cars short of the bridge. "Now slow down and take in the sights," Cassandra said. "Tell me what the Mercedes is doing."

"Hank, what are you doing?" Catherine asked.

"Sightseeing," he told her.

She glanced at a theater's marquee. "Well, I don't have any need to see a 'Real Live Fucking Show.'"

"Something for the family?" the barker in front of the theater called.

"The Mercedes is following us on the other side of the canal," Hank told Cassandra.

"Good," Cassandra said. "Turn around and head back. You'll see two policemen coming your way. They're looking for you."

They turned around and walked past the theater. For a moment, the barker looked hopeful but they kept on walking. "Is that the Mercedes you told me about?" Catherine asked.

"I can't be sure. It looks the same."

"Hank, I think you're becoming paranoid."

The Hague

Jason and Aly waited impatiently at the prison's main entrance and counted the minutes to visiting hours. Aly sat the big basket with dinner down and tried to calm an anxious Jason. "It's really too early to tell."

"I know," Jason replied.

A Far Justice

A guard opened the gate and they hurried to sign in and go through the mandatory inspections. Six minutes later, they were inside and hurrying down the long corridor to Gus's cell. He was waiting for them in the open doorway. Aly ran into his arms while Jason pulled out his cell phone and dialed the Mayo Clinic. "Michelle's waiting for the call," Jason said. He handed the phone to Gus.

His daughter's face appeared on the screen. "Oh, Dad," she said. For the first time, there was hope in her voice and tears in her eyes. "The doctor's think they've stabilized Mom."

"Can I see her?" Gus asked. Michelle pointed the videophone at Clare and the image of an older, very frail woman came on the small screen. She was lying in bed, her red, gray-streaked hair pulled to one side, and her eyes closed. She was breathing regularly, without an oxygen cannula. Gus's face softened as he gazed at his wife and slipped back in time.

Gus stormed into the hospital and headed for the surgery ward. He was wearing a sweat-stained flight suit and lines from his oxygen mask were imprinted on his face. Clare was waiting for him outside the recovery room. "He's out of the operating room and in recovery," she told him. "He's going to be okay." She reached out and touched his face. "Benjy didn't make it." For a moment, Gus didn't move. Benjy was Jason's best friend. She spoke quietly, her voice measured and in control. "They were with a bunch of kids at the lake and Benjy drove home. They were hit by a drunk driver." Gus held onto his wife. "It wasn't their fault, Gus. But they had been drinking and the police are going to charge Jason." Gus's anger flared. "For what? Being a kid?" Clare held onto him. "We'll get through this," she murmured.

"Dad," Michelle said, bringing Gus back to the moment. "They need to do another operation to harvest bone marrow and remove some lung tissue. They need a lot."

"We'll get through this," Gus murmured.

20

The Hague

Harm de Rijn took the stand Monday morning and gazed serenely over the courtroom. "Now there's a confident man," Hank murmured loud enough for the spectators immediately behind him to hear.

"Respect your elders," Melwin said as Hank stood.

"Of course," Hank replied. He walked to the podium carrying a thin leather folder much like a weapon, which was exactly how he planned to use it. He placed it unopened on the podium. He fixed Bouchard with a long look and let the tension build. "Where's Henri?"

"The court has ruled on the matter of Henri Scullanois," Bouchard replied.

Hank shrugged and turned to de Rijn. "Good morning, Mr. DeGroot."

"Good morning, Hank. I prefer to be called by my professional name."

"I understand. But unfortunately, the prosecutor identified you by your real name on their witness list. As the court has closed the witness list to additions and modifications, we must use the name your parents gave you."

Denise stood. "We have no objections to referring to the witness as Harm de Rijn."

"The court concurs," Bouchard said.

"We note that the witness list has been so modified," Hank said. He handed the clerk a small plastic jewel case holding a mini CD. "If it may please the court, this is the complete and unedited video that was presented to the court on Friday."

"Objection!" Denise shouted. "The video as shown to the court was edited for relevance."

"Then let Mr. DeGroot so testify," Hank replied, "after the court has been shown the complete video."

Bouchard conferred with Della Sante and Richter. "Overruled," Bouchard intoned. "Monsieur Sutherland, please refer to the witness by his professional name."

"Of course, your Honor. I was using the witness's name at the time the video was made for the sake of accuracy." The lights darkened and the screen descended from the ceiling. The same video shown on Friday started to play. Suddenly, the image of a destroyed tank appeared in sepia tones. Hank paused the video. "Mr. de Rijn, wasn't this excerpt, shown here in sepia, part of your original video that was aired on February 29, 1991, but was edited from the video shown to the court last Friday?"

"Yes it was."

Hank played the video and stopped it twenty-two more times, each time asking the same question and getting the same answer. When the lights came on, Hank turned to the bench. "If it pleases the court, the amended video is presented as defense exhibit one."

Denise remained silent as Bouchard looked at the other two judges. They nodded in unison. "The amended video is so entered," Bouchard ruled.

"Thank you, your Honor. Mr. de Rijn, you earlier testified that two thousand trucks and vehicles were destroyed, and over three thousand men and women burnt and dismembered. Is that correct?"

"That is correct."

"And the video, as fully restored and entered into evidence, documents what you actually saw?"

"That is what I saw."

"Yet I counted only two hundred and forty-eight destroyed vehicles on the video. That number includes seven tanks, twelve armored personnel carriers, and five mobile surface-to-air missile batteries, which were all edited from the video entered into evidence by the prosecution on Friday. Further, I counted only seventy-six bodies."

Denise was on her feet. "Objection! Objection!" She calmed down. "Obviously, Monsieur de Rijn has other sources for his figures."

"Then please present them to the court," Hank said. "As of now, you have made it a matter of record that only two hundred and forty-eight vehicles were destroyed and seventy-six people killed. Or are we dealing with something other than facts here?"

Bouchard rapped the bench with his gavel. "Your sarcasm is not called for."

"I apologize, your Honor. By the way, what is your ruling on the learned prosecutor's objection?"

"I will not warn you again, Monsieur Sutherland."

"Again, I apologize, your Honor. But my question remains before the court."

Bouchard humphed. "The prosecutor may clarify her points on redirect examination."

Hank turned to de Rijn. "How many of these seventy-six bodies were civilians?"

"They were burned beyond all recognition, but a few were women who were not in uniform."

"But you just testified they were burned beyond all recognition. Which is it, Mr. de Rijn?"

"Women were reported traveling in the convoy."

"Did you actually see them?" De Rijn shook his head. "The witness is shaking his head in answer," Hank said. "Did you actually witness the attack?"

"No."

"Do you have any direct knowledge of the nationality of the alleged aircraft that supposedly caused the deaths and destruction you saw?" De Rijn stared at him and didn't answer. "I understand why you are reluctant to answer that question. May I ask how long it was after the attack before you were present at the scene?"

"I don't recall."

Hank reached into his folder and handed two sheets of paper to the clerk who handed them to de Rijn. "Mr. de Rijn, this is a list of passengers who cleared Dutch immigration at Schiphol Airport on the evening of February 26, 1991. Would you please read the highlighted name on page two, the passport number, and destination?" De Rijn glanced at the list and handed the list back to the clerk without a word. "For the record, the highlighted name is Peter DeGroot, the passport was issued to the witness under that name, and the destination of his flight was Riyadh, Saudi Arabia. Mr. de Rijn, when did you arrive in Riyadh?" Hank tapped the folder with his right forefinger, challenging him.

"Late the next day."

"That would be on February 27, 1991. Is that correct?"

"I believe so."

"Did you drive or fly to Mutlah Ridge?"

"We had to drive."

"How long did it take you to cover the 600 kilometers?"

"I don't recall."

"Can we safely assume that you could not have arrived at Mutlah Ridge no sooner than the morning of February 28, 1991, approximately 48 hours after the attack?"

"Objection," Denise said. "Monsieur de Rijn has already testified that he doesn't remember."

"Sustained," Bouchard said without looking at Della Sante or Richter.

Hank had the passenger list entered as the second defense exhibit and picked up the leather folder as if he were finished. De Rijn started to stand, anxious to escape. "One last question, sir. Who were you working for at the time?"

"I don't understand."

"Who paid you when you were covering the Gulf War?" Hank placed his folder on the podium and tapped it with his finger.

"I was freelancing at the time."

"Really?" Hank said as he opened the folder. He extracted three sheets of paper and handed them to the clerk who passed them to de Rijn. He closed the folder. The newscaster glanced at them and paled. "Please read the first document, sir." De Rijn shook his head and handed it back to the clerk. "If it may please the court," Hank said, "this is a contract employing the witness as a reporter for the Iraqi Ministry of Information. The witness, and the Iraqi Minister of Information, who is present in the witness's anti-chamber and listed as a defense witness, signed it on November 16, 1990. And the second document, sir?" Again de Rijn refused to answer and handed it to the clerk. "The witness was shown a certified copy of the first check he received from the Iraqi Ministry of Information. It is in the amount of eight thousand dollars and was cashed on January 1, 1991. And the last document, sir?"

"It's another check," de Rijn croaked as he handed it back to the clerk.

A Far Justice

"From the Iraqi Ministry of Information in the amount of eight thousand dollars and cashed on March 1, 1991." He tapped the closed folder, challenging de Rijn to discover what was inside. "Do you deny that is your signature on the contract and two checks?"

"No." De Rijn's voice was barely audible.

"Defense enters the contract and checks as defense exhibits three, four, and five."

Bouchard hesitated, expecting to hear an objection from Denise. But there was only silence. He looked at Della Sante and Richter who nodded. "So entered."

"I have no more questions of this witness." Hank turned away from the podium. "And where's Henri?"

Bouchard ignored him and adjourned for the day.

* * * * *

Marci Lennox was in her broadcast team's van talking to her director in New York over the satellite feed. "I expected fireworks, but nothing like this. Sutherland ripped de Rijn a new one."

"And that makes us all look bad," the director added. "Play it down."

"Why? This is a hot one. It plays like this; 'Under cross-examination by Hank Sutherland, the Netherlands' premier newscaster was shown to be a paid stooge for Saddam Hussein, a liar, and seriously cast the prosecution's case in doubt.' This could have legs."

"Remember who owns us," the director warned.

"Yeah, yeah, I know. We've been bought out by Dutch interests."

"That's the way the world turns, sweetie."

* * * * *

The small group huddled around the TV in Hank's office. "That's not Marci's style," Hank said. "Normally, she'd be all over something like this."

"That's very straightforward reporting," Catherine said. "She's sticking to who, what, when, and where. Perhaps it's just as well.

171

You'll never have another day in court like this one, and I don't want it going to your head."

"Not to worry," Melwin counseled. "Today's TV coverage speaks for itself." He thought for a moment. "I seriously doubt Du Milan will be able to get de Rijn back on the stand for redirect. For that matter, I imagine most of her witnesses are running for cover. You can be sure we'll never get Scullanois on the stand, not after today."

"Which is fine with me," Hank replied.

"By the way," Catherine said, "Gus is magnificent. I think half the women in the courtroom are in love with him."

"Are you suggesting we play to that?" Hank asked.

"You'd be foolish not to."

21

The Hague

Bouchard mentally braced himself as he went through the opening ritual and asked Du Milan if there were any issues before the court. As expected, Melwin immediately stood. Bouchard smiled tolerantly, establishing a semblance of control. "What do you have for us today?"

"If it may please the court," Melwin began. "The court has established that the alleged crimes took place on February 25 and 26, 1991. Article Twelve of the Rome Statute clearly states, and I quote, 'The court has jurisdiction only with respect to crimes committed after the entry into force of this Statute.' The Statute was entered into force on July 1, 2002, after sixty countries had deposited certificates of ratification with the United Nations. Therefore, the court does not have temporal jurisdiction over this alleged crime and we ask for the immediate dismissal of all charges against Mr. Tyler." He handed the blue-covered petition to the clerk.

"Madam Prosecutor?" Bouchard asked.

Denise stepped to the podium. "As I stated in my opening remarks, the Rome Statute allows the court to reach into the past and to correct obvious crimes against humanity – crimes which were recognized by The Geneva Conventions prior to 1991. Further, the action on Mutlah Ridge occurred under a United Nations resolution. As The Geneva Conventions are integral to the United Nations and the Rome Statute, which the defense has rightfully made so clear to the court, the defendant's crimes fall under the court's jurisdiction." Loud applause engulfed the courtroom.

Melwin tried to look tolerant. "Yet the court has no jurisdiction for crimes committed before its inception."

"The court has previously ruled on *ratione personae*," Bouchard said, "but not *ratione temporis*. Therefore, we will take your petition under consideration. Madam Prosecutor, you may continue."

"The prosecution has no further need of the witness de Rijn and asks that he be excused." The audience sat in stunned silence as Bouchard excused the absent TV commentator. Denise took a deep breath. "The prosecution calls Natividad Gomez."

The woman who entered the courtroom had changed. She had lost twenty pounds, was dressed attractively, and her hair was carefully styled. "Oh, my," Melwin breathed. "She's a stunner." They listened as Denise led Natividad through the standard questions establishing her identity, and that she worked in the records section of the Air Force Personnel Center at Randolph Air Force Base, San Antonio, Texas. Denise handed Natividad a thick folder.

"Do you recognize the contents of this folder?"

Natividad went through the contents. "Yes I do. It contains August Tyler's Air Force personnel file."

"Please read the highlighted portions of the earmarked pages."

For the next hour, Natividad methodically read from the file, documenting Gus's training and assignments. Denise requested a recess for lunch just as she reached the sections covering the time he flew combat in the Gulf War.

"Good timing," Hank allowed.

"I predict a full house drooling for blood on cross-examination when we reconvene," Melwin said. "You mustn't disappoint them."

"I won't," Hank promised.

Two hours later, Bouchard led Della Sante and Richter to their seats and nodded at the cameras, enjoying the drama of the moment. "Please be seated."

Denise continued to lead Natividad through Gus's file and established that he had been assigned to the 25th Tactical Fighter Wing at Al Kharj Air Base, Saudi Arabia, on February 25, 1991, had flown a combat mission on that date, and was awarded a Distinguish Flying Cross for engaging and stopping a large enemy convoy on Mutlah Ridge. Natividad closed the thick folder and handed it to the clerk.

"Has anything been deleted from the defendant's file or modified in anyway?"

"As best I can tell, no."

Denise handed the folder to the clerk. "The prosecution enters into evidence August Tyler's personnel file." The six TV commentators in the booth hastened to explain to their audiences that the prosecution had placed Gus at the scene and proven that he had attacked the convoy.

Bouchard looked at the defense table, waiting for an objection. There was none. "August Tyler's military record is entered as prosecution exhibit two. Monsieur Sutherland, your witness." Hank came slowly to his feet and picked up his leather folder. He glanced at Natividad and then back at his folder, ratcheting up the tension even more.

Gus came to his feet. "Your Honor, may I speak with my counsel for a moment?"

"Do you require a recess?"

"No, your Honor."

Hank walked slowly to the dock, still carrying the folder, and spoke in a low voice. "Be sure the cameras can focus on your face."

Gus turned slightly toward the cameras. "Everything she said was true. Leave her alone."

On cue, Hank froze. Then he slowly nodded and returned to his table. He thought for a moment as the audience waited. He handed his leather folder to Melwin and stepped to the podium. "Where's Henri?" he asked, sotto voce. Bouchard ignored him. "Good afternoon, Ms Gomez."

The fear in her voice was painful, a living reminder of what had happened to de Rijn on the stand. "Good afternoon."

Hank's voice was gentle. "I only have a few questions. When did you remove Mr. Tyler's file from the records section?"

"I don't remember the exact date, but it was mid-October of this year."

"Are personnel files classified in anyway?"

"They're for official use only."

"Whom did you give the file to?"

"Jean Philippe."

"Do you know Jean Philippe's last name?"

She shook her head. "No."

"Was he French?"

"He said he was born in Paris."

"Were you paid money or given any presents in return for the file?"

"Oh, no."

"Have you seen Jean Philippe since then?"

Tears filled her eyes. "No."

"Do you love him?"

"Oh, yes."

"Thank you, I have no more questions." He sat down.

Denise stared at Hank, reassessing her adversary. Reluctantly, she gave him high marks for his courtroom stagecraft. "I have no further questions."

* * * * *

It was a 'walk-and-talk' shot as Marci Lennox moved down the crowded sidewalk outside the ICC's palace. "The defense team continues to rock the trial chamber with legal challenges and constant surprises. Every legal expert in the courtroom predicted that Sutherland would destroy today's witness much as he had Harm de Rijn. But Colonel Tyler intervened and called off his attack dog attorney." The director spliced in a clip of Gus talking to Hank in the courtroom with Marci doing a voice over. "A lip reader understood Tyler to say, 'Everything she said was the truth. Leave her alone.'"

The camera was back on Marci. "And much to everyone's surprise, Sutherland did."

Amsterdam

Catherine snuggled under the down comforter and cuddled against her husband. "I loved it."

"Loved what?"

"Today in court, you ninny."

"Oh. I thought you had something else in mind."

"It was great theater and the media ate it up."

"We took a chance. I wasn't sure if it would work or not. But letting her off didn't improve our case."

Does it matter?" She waited for a reply. Then, snuggling closer, "Hank, I do have something else in mind."

A Far Justice

"It worked, didn't it?"
Catherine kicked him out of bed.

22

The Hague

Hank noticed the change the moment he and Catherine got off the train from Amsterdam the next morning. A few of their fellow passengers actually nodded at them on the platform and the crowd seemed to magically part, giving them open access to the taxi rank. The cab driver jumped out to open the door and took the most direct route to the Palace. Hank decided it was time to really test the waters and told the driver to drop them off at the main entrance. Demonstrators, curious spectators, and over two hundred TV crews spilled out of the forecourt and blocked their way. Again, the crowd parted as they made their way inside. Catherine gave him a little nudge. "It worked."

"Not last night," he grumbled.

* * * * *

Denise was huddled with the assistant prosecutor prepping for the upcoming session when her husband burst into her office. She looked at him in surprise. "Chrestien! I wish you had told me you were coming. Court reconvenes in a few moments and we are pressed for time."

Chrestien shot a contemptuous look at her assistant. "Leave." The man scurried out without a word, anxious to tell everyone on the prosecutor's staff that Chrestien Du Milan was at least twenty years her senior and four inches shorter.

"What's wrong?" Denise asked.

"What's wrong? Westcot is here and talking to everyone in the EU except us."

An unspoken worry claimed Denise. Supposedly, Westcot and Chrestien were friends but that was a civilized façade. Behind the scenes they were bitter rivals and Chrestien hated the American. "Can you contain him?" she asked, refusing to show her concern.

"Of course. But the trial is turning into a fiasco."

"Perhaps Sutherland has something to do with that." Chrestien stomped his right foot and, for a moment, they stared at each other. She had never seen him so angry. "I seem to recall you saying that you'd take care of him."

Chrestien slumped in a chair as his anger slowly died away. "The security around Sutherland is tight as a drum."

"What are you talking about?"

Denise was his star pupil and his most prized possession but she was not ready for the brutal reality of his world. One of his operatives had contacted 'the Family,' a Corsican clan that supplied support services to the French underworld and the occasional terrorist group. A verbal contract was duly negotiated that was heavy on price but lacking in specifics. The Family would "disrupt" Tyler's defense team for 1.5 million euros, and, as always, the Family required full payment in advance. "We're trying to gain access to his staff," he lied.

Denise accepted that as part of the game and could live with it. "Oh, I see. Marie Doorn."

Again, the lie came easy. "Of course." Chrestien's operatives had approached Doorn, but to no avail. His anger slipped out. "Damn Sutherland! He's turned Tyler into a Sir Galahad, the strong but silent type. There's actually a fan club forming in Paris!" Chrestien shuddered at the betrayal by his fellow Parisians, who he considered a fickle lot at best. "Scullanois is in a panic. He says it will be the end of his career if he's called as a witness. I've tried to calm Renée but she says Sutherland will link our rapprochement with China to the trial." He paced the floor. "There will be the devil to pay with the EU if that comes out."

Denise tensed at the mention of Scullanois's wife. "Reassure Renée that Bouchard will not let Henri take the stand. But no one can control Sutherland."

"I may have something." Again, he considered how much she needed to know. "In Iraq." He stood. "My airplane is waiting." He kissed her good-by on the cheek.

* * * * *

The courtroom buzzed with anticipation when Gus entered the dock. He nodded at Hank and Melwin, and scanned the packed spectator section. Half a dozen women smiled at him. He sat down and glanced at his watch, wondering why the delay.

Eleven minutes later, Denise hurried into the courtroom. "Better late than never," Melwin said in a low voice. The clerk buzzed the judges' anti-chamber and called for everyone to stand. "Do not expect the same courtesy to be extended to you and me," Melwin said. The judges filed in and day six of the trial started thirteen minutes late.

Bouchard was his usual choleric self. "The court has reviewed defense counsel's petition addressing temporal jurisdiction. It is our consensus that the court has temporal jurisdiction in this matter."

Hank looked at Melwin. "Did I hear right? By what precedent or law?"

"My dear sainted grandmother called it Sod's Law," Melwin replied. He stood, a hungry look on his face, and raised his voice. "I'm not aware of any precedent supporting such a ruling. Perhaps the court can help me in this regard."

"Down boy," Hank said. He was rewarded with a murmur of chuckles.

Bouchard fixed the Irishman with a stern look. "Monsieur Melwin, you are out of order. Return to your seat." He waited while Melwin sat down. "Madam Prosecutor, are there any matters or issues that need to be brought to the court's attention?"

Denise bobbed to her feet. "There are none, your Honor." She sat down and waited for Melwin to stand. But he didn't move.

"You have nothing for us, Signore Melwin?" Della Sante asked.

"Not today, your Honor," Melwin replied. "Not that it would do any good," he added sotto voce.

"Madam Prosecutor," Bouchard said, "you may call your next witness."

"The prosecution calls Ewe Reiss."

The side door opened and an apparition ghosted into the room. Audible gasps echoed over the crowd as the scarred and mutilated man took the witness stand. When the clerk stood to read the undertaking to tell the truth, Reiss held up his right hand, palm out and the stump of his fingers spread wide to stop him. "I will not take an oath."

Bouchard leaned forward. "You are not required to take the undertaking to tell the truth if you believe it is an affront to your human dignity, Monsieur Reiss."

"The men who did this to me all swore oaths. They are not my teachers."

Denise opened her folder and uncapped her OMAS. She checked off the first item as she began her questioning. Hank gave her high marks as she led Reiss through his testimony, establishing he was a civilian diesel mechanic working in Kuwait City and had been driving a truck transporting the bodies of Iraqi soldiers when he was caught in the attack on Mutlah ridge. His face streaked with tears as he described the death of his fellow driver, also a civilian. "How was your friend killed?" Denise asked.

"We were in the middle of the convoy and not hurt by the first bombs that boxed the convoy in. Then the plane attacked again, and dropped the small bombs that fall by the thousands and explode like hand grenades. I later learned they are called cluster bomb units."

"Did you see the airplane that dropped these bombs?"

"It was the same one, the one that dropped the first bombs. It flew right over us, very low. I escaped before our gas tank exploded. But my friend was trapped in the truck and burned to death."

"Tell us about your friend and what happened."

"His name was Hassan Ghamby. He was twenty-six years old, a Palestinian who worked in Kuwait City. He supported his family who still live in Gaza." Denise let his story unfold as he told of the next horrible hours and how he had crawled into the desert and dug a hole to hide from the attacking aircraft. He was hit again but later rescued by United States Marines who got him to a hospital in time to save his life. There was no anger in his voice, only a soft, melancholy echo from the past. She asked if he had been warned that the convoy could be attacked. His "No" carried a simplicity that left no doubt he was telling the truth. Denise closed her folder, capped her pen, and thanked him.

Bouchard declared a recess for lunch.

"We need to talk," Cassandra told Hank. "We've got problems."

"Why did I know that?" Hank muttered.

* * * * *

A Far Justice

Hank sat at the defense table after lunch, his hands folded, head bowed. He pulled into himself, thinking about all that Cassandra and her team had told him. He stood when the three judges entered, not sure what to do. "When in doubt, delay," Melwin advised.

Bouchard reconvened the court. "Your witness, Monsieur Sutherland."

Hank stepped to the podium carrying his thin leather folder. Reiss's eyes were riveted on it. "Where's Henri?" Hank asked.

Bouchard rapped his gavel. "I have cautioned you before on this matter."

"Yes, your Honor, you have." He turned to Reiss with the traditional "Good afternoon, Mr. Reiss."

"Good afternoon, sir."

"Mr. Reiss, you testified that you saw the airplane that bombed the convoy and killed your friend. Could you identify any markings that identified its nationality?"

"No. It was dark."

"Are you sure there was only one aircraft?"

"There was only one at first. The others came later. I later learned it was an F-15 called the Strike Eagle."

"Were your vehicle's headlights on?"

"No. The Iraqis wouldn't let us."

"As your truck was carrying bodies, was it clearly marked with a red cross?"

"No. It had been used for carrying supplies and we didn't have time to repaint it."

"Did you fire a flare or do anything to announce your presence to the attacking aircraft?"

"I didn't have flares."

"Then how could the pilot have known you were in the convoy?"

Reiss only stared at Gus and did not answer. Hank let the silence resonate. "Mr. Reiss, what happened to the remains of Hassan Ghamby?"

"I don't know. There were so many casualties. I assume he was buried in a mass grave."

"Besides yourself, who else knew Hassan Ghamby was at Mutlah Ridge?" Denise's head came up at Hank's question. She quickly scribbled a note and handed it to her assistant with a warning look. He quickly left the courtroom. Reiss did not answer, and again,

Hank did not press him. "Mr. Reiss," his voice was soft, almost inaudible, "why were you trying to escape with the Iraqis?"

"They paid me to drive and I wanted to help Hassan escape."

"Did the Iraqis pay Hassan Ghamby to help drive?"

The apparition slowly shook his head. "No."

"You said Hassan Ghamby was a Palestinian working in Kuwait. Was he one of the Palestinians who had collaborated with the Iraqis during the occupation?"

"He said the Kuwaitis would kill him if he stayed behind."

"Mr. Reiss, I know this is painful, but was Hassan Ghamby your lover?"

A single tear streamed down Reiss's scarred face as he slowly nodded. Hank's voice was gentle. "The witness is nodding yes." Suddenly, he sensed the truth and decided to take a chance. He gently tapped his leather folder, drawing every eye in the courtroom. "You weren't really transporting bodies in the truck, were you?"

Reiss's head shook once. "No."

"What was in the truck?"

"Mostly TVs and appliances. And a Rolls Royce."

"Were they stolen from the Kuwaitis?"

Reiss lifted his head, at last free of a terrible burden. "Yes. But Hassan didn't know. He was an honest man."

"I know this has been very painful, Mr. Reiss, and I thank you for telling the truth. I have no more questions."

Tears streaked Reiss's scarred face as Denise stood. "The prosecution has no further questions but may have to recall the witness at a later time."

Bouchard adjourned the court for the day and Hank slumped in his seat as the courtroom emptied. "I can't believe I did that," Hank said.

"I'd rather you didn't do it again," Catherine told him from the other side of the railing.

"Do what?" Jason asked.

"My husband," Catherine answered, "violated one of the prime rules of questioning. He asked a question when he didn't know the answer."

* * * * *

A Far Justice

The forecourt of the palace was strangely quiet as Catherine made her way through the milling crowd towards Marci Lennox. A technician fitted her with a wireless button microphone. "Can you sense the anger?" the technician asked.

"It's confusion," Catherine answered. "Not anger." Another technician did a sound balance and they were on the air.

"Mrs. Sutherland, " Marci began, "we've seen your husband destroy one prosecution witness on the stand and then treat the next two with gentleness and understanding. Is this part of the defense's strategy?"

"It's very simple," Catherine replied. "Hank Sutherland honors the truth. Ewe Reiss is a true casualty of war, and when pressed, he told the truth."

Amsterdam

The phone in Hank and Catherine's hotel suite rang just after they had gone to bed. Hank picked it up, barely conscious. It was Jason. "I'm in the lobby. Turn on the TV. I'll be right up." He broke the connection.

"Who was that?" Catherine asked.

Hank reached for the remote control to the TV. "Jason. He's on the way up." He cycled to an English-speaking news station.

A very concerned woman newsreader was standing in front of a map of the Netherlands. "The body of Harm de Rijn was discovered in his car, an apparent suicide. The car was found in his garage with the engine running. His wife told investigators that he had been severely depressed since testifying before the International Criminal Court." A knock at the door demanded their attention.

"That was quick," Hank said. He padded to the door and let Jason in.

"There's a pretty ugly crowd outside," Jason said.

"In Holland?"

"Yeah, in Holland. I've got a security team in place. Stay inside." He didn't tell them the security team had been guarding them from the very first and that he had one guarding Aly and her parents. "But I can't locate Melwin."

Catherine was standing in the doorway to the bedroom. "Try Marie Doorn's apartment."

"What the hell is he doing there?" Hank asked.

"They seem to have clicked," Catherine replied.

"Cassandra," Hank said, "do you have Marie Doorn's address?"

Delft, the Netherlands

The light was still on in Marie Doorn's small third-floor apartment when Jason arrived shortly after midnight. He was not surprised when Marie answered his knock dressed in a silk negligee. He spoke briefly to Melwin and, satisfied that all was well, returned to his car. He wrapped a lap robe around his shoulders and used a night scope to scan the apartment building a hundred yards away. He punched at his cell phone and called for another security team. The controller told him a team was on the way, and that all was quiet at the Amstel Intercontinental and the van der Nord farm. Jason settled down to wait for the team.

"Oh, oh," he murmured. Two men were walking down the side of the apartment building, headed for the rear entrance. He bolted from the car and punched at his cell phone as he ran for the apartment. "I got two unknowns inside Doorn's building. Going in." The controller told him the security team was ten to twelve minutes away. Jason drew his 9mm Glock and chambered a round. He was through the front door and bounding up the stairs. He reached the third floor and cracked the stairwell door leading into the hallway. Nothing.

He checked the hallway again. The door to Doorn's apartment was cracked open.

How had he missed that? Before he could move, two muffled shots, little more than loud pops, echoed from the apartment. He crouched at the doorway as two more pops carried down the hall. A bitter taste flooded Jason's mouth. He was too late and two people were dead. The two men emerged from the apartment. The first one headed for the stairwell as the other closed the door and walked quickly away in the other direction.

Jason drew back into the shadows and waited. He shifted the Glock to his left hand. The door slowly opened and a man came through. He headed for the stairs and didn't see Jason at his back.

"Freeze," Jason ordered. The man was a blur of motion as he spun around and kicked at the Glock with his right foot. But Jason was quicker. He raised the Glock and caught the man's ankle with his right hand. He held him off balance, his hand a crushing vice. The man drew a small semi-automatic and fired. The bullet creased Jason's bicep and smashed into the wall. Jason reacted automatically and twisted the man's leg. The man jerked and pulled his leg free as Jason drove a fist into his chest. The assailant stumbled backwards and pitched over the side of the railing. His scream came to an abrupt halt when he bounced off the concrete floor three stories below. The semi-automatic clattered as it bounced, an ending punctuation. Jason charged down the stairs.

Outside, he saw a shadow hurrying down the walk and gave chase. The man saw him and ran. Jason breathed easily as he chased the man, in no hurry to catch him. He wanted to run him a bit to tire him out. He put on a burst of speed when the man reached a parked car and jumped inside. The engine roared to life as Jason reached the car. The man slammed the car into gear and twisted the steering wheel as Jason squeezed off a round into the windshield. He missed. But like so many European windshields, it splintered into a thousand bits and shreds, momentarily blinding the driver. Jason fired a second round through the opening. This one tore off the driver's ear. The car crashed into a parked minivan.

Jason dragged the man out of the car and spread-eagled him against the minivan. "I always give a man a choice," he said. "Talk or start bleeding." The man spat in Jason's face. "Your choice," Jason growled. He squeezed off a third shot and shattered the back of the man's right knee. He screamed in pain as Jason jammed the muzzle into his rectum, lifting him clear of the ground. "I always give a man a choice . . ."

23

The Hague

It was early Friday morning and Marci Lennox's crew switched on small high intensity floodlights, lighting the Palace's deserted forecourt. She looked into the camera. "A triple tragedy with the suicide of Harm de Rijn and the brutal murder of defense counsel Alex Melwin and his legal assistant, Marie Doorn, has stunned this small and normally placid country. Harm de Rijn had often been called the Netherlands' Walter Cronkite, and apparently took his own life after it was revealed that he was employed by Saddam Hussein's regime during the Gulf War of 1991.

"The demonstrations that swept through Amsterdam following the news of de Rijn's suicide melted away in the aftermath of the double killing which has all the earmarks of an execution-style murder. The murder is under investigation, and we are told that the trial will remain adjourned at least until Monday."

* * * * *

The four friends gathered around the conference table, each harboring their grief quietly, in their own way. Hank bent over the table, his hands planted firmly next to the stark crime photos Jason was carefully spreading out. He took a deep breath. *What would Alex do?* he wondered. Suddenly, he could hear Alex's voice. "Carry on, mate. Nail the bastards." Hank glanced at Catherine and Aly and forced his grief into a closely guarded cell to deal with later, when he could put it all in perspective and properly honor Alex Melwin.

"They're two thugs from Marseilles," Jason explained. "The one who took the header down the stairwell was the leader. The one

I convinced to talk claims 'the Family' let the contract for the hit and that's all he knows. The Rijkspolitie, that's the Dutch national police, says the Family is a group of Corsicans that provides whatever services the underworld might require, and I was lucky to get the thug to even admit the Family was involved. So we're pretty much at a deadend."

"Are the police going to charge you?" Hank asked.

"As far as the Dutch are concerned, I did them a favor."

Hank thought for a moment. "Why Alex and Marie?"

Jason shook his head. "We'll never know, not now. But I think they were going after you and couldn't hack it. So they took out who they could."

"Why would they do that?" Catherine asked.

"According to the Rijkspolitie, it's the way the Family does business. Cash on the barrelhead and it's a matter of honor to provide results."

Catherine was still confused. "Why couldn't they get to Hank?"

"Let's just say we had his back."

Catherine was very worried. "Is Hank safe?"

Jason nodded. "Oh, yeah. Count on it."

Catherine's eyes opened wide as the pieces came together. "By any chance do your people drive a blue Mercedes?"

A little smile flickered across Jason's lips. It was time they knew. "Sure do. If you get in trouble and need help, look for it or a silver Audi." He studied the two lawyers for a moment. "So where do we go from here?"

Hank paced the floor. He knew what Alex would have done if he had been the victim. "The game's changed." He opened his percom and sat it on the table. "Folks, meet Cassandra." He explained how the personal communicator worked and let them get acquainted. Then, "Cassandra, what's your estimate of the situation?"

"Losing Alex was a major setback," she replied. "He knew how to argue the legal issues and most of the judges on the court listened to him. Now that he's gone, we're very worried about keeping the Reverend Person's statement out."

"Have you been able to establish contact with Person?" Hank asked.

"Not yet. There is a report that a supply convoy got through to the mission."

"Is the airfield open?" Jason asked.

"It's reported closed," Cassandra replied.

"Gus claims that Toby would never make that statement," Hank said. "At this point, I'm willing to go with that. But we're back to the basic problem; getting him here."

"We contacted the State Department," Cassandra said. "No help there. They said the United States is hands-off in the Sudan. Even if we got to him, we don't know if he would agree to testify."

Hank stopped his pacing and looked at Jason. "If we can work something out, would you go get him?"

"In a heartbeat," Jason replied. "Toby will remember me and listen."

"Cassandra, can you make that happen?" Hank asked.

"I'll get right on it."

"So what do we do for now?" Jason asked.

"I'd suggest you pack," Cassandra answered.

* * * * *

Bouchard's opening remarks when he reconvened the court on Monday were somber and fitting, and, for the first time, Hank saw a hint of humanity as he paid tribute to Alex Melwin and Marie Doorn. Denise stood when the judge finished and added her condolences. Bouchard thanked her and turned to Hank who was sitting alone at the table. "The court will hear with favor any request for a postponement."

Gus came to his feet. "Your Honor, if I may." Bouchard granted him leave to speak. "As you may know, I had many differences with Alex Melwin when he was first appointed as my defense counsel. But as time passed, I came to trust him and respect his judgment. Alex was many things, imperfect in some ways, but in one thing constant and true. He believed in this court and what it stands for. He once wrote that 'the court is seriously flawed but at same time it is a beacon for our future.' Perhaps the best way we can honor Alex Melwin is to continue, to remedy those flaws and find that beacon that he spoke of."

For a moment, there was only silence. Then Della Sante stood and bowed her head. "You honor us, Signore."

"If there is no objection," Bouchard said, "we will continue." Routinely, he asked if there were any issues for the court. Denise said no as Hank came to his feet. Bouchard closed his eyes and took a deep breath in obvious frustration. "Yes, Monsieur Sutherland?"

"If it may please the court; reference is made to the Prosecutor's petition 'Initiation of Investigation into United States War Crimes in Iraq, March 19, 2003, to January 20, 2009.' The prosecutor was granted permission by the court to proceed with the investigation on October sixth of this year. However, she exceeded the intent of the court when she extended the investigation outside of the aforementioned dates. Therefore, the prosecutor lacked the authority to arrest and charge the defendant, and he must be released immediately." He handed the blue-covered petition to the clerk and sat down.

Denise smiled indulgently. "This is a minor matter of little more consequence than a typographical error."

"Is it?" Hank asked.

Bouchard's face went rigid. "Monsieur Sutherland, you are splitting hairs and the court agrees with the . . ."

Richter interrupted. "I find this very troublesome and urge the court to take defense council's petition under immediate review." He closed his notebook with finality.

Bouchard's face turned a mottled red, and his jaw quivered as he spoke. "We are adjourned until further notice." He stood and hurried out without waiting for the other two judges.

Hank turned to Catherine and Jason. "How about that?"

"You've openly split them," Catherine replied.

* * * * *

Denise's high-heels clicked an angry tattoo on the parquet floor when she stormed into Bouchard's office. She ripped off her robe and dropped it on his secretary's desk as she passed. "He's not to be disturbed," the secretary warned. Denise ignored her and pushed through the double doors. The secretary picked up the phone. "Aly," she began.

Bouchard came to his feet, his anger matching hers. "I'm tired of these endless challenges to the court's authority," he snapped.

"At least we agree on that. Stop him."

"And how am I to do that?" Bouchard asked.

Denise paced the floor. "Delay. Let these foolish petitions pile up."

"I can't. Richter is pressing for final arguments before Christmas and Della Sante is questioning everything now."

"Which one is dissenting on your rulings?"

"Both. Fortunately, they've split so far but, sooner or later, they will agree." The intercom buzzed and his secretary announced that Sutherland was outside. He glared at the offending instrument. "I'm in conference." The door banged open and Hank barged in.

"If you two meet once more without me, I'll file a protest with Relieu and go public."

"We are all officers of the court," Bouchard protested. "President Relieu encourages cooperation at all levels."

"But not in secret. Do you want to see how that one plays with the media?" He held the door and motioned for Denise to leave. She hesitated for a moment and then walked out.

New York, New York

Elizabeth 'Liz' Gordon, CNC-TV's premier anchorwoman hosting the evening newscast, spun around in her chair and faced the large screen, her trademark short skirt and long legs in full view. Marci Lennox was on the screen, standing in the deserted courtroom. "Marci, what exactly is going on?"

"Liz, it appears that Hank Sutherland is pounding at the very legitimacy of the court and has apparently split the three judges hearing the case."

"Is there any substance to the rumor we've been hearing over here about Iraq?"

"I can confirm that Iraq has ratified the Rome Statute and is now a member of the International Criminal Court, which makes it the third Arabic country to do so."

"What impact will that have on the case?"

"It is far too early to tell and given the unpredictability we've witnessed so far, I would not even want to hazard a guess."

"Well, it does sound exciting."

Marci grew even more serious. "Not if your name is Gus Tyler."

24

The Hague

Aly stood at the defense table arranging the folders for the day's trial. She was wearing a clerk's plain back robe and would be sitting next to Hank. She walked over to Gus when he took his place in the dock. "I'm glad you're here," he told her.

"It was Hank's idea," she said. "And I wanted to do it."

"Every friendly face helps."

The red light on the clerk's table blinked and she hurried back to the table and stood beside Hank for the opening processional. When the court was called to order, Bouchard cleared his throat. "On examination of defense counsel's petition to dismiss, the court must rely on Article Thirty-two of the Rome Statute that states 'A mistake of law as to whether a particular type of conduct is a crime within the jurisdiction of the court shall not be a ground for excluding criminal responsibility.' The court finds that the date in the prosecutor's original petition is a minor mistake of law that does not negate the jurisdiction of the court nor criminal responsibility. Petition denied."

"Why am I not surprised?" Hank said in a loud voice.

"What does it mean?" Aly asked.

"It means," he replied in a stage whisper that carried over the room, "that the court can prosecute whoever it damn well pleases." He came to his feet. "Your Honors, I am deeply concerned by the court's interpretation of Article Thirty-two which concerns the mental element required by the crime in question."

"Counsel is referring to the first paragraph of Article Thirty-two," Bouchard snapped. "The court is relying on the second paragraph, which addresses particular types of conduct and the court's jurisdiction."

"Your Honor, Article Thirty-two does not give the court an unrestricted license to hunt for targets of opportunity."

"You will come to order," Bouchard replied, his anger barely in control.

"As soon as the court comes to justice," Hank muttered as he sat down.

"Why are you antagonizing him?" Aly whispered.

"When all else fails, get obnoxious."

Denise stood. "If it may please the court." Bouchard breathed in relief as he recognized her. "May we move beyond this? As you know, the Republic of Iraq has ratified the Rome Statute, becoming the one hundredth and twelfth nation to become a member of the International Criminal Court. The office of the prosecutor welcomes Iraq on this momentous occasion."

"If I may speak for the court," Bouchard replied, "this chamber also welcomes Iraq as it joins in the march to universal justice." He cleared his throat. "If there is no further business, you may call your next witness."

"The prosecution calls General Davis Armiston."

"I was hoping I'd scared him away," Hank told Aly. She handed him the folder on Armiston. "Now it gets interesting." He split his attention, listening to Denise lead Armiston through the standard questions as he reviewed the folder. At the same time, Cassandra spoke in his ear, providing an up-to-the-moment legal analysis by her team of lawyers. Denise's questions took an unexpected turn when she asked Armiston about cluster bomb units.

"I served as the commander of the Air Armament Center at Eglin Air Force Base in Florida," Armiston replied, "and was responsible for the testing, development, and sustainment of all air-delivered munitions employed by the Air Force."

"How would you describe the weapons effects of CBU-58s as employed on Mutlah Ridge?"

"It's a wide-area denial weapon to be used on enemy troops and soft targets caught in the open."

"You referred to CBUs as 'wide-area.' Does that mean they are indiscriminate in nature?"

"CBUs are not target selective," he replied.

"So anyone caught in the open, civilian or military, will be killed."

"Given the nature of shrapnel, they are just as likely to be wounded."

"Isn't it more desirable to kill the enemy than wound him?"

"Just the opposite. A wounded man or woman takes more care than a dead one, and that consumes resources and personnel. Further, you must take care of your wounded or it adversely affects morale."

"Then militarily, it is more desirable to cause widespread harm and suffering than outright death."

"That is the nature of warfare."

"Moving on, you served in the Gulf War of 1991 with the defendant. Did you know there were civilians in the areas you were attacking?"

"It was common knowledge that civilians were in the area."

"Were these civilians warned about impending bombardments?"

"I never heard anything about that."

"Did you participate in the attack on Mutlah Ridge?"

"No. I was in crew rest in my quarters."

"Do you know who flew the aircraft that initially attacked the convoy?"

Hank was on his feet. "Objection. Hearsay. The witness has already testified he was in crew rest."

"Overruled," Bouchard said. "The witness's testimony is both relevant and compelling."

"And could have been overheard in a bar," Hank replied.

"The witness will answer the question," Bouchard said.

Armiston's face turned sad. "August William Tyler."

"General Armiston," Denise continued. "What kind of pilot was the defendant?"

"Actually a very good pilot. But he tended to be a bit of a cowboy."

"Please explain."

"He was too aggressive and disregarded the rules of engagement. Once he attacked a convoy he found outside his assigned area without authorization."

Hank objected but, as expected, Bouchard overruled him.

"What type of convoy?" Denise asked.

"It was probably carrying a Scud missile."

"Probably?" Denise asked.

"Photo reconnaissance could only confirm the presence of a fueling truck, a few support vehicles, wreckage that could have been the missile carrier, and a bus."

"But no missile?"

"It probably blew up."

"Probably. You mentioned a bus. What was it doing there?"

"Probably carrying the support crew."

"Could it have been carrying civilians?"

Hank was on his feet. "Objection. The witness has no direct knowledge of who was on the bus."

"Learned counsel is correct," Denise said. "I withdraw the question. I have no further questions. Thank you, General Armiston." She looked at Hank with anticipation and sat down.

"We were just sandbagged," Hank murmured to Aly. He stood and walked to the podium his head bowed, deep in thought. Slowly, he raised his head. "Where's . . ." He waited for a reaction.

"Henri?" a woman called from the back of the audience.

Bouchard rapped his gavel. "Another outburst from the spectators and I will order the visitor's gallery cleared."

Hank looked puzzled. "Your Honor, there have been many much louder outbursts from the audience without a reprimand from the bench. Does your warning apply to all outbursts or only those outbursts for the defense?"

"I am tired of your sarcasm, Monsieur Sutherland, and will not tolerate it."

"It is a valid observation, your Honor."

Bouchard rapped his gavel. "Proceed with your questioning."

Hank placed his unopened leather folder on the podium. "Good morning, General."

"Good morning, Hank."

"General Armiston, you testified you were in crew rest the night of the mission on Mutlah Ridge. If ordered, would you have flown it?"

"Of course. But my reaction would have been different. I would have overflown the convoy and radioed back what I had observed."

"And if then ordered to attack?"

"I would have called for a flare ship to illuminate the convoy and then only employed my weapons if I could clearly identify it as a military convoy."

Gus motioned Hank over to the dock and spoke in a low voice. Hank nodded and returned to the podium. "General, the flare aircraft you referred to were slow moving AC-130 gunships, which are limited in their ability to maneuver. Because of the high threat from surface-to-air missiles and anti-aircraft artillery batteries, they were prohibited from operating in that area. Lacking such illumination, would you have attacked or allowed the vehicles to escape?"

Denise was on her feet. "Your Honor, this is all hypothetical and of no value as the witness was not there."

"Move on, counselor," Bouchard ordered.

"Is it any wonder you were in crew rest?" Hank asked, sotto voce. "General, did the Iraqis use civilian buses to transport soldiers in the Gulf War?"

"Of course."

"Would a bus traveling with a military target be subject to attack?"

"Under most circumstances, yes. But in this case, the convoy Captain Tyler attacked was out of his area of operations, and he had not received authorization to engage the enemy or employ his ordnance."

There was no objection from Denise about Armiston's use of Gus's military rank so Hank ran with it, eager to validate Gus's military standing. "So the then Captain, later Colonel, Tyler should have let the Scud missile escape into the desert."

"A suspected Scud missile," Armiston said. "Bomb damage assessment never confirmed there was a missile on the TEL."

"General, when you flew combat missions in the Gulf War, did you attack vehicles?" Armiston confirmed that he had. "Did you always know exactly what the vehicle was?"

"I always had a high degree of confidence that it was a valid target or I would not have employed my ordinance."

"Then you trusted the targets had been properly validated by your commanders."

"That's correct."

"Did you ever employ CBUs?"

"Of course."

"Did you then, or as the commander of the Air Armament Center consider them a weapon of mass destruction?"

"The issue was never raised."

"I see. Did it ever occur to you that it could be an issue?"

"I never thought about it."

"General, why are you here?"

"Objection," Denise called.

"The question goes to motivation," Hank replied.

Bouchard glanced at Richter and Della Sante who nodded. "The witness may answer the question."

"As I had served as the Supreme Allied Commander, Europe, it was an obligation I could not ignore."

"And it is not personal in anyway?"

"Of course not."

Hank walked to the defense table and Aly handed him a thick document printed on oversized paper with a green cover. He handed it to the clerk who passed it to Armiston. "General, do you recognize this document?"

Armiston threw a quick look at Denise. "It's a US Air Force accident investigation report."

"Are you the pilot named in this report?"

Denise was on her feet. "Objection. The report is for official use only. Further, this court cannot verify the authenticity of the report. Therefore, it has little probative value."

"Sustained," Bouchard said.

Richter cleared his throat for attention. "The defendant's personnel records were also classified 'for official use only.' Yet they were allowed into evidence."

"The source of those records," Denise replied, "was in court and was cross-examined as to their accuracy."

Richter stared at her, appalled by her reasoning. "Need I remind the prosecutor that the subject of this accident report is on the stand, and subject to your examination? It is my opinion that the accident report be allowed."

"And mine," Della Sante said.

Bouchard was stunned. He had just been overruled in open court. "So ruled." The words almost choked him.

Hank turned to Armiston. "Please read the highlighted passages on the marked pages."

Armiston's face flushed as he read. "Findings: the primary cause of the accident was an induced compressor stall caused by the pilot when he cross-controlled the aircraft on final approach. Further, the pilot did not immediately institute the correct emergency procedures which could have averted the resulting crash." He turned the page. "Recommendations: subparagraph four. As investigation revealed that the pilot was involved in two earlier aircraft incidents, the Board recommends a Flight Evaluation Board be convened to evaluate the pilot's suitability to remain on flying status."

"What was the first incident?" Hank asked.

"I don't remember."

"You'll find it in Annex C, page C-12. Will you please read the highlighted passage?"

Armiston closed the report and handed it to the clerk. "Apparently not," Hank said. "Is it true that the first incident occurred when you attempted an approach into Ramstein Air Base, Germany, but landed on a nearby autobahn?"

"Yes, but . . ."

Hank looked at him expectantly. Armiston shook his head, reluctant to say more. "Is it true the second incident occurred when you became lost flying a low level mission over Germany and had to make an emergency landing at Frankfurt Airport where you flamed out for fuel starvation on the runway, closing the runway and causing sixteen civilian airliners to divert to alternate airfields?"

"Weather was a factor," Armiston said.

"I take it that means 'yes.' How did the accident investigation board learn of these two incidents?"

"Tyler told them."

"Were you under his command at the time of the incidents?"

Armiston snorted. "I was never under his command. We were both lieutenant colonels and assigned to the same wing. I was the chief of plans and Tyler was a squadron commander. I only flew with his squadron to maintain flying proficiency."

"What were the results of the Flight Evaluation Board the accident board recommended be convened to determine your suitability to continue flying?"

"It was never held."

Hank opened his leather folder and pulled out two documents. "Why?"

"I was reassigned to AFMC, Air Force Material Command, and the commander ruled there was no need to convene a flight evaluation board."

"Was the commander of AFMC related to you in any way?"

Armiston hesitated before answering "He was my father-in-law's brother."

Hank nodded and returned the documents to the folder. "Defense enters the Accident Report as defense exhibit five."

There was no objection from Denise, and Bouchard checked with Richter and Della Sante before ruling. "So entered."

Hank turned away from the podium as if he were finished. He stopped and opened his leather folder. "I do have one last question. Besides the accident and the two landing incidents, are there any other blemishes on your record?"

"I served with distinction throughout my career."

Hank closed the folder. "I take it that means 'no.'" His voice was heavy with contempt. He sat down.

"Your witness, Madam Prosecutor," Bouchard said.

Denise stood. "The prosecution has no further questions."

"Smart move," Hank said, sotto voce, as he stood. "The defense has no further questions at this time but reserves the right to recall the witness."

Bouchard declared a recess for lunch. "Well," Hank told Aly, "we now know why the good General is testifying."

"We do?"

The moment the judges were out of the room, Hank turned to Catherine. "Get to Marci and blow the whistle on Armiston."

"Will do," she said, pushing her way through the crowd.

"Aly, notify the Victims and Witnesses Unit that we will recall Armiston to the stand the same day as Secretary Katelhong." He gave a disgusted snort.

* * * * *

Marci looked into the camera. "General Armiston was the second witness who fared badly under cross-examination by Hank Sutherland." She turned to Catherine and tipped the microphone in her direction. "Is this trial turning in favor of Gus Tyler?"

"I wouldn't say that," Catherine replied. "The prosecution needed Armiston to prove that Gus disregarded the rules of engagement. However, Hank cast doubt on his credibility and the judges saw quite clearly why Armiston was willing to testify. He is tying up the loose ends in his past that could seriously hurt his upcoming bid for the presidency."

"And that loose end is Gus Tyler," Marci added.

"Exactly. A conviction will discredit the man who questioned his competence as a pilot and his integrity as an officer."

* * * * *

Gus was back in the dock waiting for the afternoon session and motioned for Hank to come over. "What's up?" the lawyer asked.

"There are five or six women in the audience who keep looking at me and smiling. I think one's flirting."

Hank looked and saw a group of attractive women ranging in age from their mid-thirties to early fifties. "The ones down front on the left?"

"That's them. It's getting embarrassing."

Hank chuckled. "Courtroom groupies. Maybe we're doing something right. Don't worry about it but I'll get Cathy's take."

"Should I smile back?"

"A little nod of recognition wouldn't hurt."

"How's it going today?"

"So far, pretty good. Du Milan needed Armiston to show you didn't follow the rules. That backfired. I expect she'll trot out a few weapons experts to testify why CBUs are prohibited. She has three big problems. She has to prove civilians were in the convoy, you knew it, and that Reiss's buddy, Hassan Ghamby, was indeed killed there. So far, the court only has Reiss's uncorroborated testimony on that."

"What about Toby?"

The red light on the clerk's table blinked. "He's still caught in the Sudan and can't get here to testify, but Du Milan will try to get his statement read into evidence." He returned to his seat as the judges trooped in.

The afternoon unfolded much as Hank had predicted. Denise first called a French doctor who had reached the convoy within hours after the attack. He testified that he had treated many casualties dressed in civilian clothes, including three women. Later, he worked in a mortuary to help establish identifications. Based on a bracelet, one of the bodies was identified as Hassan Ghamby. The photos he produced were extremely grisly and admitted into evidence. On cross-examination, Hank asked the doctor if he could identify the exact body in the photographs that had been wearing the bracelet. The doctor replied that he couldn't be certain, as it was so long ago. "So it could have been found on the body of a soldier," Hank said.

"Then why were they dressed as civilians?" the doctor asked.

"They're called looters and deserters," Hank replied.

Denise next called a witness claiming to be an expert on weapons of mass destruction. Roger Marks was a nondescript Englishman with thinning blond hair, and paunchy from lack of exercise. He swelled with importance as Denise led him through the standard opening questions, establishing his bona fides as an expert witness who had been in Kuwait during the Gulf War examining weapons effects.

At first, Hank dismissed him as a puffed-up martinet. Then he caught it. Roger Marks was a man filled with resentment at the world for not recognizing his worth and rewarding him accordingly. It didn't matter that what the world saw was mediocrity with a mini cassette recorder. Marks wanted his fifteen minutes of fame and this was his chance. He grew with self-importance as he lectured the court on CBUs, and concluded by claiming that the weapon was designed to cause unnecessary suffering and injury, and in violation of the international law of armed conflict and the Geneva Conventions.

Satisfied, Denise ended Marks's testimony by having him read the list of prohibited weapons in the annex to the Rome Statute, which included CBUs."

Hank opened his cross-examination by asking "Were CBUs listed as a prohibited weapon in the annex in February of 1991?" Marks replied that the annex did not exist in 1991. Hank looked puzzled. "So a pilot dropping CBUs in 1991 had no way of knowing he was employing a weapon that would be prohibited in the future."

"He should have!" Marks blurted. Laughter rippled across the courtroom.

Hank shook his head and gave Marks a patronizing look. "The defense has no further questions for this witness at this time but reserve the right to recall him later." Denise wisely declined redirect and Marks gratefully escaped. Hank handed the clerk a familiar blue-covered petition. "At this time, we respectfully request the court to dismiss the charge of employing prohibited weapons."

"Court procedures require such petitions to be submitted at the beginning of the day's session," Bouchard told him.

"I beg the court's indulgence," Hank replied. "It is submitted for the sake of efficiency."

"And the basis for your petition?" Bouchard asked.

"Ratione temporis," Hank answered. "The prohibition of retroactive crimes and punishments is fundamental to all human rights laws. Further, Article Twenty-two of the Statute specifically states that a person cannot be held criminally responsible by the court for a crime that was not prohibited at the time it took place."

Denise stood, fuming with anger. "This a waste of the court's time. The court has ruled previously ruled on this very issue and now the learned counsel for the defense is asking the court to reverse itself. Further, the standard adopted by the European Court of Human rights with respect to prosecuting crimes not prohibited at the time is that they must be foreseeable as being such."

Hank knew he was spinning his wheels but he was determined to keep battering at the court and ratcheting up the pressure on Bouchard. "And now the court has before it a specific instance to measure that standard against. Further, I would like to remind the court that Article Eleven limits the court's jurisdiction to . . ."

Bouchard rapped his gavel and interrupted. "Learned counsel for the defense will not lecture the court on the Statute. However, the court will take your petition under advisement. We are adjourned until tomorrow morning at ten o'clock."

* * * * *

Chrestien glared at the offending TV. He grabbed the remote control and flicked it off. "The bitch," he muttered.

Denise padded out of her kitchenette with a large bowl of ice cream. She cuddled beside him on the couch, her bare legs curled up. "The wretched Marci Lennox?"

"Of course. I want to see her reaction tomorrow."

"Chrestien, I don't want to do it."

He stroked her thigh, sensing something was wrong. Was he losing control of his wife? That was the one thing he could not tolerate. "It's your last chance to muzzle Sutherland before he presents his case."

"It's wrong."

He squeezed her thigh. Hard. "Don't be stupid."

* * * * *

Gus stretched out on his bunk after Derwent left, his fingers intertwined behind his head as he listened to the soft night sounds of the prison. A soft moaning from down the corridor drifted under the door and blended with faint aftermath of the psychiatrist's perfume. Scent and sound blended as the sleeping pill started to work.

Clare nudged him. "Okay, what's bothering you?" He blinked, coming awake. Clare was in bed, fresh from a scented bubble bath. "You were moaning," she told him. "Something's been bothering you all evening." He reached out and she cuddled in his arms, her head against his chest. "Jason will be alright. You got his attention. Wendy's folks aren't going to do anything." Wendy's father had caught Jason and her in bed. Gus gave a little nod. "I didn't know she was eighteen," Clare said. "My God, Jason's only fourteen. What was she thinking of?" Gus let her talk. "It's Armiston," he finally admitted. "I can't let him fly the jet. He's too damn dangerous. Head up and locked most of the time." Her hand sneaked up his chest and caressed his cheek. "Do what you have to do." Her left leg wrapped around his right knee and she cuddled closer. "Pay attention," she ordered.

25

The Hague

Hank studied Bouchard as he sat down and convened day nine of the trial. "Now there's a man with a mission," he told Aly."

"Is that good news?" she asked.

"Not for us.'

"Good morning, Bouchard began. "The court has reviewed defense counsel's petition to dismiss the charge of using prohibited weapons under the provisions of Article Eleven and Twenty-two. The court finds no substantive reason to reverse its prior ruling. Further, the consensus of the court is that the widespread and indiscriminate effects of cluster bomb units were well known to all at the time of employment. Therefore, the standard adopted by the European Court of Human Rights that their eventual prohibition could have been logically foreseen applies. Petition denied."

Applause broke out in the courtroom, and Aly held onto Hank's hand. "Why am I not surprised," he said, sotto voce.

Bouchard ignored the disturbance but Gus looked at the audience and made a dampening motion with his right hand, urging them to stop. They did and he gave them a nod in thanks. "Before we proceed," Bouchard said, "are there other issues for the court to consider?"

Denise stood. "If it may please the court, there is a petition for your consideration. As the court is aware, the Republic of Iraq has recently joined our ranks. We have received a petition from the president of Iraq requesting that the defendant be transferred to their custody upon termination of this trial."

"What is the purpose of such a transfer?" Bouchard asked.

"For the defendant to be held for trial in another matter. It is their contention that he bombed civilian vehicles lost in the desert at a time and place other than Mutlah Ridge."

"We know where that came from," Hank said as he came to his feet. "Your Honors, Iraq has the death penalty, which the Statute specifically prohibits. To extradite Mr. Tyler would subject him to Koranic law and certain execution."

The flicker of a smile crossed Bouchard's lips. "The court does not 'extradite' but 'transfers.'" The flicker turned into a self-satisfied look. It was payback time. "Further, Article Eighty of the Statute, which addresses the penalties of which you speak, clearly states that 'Nothing in this Part affects the national application by States of penalties prescribed by their national law.' However, we will take the prosecutor's petition under review."

Cassandra spoke in Hank's ear. "We didn't see that one coming. Sorry."

"Neither did I," Hank admitted.

"Madam Prosecutor," Bouchard intoned, "please call your next witness."

Denise came to the podium. "It is our intention to call the Reverend Tobias Person as a witness. Unfortunately, Reverend Person is currently in the southern Sudan at his mission where there is a great deal of unrest and fighting. Consequently, the Victims and Witnesses Protection Unit has determined that any travel at this time would endanger Reverend Person's security and very life. Therefore, the prosecution calls Watban Hamza Horan."

Cassandra was there for Hank, her voice urgent. "Horan is not on the witness list. He's a Palestinian lawyer who works for the court and does official translations."

"Objection," Hank called, coming to his feet. "There is no Watban Horan on the witness list."

"Monsieur Horan," Denise replied, "is not a witness but an officer of the court. It is in that capacity that he is entering a sworn statement by Tobias Person into evidence."

"Your Honor," Hank protested, "the defendant has the right to examine all witnesses against him. We cannot cross-examine a statement. Further, as we have called the Reverend Tobias Person as a witness for the defense, to admit such a statement, without examination by the defense, is highly prejudicial to the defendant."

Bouchard was in his element. "I'm quite sure defense counsel is aware of Article Sixty-eight that requires the court to take appropriate measures to protect the safety of all witnesses. To that end, the court may allow the presentation of evidence by electronic or other special means."

Hank kept hammering away. "Need I remind the court that Article Sixty-eight is primarily concerned with crimes involving sexual, gender, or violence against children?"

Denise stood. "But not limited to," she added, quickly sitting down. Bouchard turned to Della Sante and then Richter. Both nodded.

"They owe him on this one," Hank murmured to Aly.

"Overruled," Bouchard said.

"Your Honor," Hank said, "We need to confer for a moment." Bouchard granted his request and Hank quickly explained to Gus what was going to happen and what he wanted Gus to do. He returned to his seat.

\ A strange little man entered the side door. He appeared to be in his late fifties, rotund, and with wisps of gray hair sprouting from his balding head like clumps of crabgrass. He recited the undertaking to tell the truth in French and spoke in full and resonant tones worthy of a Shakespearian actor. Denise spoke in French and went through the introductory routine. She established that Horan did not speak English, had traveled to the Sudan with a clerk of the court, and taken a sworn statement from Tobias Person. The clerk handed Horan a thin document to read. Horan turned to the first page and started to read in French.

Gus was on his feet. "Your Honor, Toby doesn't speak French."

"What's he doing?" Aly whispered.

"We're going through the backdoor on this one," Hank replied in a low voice.

"You can listen to an official translation," Bouchard said. "A headset is beside your chair."

"I speak French," Gus said.

"Please be seated," Bouchard said. Gus didn't move. "Sit down." Gus refused to move and Bouchard's face turned bright red. "The defendant is out of order. Counsel, tell the defendant to sit down." A murmur worked through the spectators.

"Your Honor," Gus said, "you mentioned 'other electronic means.' Why can't the court contact Toby by satellite phone?"

Now it was Hank's turn. "Defense will not object to the Reverend Person testifying by satellite relay or radio."

Denise turned to Gus. "The prosecution tried to establish contact as recently as this morning but all communications are cut off. Given the current situation in the area, we do not foresee contact being established in the foreseeable future."

Bouchard conferred with Richter and Della Sante. "The court will hear the statement," he announced.

Gus sat down as Hank donned his headset. He half-listened, waiting for the telling part he knew was coming. Horan read with dramatic intensity but the translator's voice was flat and without emotion.

"Question: Were you flying with Captain August Tyler when you attacked the convoy on Mutlah Ridge?

"Person: Gus Tyler was my nose gunner, and one great pilot.

"Question: Was it your intention to attack the convoy?

"Person: That's why we were there.

"Question: What weapons did you use?

"Person: Snake Eyes, that's a 500-pound bomb, and CBUs.

"Question: Are these Snake Eyes or CBUs precision weapons?

"Person: Absolutely not. That's why we called them dumb bombs.

"Question: Were you aware that civilians were in the convoy?

"Person: Absolutely.

"Question: Did you take all reasonable precautions to minimize civilian losses?

"Person: Well, we were preoccupied at that particular moment.

"Question: Were you aware that civilians are protected by the Geneva Convention?

A Far Justice

"Person: We were all briefed on the Geneva Conventions." Horan finished reading the statement and an expectant hush fell over the courtroom as Denise adjusted her reading glasses and turned a page of her notebook.

"Do you affirm that the statement by Tobias Person is complete and unabridged?"

"I so affirm," Horan intoned in French.

Denise looked over her glasses at Hank. "The statement is entered as prosecution exhibit two hundred and fifty-three." Every head turned to hear Hank's objection.

Hank came to his feet as Cassandra whispered that there was no way the judges would sustain any objection against admitting the statement. Hank bit the bullet. "The defense has no objection to the statement, as read by Mr. Horan, being entered into evidence."

"So entered," Bouchard intoned with finality.

Denise turned to the judges, and bowed her head. "If it may please the court, the prosecution rests." She sat down as Horan stood to leave the stand.

Hank came to his feet. "Please, sir, the defense has some questions." Horan looked at him, uncomprehending. Hank gave him an encouraging look. "It is traditional, you know."

Bouchard rapped his gavel. "As the statement was taken by an officer of the court, and it is complete and unaltered, the statement speaks for itself."

"Your Honor, it is not the statement, as read, that is under question. That is why the defense had no objection to it being entered into evidence. However, the circumstances surrounding it require clarification."

Della Sante, obviously upset, dominated the conversation as the three judges conferred. A decision was reached. "We will allow some clarification but nothing else," Bouchard announced.

Horan sat down, a very unhappy man. Denise had assured him that as an officer of the court, he would not be subject to cross-examination. He donned a headset. "Mr. Horan, do you speak any English at all?" Hank asked. Horan listened to the translation and answered in French, saying that he did not speak English. "In what language did you conduct the interview?" Again, they went

211

through the process and Horan said that the interview was conducted in Arabic as the Reverend Person was very fluent in Arabic and did not speak French.

"Was the interview taken down in shorthand or recorded electronically?" Horan replied that the clerk, who did not speak Arabic, recorded it. He then translated the recording into French as the clerk replayed it. The same clerk then typed the hardcopy that was read in court.

"Did you ever have possession of the original disk?" Horan replied that the disk had been in possession of the clerk and that he had never touched it. Hank turned to the bench. "Given the importance of Reverend Person's statement, and as it has been entered into evidence, it is only fair and reasonable that the original recording be submitted to an impartial panel of translators appointed by the court to authenticate Mr. Horan's translation."

The judges again conferred for a moment. "The court agrees," Bouchard said. "The original recording will be surrendered to the court."

Horan glanced nervously at Denise. He spoke in French and the translator repeated his words in English. "The clerk had the disk but we can't find it."

Hank let his disgust show. "Your Honor, please direct the clerk to produce the disk."

A burst of French exploded from Horan, and Gus threw up his hands in frustration. A low din swept across the courtroom even before the translator was finished. "We can't do that because she is dead. That's why we can't find the disk."

Cassandra's voice was almost drowned out in the hubbub. "Call for an adjournment. Ammo is on the way."

Hank was incredulous. "Do I understand that the clerk was Marie Doorn?"

"That is correct," Denise said.

"Your Honor," Hank shouted in the uproar sweeping the room, "the defense requests an immediate adjournment."

"We are adjourned until tomorrow morning at ten o'clock," Bouchard said.

Everyone stood. "So it was Marie they were after," Hank said in a low voice to Denise. "Not me or Melwin."

"I can't believe that," Denise protested.
"Just how much coincidence do you believe in?"

New York

It was a trans-Atlantic roundtable discussion with Liz Gordon in CNC-TV's New York studio and Marci Lennox in the ICC's studio in The Hague. "Marci," Liz said, "it looks like total chaos from here. What is going on?"

"It's a war zone over here," Marci began. "First, there was the bombshell when Iraq demanded the ICC transfer Colonel Tyler to their custody to be tried on an unrelated charge of bombing a civilian bus during an unauthorized mission in the desert. The court has yet to rule on that. Then there was controversy over the Reverend Person's statement that clearly states Colonel Tyler knew they were attacking civilians in the convoy. This is the prosecutor's smoking gun that can convict the Colonel."

"Will Sutherland be able to get it thrown out?"

"I think," Marci replied, "that it all depends if they can find the original disk."

"The prosecution has rested its case. So what can we expect from Sutherland?"

"There is some confusion as Horan is still on the stand. We don't know which of his witnesses Sutherland will call, but everyone is waiting to see if Colonel Tyler will testify."

"How well is Sutherland doing so far?" Liz asked.

"On the face of it, very well. So far, he's managed to cast doubt on every aspect of the case and totally discredited two of the prosecution's main witnesses. What he will do with Horan and Person's statement remains to be seen. The ICC tries to blend two legal systems, the European accusatorial system and our adversarial system. The judges are not used to a situation where a skilled and aggressive lawyer can drive the court and take control away from a weak judge."

"If Colonel Tyler is turned over to the Iraqis," Gordon asked, "will he be tried under Koranic law?"

213

"Unfortunately," Marci replied, "that does appear to be the case."

Gordon faced the camera. "The video we are about to show is very graphic and violent. We urge you not to watch if you are upset by violence or let children under the age of seventeen see it. It shows a public execution last week on the main square of Basra in Iraq. An Islamic court, operating under Koranic law, had convicted a man of murder earlier the same day. Again, we must warn you not to watch if you are upset by violence."

The screen cycled to a scene in Iraq. A truck dumped a load of sand in front of a small front-loader that quickly smoothed it out. A convoy of vans drove up and police established a cordon around the sand as a hooded and bound man dressed in white was dragged out of a van. He was forced to his knees on the sand as his executioner carrying a short sword walked up behind him. The man's hood was jerked off as the executioner raised his sword. The sword flashed in the noon sun and the man's headless body gushed blood onto the sand.

"Justice is swift in Iraq," Liz Gordon said.

Marci had the last word. "Above all this, we're seeing the real Gus Tyler, calm and resolved in the face of adversity, and confident that he will find justice. But Hank Sutherland has his work cut out for him." They were off the air.

"Liz," Marci asked over the satellite feed, "where did you get that video?"

"A woman named Cassandra who works for a research company sent it over about twenty minutes ago. Keep up the good work, Marci. Think Emmy."

"A girl can never get enough of those."

The Hague

The three judges forming the presidency of the ICC stood when Denise entered the ornate conference room where they conducted their deliberations. They all sat in a tight cluster and Denise braced herself for the judicial scolding she was about to receive. "My dear," Relieu began, speaking for the other two judges, "whatever were you thinking of?"

Denise summoned all of her cultural superiority and fixed him with a condescending look. "Whatever are you talking about?"

"You rested your case prematurely," Relieu replied.

"I assumed I was dealing with competent judges and once the Person statement was admitted into evidence, my case was proven. What else did they need to hear? After all, we are a court of jurisprudence, not a theater for entertaining the public."

"But my dear," Relieu replied, "we are both. You had reached the climax of your case. Now you must put a conclusion on it before Sutherland has the opportunity to do it for you. The evidence you submitted to the court proves Tyler's guilt. It remains for you to vest it with complete moral authority. Only then will the court's preeminence on the world stage be assured."

The elderly Spaniard considered the court's best political tactician leaned forward and held her hand. "I will explain to Bouchard how to keep your case open. It is really a very simple matter. But you must do the rest."

Denise gave him a pleading look. "What do you suggest?"

* * * * *

Gus heard the familiar click of heels in the corridor and quickly sat on his bunk. He wrapped his arms around his knees, clasping them to his chest as Therese Derwent burst into the cell. She sat beside him and took his hand. "You saw it?"

"The execution? It was on the late news."

"It was horrible," she said.

He stared at the wall. "What's going to happen is going to happen."

"It's barbarous. The court will never allow it."

"Wouldn't it?" He fixed her with a sad look. "Theresa, they're a bunch of clowns." He waited for her reaction.

Her eyes glowed at the sound of her name. "I won't let it happen."

"There's not much you can do about it. I'll get through it."

"I have a sedative, if you need it."

"I could use something to help me sleep."

She opened a small packet and gently placed the capsule between his lips. Then she held a cup of water for him to drink. She sat down as he relaxed. "Everything will be fine," she said.

26

The Hague

Bouchard's secretary worked to hide her smile when the judge entered his office the next morning. "You are wanted in the presidential chambers," she said. She added "immediately" to get his attention and watched in satisfaction as he scurried out the door. She picked up the phone. "Aly," she began.

The Belgian judge was panting when he entered the presidential conference room where the three presidents of the court were waiting. As with Denise, Relieu spoke for the other two men. "This is turning into a fiasco. Two things must happen if we are to maintain the dignity of the court. You must regain control, and there must be a conviction."

"I see no problem obtaining a favorable verdict. The statement by Tobias Person is proof of Taylor's guilt, which is obvious even to Della Sante. But Sutherland is impossible to control. He uses everything against us."

"Gaston," Relieu fumed, "coordinate your actions."

"If Sutherland learns I spoke to Du Milan without him being there . . ." He shuddered. "He has spies everywhere."

"We are aware of that disturbing fact," the Spaniard said. "So we have done it for you. When you reconvene this morning, ask a very simple question and move forward. Everything will be back on track." He leaned forward and spoke in a low voice.

* * * * *

Hank paced the holding cell outside the main courtroom. "Don't expect a quick ruling on the Iraqi petition," he told Gus. "They want to hold it over our heads so we'll roll over and take a conviction; better a Dutch prison than being transferred to the Iraqis."

Gus adjusted the tie Derwent had given him. "Hank, reality check. The verdict was in before the trial ever started and this thing with Iraq is just one more way the system is stacked." He turned and faced the lawyer. "It's like flying combat – when all else fails, select guns and put the pointy end of the jet in their face."

"It's not too late for damage control. I can still cut a deal."

"How does a simple 'no' sound?"

Hank's respect for the pilot went over the moon. "Gus, you are one amazing guy."

"Let's go do it," the pilot said.

"Guard," Hank called, "we're ready." Two guards escorted them to the courtroom. Gus led the way in as over half the audience stood. "I'll be damned," Hank said in a low voice.

"Without doubt," Gus said. "Go get 'em."

Hank joined Aly at the table and waited for the tenth day of the trial to start. "Break a leg," Cassandra whispered in his ear.

"You are encouraging," he murmured as the judges entered.

Bouchard quickly disposed of the opening formalities without ruling on Iraq's petition for custody, and recalled Horan to the stand. "Monsieur Sutherland, you may continue."

Hank came to the podium and sat his thin leather folder down unopened. "Good morning, Mr. Horan. Have you found the missing disk?" They waited for the translation. Horan replied that they had searched all night to no avail. "I see. Are you totally impartial in this matter?" Horan swelled with indignity and angrily replied that he was. "I see," Hank said as Aly handed him a videocassette. He relayed it to the clerk. "If it pleases the court, this was aired by the BBC on September 11, 2001."

"Objection," Denise said. "Monsieur Horan is a member of the court and is not here as a witness."

"As the member of the court cannot produce the electronic recording in question," Della Sante replied, "the court must satisfy itself that there are no irregularities in his conduct." Bouchard glared at her for pre-empting his authority.

Richter tapped his microphone for attention. "I am also deeply concerned about the missing disk and agree."

A Far Justice

"Overruled," Bouchard said. "The court will view the videocassette." The room darkened as the screen descended.

The logo of the BBC World News flashed on the screen as the commentator spoke. "The Palestinians in the town of Nabulus on the West Bank reacted spontaneously to the announcement of the destruction of the World Trade Center." A black-robed woman laughing and dancing in the streets filled the screen. The image froze as the lights came back on.

"Mr. Horan, do you recognize the woman on the screen?"

"No," Horan replied in English without waiting for the translator.

Hank arched an eyebrow but said nothing as he opened his leather folder and pulled out the front page of an Arabic language newspaper. He handed it to the clerk who relayed it to Horan. Horan held up his hand and refused to touch the newspaper. "Apparently," Hank said, "the witness does not recognize his own sister. Mr. Horan, will you be so kind as to translate for the court the caption under the newspaper photo that shows you with the same woman we see on the screen in front of the court?"

"She is my sister," Horan said in English.

"We're speaking English now?" Hank asked.

Bouchard banged his gavel. "You will not badger an officer of the court, Counselor."

"I apologize, your Honor. I have no more questions of this witness." He turned and looked at Denise.

She led Horan through a series of gentle questions, trying to show he was an impartial and dedicated officer of the court. But what emerged was a rigid and dogmatic man claiming he was above all criticism because he shared the court's authority. Della Sante's body language was ample indication that she was disgusted with Horan. Denise finally managed to end it. "We have no further questions."

Hank stood. "The defense has no further use of this witness." Horan bolted from the witness box and out the side door. "The defense enters the video and newspaper article as defense exhibits seven and eight."

Denise objected but Della Sante's expression and gestures were clear evidence that she wasn't having it. After a few moments of intense discussion at the bench, Bouchard composed himself and

219

turned to the courtroom. "Objection overruled. So entered. As it is after twelve o'clock, the court is in recess until two this afternoon."

Hank turned to Catherine and Jason who were in their usual places behind the bar. "I'll file a motion to exclude Person's statement tomorrow."

"I don't think that will do much good," Catherine replied.

"That is a very safe statement," Cassandra murmured in his ear, her voice edged with cynicism. "The court is still in its formative stages and cannot afford the luxury of questioning its rules and procedures, much less its own officers." Hank stood up to stretch. "By the way," Cassandra said, "Suzanne Westcot is waiting in the hall outside."

"I believe I'm being summoned," Hank said. He led Catherine and Jason outside as Aly gathered up the files and folders on the table and followed them.

Suzanne was pacing the floor and wearing a stylish warm-up suit that made her look all of eighteen years old. "I just got here," she said. She tossed her blonde ponytail and looked even younger. She gave Jason a serious look and lowered her voice. "Max thinks we can get a helicopter into Mission Awana. Getting out may be more difficult."

Jason didn't hesitate. "Let's go."

"It will be dangerous," Suzanne said.

"His bag is in my car," Aly said, her voice strained, tears in her eyes.

Jason wrapped his arms around Aly, engulfing her. "Hey, I do this sort of thing for a living. I'll be back. With Toby."

Tears streamed down Aly's face. "I know." Jason kissed her and followed Suzanne down the hall. Catherine handed Aly a Kleenex to dry her tears "Did you see that look in her eyes?" Aly asked. "Mark my words, she'll make a play for him."

Catherine touched her arm. "I don't think that's a problem with the Tyler men."

* * * * *

Two hours later, Hank followed Aly into the packed courtroom. "No one left for lunch," she told him. "They were afraid they would lose their seats."

"It's the best show in town."

They waited as Bouchard reconvened the court. Bouchard adjusted his glasses, studied Denise, and asked the question Relieu had counseled. "Has the prosecution rested?"

"Damn," Hank allowed under his breath.

Without the least embarrassment, Denise approached the podium. "No, your Honor. The prosecution calls Doctor Gustav Schumann." Every head in the courtroom turned towards the side door as a collective silence held the room spellbound. The door opened and a tall and bent old man shuffled into the courtroom, his massive mane of gray hair instantly recognizable. His face was drawn and haggard from the mere exertion of walking, and few doubted that he was near death. His two canes played a slow tattoo on the floor as the audience came to its feet out of respect.

"Alex, we need you," Hank moaned to himself. Aly pushed a thick folder across the table, her face filled with worry. "I'm surprised he's up to it," Hank said quietly.

Cassandra was there, speaking quietly in his ear. "After Horan, Du Milan needs to end on a high note. She wants to cloak her case with moral authority. Schumann can do that for her."

"Tell me," Hank muttered. Gustav Schumann had been born in East Prussia and after World War II, had challenged the barbarism of his Soviet masters. He had spent most of his life in and out of East German jails where he had been repeatedly tortured and thrown into solitary confinement. But his jailers had not broken his spirit and he had emerged as the conscience of his generation. He had led the crusade for creating the ICC, and it was his voice that demanded universal justice for the oppressed of the world.

Then it happened. The old man stood more erect and moved with confidence as he took the stand. His head was up and his hazel eyes flashed with defiance. Gustav Schumann was about to fight one more, and perhaps his last, battle.

Cassandra was still there. "Melwin developed a strategy, but we really didn't think he would be able to testify. It's in the folder." Hank opened the folder and started to read, splitting his attention as Denise began an almost reverential questioning. Hank listened, automatically searching for the weakness or misstep that could impeach his testimony. "Do not object" was written in bold letters in Melwin's notes and underlined twice. Hank gave Denise high marks as she led

Schumann through the opening formalities, reinforcing his authority. Finally, Denise came to the heart of Schumann's testimony.

"Did you serve on the Commission of Inquiry for the International War Crimes Tribunal in its investigation into United States war crimes against Iraq?"

"I served as the chair of the commission from its inception through May of 1991."

"Please relate for the court the purpose of the commission."

"The purpose of the commission was to document the systematic destruction of the civilian infrastructure in Iraq during the Gulf War of 1991. Our investigators traveled over 2,000 miles in Iraq during a time when the United States was flying over 3000 bombing sorties a day. It was their goal to document the atrocities being committed by the United States. In that, they more than succeeded."

Hank marveled as he followed Melwin's notes and listened to Schumann's testimony. The Irishman had outlined the testimony he was now hearing, and annotated every major point and how the judges would respond. Again and again, Melwin had written "Do not object." Bouchard finally declared a recess to give the old man a chance to recuperate.

"What was Melwin's game plan?" Hank asked Cassandra.

"He seemed unconcerned and never confided in me," she replied.

"Nor me." Hank scanned the folder, looking for any clue on how to challenge Schumann's testimony. The fact that Schumann's testimony was all hearsay mattered little and Melwin had calculated the judges would rule it truthful, voluntary, and trustworthy. Hank stopped his search when the court reconvened and Denise resumed her questioning. She turned to the Highway of Death.

Hank's head came up when Schumann said, "The investigators spent a full day examining the carnage. Many weapons of mass destruction had been used, such as cluster bomb units and napalm." A loud murmur swept the courtroom at the mention of napalm and grew in volume. Bouchard let it grow before gaveling for order.

Hank looked at Gus who shook his head. The pilot mouthed the words "No way."

Denise was surprised by the mention of napalm but an inner voice urged her to caution. "This is a very serious charge, Doctor.

What evidence was presented to the commission substantiating the use of napalm?"

A confused look crossed Schumann's face. "That was some time ago and I don't recall the details. It is all in our report." Denise nodded and moved on.

Cassandra's legal team was on it. "It was only an allegation," she told Hank. "There is absolutely no evidence in the report about the use of napalm. He's an old man and it will look bad if you beat him up on the stand." Hank understood and listened as Denise continued her questioning. It was late in the afternoon when she finished and stepped away from the podium. She nodded briefly in Hank's direction, her face a mask.

"As it is late," Bouchard said, "perhaps it would be best to resume tomorrow."

Hank closed the folder and saw the two short notes scribbled in Melwin's scraggily scrawl on the back cover. He knew what to do. "Your Honor, I only have a few brief questions and unless the prosecutor has further questions, it will not be necessary for Doctor Schumann to return tomorrow."

Schumann gave Hank a weary look. "Let's end it."

"Thank you, Doctor. You testified that the name of your organization was 'The Commission of Inquiry for the International War Crimes Tribunal.' Is that correct?"

Denise was on her feet. "Objection. Relevancy. This is a matter so trivial it demeans the court and the witness."

"Your Honors," Hank responded, now certain he was on the right track, "we have heard compelling testimony. But it is secondhand and hearsay at best. I am merely trying to establish the framework in which it was originally presented to determine its relevancy to these proceedings."

The judges conferred briefly. "Objection overruled," Bouchard said. "Doctor Schumann may answer the question."

"That is the correct title."

"Did the United Nations create this International War Crimes Tribunal?"

"No."

"Was this International War Crimes Tribunal formed by the International Court of Justice?"

"No."

"May I ask who created this so-called International War Crimes Tribunal?"

Schumann was indignant. "Our charter, sir, was conveyed by humanity, the oppressed of the world who seek justice. It was our belief that the evidence presented by the commission was so compelling that the world could not ignore it."

"Let me rephrase the question, Doctor. Under whose authority was a charter granted to the International War Crimes Tribunal?"

The two men stared at each other, locked in a contest of wills. "The International War Crimes Tribunal has yet to be formed," Schumann admitted.

"I have one last question about your investigators. Was your commission formed before or after your investigators traveled through Iraq and Kuwait?"

"It was formed after they returned from Iraq," Schumann replied.

"Thank you, Doctor Schumann." Hank turned to Denise and murmured, "Your witness," daring her to continue the cross-examination.

She stood, and for a moment, Hank thought she would accept the challenge. "We have no further questions. Thank you, Doctor Schumann. It has indeed been a rare privilege to hear you speak and share your wisdom."

The audience broke out in applause as Schumann made his way out. Bouchard let the applause crescendo and die away naturally. Sensing the moment was right, Denise turned to the judges and bowed. "Your Honors, the prosecution rests."

"We are adjourned until the usual time tomorrow," Bouchard intoned.

Hank sat back in his seat and threw his pencil on the table. "Good recovery," Cassandra said. "Was it you or Alex?"

"It was Alex." Hank grabbed the folder and read from the back cover. "One: No war crimes tribunal existed. Two: the commission is a publicity stunt to embarrass the UN."

"We've got a major problem. The media is going ballistic over Schumann's charge of using napalm. You're going to have to defuse it without going after Schumann."

"That's going to be tricky," Hank replied.

A Far Justice

* * * * *

The riot police lowered their visors and locked their shields together as the mass of humanity surged down Scheveningseweg, the broad boulevard leading towards the ICC. Marci Lennox's burly camera crew elbowed their way through the reporters who were clustered behind the police line and cleared a space for Marci. She tossed her hair into place and spoke into the camera.

"The Dutch police tell me that they have never seen a demonstration of this size form so quickly and with such emotion." She glanced down the street, her worry obvious. "Even from here, I can hear the chant of 'Napalm, Napalm' being repeated over and over." A cameraman raised a micro camera mounted on a telescopic pole to get a better view. "The officer I spoke with estimated over five thousand demonstrators had gathered on the beach, but their numbers have obviously grown."

"Marci," her director interrupted, "the police say we gotta get out'a here."

She knew the feed was live and played it. "This demon- stration is the immediate fallout of Doctor Schumann's charge that the United States used napalm on Mutlah Ridge. As far as public opinion is concerned, it is the smoking gun that has convicted Gus Tyler."

"Marci!" her director yelled. "We gotta go. This is turning into a riot."

"Hold on," Marci said. She glanced at the micro camera's monitor. Leading the mob was Ewe Reiss. "Zoom on him." Reiss surged into view, filling the monitor, his face triumphant as the first paving stone arced over the police line. "Run!" Marci shouted.

* * * * *

Bouchard took the call from Ziba Katelhong about the time Jason's Lufthansa flight to Addis Ababa, Ethiopia, pushed back from the terminal at Frankfurt, Germany. The judge listened for five minutes without saying a word. Then, "We're in total agreement, Madam Secretary." Again, he listened. "Can I rely on your complete backing?" He grunted in satisfaction at the answer. "Is the suite at Des Indes to your satisfaction?" As he expected, The Hague's premier five-star luxury hotel was barely up to the task of meeting the

Secretary General's needs but it would have to do. He broke the connection and leaned back in his chair, his hands folded across his paunch. Slowly, and with relish, he selected the words he would use. He was back in control and it was just a matter of picking the right moment.

27

The Hague

Bouchard was braced for the inevitable when he reconvened the court at exactly nine A.M. on Friday, December 17. He smiled indulgently at Hank. "And what do you have for us today?" he asked.

Slowly, Hank walked to the podium and handed the head clerk his latest petition. "As the prosecutor cannot find the original recording of Reverend Person's statement, we petition the court to exclude the statement as presented by Watban Horan."

"Your Honors," Denise said, "Monsieur Horan was acting as an officer of the court. There is no reason to disallow the statement."

Hank was ready. "Lacking the original electronic recording, the accuracy of the translation cannot be verified. Further, Watban Horan demonstrated a working knowledge of English, which he had denied under oath. Is the court to assume this is the only thing he lied about? Finally, there is the question of his motivation. Does his family loyalty exceed his loyalty to the court?"

"The court will take your petition under advisement," Bouchard said. "You may present your defense."

"If it may please the court," Hank began. "The issue before us is amazingly simple: What law applies in combat? Is it criminal law as defined by the Rome Statute or the international law of armed conflict?"

Bouchard smiled. "You're getting ahead of yourself, Counselor. Save your legal arguments for your closing statement."

"I'm simply trying to clarify the basic issue."

"Call your first witness," Bouchard ordered, cutting him short.

Hank started to protest but thought better of it. "We recall General Davis Armiston to the stand."

The chief clerk stood. "General Armiston is not available at this time."

"I see," Hank said. "The defense calls Henri Scullanois to the stand."

Denise was on her feet with an objection as Bouchard rapped his gavel and said, "Counsel is out of order."

"Ah," Hank murmured. "Let justice be done." Before Bouchard could respond, "The defense recalls Secretary General Katelhong." The side door opened and the Secretary General swept into the room, surprising Hank. "I'll be damned," he said under his breath. "I didn't think she would show."

"Is this good?" Aly asked.

"It could be," Hank answered. "I'm surprised Du Milan didn't tell her to stay in New York."

"I don't think anyone tells Madame Katelhong what to do," Aly said.

Bouchard welcomed the Secretary General and reminded her that she was still under oath as Hank opened his leather folder. "Thank you for returning, Madam Secretary."

"I do so in the interests of justice," Katelhong replied.

"Madam Secretary, the court has heard gripping testimony by Doctor Gustav Schumann . . ."

Katelhong cut him off. "I have reviewed, in detail, all of Doctor Schumann's testimony. It was an eloquent testimonial to the senseless brutality of war."

Applause echoed over the courtroom and Hank studied Bouchard, certain the judge would allow Katelhong to say whatever she pleased. "Madam Secretary, in your previous testimony, you stated that the Gulf War of 1991 was under a United Nations mandate. Therefore, why hasn't the United Nations investigated these alleged 'war crimes' committed in its name as claimed by this so-called Commission of Inquiry?"

"I cannot answer the question as I was not part of the United Nations at that time."

"But as the prosecutor has pointed out, there is no statute of limitations on murder. Is this the first time these alleged crimes have come to the attention of the United Nations?"

"Again, I cannot answer that."

A Far Justice

Hank decided to bait her. "Of course. If the answer is 'no,' then there was no substance to the allegations because no war crimes were committed. If the answer is 'yes,' then the United Nations was, and is, derelict in its duty, or perhaps the ultimate authority responsible for the commission of the alleged war crimes."

Denise stood to object but Katlehong raised her hand, silencing the prosecutor. For a moment, the courtroom was deathly silent. "War is a crime, Mr. Attorney." She warmed to the subject and Bouchard let her speak. Much of what she said was a pure recitation of Schumann's testimony from the day before but she started to repeat certain phrases. "There is no statute of limitations on aggression . . . the civilized world cannot permit the wanton murder of innocent civilians . . . the civilized world must stop genocide."

When she finished, applause swept the room. "Madam Secretary," Hank said, "your sentiments are shared by everyone in this room. We all know that war is a brutal business with its own grim calculus." He wondered how much more he could say before Denise objected and Bouchard cut him off. "However, this is a court of law that must deal with the hard facts of reality." Denise was coming out of her seat. "I have one last question." He waited for Denise to sit. "Can you provide the court with any evidence that directly links the defendant with committing aggression, wantonly murdering innocent civilians, or committing genocide?"

Katelhong stared at him. "No. But let me add this. You, sir, by your constant attacks on this court are damning the future."

"But Madam Secretary, we are in a court of law, and we are concerned with justice in the here and now. I have no more questions."

Denise immediately stood. "The prosecution has no further questions, and I wish to thank Madam Katelhong for taking her valuable time to appear before this court."

Ziba Katelhong rose majestically and marched from the court. Bouchard ordered a recess for lunch, and Hank walked over to the dock to speak to Gus. "That lady swings one big bat with the judges," the pilot said.

Hank looked at the empty bench. "Indeed she does. But Della Sante got the point. Hopefully, Richter did too."

"Which is?"

"That Schumann's testimony had nothing to do with the facts of this case. Because of public opinion, I couldn't go after him, but Katelhong was a different story."

Two hours later, they were back in session, and Hank called Andre Bolland, France's patriarch of international law. The elderly man marched to the witness stand with a bearing and the dignity conferred on members of the *Institut de France*, that unique society charged with maintaining the intellectual and cultural integrity of France. For the next few hours, Hank led Bolland through the intricacies of international law. "So," Hank concluded, "there is no inherent prohibition in the killing of innocent people in war?"

"Not if it occurs during an attack on an objective or target that is of military value," Bolland replied. Hank thanked him and turned to Denise.

"Professor Bolland, I only have one question. "Is a civilian traveling in an escaping military convoy taking a direct part in hostilities?"

Bolland shook his head. "Taking a direct part? No." Denise thanked him and sat down.

Hank stood. "Doctor, is pillaging a war crime?"

"Of course. Looters can be summarily executed in the act."

"Is transporting stolen goods part of the act of pillaging?"

"Of course." Hank turned to Denise. The old man looked very disappointed when she waived re-examination.

Bouchard checked the time and adjourned for the weekend. Aly gathered up their folders and returned to the office while Hank followed Gus to the holding cell. Gus was amazingly upbeat as they rehashed the day's testimony. "I can actually see some light here," he said.

Hank had seen it before. "It always feels good when you can finally swing back."

"Jason arrived in Addis Ababa," Cassandra said, interrupting them.

"That was quick," Hank allowed. "What happens now?"

"He's made contact with a helicopter crew from Westcot Oil who will fly him to Mission Awana tonight. The flight is about 450 miles each way, about three hours flying time. They should be back here by Sunday night. Westcot oil flies Super Pumas because it has a good safety record." Hank relayed the information to Gus.

"A helicopter made by the Frogs," Gus moaned. He thought for a moment. Then the old grin was back. "Hell, if it ain't hard, it ain't worth doin'."

The two men talked for a few more moments before the guards came to take the pilot back to his prison. Hank watched Gus disappear down the corridor, amazed by his strength and resilience. He wondered if he could do half as well, and silently prayed that he would never have to find out. He couldn't believe it, but for a moment he envied Gus. How many men had a chance to see all they were held up to the world's scrutiny? To find out if their self-image matched reality? And to learn in the end that the image they held close to their hearts was enough.

Addis Ababa, Ethiopia

Jason huddled on the helicopter's jump seat between the two pilots and shivered. "Damn, it's cold," he moaned. He hated the waiting and wished they would get moving.

"Didn't anyone tell you Addis Ababa gets cold at night, Mate?" the short copilot said. "The field elevation here is over 2300 meters." Jason did a mental conversion and came up with 7600 feet.

"Where's your coat?" the pilot asked. He spoke with a heavy German accent.

"Lost it with my suitcase."

"Ah," the pilot replied. "You didn't pay the 'consideration' when you came through customs."

"You mean bribe the inspector?"

"That's the way the system works," the pilot said. He checked the time. It was 0130 hours Saturday morning. "We'll be starting engines in a moment." The lights in the control tower went out and only the rotating beacon on top marked the night. "The field is supposed to stay open until 0200 but they always go home early." The two pilots went through the engine start drill and the Super Puma's big four-bladed rotor started to turn. The cabin heat came on. The copilot called the tower and asked for permission to taxi and takeoff. There was no answer, which was exactly what the pilots wanted. There would be no record of Westcot Oil's helicopter ever having been at Bole International Airport.

The helicopter lifted off and departed to the south, avoiding the built-up areas around the city before turning westward. "Make yourself comfortable," the pilot said. "We will land at Beica to refuel while we're still in Ethiopia, then on into Awana. Want to get there before first light while the Arab *arschfickers* are still asleep."

"I do appreciate this," Jason said.

"No thanks needed," the copilot said. "We can take a six month vacation for what Westcot is paying for this flight."

Jason crawled into the passenger compartment and went to sleep, now comfortably warm. The copilot woke him ninety minutes later and told him to strap in for the landing at Beica. The refueling went quickly and they were airborne in less than twenty minutes. "Be on the ground at Awana in seventy-five minutes, mate," the copilot told him. Jason stretched out on the seat and went back to sleep.

Jason wasn't sure what woke him but he sat upright, aware that something was wrong. He listened for a moment and realized they were flying on one engine. He scrambled into the jump seat between the pilots and jammed a headset over his ears. "We're losing power," the pilot told him. "Probably contaminated fuel at Beica." His baldhead gleamed with sweat. "We need to land."

"Where are we?" Jason asked.

The copilot pointed to the moving map display on the instrument panel that was slaved to the GPS. "Seventy-five miles to the mission. We're still over the Sudd. That's a swamp where the Nile gets all dammed up. Bloody big place."

"Can we land in a swamp?" Jason asked.

Again, the copilot pointed to the moving map, his worry now obvious. "There's a village and high ground ahead of us. Fifteen miles."

The right engine changed pitch. "Are we going to make it?" Jason wondered.

"Don't have a choice now do we? Might be a good idea if you strapped in back there."

Jason did as ordered and counted the minutes. If they were going 120 MPH, it would take seven and a half minutes to reach the village. Exactly eight minutes later, the right engine quit. "Brace yourself!" the copilot called. The nose of the Super Puma came up at a steep angle. "We're going to auto gyro in. Landing light on." Then, "Ah shit!"

A Far Justice

The helicopter crashed down into a mud and wattle hut. For a moment, Jason couldn't move. They were still right side up and intact. Then the copilot was out of his seat and coming towards him. He gestured at the pilot who was right behind him. "His landing, Mate. Not mine." The two pilots wrenched the side door back and jumped out. Jason fumbled at his seatbelt but it was jammed. He was vaguely aware of smoke and a fire burning behind the helicopter. He heard shouts and a loud commotion as he finally freed himself. He stood in the doorway and felt sick. The crash had killed the people sleeping in the hut. The big rotor had cut one person in two and there was blood and body parts scattered over the wreckage.

Jason pushed through the wreckage in time to see a large group of angry villagers pushing and shoving the two pilots to the ground. A machete flashed in the flickering flames. A woman pointed at Jason and yelled. A man holding a bloody machete walked towards him, shouting in a language he did not understand. Jason held up his hands. "Mission Awana!" he shouted. "Mission Awana!" It was all he could think of.

The man stopped and spat out a torrent of words. Someone shouted a reply and Jason thought he heard the words "duh nah" five or six times. The man turned back to Jason, his face a mask.

28

The Hague

The halls of the palace were deserted when Hank and Catherine arrived Saturday morning. The smell of freshly brewed coffee lured them down the corridor and grew stronger as they reached their office. "Aly," was all Hank said. "I wonder if she went home last night?"

"Probably not," Catherine replied.

They pushed through the door to find the young woman pacing the floor. Without a word, Aly rushed up to Hank and handed him his percom. "You left Cassandra here last night. She's been buzzing for the last five minutes. I tried to answer, but she doesn't recognize me."

"Damn," Hank moaned. He flipped the lid open and Cassandra's face appeared on the screen. "I'm afraid there's bad news. Jason's helicopter is missing. We know it refueled at Beica in Ethiopia early this morning but it never reached the mission. We also have satellite imagery of a helicopter that crashed into a village in the Sudd not too far from the mission." The voice grew worried. "The photo shows the bodies of two men wearing white shirts and dark pants staked out on the ground near the wreckage. One's bald and the other is too short to be Jason. We think they're the pilots."

"But no trace of Jason," Hank said.

"None."

"Well, that's good news of a sort." He thought for a moment. "I'm going to have to tell Gus. Can you give me a print-out of the photo?"

"It's pretty gruesome," Cassandra warned.

"Gus can take it."

Hank didn't recognize the woman sitting in the cell with Gus. "I don't think you've met Doctor Therese Derwent," Gus said. They shook hands in the European manner and Hank introduced Catherine and Aly.

Derwent read the situation correctly. "Perhaps I should leave."

Hank sensed the psychiatrist was an ally and shook his head. "Gus, we've lost track of Jason." He repeated all that Cassandra had told him and showed him the photo.

Gus's face turned to stone. "That's not him."

"I helped Jason pack," Aly said, fighting her tears. "He didn't take a white shirt."

"May I?" Derwent said, taking the photo. "I did field work in tribal villages in Africa. The bodies were left as a warning. If they had killed Jason, they would have displayed his body with the other two."

Gus stormed out of the cell and paced the corridor. Hank started to join him but Derwent motioned him to stay back. "Give him time to work it out," she said.

Gus slammed the palm of his hand against the steel door, sending an echo down the hall. Twice more he pounded the door without saying a word. Slowly, he reined in his emotions. He stood in the doorway as his breathing slowed. He spoke quietly, his voice under tight control. "God damn them to hell."

"Tribal Africans have a simple, very primitive justice," Derwent explained.

"Not them," Gus said, his anger still boiling below the surface. "I understand where they're coming from. It's the bastards here. They live in some sort of fucking parallel universe where they have absolutely no responsibility for their actions."

"You mean the court?" Derwent said, pushing him to focus his anger. Only then could she defuse it.

"Who the hell else? Look at Du Milan. She hasn't got a clue what real life is like. It's no concern to her that Jason is in harm's way because of what she did to nail me. It's like 'Hey, I can do whatever I want because 'humanity' demands it. Tell me that's justice."

"That's not what justice is about," Hank said quietly.

Gus looked at his friend. "I know that, Hank. You want to make things better; you care about righting a wrong and protecting the innocent." His anger was back. "But that is the last goddamn thing on her agenda." He stalked back into the corridor, still seething with anger. Aly rushed out after him, tears streaming down her face. He held her in his arms as she cried. "It's going to be okay, Love," he murmured.

"How?" she asked.

Gus looked around to be sure they were alone in the hall and whispered in her ear as he pressed Suzanne's business card into her hand. She nodded and held on to him, still crying.

* * * * *

Catherine held Hank's arm tightly as they walked past the guard's console in the main entrance hall. Hank paused long enough to sign out. He glanced at the bank of TV monitors in front of the guard. "The shrink Derwent is right behind us," he said. "I think she's in love with Gus."

Catherine smiled at him. "You idiot. She likes him, but she's too European, too much of a professional to let herself fall in love."

Hank cocked an eyebrow. "Woman can do that?" The guard pressed a button under the screen monitoring the main entrance and the heavy entrance door slid silently back. They walked arm-in-arm into the cold, blustery afternoon.

"Hank, I know you're feeling responsible for Jason."

"It was my idea to send him there."

"Don't do it," she cautioned.

"Do what?"

"Blame yourself. You're not responsible for what happened."

"I wish it were that simple."

The Sudd, Southern Sudan

Flies buzzed around Jason's head as he lay on the ground, his feet and hands tightly bound. A girl of about nine or ten years of age came into the hut and brushed the flies off his face. She helped him sit up and held a plastic jug to his lips. The warm water trickled down his throat as she carefully let him drink. "Where am I?" he asked.

"The name would mean nothing to you," a woman's voice said. Jason tried to focus on the speaker standing in the doorway, but the bright light framed her and he could only see a heavyset figure dressed in combat fatigues. She stepped into the hut and he had a better look. Her hair was cut extremely short, and he guessed her age around thirty-five. Her brown eyes and dark skin radiated with energy, and she moved with the same rippling grace as the village women. Like them, she was a tribal African, yet she was different.

"What happened to the pilots?" Jason asked.

"Dead," the woman answered. "They killed seven people when they crashed into to the hut, all women and girls. The family killed them." She said a few words in Dinka and the girl untied the knots that bound him.

"Thank you. My name is Jason Tyler and I'm looking for the Reverend Tobias Person at Mission Awana."

The woman stared at him, her face unreadable. "I'm D'Na." to Jason's untrained ear, her name sounded like 'duh nah,' the two words that had saved him.

29

Mission Awana, Southern Sudan

The two high-wheeled all-terrain pickups hurtled down the dirt track and slammed to a stop in front of the makeshift roadblock, sending a cloud of dust over the sleeping guards. "What the . . .?" Jason muttered, coming awake. It was still dark and he slowly got his bearings. He was wedged in the cab of the lead pickup between the driver and D'Na. "Who the hell are they?"

"Arab militiamen," D'Na told him. "The Sudanese Army pays them to blockade the mission."

Jason was confused. "But that's where we want to go, right? So why are we stopped here?"

D'Na gave him a condescending look. "We are stopped so we can bribe them to let us in."

"Right. So they'll take your money and let us through."

"They like the money," D'Na said. "And they understand." She pointed to the top of the cab and made a shooting gesture with her forefinger and thumb, indicating the heavy machine guns mounted above the cab of each truck. "They are paid to blockade, not to fight." She got out and struck up a friendly conversation with the guards. Money exchanged hands and she climbed back in. "All is good as long as the army is busy fighting the rebels."

"Lovely," Jason said to himself.

D'Na laughed. "Welcome to Africa." They rode in silence as the two trucks raced down the rutted track, leaving a cloud of dust glittering in the first rays of dawn. "I love this time of day," D'Na said as they barreled into the mission compound. "All is new and fresh." The trucks coasted to a stop in front of a rambling single-story house with a tin roof and wide verandas. "Mission House," she announced. It was the heart of the mission. "And my husband." Toby Person was standing on the veranda waiting for them.

The Hague

Aly stood in the early-morning light and gazed out the office window. Below her, a woman hurried across the palace's forecourt, bundled up against the cold wind sweeping in off the North Sea. But Aly didn't see her. Catherine switched on the lights and was surprised to see her standing there. "You startled me," she said. "How long have you been here?" Hank was right behind her.

"All night," Aly replied, her voice heavy with despair. "I keep hoping to hear something."

Catherine took her in her arms and held her, pulling her back from the dark abyss threatening to claim her. "Don't give up hope," Catherine murmured. She sat Aly down and handed her a cup of coffee. "We'll find him."

Hank nodded in agreement. He looked at the calendar. It was Sunday, December 20, and Jason had been missing for over twenty-four hours. He wanted to reassure Aly but he knew the odds.

"My father has a question that's been bothering him," Aly said. "Why do you hate the court?"

Hank welcomed the chance to talk, anything to get his mind off Jason. "I don't hate it. Who can argue against prosecuting true war criminals and thugs who commit genocide? But I remember Alex once saying the court, in its zeal to get the bastards, is mucking it up. He knew the Rome Statute conflicts with our Constitution and the US can't join. That doesn't mean the two can't coexist. But the moment the court asserted its jurisdiction beyond the countries that have ratified the treaty creating it, it became a political animal, a perversion of the law that Alex loved and respected. He was right to fear for the court."

Aly started to cry. "Why Gus? He isn't a war criminal."

"No, he's not. He just happened to kill a lot of people in combat."

"Does that mean he's a political prisoner?"

"Yeah, it does." Hank's jaw hardened. "And I'll destroy the court if that's what it takes to free him."

A Far Justice

Mission Awana

Jason wondered if he was in the same world. A shower, shave, and clean clothes had worked a magic he had never experienced. Now he was sitting in the large open room in Mission House as two golden children played at a game of sticks on the floor. He sipped at the cool herb drink that carried a special power of its own. D'Na swept into the room, a transformed woman. She was wearing a sarong-like wrap that reached to her ankles. A pattern was woven into the cloth that changed with the light as if it had a life of its own. The two children ran to her and cuddled to her side. Her laughter filled the room.

"Any luck this time?" Toby said, a sad look on his face.

"No." She gestured at Jason. "Just this one."

Toby explained. "D'Na follows slavers around and tries to buy the children back. Slavery never died out in this part of Africa. The Sudanese consider the Dinka and Nuer subhuman, and a twelve-year-old virgin can bring up to ten thousand dollars in Omdurman. Unfortunately, Islam only discourages slavery, not prohibit it, which is enough to open the window." Toby's face turned hard. "We've experienced a resurgence in the last ten years."

"Why doesn't the United Nations stop it?" Jason asked.

Toby gave him a disgusted look. "And violate Sudanese sovereignty? If the UN got involved simply because the Sudanese were engaged in a little slavery and genocide in their own country, what country would be next?"

Jason was shocked. "Genocide? I thought they ended that five, six years ago."

Toby shook his head. "They stopped the genocide in Darfur, five-hundred miles to the northwest of here, and signed a so-called permanent cease-fire. They do that every now and then but it's temporary at best. We're caught in a civil war between the Arab north and African rebels in the south. It's been going on over fifty years and I don't see it ending soon." He unfolded a map and spread it out for Jason. He pointed to large tracts of land blocked in with squares and rectangles.

"The prize is oil. These are the oil concessions located about a hundred miles to the west of here. The oil reserves are not huge like the Middle East but they're nothing to sneeze at – about the size of

241

Columbia and Venezuela. The government in Khartoum parceled the concessions out to foreign consortiums and takes eighty percent of the gross. We never see a bit of it down here, and as far as the government is concerned, the tribes are unbelievers and not entitled to a cent. To make their point, the Sudanese Army has recruited Arab militias called Janjaweed to drive the tribes out of the concessions.

"For the most part, they've left us alone. The mission has a fairly high visibility in Europe and the States, so rather than draw attention to what they're doing, Khartoum has ignored us. It was working until an exploration team from Westcot Oil discovered a large reserve in block five, here." He tapped an odd-shaped, penciled-in area on the map that was located two hundred miles south of the mission.

"Dad said that Westcot Oil had bailed out of the Sudan," Jason said.

"It had. But it got back in when Max Westcot bought the Canadian consortium that holds the concession to block five, which the rebels control. But Khartoum has a greedy eye so they called for jihad against the rebels to get it back. The rebels fought back and turned the area south of the river, that's the Bahr el Ghazal, or the White Nile, into a no-man's land. Unfortunately, we're in that no-man's land. The rebels want to make the White Nile the de facto boundary and Juba their capital." He pointed to the large town 350 miles south of the mission, on the far side of the oil concession. "Unfortunately, we're caught between the Sudanese and the oil – a victim of geography. There was some heavy fighting here two years ago when the US Air Force was flying C-130s out of the mission for the UN Peacekeepers. We were almost overran and destroyed, but things have calmed down – for now."

"Why don't you move to some place where it's safer?" Jason asked.

Toby waved his hand at an aerial photograph of the mission hanging on the wall. "The mission goes back over a hundred years and I can't walk away from it." He looked at his children. "There are two more very important reasons. This is their home."

"And the other reasons?"

A wry grin crossed Toby's face. "Because it's the right thing to do?"

"You sound like my Dad."

Toby stood up. "It's time for church."

A Far Justice

Toby led his family and Jason to a makeshift amphitheater on the side of a low hill facing north. Jason sat on the rough planks that served as benches and the two children bounded into his lap as Toby unpacked a lunch basket. It was a simple meal of bread, cooked vegetables he didn't recognize, and a cool drink of the same herb tea. Groups of families wandered in and found places under the canopy of fronds and tree branches as they unpacked their lunches. Their numbers kept growing until Jason estimated the size of the crowd at over a thousand. Everyone was talking, laughing and eating. "When does it start?" he asked.

"When the time is right," Toby replied. "We're on African time here. Be patient." A song leader stepped to the front and started to sing. One by one, the families stopped eating and joined in. Soon, all were singing and they were a congregation.

"It's beautiful. I wish I understood the words."

"It's a local dialect of Dinka," Toby explained. "They're great singers." He translated. "We give thanks, Oh Lord, we give thanks. We give thanks for our food, we give thanks for each other." A lone woman sang out and, again, Toby translated. "I give thanks for tomorrow." The congregation repeated it and a man gave his personal thanks. Again, the congregation sang back. The song continued for almost ten minutes before it died away and the families went back to their lunch.

"Who wrote it?" Jason asked.

"No one really wrote it," Toby answered. "I sort of started it one time and it took on a life of its own." Another song leader stepped forward and began to sing. Again, the people joined in. "They're singing about their families." This time, Toby joined in and Jason was surprised by the rich quality of his voice.

The congregation continued to sing until the sun reached its zenith. Toby made his way down the hill, touching people as they extended their hands to him. He stood in front and spoke for a few moments in Dinka. Then he raised his right hand. He chanted a few words of benediction and the congregation responded. It was over and they made their way back to Mission House.

They sat on the veranda as a gentle breeze cut the heat of the day. "So what is worth the lives of two pilots and an expensive helicopter to bring you here?" Toby asked.

243

"It's about my Dad," Jason said. He talked quietly, relating the entire story. Not once did Toby interrupt him. When Jason finished, Toby walked into Mission House and returned a few moments later with a mini CD player. Without a word, he fast-forwarded it to the section he wanted and let it play. A stream of Arabic filled Jason's ears but Toby's voice was unmistakable. Then Toby translated.

"Question: Are these Snake Eyes or CBUs precision-guided weapons?"

"Answer: Absolutely not. That's why we called them dumb bombs.

"Question: Were you aware that civilians were in the convoy?"

"Answer: Absolutely not."

Toby hit the stop button. "Son of a bitch," Jason whispered. "The fuc . . ." he caught himself in time.

"The fucker lied," Toby said, completing the sentence. "Will it do any good you getting this to The Hague?"

"Based on what I've seen of the court so far, I doubt it. We need to get you on the stand."

Toby pulled into himself. "I can't leave."

D'Na took charge. "Yes, you can. We don't need you to run the mission."

Toby touched her cheek. "My warrior queen."

"Any chance we might get a message out?" Jason asked.

"We can try," Toby replied. "Landlines have been cut for weeks, and the Sudanese Army is jamming the HF radio and satellite communication channels, which they do periodically. They claim it is because of the so-called 'emergency' they've created."

The Hague

It was late Sunday afternoon when Hank and Aly trooped into Gus's cell. Aly carried a pizza box and deposited it on the table. "I hope you like *pannekoeken*." She opened the box to reveal what looked like a big pizza.

"They're great," Hank added. "It's more like a big crepe with all the goodies piled on top. Dig in before it gets cold." The three sat at the table and devoured the pancake. When they were finished, Hank called Cassandra and asked if there was any news on Jason. His face lit up at her reply. "I'm with Gus, go loudspeaker please."

Cassandra's voice filled the room. "A listening station monitored a garbled high-frequency radio message from Mission Awana. There was a reference to a Tyler but the rest was lost in static, probably jamming."

Gus pounded the table. "Damn! He's alive."

"We can't be sure," Cassandra cautioned. "The Sudanese Army and the rebels are fighting north of the river, about ten miles away, and jamming all communications. Arab militiamen have sealed the mission off. The situation down there is very unstable and fluid, to say the least."

There was no doubt in Gus's mind. "You don't know Jason. He's alive. Can you get him out?"

"We've contacted the State Department," Cassandra explained. "As expected, they refuse to get involved in the Sudan."

"I'll contact Max and see what he can do," Hank said, breaking the connection. Without a word, Hank handed Gus his cell phone to call home.

Michelle answered on the first ring and her voice matched the concern on her face. "The doctors say Mom has definitely stabilized, and I think there's been some improvement. Is there any news on Jason?"

"We're pretty certain he's at the mission." Gus replied. "We can't be absolutely sure, but don't give up hope."

"We won't."

"I love you, hon."

"We all love you," Michelle said. Gus ended the call and returned the phone.

Île St-Louis

Ziba Katelhong decided the Hôtel L'Abord met her standards, and she resolved to have one like it. She sighed and turned to face its owner and her two other guests. "The United States is pressing the General Assembly for action on China. I have the Security Council under control but I am worried about what is happening here. You must contain the situation." She gave them a meaningful look

"Max Westcot is in Europe talking to everyone," Chrestien Du Milan said.

"Which is why I'm here," Katlehong replied. "The Dutch prime minister is spending the holidays with him in Spain. No surprises, please."

Renée Scullanois was worried. "Are we seeing a *rapprochement*?" She had often cautioned her husband, Henri, about the Dutch penchant to act on their own.

The Comtessa Eugenie stomped her foot in frustration. "That must not happen." The old woman's face was livid at the idea.

Ziba sat beside her and stroked the back of her hand. "My dear Eugenie," she began. The old woman stiffened at the familiarity but said nothing, "The Dutch and the Americans have a long tradition of friendship that defies rationality. It is something I must deal with. But I believe the Dutch will act in their own interests."

The Comtessa gave the Secretary General a cold look. "Insure they do. We will do whatever is necessary on our part." She gave Chrestien and Renée a knowing look. "I believe dinner is ready." She escorted them into the formal dining room, and Ziba Katelhong decided that the Hôtel L'Abord would do just fine as her new home.

30

Mission Awana

D'Na stopped the high-wheeled pickup truck a half-mile short of the roadblock. "Wait here," she told Toby and Jason. She got out and disappeared into the early-morning dark with Hon and Paride, the two Dinkas accompanying her. All three were armed with MP5s, a nine-millimeter submachine gun made by Heckler and Kock. "She's good at this sort of thing," Toby told Jason. They waited in silence until the three returned, materializing out of the shadows like ghosts.

"They're all asleep," D'Na said. "We'll take the truck through and meet you on the other side." Jason gave her a questioning look. "I can bribe a white man into the mission, but never out of it," she explained. "They would shoot you the moment they saw you trying to leave." She snorted at Jason's confused look. "This is Africa, man. It doesn't have to make sense." She knelt and drew a rough map in the dirt. "Go this way through the fields and stay south of the roadblock." She etched a crossroads on her map and drew in a small compound. "You wait here. I'll stay here and take the truck through at first light. We may be in a hurry." She stood up and brushed her hands. For a moment, she and Toby drew close and touched hands

The two Americans adjusted their night-vision goggles and made their way between small fields that had been recently tilled. At one point, Toby stopped and knelt to survey the work. He ran the earth through his fingers. "They're doing it right," he announced. Satisfied, he led the way into the low brush, and they could see the dying glow of campfires. "The roadblock," Toby whispered. They froze as a man stumbled half asleep out of the bushes, less than three yards in front of them. Jason drew his knife and motioned Toby into a crouch. The man was oblivious to the danger behind him as he relieved himself. Finished, he grunted and disappeared back into the shadows. Jason counted slowly to ten and motioned Toby forward. Within minutes, they were clear of the roadblock and were nearing the crossroads and compound for the rendezvous with D'Na. Now they had to wait.

Toby ripped off his night vision goggles as the first light of dawn etched the eastern sky. "Dawn comes up fast in the tropics," he told Jason. He pointed to the knife on Jason's belt. "Would you have?"

"Almost did," Jason admitted. Toby nodded, accepting the truth of the situation. In the distance, they could hear a vehicle coming down the road. It came at them fast with D'Na standing in the back with Paride, the taller of the two Dinkas. The truck slowed and the waiting men barreled into the back. "How did it go?" Jason asked.

"Not good," D'Na admitted. "They wanted to discuss it, which means they wanted the truck. I threw a roll of money at them but they needed a little more persuasion." Paride laughed and patted the machine gun mounted over the cab.

D'Na rode with them a few more miles before pounding on the roof of the cab signaling the driver to stop. "Hon's a good driver," she said. "He and Paride will go with you and bring the truck back." She and Toby climbed down. Again, they stood close and touched hands. Then they gently kissed. "Go," she commanded.

Toby never took his eyes off her as they sped away. "Will she be okay?" Jason asked. Toby didn't answer.

The Hague

Gus entered the dock at exactly 9:55 Monday morning and studied the audience. Most were still wet from waiting outside in the driving rain howling in from the North Sea. His rooting section was there and had grown. *That's encouraging,* he thought. He stood when the judges entered and waited to see if Della Sante looked at him. She didn't, which was an indicator of the way it would go. Bouchard called the court to order. *Go ahead, you prick.*

"The court," Bouchard began, "has reviewed defense counsel's petition to exclude the sworn statement of Tobias Person taken by Watban Horan, an officer of this court. As Monsieur Horan was acting in his official capacity, and as the statement was entered into evidence consistent with Article Sixty-eight of the Rome Statute, there is no cause to exclude the statement. Petition denied."

Gus stared at Bouchard. *No surprises there, asshole.*

Hank was on his feet. "Your Honor, the defense must take exception." He hesitated for a moment, reluctant to openly cross the Rubicon. The lawyer in him urged caution but another voice said it was time. "Such an interpretation strikes at the very heart of admissibility of evidence."

Denise was ready. "My learned colleague has been trained in common law with its complex and technical rules for presenting evidence to a jury of laymen. But we are not dealing with a jury of common citizens, but with a panel of preeminent jurists fully trained in the law and experienced in the weighing of evidence."

Hank turned to her and entered the waters. "But as the prosecutor cannot provide the original recording of Reverend Tobias's statement, the court's ruling not only is prejudicial but it is inconsistent with the rights of the accused to a fair and impartial trial."

Bouchard's face turned bright red and his breath came in short bursts as the full meaning of Hank's accusation hit home.

Shack! Gus thought.

The judge's mouth opened but no words came out. Della Sante came to his aid and handed him a glass of water. Slowly, his breathing slowed. Della Sante shot Hank a withering look and sat down.

Gus worked to keep a concerned look on his face. *Gotcha there, didn't he?*

"Your exception is so noted," Bouchard finally managed to croak. "Is there any other business for the court to consider?"

Denise stood. "There is none, your Honor."

Hank came to his feet; now well into the waters of open conflict. "If it may please the court. The defense is in the process of establishing contact with the Reverend Tobias Person in the hope that he can appear in this court. We have reason to believe that the defendant's son, Jason Tyler, has reached Mission Awana in that endeavor."

Denise popped to her feet. "Your Honors, we must take exception. The defense cannot be permitted to ignore the rulings of the Victims and Witnesses Unit whose sole concern is for the safety and protection of the Reverend Person. The court's procedures must be adhered to if we truly value human life. To recklessly send a private individual in such an attempt is nothing more than cowboyism and a blatant disregard of the will of the court."

Now we're cowboys? Gus thought. *Oh, I hope so.*

"Perhaps," Hank said, now swimming hard in the current, "the court should employ more cowboys if it wants to accomplish anything in the real world."

"The prosecutor's exception is also noted," Bouchard said, still having trouble breathing. "What is your point, Monsieur Sutherland?"

"The defense respectfully requests a two-week recess to allow time to safely bring the Reverend Person to The Hague. This would coincide with the court's recess over the holidays and extend it a few days to Monday, January third."

Della Sante, now concerned with Bouchard's blanched look and ragged breathing leaned over to talk to him. Richter leaned in from the other side and listened. Bouchard's lips moved and both jurists nodded in agreement. Della Sante turned to her microphone. "As the holidays are upon us, the court will adjourn early; however, we will reconvene as originally scheduled on Wednesday, December 29."

The clerk called for everyone to stand as Della Sante helped Bouchard out the door. Hank followed Gus into the holding cell and closed the door for privacy. "Well, we've got eight days to get Toby here," Hank said.

"Jesus H. Christ, Hank. I thought Bouchard had a heart attack when you accused the court of being prejudicial."

Hank's face turned rock hard. "That was the idea."

* * * * *

Marci Lennox checked her hair in the mirror and decided to go with the wind-blown look, not that she had a choice. The storm off the North Sea was starting to build again, and she envied Catherine Sutherland's hairstyle that seemed to defy the weather. Marci nodded at the cameraman and he switched on the lights, illuminating that corner of the forecourt of the ICC's palace. "Today left little doubt that Hank Sutherland was on the attack as he accused the judges of violating Gus Tyler's rights to a fair and impartial trial." She turned to Catherine. "Mrs. Sutherland, what exactly is your husband trying to accomplish?"

"He's stating the obvious. What we are seeing could never happen in a court stateside or in England. The admission of Reverend Person's statement into evidence violated Colonel Tyler's right to confront the witnesses against him in court, a right that is guaranteed every American citizen."

"But this isn't the United States," Marci said "and Colonel Tyler does not enjoy the rights provided by our constitution."

"Which is exactly why the United States is not a signatory to the Rome Statute."

Marci changed the subject. "Will you stay here over the holidays to be with Colonel Tyler?"

"No. I'll be going home to be with our boys. Hopefully, Hank can join us for a few days."

Marci ended it. "This is Marci Lennox from The Hague signing off until January 29, when I'll be back for the next round of fireworks." Her director gave her the cut signal and she lowered her microphone. "Catherine, who is your hair stylist?"

Southern Sudan

"We've come a hundred miles," Toby said. "No one could have done it better. Well, done." Hon, the heavyset Dinka driving the truck, smiled at the compliment. Although it was the dry season and the swamps had receded, it had been difficult navigating through the open savannah and avoiding mud holes while staying clear of the rut that passed for the main road. "We need to pitch camp before it gets dark."

Hon nodded and inched the truck through the drying grass. He found a low mound as night fell and guided the truck to the center. The four men got out and stretched, walking around the remains of an old campfire. Jason bent over and studied a pile of dung. The Dinka were cattle herders and placed great value on their animals, but this was different. He found a flashlight in the truck and walked around the area while Hon and Paride gathered up dry dung to make a fire. The smoke would help keep the insects away. At one point,

Jason squatted and traced a distinctive print. It all came together. "I didn't know you had horses down here."

Toby's face froze. "We don't. The climate is too unhealthy for them."

"Janjaweed," Hon and Paride said, almost simultaneously. The fear in their voices was obvious. Jason shook his head, not understanding.

"The Janjaweed are Bagara horsemen," Toby explained. "The Bagara are Arabized cattle nomads from Kordofan and Dufar. About fifteen years ago, the Sudanese Army recruited them as a militia and turned them loose on the Dinka and Nuer villages in the oil concessions, all well to the northwest of here. But they've been quiet for the last few years."

"Are they Muslim?" Jason asked.

"More or less," Toby replied. "They belong to the Ansar Sunni sect and are very warlike."

"So what in hell are they doing down here?" Jason wondered.

"Slavers," Paride answered.

Toby shook his head. "They'd have trucks if they were doing that. It's a raiding party."

31

Southern Sudan

The sun was rapidly sinking when Hon stopped the truck. "Good place, Boss," he said. Toby nodded. Like the others, he was dead tired. They had been traveling since sunup, pressing ahead as fast as they could but on constant alert for the Janjaweed. They only had a few minutes before it was dark and Jason stood on the cab of the truck and scanned the flat grasslands with his binoculars.

Jason pointed to a heavy plume of smoke drifting in the still air. "According to the map, that smoke is coming from a village." He motioned for Hon to pull behind a thorn tree for cover while he quickly camouflaged their tracks in the rapidly fading light.

"We might get some uninvited guests," he told Toby. "We need to spread out and set up mutually supporting fighting positions. You and Hon next to the truck, and Paride and me over there." He pointed to a pile of heavy brush.

"You'll need to rig mosquito nets," Toby warned.

"And don't sleep on the ground," Jason added. Africa was a stern teacher and he was learning very fast.

They set up camp and ate a cold meal. The night was amazingly noisy with insects and strange sounds, and, in the distance, the burning glow that marked the village. Toby tried to get some rest, but sleep wouldn't come. He sat in the cab of the truck and stared into the night. Finally, he woke Jason. "I want to check on those villagers."

Jason hesitated, considering the wisdom of it. But there was something in Toby that could not be denied. "Let me do it while it's still dark. Hide in the night." He spoke to Paride, who spoke excellent English, and explained what he wanted to do. The tall Dinka instinctively understood and readily volunteered. The two men charged their Heckler and Kock MP5 submachine guns, and adjusted their night vision goggles. With everyone in radio contact, they moved out in the early-morning dark. Jason took the point with Paride slightly behind and to his right. Toby and Hon stayed behind to guard the truck.

The burning smell grew stronger as the two men approached the village. Jason motioned Paride to a halt and studied the village through his NVGs. Little was recognizable and what had been a village of huts gathered in family compounds was now a pile of debris. Two fires were still smoldering and giving off a terrible stench. Jason keyed his radio. "No signs of life."

"We're coming up," Toby replied.

Jason and Paride waited and before too long, they heard the approaching truck. "Stop where you are and come on foot," Jason radioed. "Leave Hon to guard the truck." Moments later, Toby emerged out of the shadows carrying the truck's first aid kit. "I don't think you should go in," Jason cautioned.

Paride agreed. "Only death is there.

"I don't have a choice," Toby said. His voice was soft but Jason heard the resolve. He knew when to follow. The three men moved through the remains of the village and skirted a pile of dead bodies. Women, children and men had been herded together and cut down with submachine-gun fire. Two dogs were ravaging the remains, their muzzles bloody. Jason swung his MP5 around and fired a short burst, killing the dogs. He motioned Paride forward, and they worked their way towards the smoldering fires on the far side. Jason got there first and froze. Two bodies were staked out spread-eagled over beds of charcoal. "Oh, my God," he whispered. "They burned them alive. Who would do something like this?" "Janjaweed," Toby said from behind them. "Now you know our enemy." He turned to leave but movement caught his eye. Jason also saw it and whirled around, raising his MP5. "Don't shoot," Toby commanded.

The Hague

Hank's footsteps echoed down the empty corridors of the palace. "Two days before Christmas and the place is like a tomb," he said to himself. He pushed through the doors into his office where Aly was waiting for him. "Sorry," he told her, "there's no word on Jason." She nodded without a word and handed him a mug of freshly brewed coffee. "Thanks. I need three to jumpstart my heart."

She tried to manage a smile but failed. "How is Catherine?" she asked.

"Made it home safe and sound and is in overdrive with the boys getting ready for Christmas. I'm booked out on a flight at noon but wanted to see you and Gus before I left."

The phone rang and Aly answered. "It's Winslow James, the American Embassy." An image of the effete little man flashed in Hank's mind. He pulled a face and took the handset.

"This is Winslow James, the deputy charge of mission speaking. Are you aware that the State Department has restricted travel to the Sudan and military personnel are specifically prohibited from entering? I'm calling to inform you that your actions have forced us to lodge an incident report with the Pentagon, and with the Department of Justice."

"Jason Tyler is going after the one witness who can keep Gus from going to prison for a very long time. A witness, I might add, that the State Department hasn't done squat-all to help bring here."

"That does not justify your actions," James retorted. "I cannot tell you how you have humiliated your country with these cheap tricks of yours in court, and your feeble attempts to embarrass the French foreign minister."

"Really? I cannot tell you how embarrassed I am that my country allowed Colonel Tyler to be put on trial."

"There is a distinct possibility that the Netherlands will declare you persona non grata at the conclusion of the trial. Another embarrassment that I must deal with."

"Relax. They'll only do that if we win. Have a merry Christmas." He slammed the receiver down. "What a prick. Well, I've pissed off the State Department so I must be doing something right." He gathered up his gloves and briefcase. "Let's go see Gus."

Southern Sudan

Toby bent over the young woman in the early-morning light and performed triage in the middle of the destroyed village. Even with a modern operating room and a team of skilled doctors, he doubted she would survive her horrendous wounds. He spoke quietly and made her as comfortable as he could. There was nothing he could do. Then he squatted in front of her four-year-old daughter. He cooed to the little girl in Dinka as he closed the deep gash in her left arm, and, for a brief moment, there was hope in her eyes. Then the fear was back. Toby stood. "How many?" he asked.

"Five all told," Jason answered. "We found three more." A seven-old-girl stood beside him holding an infant. A little boy peaked from behind Hon and then ran to Toby, his hand over his right eye. "They were small enough to hide," Jason said. Toby bent over and gently moved the toddler's hand aside. He examined his eye, flushed it as best he could, and gently removed a splinter. "What now?" Jason asked.

"They go with us in the truck."

"We haven't got enough room," Jason replied, gesturing at the woman.

"We're not taking her," Toby said. The pain in his voice reached into Jason, tearing at his humanity. It was a decision he could not have made.

Gunfire echoed in the distance and they heard the sound of the truck's racing motor. "Janjaweed!" Hon's voice shouted over the radio as the distinctive clatter of an AK47 reached them.

"Paride!" Jason ordered. "Get them to cover. Over there." He pointed to the far side of the village and a dense stand of brush. Toby scooped up the infant and toddler with the wounded eye as Paride hustled the two girls to safety. Jason picked up the woman and started to follow. He felt the life go out of her and gently laid her beside the ruins of a mud and wattle hut. He hoped it had been her home.

The gunfire was much closer and he saw the cloud of dust kicked up by the speeding truck. Jason keyed his radio. "Hon, what's happening?"

"Janjaweed behind me. Seven, maybe eight. They ride horses and yell they only want truck. I no believe and outrun them."

"Drive straight through the village and pick me up." Jason checked his MP5 and moved to one side. His eyes narrowed as the sound of the approaching truck grew louder. A short burst of gunfire split the air and he knew the Janjaweed were not far behind. "If they want the truck, they're gonna have to earn it," he said to himself. The truck barreled into the village and Hon slammed on the brakes. Jason

A Far Justice

piled into the rear. "Go! Go! Go!" Hon mashed the accelerator and the truck sped ahead as Jason loaded the heavy machine gun mounted over the cab. He slapped the receiver closed and chambered a round. He fire a short burst, clearing the weapon. "Go back!" he roared.

Hon slewed the truck around as three horsemen charged through the village, coming straight at them. Simultaneously, they realized the danger and jerked their horses to a halt to reverse course. Jason fired a long burst, cutting into them, shredding the men and horses. Hon jerked the truck to the right as a volley of submachine gun fire split the air where they had been a fraction of second before. Jason found the mounted shooter hidden behind the debris of a destroyed hut. He raked the hut with a long burst, sending up a cloud of wooden debris. The horse reared and threw the Janjaweed, but he never lost the reins and dragged the horse down onto its side and safety. Now he waited.

Two more horsemen came at the truck, both firing from the hip. One slug ripped into the truck's windshield barely missing Hon. It exited the rear of the cab and cut a crease in Jason's right thigh. Jason brought the heavy machine gun to bear and raked the horsemen as pain shot up his leg. The Janjaweed and horses went down in a bloody heap. Automatically, Hon slowed as they passed and Jason emptied his MP5 into the men and horses. Then they were clear of the village. "Go back!" Jason ordered.

Hon spun the truck around and slammed to a stop. A lone Janjaweed holding a woman astride his saddle as a shield was coming at them. Jason thumbed his MP5 to single shot, aimed, and squeezed off one round, hitting the horseman's right shoulder. He shrieked in pain. Jason fired again and the round ripped into the Janjaweed's throat, cutting his scream off in full flow as his mouth worked, forming sounds that could not come. The woman broke free and ran, but another Janjaweed chased after her. He swung a machete and cut her down. Hon reacted automatically and gunned the engine as he twisted the wheel, going after the Janjaweed. Jason mashed the trigger of the heavy machine gun but missed.

The rider was a superb horseman as he guided his horse through the village, running for safety. But the determined Hon closed on the fleeing man and Jason was able to bring the machine gun to bear. He squeezed off a round, but the weapon misfired and blew the bolt back. Fortunately, Jason was wearing goggles and only suffered minor flash burns. The truck coasted to a halt. "Engine dead," Hon yelled. An

AK47 slug had punched a hole in the radiator and holed the engine block. "Look out!" the Dinka yelled.

The Janjaweed had spun around and instantly realized what had had happened. He charged the truck, firing wildly and driving Hon and Jason to the ground. Jason returned fire with his MP5, and emptied the clip. He missed. Now the Janjaweed was almost on them and Jason jumped directly into the path of the charging horse, denying the Janjaweed a shot.

At the last moment, Jason feinted to his left and then back to the right, on the horseman's left, certain that the tribesman was right-hand dominate. He grabbed the horse's mane with one hand and the Janjaweed's bandoleer with the other. Jason was a big man and threw his weight against the horse, and the two men and the horse went down in a heap. Jason rolled over the man and grabbed his AK47. At the same time, he jammed his elbow into the rider's sternum, knocking the wind out of him. The horse struggled to its feet and bolted free. Hon grabbed its reins, dragging it to a halt.

Jason stood the Janjaweed up and examined his clothes. "What do we have here?" His prisoner was no ordinary Janjaweed. He keyed the radio to check in with Toby while Hon lashed the Janjaweed to the truck. "We got 'em."

Toby's voice came over the radio. "You two okay?"

"I got nicked, Hon's fine. One hell of a driver. But the truck's disabled."

"Paride's a good mechanic," Toby answered, "and I've got the first aid kit. We're on our way. Patch and repair as necessary." Jason sat on the truck's tailgate and waited as Toby and Paride, along with their flock of children, made their way back. Toby stopped and told the children to wait in the shade of a low bush. They had been through enough and he didn't want them to see the carnage of what had been their village.

Suddenly, the Janjaweed who had been hiding in the debris of the destroyed hut bolted for safety. He was up and mounted and racing for the children, fully intending to use them as cover to make his escape. He turned and fired his AK47 from the saddle, driving Jason and Hon down. He galloped past the children and fired at them. But Paride was there. He stood and emptied his MP5, killing the Janjaweed and his horseFor a few moments, there was only silence. "Where's Toby?" Jason yelled.

"There!" Paride shouted. Toby was lying over the infant he had been carrying, his blood soaking the ground. The captive Janjaweed laughed.

Hon turned and shot him in the head.

32

Southern Sudan

Paride sat on the truck's fender, his feet in the engine compartment as the sun beat on his back. "Bullet make big hole in engine. Water all run out. Sorry, Boss, no can fix." Without a word, Jason walked to the rear of the truck where Toby was resting in the shade of a tarp they had rigged.

"The truck's kaput, and my friend, and you've got two nasty holes in your body. We need to get you to a doctor."

Toby managed a grimace. "I am a doctor. You've got me pretty well patched up, and I'm not too worried about the wound in my side. Didn't hit anything vital. Left leg's a problem. I don't think I'll be walking."

"Where's the nearest town?" Jason asked.

"Duk Faiwil, about ten miles south of here. It's about halfway between the mission and Juba, 180 miles either way."

Jason thought for a few moments. "Paride, strip down all the weapons but the two MP5s, and bury the pieces. Hon, bring the horse over here." While Hon rigged three packs, Jason tied the ends of two long poles to the saddle to make a travois. Then he lashed a litter across the back of the poles, creating an A-frame. When it was ready, they carefully lifted Toby onto the litter. "The kids can carry the canteens," Jason said. He still had a problem. "Reverend, can you hold the baby?" Toby nodded and cradled the infant next to him.

The three men hefted their packs and set out. Jason led the way with Paride shepherding the two girls and carrying the little boy. Hon brought up the rear leading the horse and dragging Toby on the travois. But the ride was too bumpy and the wound in Toby's side quickly reopened, bleeding profusely. He stayed conscious long enough to tell Jason that he had to cauterize the wound to stop the bleeding and then stitch it up. Jason stuffed the cleanest rag he had into the wound and pressed against it with his hands.

Hon ran back to the truck for the tool kit while Paride built a fire. Within minutes, Hon was back and the ends of a lug wrench and two screwdrivers were in the fire, heating up. "Please, God," Jason prayed, "help me do it right."

"God's neutral when it comes to this," Toby murmured, coming awake. He told Jason how to use the pointed end of the lug wrench and then how to finish up with the screwdrivers to seal the small arteries. "Do it quick," Toby ordered. The smell of burnt flesh wafted over them. Finally, Jason was done and wrapped the wound with a fresh bandage. Toby was still conscious and his face was bathed in sweat. "Don't want to do that again," Toby admitted.

Jason told Hon to strap their backpacks to the horse's saddle while he and Paride disassembled the travois. They suspended the litter from the two poles, and, with Toby aboard and holding the infant, they shouldered the poles. They walked slowly down the rutted track in tandem, the litter swinging between them. Hon followed close behind, carrying the toddler and leading the packhorse and the children. The sun, the heat, and the humidity bore down, demanding a ferocious toll.

Late that afternoon, the infant died in Toby's arms. Jason squatted in the sun as Hon and Paride scrapped out a shallow grave. He listened as Toby sang softly in Dinka, the same song he had heard at the mission's church. Toby kissed the infant's cheek. Jason took the small body and gently placed it in the grave. He stood, forever a changed man.

* * * * *

It was late the next day and Hon and Paride walked side-by-side, leading the way as each shouldered one pole of the litter. Behind them, Jason shouldered both poles, carrying the backend of the litter. The oldest girl led the horse, which was now carrying their packs and the two other children. The horse was rapidly weakening under its load and in the heat. The American didn't know how much longer he could keep pressing the men and hoped they were near the town. Twice, they had to take cover as armed men passed, and it was, without doubt, the longest ten miles and twenty-four hours in his life.

A Far Justice

The two Africans stopped. "Duk Faiwil, Boss," Paride said. "Straight ahead."

They all slowly sank to the ground, totally exhausted. The men breathed heavily. Finally, Jason came to his feet and checked on Toby. He was semi-conscious and sweating. "We got to get some antibiotics in you," Jason said. He thought for a few moments. "Paride, can you trade the horse for antibiotics for the Reverend?"

"Don't think so, Boss. Medicine hard to get and horses not worth much. Too bad no have cows. But for Reverend, they will give medicine." The three men shouldered the litter and the small caravan made its way into town. A strange sight greeted them as brightly dressed Dinkas and Nuers mingled with refugees flooding into the small town. A haphazard array of decorations covered market stalls. It was uniquely African as harsh reality collided with a festive mood. "Christmas tomorrow, Boss," Paride said.

"I forgot," Jason admitted.

Paride spoke to a tall young man and was given directions to a sprawling compound crowded with people sitting on the ground. A faded sign announced they had found the hospital. They carefully lowered the litter to the ground and Paride worked his way inside, calming hostile voices and shouts for jumping the line. He was back in a matter of minutes leading a doctor, nurse, orderly, and two guards. "They all know Reverend Person," Paride said. "He very important man in Sudan."

Toby spoke quietly to the doctor who occasionally nodded. Jason did not understand a single word but heard an authority in Toby's words that could not be denied. The doctor pointed at the children. "There are a few refugees from their village here." He spoke to the nurse who took charge. She barked at the orderly, picked up the toddler, and led the two girls into the hospital compound.

"Will they take care of them?" Jason asked.

Hon looked at him for a moment. He had to make the American understand. "A village is a big family. Everyone have uncle or aunt. Children are future of family. No children, no future."

The guards stayed with the horse and packs while they carried Toby inside. Paride and the doctor engaged in a lively conver- sation. When Toby was in the operating room, Paride pulled Jason aside and spoke in a low voice. "Doctor says there is much fighting to north and many people come this way. Some people say Sudanese Army attacks

Mission Awana but no one knows for sure. Nurse says Army patrol drive through town last night."

"Did she say how many troops?"

"Not many, maybe twenty. She says they have two armored cars and a truck."

"Damn, that's not good. We need a vehicle to get out of here."

"Don't worry, Boss. I go get one. Doctor says they have a telephone." Paride pushed through the crowded room and disappeared into the compound.

Jason and Hon wandered around the compound until they found an office guarded by two armed men. Hon spoke to them in Dinka and money passed hands. One of the guards opened the door and allowed them in. Inside, a young man sat behind a desk talking on the telephone, speaking a southern dialect of Dinka. He ignored them. "He's talking to his girlfriend in Juba," Hon whispered. The young man finally looked at them, his eyes cold and unblinking.

"The phone is for official business only," he said, switching to perfect English.

"This is official," Jason answered. "We're taking the Reverend Tobias Person of Mission Awana to Juba. He has been badly wounded and we need to arrange transportation and medical treatment."

The young man ignored him and returned to his phone call, speaking Dinka. After a few minutes, he again looked at them. "A call will be five-hundred dollars US"

"I lost all my money and credit cards when my helicopter crashed. If you give me a bill, I will make sure you are paid when we reach Juba." The young man stared at Jason, his face a mask, his eyes lifeless. He waved his hand in dismissal and turned to the window, renewing his telephone conversation. He laughed.

Jason's jaw hardened in anger and Hon touched his arm. "Time to go, Boss." The Dinka looked at the door. Jason stormed out, only to be stopped by the guards who demanded more money. Hon again handed over a few Sudanese dinars and hustled Jason outside. "It's okay, Boss. Some people give, some people take."

They made their way back to the horse and Jason untied one the packs. He pulled out an MP5 and strapped on a web cartridge belt. "That won't happen again." He threw the other MP5 to Hon who looked very worried. "Pay the guards," Jason ordered, leading the horse into the shade. Now they had to wait for Paride to return.

The Hague

Aly joined the large crowd milling in front of the Hugo Grotius prison on Christmas afternoon, and, like the others, waited impatiently for a guard to open the doors leading inside. At exactly two o'clock, the outer gates slid back and a guard unlocked the inner glass doors. The crowd surged in, carrying food and gifts. Aly joined the line and waited patiently to sign in and go through inspection. Gus was waiting for her, his cell door open. "It's one big open house," he said. "There is no way they'd do something like this in the States, not even in a minimum security prison like this one."

"Our prisons are different," Aly explained. "Rehabilitation is the goal, not punishment." She smiled. "Hank called this morning with news. He said to tell you that the NSA monitored a telephone call from a town called Duk Faiwil in the southern Sudan. A young man was talking to a girlfriend in Juba and said there was an American with a missionary at the hospital where he worked. The man said the American had lost all his money in a helicopter crash so he couldn't pay for a phone call."

Gus exploded. "Jason and Toby!" He slowly calmed. "If Hank knows, Max Westcot knows. Max will get them out. Count on it."

Therese Derwent knocked on the open door. "Count on what?"

Gus smiled. "Bringing good news."

Derwent stepped into the cell with three plastic carrier bags. "Dinner," she announced. She looked at Aly. "Please join us." Gus sat on his bunk as the two women talked and enjoyed their easy conversation. Within minutes, Derwent had set the table and handed him a bottle of wine to open. "The superintendent only allows one per family," she cautioned. The food was as close to a traditional American Christmas dinner as the psychiatrist could manage with sliced turkey, stuffing, vegetables and all the trimmings. When they had finished, the three walked the corridors, exchanging Christmas greetings and chatting with the other prisoners and their families.

Finally, they were back in Gus's cell and Aly handed him a cell phone to call home. Gus eagerly dialed the Mayo, hoping the timing was right and Clare would be awake and able to take the call. His daughter answered on the first ring. "We've been waiting," Michelle said, her voice radiating with happiness. She turned the camera towards Clare who was sitting up in bed, her hair carefully arranged.

Her lips moved and she smiled as Michelle held the phone close. "Merry Christmas, darling." Her voice was weak but clear and distinct.

Gus smiled as tears coursed down his cheeks. It was the first time he had heard her voice since leaving home in late September. Aly and Derwent stepped into the hall to give them privacy. "I envy him his Christmas," the psychiatrist said.

"He deserves it," Aly told her. She considered her next words. "You don't really know him."

The psychiatrist gave her an indulgent smile. "I think I do."

33

Duk Faiwil, Southern Sudan

Jason glanced at his watch and tried to go back to sleep. It was still dark and the hospital compound was quiet, perched on the edge of morning. The hut he shared with Hon had lost its stifling heat and was comfortable enough, but frustration laced with anger twisted his stomach into a hard knot, driving the last vestiges of sleep away. He glanced at his watch again. But other than the passage of a few minutes, nothing had changed. It was still Wednesday morning, December 29, and Toby was still in the hospital running a vicious fever. They had to get Toby to Juba and proper medical care but he hadn't been able to find transportation and Paride still hadn't returned after three days. "Too damn many 'stills,'" he muttered to himself.

The knot in his stomach tightened as his mental alarms screamed at him, warning him that the trial was entering its final stages, and they were marooned in this forsaken Sudanese town. His right hand flashed out and he squashed an insect between his thumb and forefinger before it could bite the still sleeping Hon. At least he could still do that. He stood in the open doorway as the hospital compound slowly came to life. What had D'Na said about morning in Africa? It was the best time of day when all was new and fresh. He wanted to believe that.

A commotion outside the compound drew his attention and woke Hon. "Something is going on," Jason said.

"I go see, Boss," Hon said. "I try to find food."

"That would be nice," Jason said, trying to ignore the hunger that was part of their life. Hon pulled on his T-shirt and headed for the gate while Jason sat in the doorway. A fact of life was that one of them always had to stay and guard their meager possessions or they would be stolen.

Hon came back, running for all he was worth. "Boss! Soldiers come!"

"Pack up," Jason ordered. "I'll go get the Reverend." He ran for the hospital as the sound of approaching helicopters beat at him. He looked up as two tan colored helicopters flew low over the town. Their distinctive roundels flashed in the sun – Sudanese Air Force. A third helicopter flew past. A wall of people rushing out of the compound blocked his way but he managed to push and shove his way into the ward where Toby was staying. Fortunately, the missionary was sitting on the edge of the bed and pulling on his clothes. His face was bathed in sweat and he swayed from the effort. Jason knelt down and slipped on Toby's boots, quickly tying them.

Toby tried to stand but he didn't have the strength. Jason helped him to his feet and carried him piggyback out of the hospital. Hon was waiting, packs shouldered and holding their two MP5s. "Let's go," Jason said, joining the crowd of people surging through the small town and fleeing to the south. Four teenagers split off from the gangs ransacking the marketplace and surrounded them. One grabbed at the packs Hon was carrying and dragged him to the ground while the second one grabbed the MP5s. The last two pushed at Jason and snarled. The first two stripped the packs and MP5s away from Hon and ran, disappearing into the crowd but the other two kept coming at Jason. He dropped Toby to the ground and drove his right fist into his closest attacker's sternum, knocking the wind out of him. A hard kick to the knee sent his assailant to the ground screaming in pain. The last one drew his machete and swung at Jason. But the big American's reflexes were rattlesnake quick and he feinted to his right, avoiding the machete. The teenager started to swing, and then checked it. He grinned wickedly as he parried and thrust, coming at Jason. A short burst of heavy machine gun fire cut into the young thug, almost chopping him in two. Jason dropped to the ground and rolled, using the teenager's body for cover. "It's okay, Boss," Paride yelled.

"Man, am I glad to see you," Jason called.

Hon struggled to his feet, still dazed but not hurt. He blinked his eyes, his face fearful. "What . . .?" he asked, pointing at the high-wheeled armored personnel carrier stopped behind Paride. Four heavily armed white men clambered out the back. A big, burley, blond-haired man was the last to climb down.

"It's called a Wolf Turbo, Mate," the man said.

"They are friends," Paride said. "They find me."

The man stuck out his hand to Jason. "Hans Landerrost." They shook hands. "You are the devil to find. Paride here tells me the Reverend is wounded." He spoke with a South African accent. "We have an airfield near here." The Afrikaner looked up as two more Sudanese helicopters flew over. "This is getting bloody fuckin' interestin'."

The bark of AK47s echoed in the distance.

The Hague

Gus made small talk as they waited for the trial to reconvene. "How was Christmas?"

"Strange enough, one of the best we've had," Hank answered. "Catherine hit the ground running when she got back, but for some reason eased off. We didn't go through all the usual hoopla and spent Christmas Eve decorating the tree."

"Is Catherine coming back?"

Hank allowed a little smile. His wife was his best friend and anchor. "She'll be here tomorrow."

"So what's on the agenda for today?"

"We have to discredit Schumann's testimony. Fortunately, his charge about using napalm is bogus so we can tie that can to his tail."

"Unfortunately," Gus admitted, "we did use it."

"Ah, shit," Hank moaned. "Are you sure?"

"Yeah. The Marines used it at least once. I'm not sure where or when."

"Was napalm used on Mutlah Ridge? By anyone?"

"No and no," Gus answered.

"Did the Air Force ever use napalm in the Gulf."

"Not that I'm aware of. The Air Force stopped using it back in the seventies in Vietnam. It was a crappy weapon to begin with, and not very effective. Tactically, CBU's are much better. The canisters separate clean from the aircraft with a good trajectory. You always know where they're going and it really chews up the bad guys without all the bad publicity."

Cassandra whispered in Hank's ear, outlining a strategy her legal team had devised. Hank visibly relaxed. "I can handle this," he promised. It was time, and he left for the courtroom where Aly was waiting. Every seat in the courtroom was taken and an expectant hush fell over the crowd when Hank entered the side door. He sat down and handed Aly his percom. "There's a message from Cassandra I need printed out. Also, we need to recall Roger Marks, one of Du Milan's weapons experts. Is he available?"

"I'll find out," she replied. She hurried out of the courtroom as Gus was escorted to the dock. The red light on the clerk's desk flashed and they were back in session.

Hank studied Bouchard's face as he sat down, looking for signs of ill health or strain. Then it hit him – the judge was wearing makeup. "This court is in session," Bouchard intoned. "We hope all enjoyed their holidays and are ready to bring these proceedings to a timely conclusion."

Hank stood to test the waters. "Is time now a factor, your Honor?" Given the political situation in the United Nations, he strongly suspected that it was.

Bouchard humphed. "Of course not. As is the custom of the court, does the prosecution or defense have any business to bring to the court's attention?" Denise said the prosecution had nothing for the court.

Hank wondered when the judges would rule on the petition to transfer Gus to Iraqi custody. He decided Bouchard had to pick the right moment, probably the day Gus took the stand. "The defense has nothing . . . " he let his voice trail off and relief spread across Bouchard's face. ". . . at this time," Hank added, ratcheting Bouchard up a notch. Aly rejoined him and handed him a five-page printout from Cassandra.

"Roger Marks is hovering in the witness lounge," she told Hank. "He wants to be recalled to the stand."

"The guy really needs his fifteen minutes of fame," Hank replied. "I think we'll give it to him."

"Call your next witness," Bouchard said.

Hank suppressed a smile at what was coming next. Aly read the signs right and said, "Don't get full of yourself."

"The defense recalls Roger Marks to the stand," Hank said. He waited at the podium while the Englishman entered the side door. He was the same man as Hank remembered, nondescript, paunchy, and desperate for his time in the sun. The same anger and frustration Hank had sensed the first time was still there.

Hank waited while Bouchard thanked him for returning and reminding him that he was still under oath. Hank decided that a few ego strokes were in order. "Mr. Marks, let me also thank you for sharing your valuable time and expertise with the court. From your prior testimony, it was established that you were present in Kuwait during the Gulf War. Can you elaborate on exactly what you observed?"

"Objection," Denise called. "This is a new line of questioning. The rules of the court specify that cross-examination must be confined to Mr. Marks prior testimony."

"Mr. Marks testified earlier that he was in Kuwait. I am now asking for specifics."

Bouchard spoke quietly to Della Sante and Richter. "The objection is overruled,"

Marks swelled with importance as he related how he was a reporter for Scientifica Europa, a quarterly journal published in France. He had arrived in Saudi Arabia a week before the land phase of the war started and had spent over three months examining the environmental damage caused by the war. For the next hour, he expounded on how he had documented the effect of weapons on the environment. Hank's patience was rewarded when Marks mentioned that he had been to Mutlah Ridge. It was the opening Hank needed and he held his breath to see if Denise would object. Marks continued to talk without an objection from the prosecutor.

"Mr. Marks, based on your investigation and documentation, what specific weapons did you discover in your research?" Again, Marks was effusive in answering and listed every type of weapon and the associated damage he had discovered. "Mr. Marks, you stated you were on Mutlah Ridge. Was this before or after the fleeing Iraqi convoy was destroyed?"

Denise finally realized where Hank was going. "Objection! Mr. Marks presence on Mutlah Ridge is new evidence and beyond the scope of defense counsel's cross-examination."

"The witness testified earlier to being in other areas in Kuwait without objection," Hank replied.

Della Sante leaned into Bouchard and spoke rapidly, her voice inaudible but her face animated. Bouchard grumped an answer and Richter's mouth moved, saying something in German. Bouchard straightened up. "Objection overruled. The witness may answer the question."

"I arrived at Mutlah Ridge the day after the attack and spent over forty-eight hours examining the battlefield."

"Did you discover any evidence supporting the allegation that the coalition forces used napalm at Mutlah Ridge?"

Marks hesitated, fully aware of Schumann's testimony. He did not want to answer the question. He looked at Denise who stared at him. He gulped. "No. But my test kit was exhausted."

"Why did you need a test kit?"

"Napalm leaves a distinct chemical signature. I had tested many areas for napalm and was out of test chemicals."

"You testified earlier that you interviewed many doctors about the wounds they treated. Were napalm burns ever mentioned?"

Marks' "No" was barely audible.

"In earlier testimony by Doctor Gustav Schumann, the court was told about another team investigating weapons employed by the coalition forces in Iraq." He passed two pages of the trial transcript to Marks. "Would you be so kind as to read the highlighted passages?" Marks swallowed, his throat now dry, and started to read. His flat, dry drone stripped away the emotional impact that Schumann had created. Hank leaned forward when Marks reached the critical passage.

"Prosecutor: What weapons did the investigation team document had been used by the coalition forces against the Iraqis?

"Schumann: The list is long. There were, of course, the so-called 'smart bombs;' cluster bomb units, or CBUs; anti-tank missiles, cruise missiles like the Tomahawk; the standard conventional bombs, and many more that I do not recall at this moment, for which I apologize.

"Prosecutor: We understand, perfectly, Doctor. Did your investigators document the weapons used on Mutlah Ridge, the Highway of Death?

"Schumann: The investigators spent a full day examining the carnage. Many weapons of mass destruction had been used, such as cluster bomb units and napalm."

A Far Justice

Hank moved in for the kill. "Did you encounter Doctor Schumann's investigators while you were at Mutlah Ridge?"

"Yes."

On cue, Aly handed Hank the same thin leather folder he had used in examining Harm deRijn. Marks stared at it, his lower lip quivering. "Please be more specific as to when and where you encountered Dr. Schumann's investigators."

"We were escorted as a group for safety and had to stay together for the entire time they were there."

"Yet, you discovered no evidence that napalm had been employed against the Iraqis. Is that correct?"

Marks hesitated, desperate to avoid answering. He looked at Denise who stared at him. He gulped when Hank opened the leather folder. "I found no evidence of napalm."

Hank closed the folder. "Thank you for your honesty." He sat down.

Denise was on her feet, determined to salvage what she could. "Did you specifically ask the doctors you interviewed about napalm burns?"

"No, I did not."

"Did you observe casualties suffering from burn wounds?"

"Yes, many times."

"Did you observe burnt-out vehicles on Mutlah Ridge?"

Marks was recovering. "Countless times."

"Could napalm have set those vehicles on fire?"

The old Marks was back, pedantic and confident. "It's possible."

"Thank you, Mr. Marks." Denise sat down.

Hank took the podium. "Was the burn damage to the vehicles you observed on Mutlah Ridge consistent with conventional bomb damage and gas tanks exploding?"

Marks answer was painful. "Yes."

"Did you observe this type of destruction and burn damage in areas other than Mutlah Ridge?"

The Englishman was desperate to escape. "Yes."

"We must be absolutely clear on this point, Mr. Marks. Did you test for napalm in those areas where you had observed similar bomb damage?"

Denise was on her feet. "Objection. This question had been asked and answered earlier."

"Mr. Marks," Hank replied, "testified that he had tested for napalm in 'many areas.' We are now establishing specific areas."

The judges conferred briefly and Bouchard frowned. "Objection overruled. The witness may answer the question."

Marks managed a strangled "Yes."

Hank pressed him hard. "Did you ever find any evidence of napalm?" Marks shook his head. "Please answer the question." Again, Marks shook his head. "Please answer the question for the record."

"I never found any evidence of napalm," Marks finally admitted.

Hank sat down and Denise wisely declined to continue the cross-examination. Bouchard looked tired and conferred briefly with Della Sante and Richter. They both nodded and he adjourned the trial until the next morning.

"Hank," Cassandra whispered in Hank's ear, "you didn't know if Marks had discovered napalm when you opened that line of questioning. Don't do that to me again."

"It was a calculated gamble," Hank admitted. "I was almost certain Marks would have brought it up if he had. Besides, if Du Milan had discovered it, she would have been screaming like a banshee from hell long before this."

"You can bet she's looking for it now," Cassandra cautioned.

* * * * *

Marci Lennox was holding forth in the forecourt of the palace. She was wearing a stylish cut navy style pea jacket and her hair, now cut exactly like Catherine's, caressed her face in the gentle breeze. She looked into the TV camera. "Hank Sutherland came out swinging today as the trial of Gus Tyler resumed. The veteran lawyer masterfully used one of the prosecution's expert witnesses to impeach the testimony of Gustav Schumann and refute the allegation that the coalition forces had used napalm on the highway of death. How Du Milan will recover remains to be seen." She fed a few questions to her director and then recorded the answers. She concluded with, "Moments ago, one veteran court observer told me that the momentum of the trial is swinging in Gus Tyler's favor. The only question is: can Hank Sutherland maintain it?" She was off the air.

"Nice hairdo," her producer in New York said.

A Far Justice

Southern Sudan

The Wolf Turbo coasted to a halt in the middle of the road and Hans Landerrost listened to the sounds in the dark. "Trouble," he said in a low voice, hearing something that Jason had missed. Landerrost climbed out of the personnel carrier and adjusted his night vision goggles. "Wait there," he ordered, motioning the personnel carrier off the road. His men quickly spread out and set up a defensive perimeter. Landerrost spoke quietly to his second-in-command, an equally large man named Simon, and disappeared into the night. Jason gave the Afrikaner high marks and there was no doubt that he was a highly skilled mercenary. Within minutes, Landerrost was back "There are soldiers on the road ahead of us."

"Toby's fever is up," Jason said. "We need help."

"We're almost there, mate." He checked his GPS. "The airfield is three kilometers ahead. He stared into the night, his face hard. "We'll get there as soon as those fuckin' bastards move on." He settled into his seat and fell asleep. Thirty minutes latter, the sound of a diesel engine cranking to life split the dark. "Now that's a big bugger," Landerrost said, instantly awake. The diesel engine revved and the vehicle clanked into gear. The sound was slowly swallowed by the night.

"I didn't hear the clatter of tank tracks," Jason said. "Maybe an armored car."

"That's fuckin' more than enough," Landerrost replied. He climbed into the personnel carrier and stood in the crew compartment, the upper half of his body above the open top. Again, he listened with a unique sixth sense. "They've gone." Landerrost keyed his small walkie-talkie. "We found what we were looking for. Coming in."

"We've got a mine field out," a voice replied. "Come through the swamp."

Landerrost grunted a reply in Afrikaans and guided the truck through the tall grass using a GPS. The ground turned to mush and the big wheels spun, barely maintaining traction as they crossed a swampy area. Finally, they were on solid ground and Jason could see a cluster of buildings. They drove past a portable drilling rig and a stack of pipes and crates. Jason scanned the big compound. Someone had sank a lot of money in it. "Welcome to Westcot Five," Landerrost said.

"Block five, the oil concession?" Jason asked.

"Right on. Mr. Westcot seems to be bloody fuckin' interested in you, and whatever Mr. Westcot wants, well, you know the rest, mate."

34

The Hague

Catherine burst into the office twenty minutes before the court reconvened. Aly was right behind her carrying her suitcase. Hank looked up from his desk. "Bad flight?" he asked, coming to his feet.

"Straight from hell," she answered. They embraced and Hank's morale took a quantum leap upward. His best friend and counselor was back. "Any news on Jason and Toby?" Hank shook his head. "I take it the strategy of the day is delay."

"It's about all I can do." Hank replied. "I've got a few witnesses left for today and I expect Bouchard will call for a short break over the New Year." He donned his robe and they followed Aly down the hall. "I may be able to get a delay until Tuesday, Wednesday at the latest. But Du Milan is pressing for a conclusion."

"Bouchard is listening to her," Aly added.

Hank gave her an appreciative look. "Aly's got the building wired for sound," he said. "I've got to see Gus before we start. See you in court." They parted as Hank headed for the holding cell. He expected a ruling on the Iraqi petition for custody at any time and had to warn the pilot.

The court reconvened at exactly ten o'clock and much to Hank's relief, Bouchard did not issue a ruling on the Iraqi petition. He called his next witness, a US Air Force historian who specialized in the Gulf War. Hank took longer than usual establishing the historian's credentials and Bouchard grew impatient, fully aware of Hank's strategy. "Did the United States Air Force employ napalm in the Gulf War?" Hank asked.

"No," the historian answered, "nor did the coalition forces."

Hank winced inwardly. He had told the historian to answer all questions simply and truthfully, and above all, not to elaborate. The man had failed on all counts. Denise had to know by now that the Marines had employed napalm, and he shuddered at how she could turn the historian's lie against Gus. He glanced at Catherine who nodded, urging him to address the problem now. "As it is impossible to prove a negative, how can you be so certain the Air Force never employed napalm?"

"I have a complete listing of the United States Air Force's order of battle which includes all personnel, weapons, and weapons systems. The Air Force did not have napalm in its inventory. The logic is simple; to employ a weapon you must first have it."

"Do you have a similar order of battle for all the other services, such as the US Navy, Marines or Coalition air forces?" Hank asked, desperately hoping the historian understood that he was running cover for his lie.

"No, I do not."

"Then you cannot speak with the same assurance in regards to the use of napalm by the Navy and other services."

"No, I cannot."

Relieved, Hank moved on and dragged the questioning into the late morning by going over old ground and reconfirming evidence presented to the court. Frustrated, Bouchard kept pressing Hank for relevance and finally called a recess for lunch. Hank slumped in his chair while Aly gathered up their files and folders. Catherine waited patiently until the courtroom was empty and Aly had left. "At this stage, momentum is everything," she told him. "And you're losing it. Napalm is a pushbutton issue for Europeans but I think you've defused it. Show the judges something new."

"Without Toby, I've only got Gus left."

"Then ask for an early adjournment for New Year's."

Aly hurried back in. "Suzanne Westcot is in the office," she told Hank. "She wants to speak to you immediately." Hank rushed out with Catherine in close pursuit.

Suzanne was waiting in the outer office, a big smile on her face. "He's inside." The man waiting in Hank's office was a bull of a man, slightly over six feet tall, barrel-chested, with salt-and-pepper hair cut in a brush cut, and the brightest blue eyes Hank had ever seen. "How's Gus doing?" he asked.

A Far Justice

* * * * *

The court was back in session and 33ank rapidly wound up the historian's testimony. Denise declined cross-examination, her tone and body language adequate testimony to what she thought of the witness. "The defense calls Colonel James Cannon," Hank said. The courtroom's side door opened and Cannon came through. He walked with an athletic gait and seemed to fill the room with his presence. His charcoal-gray blazer fit perfectly and his tailor had wisely not used shoulder pads. His corded neck muscles strained at the collar of his black turtleneck when he jerked his head at Gus in acknowledgment. The clerk handed him the declaration to tell the truth and he read in a voice that echoed with command and discipline. He ended with "So help me God."

Hank established Cannon's identity and his relationship to the defendant. Although they had less than two hours to prepare, Hank knew he could rely on him. "Colonel Cannon, as the wing commander at Al Kharj Air Base, did you ever order your aircrews to employ napalm?"

"No. The Air Force did not stockpile napalm or train for its use."

"Please explain."

Cannon warmed to the subject. "To begin with, napalm is one squirrelly weapon that is difficult to deliver. The canisters do not separate cleanly and often tumble and hit the underside of the aircraft. Lacking a precise trajectory, they do not provide the accuracy we demand from our weapons systems."

Hank glanced at Denise and her body language said it all. She knew. It was time to give the judges something to chew on. "To the best of your knowledge, was napalm ever used in the Gulf War?"

"The Marines did employ napalm in one operation." The gasp from the spectators was audible as the reporters in the media booth broke the news to their listeners.

"Please explain."

"The Iraqis had dug an extensive network of trenches in the desert and then filled them with oil. It was a tactic they developed in the Iran-Iraq war in 1988. When the Iranians attacked, the Iraqis ignited the oil and fried the attacking Iranians. Rather than repeat that experience, the Marines used napalm to ignite the oil. As I recall, the

Marines dropped approximately 500 canisters of Mark-77s." He thought for a moment. "I believe that was on February 23rd."

Hank couldn't help himself. "So the Iraqi tactic misfired."
"It was more like a backfire," Cannon replied.

"Colonel Cannon, you were the wing commander on February 25, 1991, at Al Kharj Air Base. What happened that night?"

"The Black Hole, that was the Special Planning Group that ran the air war out of Riyadh, called around ten P.M. local time. Sensors had picked up a mass movement of vehicles out of Kuwait City and Intelligence had confirmed that Saddam was trying to extract his army." For the next fifteen minutes, he held the courtroom spellbound as he related how he had launched every aircraft he could to pound the convoy into oblivion.

"What did you tell your pilots?" Hank asked.

"I reminded them what the Iraqis had done to the Kuwaitis and told them that should put a little hate in their hearts."

"Were you concerned about civilian casualties?"

"A commander is always concerned when innocent people are in harm's way. But we had warned the Iraqis that anyone moving in a military formation was a legitimate target. If they wanted to avoid attack, they were to stay put and look, and act, as friendly as possible. If they had to move, do it by foot and not in vehicles."

"What weapons did you employ on Mutlah Ridge?"

"Everything we could throw at them. But since it was a wide-area target, mostly five hundred-pound bombs and CBUs."

"Did you ever employ weapons of mass destruction?"

"No."

Hank turned and looked at Gus. They had come to the moment they had discussed endlessly. Now it was here, but not the way they had planned. Gus gave a sharp nod and mouthed the words "Go for it." Hank turned to Cannon.

"Was August Tyler under your command that night?"

"Yes."

"Did you order Gus Tyler to attack the convoy?"

"I asked him and he volunteered."

"Please tell the court why you wanted Gus to lead the mission."

"Gus Tyler and Toby Person were the best crew I had, and I could rely on them to do the job."

"Was Davis Armiston under your command at the time?"

"Unfortunately. He was a marginal pilot at best. We had put Toby Person in his backseat to keep him alive and only gave him the puffballs."

Gus interrupted. "Your Honor, may I confer with my counsel?" Bouchard granted his request and Hank moved over to the dock. Gus was careful to shield his mouth from the lip readers he knew were watching. "These clowns made up their minds weeks ago and it doesn't matter what Jim says." He quickly outlined what he had in mind. Hank's first reaction was to dismiss it out of hand. Then he reconsidered.

"This just got interesting," Hank conceded. He returned to the podium. "Thank you Colonel Cannon. The defense has no more questions at this time but may need to recall you to the stand at a later date."

Denise sprang to her feet, eager to get at Cannon. "Colonel, what were these 'puffballs' you spoke of?"

"The non-demanding, milk-run missions we normally reserved for the French."

Denise ignored the titter of laughter behind her. "You told your pilots" – she looked at her notes – 'that should put a little hate in your heart.' Why did you inflame your pilots to kill Iraqis?"

Cannon almost smiled at how easy it was. "I also told them to 'Bomb the livin' hell out of them and render the bastards.' It has to do with motivation. The best way to minimize casualties on all sides is to press the attack and end it as quickly as possible. Sun Tzu explained it two and a half-millennia ago in 'The Art of War.' There's absolutely nothing new under the sun, or the moon, for that matter when it comes to combat. Do it the NATO way and you kill more people."

"NATO does not 'kill more people.'"

"Kosovo, 1999," Cannon answered. "That could have been over in three nights if NATO had gone after the right targets. As it was, they dragged it out and caused many unnecessary casualties."

"History amply justifies what NATO did."

"But not the way NATO did it."

"We are not in a debate, Monsieur Cannon. Confine yourself to answering the questions."

"Ah shucks, Ma'am, you brought it up."

An alarm bell went off in Denise's mind, warning her to exercise caution. She ignored it. "You said that you chose the defendant to fly the mission because you could rely on him to 'do the job.' Exactly what was the 'job' you were referring to?"

"To stop the Iraqi army from retreating and regrouping. We wanted to fight them once, not twice."

"By your own admission, you used cluster bomb units, a weapon designed for widespread and indiscriminate killing and maiming, to do this."

"Widespread and indiscriminate killing compared to what? You ever see what a two thousand-pound JADAM does when it comes through your bedroom window? CBUs are a wide-area weapon because targets get scattered over a wide area. There's nothing indiscriminate about CBUs if the pilot presses the attack and hits his target, which is exactly what Gus did."

Denise scoffed. "From the safety of a supersonic jet at high altitude."

"CBUs are not a precision guided, stand-off weapon. You don't deliver CBUs above the Mach from forty thousand feet. You have to go subsonic and get down in the weeds and rocks, up close and personal, while the bad guys are doing their damndest to ruin your day. It's an equal opportunity chance to get killed."

The assistant prosecutor passed her a note. *This is going badly. End it.* Denise gave the hapless man a withering look as she crumpled the note and dropped it to the floor. "You testified the Iraqis had been warned not to move in vehicles and act 'as friendly as possible' if they didn't want to be attacked. How were they warned? Perhaps by the BCC World Service's broadcasts in English?"

Cannon reached into his blazer's breast pocket and pulled out a folded piece of paper. He carefully smoothed it out to reveal a leaflet the size of a dollar bill. He handed it to the clerk. "We dropped five million of these over the Iraqis. Plastered Kuwait with 'em. It's a safe conduct pass telling them to not move but if they did, to travel only on foot without weapons. The front is in Arabic with an English, French, and Farsi translation on the back."

The clerk passed the leaflet to Denise. She glanced at it and dropped it disdainfully to the floor. "Are we to assume this reached the Iraqis?"

Cannon answered with a straight face. "Not this particular leaflet. But Intelligence reported the Iraqis were using the rest of the five million as toilet paper. We don't know if they read them or not, but we're pretty sure they made contact." Laughter swept the courtroom.

Denise froze, now fully aware of the threat in front of her. She had never met anyone like him, confident and eager to engage in combat under any circumstances. There was no doubt that he was playing with her and wanted more. She glanced at her notes. "Colonel Cannon, what is your current profession?"

"I'm an aerial assassin."

Denise looked at him in horror, certain that he had spoken the absolute truth. He looked back, much like an eager rottweiler contemplating its next meal, and she knew, without doubt, that she was on the menu. "I have no more questions at this time."

"Monsieur Sutherland, do you have any questions?" Bouchard asked.

Hank retrieved the leaflet and handed it to the clerk. "We enter the safe conduct pass as defense exhibit nine." Bouchard waited for an objection from Denise, which did not come. The other two judges nodded and he ordered it entered. "Thank you, Colonel Cannon," Hank said. "We have no further questions at this time."

Denise came to her feet, still in an obvious state of shock. "If it may please the court. As it is late and tomorrow is New Year's Eve, may we adjourn until Monday?"

"The defense has no objection but would prefer to reconvene on Wednesday," Hank said.

"Your Honors," Denise replied, "the prosecution sees no reason for more delays at this time." The judges conferred and Bouchard recessed the trial until Monday.

"Justice delayed is justice denied," Hank muttered, his voice heavy with sarcasm.

* * * * *

The two men met in the holding cell and clasped hands as the defense team crowded around, all eager to share the moment. "A fine mess you got yourself into here, Gus," Cannon said.

"Thanks for coming."

"Wouldn't have missed it for the world. How's Clare doing?"

"Not good. She's in the Mayo undergoing an experimental procedure that Max Westcot's people came up with."

Aly stood against the wall with Catherine and listened as the two men talked.

For a few moments, they totally dominated Aly's world and she truly understood the words "bigger than life." She loved Jason unreservedly, but she was attracted to the sheer animal magnetism radiating from Cannon. Hank stood alone, quietly smiling to himself. And there was Gus, unchanging and unafraid of his future. "Where do they find them?" she asked Catherine.

"I wish I knew," Catherine replied.

Aly was back in time, remembering when Jason took his reenlistment oath. "They're a band of brothers, true to each other."

"And to us," Catherine added. Hank edged over to her side and held her hand.

Cannon turned to Hank. "You do good work, counselor." He handed the lawyer a videocassette. "I believe you were looking for this. Mutlah Ridge." It was the airborne video from Gus and Toby's attack on the convoy.

Hank carefully checked the cassette to make sure the seals were still intact. They were and he exhaled loudly in relief. Slowly, a big smile spread across his face as he held the cassette up. "Now it really gets sporting. Thank you."

Cannon nodded and looked at Gus. "Anytime you want to come to work for me, just tell General Hammerly. Well, is there anything else I can do for you?"

"Any chance you can help us find Toby Person?" Hank asked.

Cannon looked interested. "Where is he?"

"Lost some place in Southern Sudan," Hank replied.

"He's with Jason," Gus added. "I believe Max Westcot is looking for them."

Cannon thought for a moment. "I can help." The three men looked at each other, an unspoken understanding between them.

"Would someone tell me what's going on here?" Aly demanded.

"Sorry, young lady," Cannon replied. "It's way above your pay grade."

Southern Sudan

Landerrost switched off the radio and closed the cover of the control panel when Jason came through the door of the compound's communications shack looking clean and rested. He had collapsed after taking a shower and slept all day Thursday in air-conditioned comfort, only waking in the early evening. "How's Toby doing?" Jason asked.

"Resting comfortably," Landerrost replied. "Leon is taking good care of him." It was an understatement. Leon, a scrawny Frenchman who had learned his tradecraft as a medic in the French Foreign Legion, had pushed everyone aside the moment he saw Toby and went to work. Within an hour, he had pumped the missionary full of antibiotics, cleaned his wounds, replaced many of the sutures, and bathed him while carrying on a loud, and very obscene tirade about incompetent doctors.

"I can't thank you enough," Jason said. "I hope the antibiotics do the trick."

The Afrikaner shrugged. "We gave him all we had. But not to worry. I got a message out and a helicopter will be here tomorrow or Saturday night at the latest. It will fly you to Addis Abba. From there, the company has laid on a jet to fly you to Europe. You should be back in Holland no later than Monday."

Jason glanced at the small radio. "Isn't that one of those new jam-proof satellite transceivers?" Landerrost didn't answer. "NATO doesn't even have it yet."

"We're not NATO," Landerrost replied. He handed Jason a printout. "This came in about an hour ago." Jason read the short message and his face paled. "I'll leave it up to you to tell the Reverend."

"Do I have a choice?" Jason answered.

* * * * *

Jason held the message for Toby to read while Leon hovered in the background. Toby shook with a slight tremor as his eyes closed. "I should have never left the mission." His voice was almost inaudible. "I could have saved them."

Jason bathed his head with a wet cloth, feeling the fever that was wracking his body. "We only know the Sudanese Army over- ran the mission. We don't know how many survived."

"They're dead. This is Africa. The mission . . . gone."

"Then we'll rebuild," Jason said. Toby quieted and fell asleep.

"Let him rest," Leon said.

"How bad is he?" Jason asked.

"I've seen worse, but they all died. I'm going to bed. Call me if his fever goes up." Jason sat with Toby, occasionally bathing his head, and checking his temperature. It was still over 103 degrees and showed no signs of relenting. He dozed off.

The intercom buzzed, jolting him awake. "The fuckin' bloody kaffirs are back," Landerrost said. "We need to talk. I'm in the radio shack." Jason acknowledged the call and hurried outside, only to stop dead in his tracks. The first light of dawn etched the far horizon, and the compound was ringed with a fiery glow as an acrid smoke washed around him. He covered his mouth and nose and ran for the communications shack, finally breaking clear of the smoke. He blinked his tears away. The tall grass that surrounded the compound was on fire and he could see dark figures running through it with torches, feeding the fire and keeping it alive. A flash and a geyser of earth erupted skyward when one of the soldiers stumbled into the minefield.

Instinctively, Jason ran for cover, trying to reach the cement-block communications shack. An incoming mortar shrieked overhead and Jason fell to the ground, his arms wrapped over his head. The communications shack erupted, engulfing him in a wave of smoke and debris.

35

Southern Sudan

Jason walked through the still smoldering wreckage of the compound's communication shack in the early morning light. He pushed part of the roof aside and stared at Landerrost's dismembered body. "One mortar round," he said to himself. "Over here!" He waited but no one answered his call. "What the hell?" He worked his way out of the wreckage but didn't see anyone. He headed for the infirmary where he heard loud voices arguing in Afrikaans. The eight men crowded around a desk fell silent when he entered. "I found Landerrost's body and need some help."

The men ignored him and kept talking among themselves. Jason listened without saying a word, and within minutes sensed what was wrong. Without Landerrost, they were a leaderless mob, pulling apart in their confusion and fear. Finally, they decided to negotiate their way out, but no one was sure exactly how. Only Leon, the medic, said it was a bad idea. "No one can negotiate with those bastards. They only understand what comes out of the muzzle of a gun." He was shouted down and Simon, Landerrost's old second-in-command, said he would try to make contact on a walkie-talkie.

Jason held back and spoke to Leon, anxious to find out exactly what they had to defend the compound. "There's just the eight of you, right?" Leon nodded an answer and Jason asked about weapons. Leon's reply was not encouraging. They had a heavy 7.62 mm machine gun, fifteen M16 assault rifles along with a healthy supply of ammunition, two hunting rifles, and four 9 mm Browning automatic pistols. "Any dynamite?" Jason asked. The medic estimated they had three or four cases. "Show me the minefield," Jason ordered.

The grass fires were still smoldering as they walked the compound's perimeter. Jason stopped, taking the lay of the land. Because of the fires, he had a clear field of view that reached to the main road approximately a kilometer away. He could see a truck, a personnel carrier, and soldiers milling about. "Why don't the bastards attack?" Leon asked.

"They know there's a minefield between us and them," Jason answered. "I count fourteen of them and since they only fired one mortar round, I expect they're waiting for reinforcements."

"You've done this before?" Leon asked.

"Oh, yeah," Jason replied. He was starting to take charge.

Île St-Louis

Chrestien Du Milan fumed at the summons from the Comtessa Eugenie but his strong sense of survival, not to mention common sense, urged him not to ignore it. Consequently, he dutifully presented himself on Friday morning at the Comtessa's magnificently restored mansion. He carefully hid his impatience as he waited for the old woman to receive him. Finally, the Comtessa was ready and he was escorted into her bedroom. He rushed over to the bed and bussed her cheeks before being waved to a nearby chair. A butler pushed a teacart to his side and poured him a cup of coffee.

The old woman shifted her weight against the pillow and a maid hurried over to adjust it and rearrange the exquisitely embroidered bedspread. The Comtessa waved the maid and butler out of the room. She eyed Chrestien as she sipped her tea. "It is not going well in The Hague," she began.

Chrestien sighed. "Nor in the United Nations."

"Nor here," she added. They sipped in silence. "We may have to take protective measures . . . what is the terrible expression the Americans are so fond of?"

"I believe the words you are seeking are 'damage control.'"

"Ah, yes. Damage control. There may have to be sacrifices."

Chrestien knew where the conversation was going. The Chinese gambit was stalled in the UN and they had to prepare for the worst. They needed a scapegoat and it was time to bargain. "Perhaps you are thinking of sacrifices in New York."

The Comtessa gave him a cold look. "My son . . ."

"Forgive me, Comtessa. I had forgotten he was our ambassador to the United Nations."

"I was thinking of The Hague," the old woman said. "But only if we should we fail there, of course."

"Of course," Chrestien said. They were both on the same page. "But if there is also failure in the United Nations, there also will have to be repercussions here."

"Of course," the Comtessa said, thinking of another name. "Perhaps you should speak to Renée. I do hope she is bored with Henri."

"I will see her tomorrow evening."

The Hague

Rank after rank of protestors, their arms linked, marched passed the Palace of the ICC. They were laughing and joking until they neared the banks of TV cameras clustered in the forecourt. Then their shouts grew loud and angry as they were herded past the lines of police blocking their way into the forecourt. "Hang the bastard now! Hang the bastard now!" they chanted. Occasionally, a protestor would break free and toss a placard over the police line to litter the forecourt.

Marci Lennox stood well back, next to the entrance as she spoke into a microphone. "The Dutch police cannot enter the court building as it is an international zone that enjoys extraterritoriality, much like a foreign embassy, and is beyond their jurisdiction. However, the Dutch have reinforced their barricades to ensure the protestors stay well clear. Fortunately, this protest is more orderly and controlled than the one we experienced on Thursday. But emotions are high and the anger is growing."

A lone church bell tolled in the distance as the last of the protestors marched by. "It is now noon on this cold and blustery New Year's Eve," Marci said. The cameras swung as another, much larger mass of people approached the court. But this group was different. They were all well-dressed and walked in somber silence as their leaders carried a photo of Gus surrounded by a wreath of flowers. The cordon of police parted and the flower bearers carefully placed the wreath in the forecourt. Then they passed on. "The banner on the flowers is in Dutch. It says, 'Justice for the innocent.' This, I am told, is the way the Dutch show the world how to disagree."

Southern Sudan

Jason watched the Russian-built helicopter, code named Hip by NATO, as it approached. It hovered above the compound and slowly pivoted, sweeping the area. The tan paint and roundel announced it was from the Sudanese Air Force. "Doing a little reconnaissance," Jason grumbled to Leon. The helicopter settled to the ground and the five-bladed rotor spun down. Six heavily armed soldiers jumped out and set up a defensive perimeter. "Trusting souls," Jason said. The man who got off next was wearing a Sudanese Army uniform and a white kaffiyeh, the traditional headdress of the Middle East. "A colonel," Jason added.

Leon keyed on the kaffiyeh. "He's a Wahhabi. Not good."

The colonel was a tall, heavy-set man and needed a shave. He looked around contemptuously and fingered the flap on his holster. Satisfied that all was secure, he barked a command in Arabic and the soldiers lowered their weapons. "Now that's an arrogant bastard if I've ever seen one," Jason said.

Simon, still holding a walkie-talkie walked towards the colonel and extended his hand in friendship. The colonel ignored it. "I am Colonel Nasir al-Rahman. You are?"

"Simon Dreyer, the assistant manager. Welcome to Westcot Five."

"What do you want to talk about?"

"We have been directed by our headquarters to leave," Simon lied. "Of course, anyone who assists us will be amply compensated by Westcot Oil."

Al-Rahman grunted. "Unfortunately, I cannot negotiate what you desire. However, if you will come with me, my general will hear what you have to say."

Jason took the colonel's measure. "I don't trust the bastard any further than I can throw him."

"If that far," Leon muttered.

"I'm leaving," the colonel said. "Stay or come." He spun around, issued fresh orders, and climbed on board the helicopter. The turbo shaft engines spun up as the soldiers hurried to load. Simon was the last to climb aboard.

* * * * *

"He's been gone too long," Jason said. It was Friday evening and four hours had passed since Simon had left with the Sudanese Army colonel.

"It was a dumb idea," Leon grumbled. He pointed to the north. "There. A helicopter."

"It's a Hip," Jason said. "I think it's the same one." The helicopter settled at the far side of the compound, the side cargo door slid back, and a bundle was thrown off. The door closed and the helicopter took off as Jason ran towards the bundle that was wrapped in a blanket.

Leon was right beside him when they reached what looked like a body. The two men quickly unwrapped the bloody blanket and examined what was left of Simon. "God damn them to hell!" Leon shouted. "They cut off his head." Four other men joined them and stared at the body.

"What do we do now?" one asked.

Jason took charge. "We start digging."

36

The Hague

The lights were on when Hank and Catherine walked into the office early Saturday morning. Aly was sitting at her desk reading Friday's edition of Le Monde. "Happy New Year," she said, her heart not really in it.

Hank and Catherine chorused a "Happy New Year" back. "What are the Froggies saying about us now?" Hank asked.

"They called the court 'besieged' and spanked Du Milan for the way she handled Cannon. One writer said they've got the wrong man in the dock and nominated Cannon."

Catherine laughed. "I wouldn't want to be the cop who tried to arrest him."

The TV in the corner came on of its own accord and Cassandra's image filled the screen. "Would you be kind enough to turn on your percom?" she said. The screen went blank.

"How did she do that?" Hank wondered.

He opened the communicator's cover and Cassandra's voice came over the small loudspeaker. "Mr. Westcot asked me to tell you that one of his teams found Jason and the Reverend Person. They are safe and are at a Westcot compound approximately one hundred miles north of Juba. Jason is fine but the Reverend is badly wounded. Mr. Westcot is sending a helicopter to pick them up and expects they will arrive in The Hague late Monday afternoon."

Aly threw her arms around Hank and hugged him for all she was worth. He had trouble breathing. "Cassandra," Hank finally managed to choke, "will Person be able to testify?"

"I believe so," Cassandra replied.

Hank pointed at his office. "Aly, please join us." She quickly filled a carafe with coffee and followed them inside. She filled Hank's coffee mug. "We have to make a decision," Hank began. "Do we press ahead and put Gus on the stand Monday or do we delay until the Reverend is here and ready to testify? I can call four or five more witnesses and blow a lot of legal smoke, but that would only increase Bouchard's blood pressure and might be counterproductive."

"After Cannon's testimony," Catherine said, "we have momentum with the media. I don't think we want to lose it."

"There is much gossip in the building," Aly added. "The court is very sensitive to public opinion and the demonstrations yesterday upset the presidents, especially Relieu." Hank nodded at the news. The Dutch secretaries' mutual protection and gossip society was alive and functioning well.

Catherine considered the tradeoffs. "Gus has definitely connected with the audience and they want to hear him. I think he will play very well with the media once he's on the stand."

"Is he ready?" Aly asked.

"We've been preparing for weeks," Hank replied. "We've got all weekend to polish his testimony. He's ready – and eager."

Aly was still worried. "What will Du Milan do to him on cross-examination?"

"After going through the grinder with Cannon," Hank answered, "she'll be tiptoeing very carefully, which is one reason to press ahead now, before she regains her confidence. If Gus does falter, I'll jump in with an objection and give him enough time to recover. If that doesn't work, I should be able to recover on redirect. But he's not going to stumble."

"Put him on the stand Monday," Catherine advised. "Maintain the momentum and finish it off with the Reverend on Tuesday. Use Person like Du Milan used Schumann." Aly nodded in agree- ment.

"Let's go talk to Gus," Hank said. He looked at Aly. "You want to tell him the good news about Jason and Toby?"

"Oh, yes," she whispered.

Southern Sudan

Jason led Leon and the small band of six Afrikaners around the perimeter of the compound while Hon and Paride followed a few steps behind, not sure of the South Africans. The big American stopped when they reached the runway on the eastern side of the compound and jumped into a freshly dug foxhole. It was a defensive fighting position, or DFP for short, and little more than a rectangular-shaped, shoulder-deep hole scooped out by a backhoe. "DFPs are wonderful things," Jason said. "But don't get too attached to the one you're in and remember we got more for fallback." He pointed out the deep shaft, approximately a foot in diameter sunk in the bottom corner of the DFP. "If someone lobs a grenade at you, don't throw it back, kick it in here. Take cover, protect your ears, and open your mouth. You're going to have visitors who think the grenade morted you. Hopefully, you'll be able to convince them you're alive and well."

He showed them how to quickly climb out and roll into the hollow depression that had been scraped out immediately behind the DFP. "This is for temporary cover only." He stood, dusted his hands, and traced a crude map in the earth. He started by sketching in the White Nile that ran south to north. Working eastward, he drew in a swampy area. He skipped a space and made an oval for the compound. Next to the eastern side of the compound, he drew in the mile-long packed-gravel runway that ran parallel to the Nile. On the far side of the runway, he drew in the minefield that arced around to the swamp and sealed them off. He skipped another space and scratched in the road that was located a kilometer to the east, and, like the runway, ran parallel to the Nile.

"The bad guys are on the road and will have to cross the area they conveniently torched last night. That puts them in the open and we can get in a little target practice. If that doesn't send them into reverse, it should speed them up and they'll charge right into the minefield. If they get through the mines and reach the runway, they'll come under our overlapping fields of fire." He drew in a series of five Xs stretched along the compound's side of the runway. "These five DFPs next to the runway are approximately a hundred meters apart and are our main line of defense."

He drew in ten more Xs scattered throughout the compound that formed a rough triangle using the original five Xs along the runway as the base. The last X, the apex of the triangle, was less than fifty meters from the marshy area that led into the swamp. "If we can't stop them at the runway, or if they flank us, we fall back into the compound. Give ground progressively, and fall back to the DFP immediately behind you." He held up a walkie-talkie. "Everyone has one. Stay in contact so we can coordinate our actions and know where the other teams are."

"What happens if we can't hold the compound?" Leon asked.

"Then we're having a very bad day and we fall back into the swamp." He tapped the last X. "Whoever gets here first covers the other teams so they can escape into the swamp."

"There's crocs out there," Leon grumbled.

"No one said it would be easy," Jason replied. He answered a barrage of questions, and when he was satisfied they all had the big picture, broke the Afrikaners into three teams. He assigned each team to a DFP in the forward line next to the runway, leaving the DFPs on the end unmanned. "Leon, you're with me. We go where needed."

One of the Afrikaners gestured at Hon and Lam. "What about them?"

"They're the reserve with the machine gun," Jason explained.

Leon exploded in a torrent of French invective that defied translation. "You're giving them the machine gun?" he finally managed in English.

"You need to see something," Jason said. He motioned for the men to follow and led them to the nearby Wolf Turbo that was armed with the heavy machine gun. "Hon, blindfold Paride." The Dinka did as ordered and Jason said, "Paride, you climb aboard and strip the machine gun. Hon, you mix up the pieces. Paride, you put it back together. Go!" The men watched as Paride jumped into the truck and field stripped the heavy machine gun, dropping the components to the floor. Hon was right behind him and mixed them up. Without missing a beat, Paride fell to the floor and sorted the pieces. He then quickly reassembled the weapon. "Any questions?" Jason asked.

"Good enough for me, Boss," one of the Afrikaners said.

* * * * *

"Boss, wake up." Jason stirred and blinked, coming awake. Leon was hovering over him waving a handheld VHF radio in excitement. "It's the helicopter. Fifteen minutes out." The relief in the Frenchman's voice was almost painful to hear.

Jason checked his watch. He had been asleep less that two hours and it was still Saturday. "As promised. How's Toby?"

"Much the same," the medic answered. "It looks like we won't need your little holes in the ground."

"I can live with that," Jason said. They stepped outside into a starlit night. "Look at that," Jason whispered, awestruck by the beauty arching above him. He heard the beat of the helicopter's rotor in the far distance. "Tell them to land on the west side of the compound and not the runway." He strained to see the helicopter but it was flying lights out. For the first time in what seemed like years, he truly relaxed. They were going home.

Before Leon could key the VHF radio a streak of flame shot across the sky and homed on the helicopter. "Merde!" Leon shouted. The shoulder-held surface-to-air missile scored a direct hit on the left intake of the inbound Puma and the aircraft disappeared in a fireball.

"Happy fuckin' New Year," Jason growled.

The Hague

Gus and Hank huddled over the small table in Gus's cell on Sunday afternoon. They had been working on Gus's upcoming testimony for over three hours, and their faces were bathed in sweat. "Why's it so damn hot in here?" Hank moaned.

Cassandra chuckled, her voice sweet and clear over the percom's loudspeaker. "They're still bugging the cell so I'm playing with them. I think they've figured it out and turned up the heat in retaliation."

"What are you doing?" Hank demanded.

"Well," she admitted, "rather than just jam the bugs in the cell, I've captured the prison's entire surveillance system and linked it to the Sunday Morning talk shows in the States. That's all they can see or hear. They are very upset."

Gus roared with laughter. "Talk about cruel and unusual punishment!"

Hank shook his head. "You've been locked up too long. Open the door and let's get some cool air in here. We can get back to this later." Gus did as the lawyer asked and propped the door open. The corridor was full of Sunday visitors and before too long, Gus's fellow inmates were bringing their friends and families by to introduce them to the jail's most famous prisoner. Gus was very courteous and shook hands with them all. He tried out the Dutch he had learned while locked up, and that seemed to please them even more. "What do you make of all this?" Hank asked Cassandra.

"The Dutch like him," she answered. Hank nodded in satisfaction – their strategy was working. He almost laughed when an elderly Dutch couple asked Gus to pose with them for a photo. Digital cameras magically appeared and Gus was the star of the moment. "Hank," Cassandra said, "fresh satellite coverage from the Sudan is coming in. It looks like the Sudanese Army attacked Reverend Person's mission."

"How bad is it?" Hank asked.

"Most of the buildings have been burned or knocked down, and I've counted over a hundred bodies. There are tank track marks all over the ground, which is why we think it was the Sudanese Army."

"Not good," Hank muttered. "We'll have to tell Gus." He caught the pilot's attention and motioned him back into the cell. Gus closed the door and Cassandra quickly repeated the news.

"Damn," Gus said. Anger etched his words. "This never would have happened if Jason hadn't gone down there to get Toby."

"Don't go there," Hank cautioned. "This has nothing to do with Jason or you. The killing in Africa started years ago and, sooner or later, this was going to happen. We can't stop it. Only the Africans can, so don't go blaming yourself just because you happen to be standing too close to it."

Gus accepted the truth of it and asked, "Any word on Jason and Toby?"

"It's not good," Cassandra warned them. "The helicopter should have arrived at the compound last night and returned to Addis Ababa by now. We haven't heard anything."

Hank fell silent and considered the options. "Maybe we need to delay and not put you on the stand tomorrow."

Gus stared at the closed cell door, seeing all the people on the other side. "Hank, you are one incurable optimist. We've been over this before. Whether Toby shows or not, the verdict is in, two to one to convict."

"Who's the one?" Hank asked.

Gus didn't hesitate. "Della Sante. Watch her face when Bouchard or Du Milan are talking. She detests old Gaston and hates Du Milan. I think it's an Italian thing, keeping the younger, more attractive woman in her place. Hank, we've got momentum so let's keep pressing ahead. Its damn the torpedoes time."

Hank's fingers drummed a tattoo on the table, his eyes hard. "Two to one," he said to himself. Gus's take was the same as Catherine's.

Southern Sudan

Jason sat at the workbench and dusted off the small satellite communications radio Leon had dug out of the wrecked radio shack. Other than a dent in the cover, it appeared to be good condition. "It should work," he told the Frenchman. Leon snorted and cursed. Although Jason didn't understand a word, his meaning was loud and clear. Jason turned it on and the power light glowed red. "The battery's almost dead." Leon cursed again. "Hold on," Jason said. He pressed the button activating the emergency locator beacon and waited. The transmit light flashed green for a few seconds as the power light dimmed and went out. "It's dead," Jason said.

Leon swore again when a burst of submachine gun fire echoed in the night. Jason shook his head. "Maybe a kilometer away," he told Leon. "I hope it's not Hon." The Dinka had been gone for over three hours reconnoitering the area and Jason was worried. The two men walked outside as the rattle of an AK47 reached the compound. They froze as more gunfire erupted. It slowly tapered off, only to re-ignite. "They waste a lot of ammo," Jason said.

"There," Leon said, pointing into the night. Hon emerged out of the shadows and walked slowly towards them, exhausted but unhurt. Jason handed him a water bottle and waited while he took a long drink and caught his breath.

Hon pointed at the road. "I get close and see many soldiers. I count sixty-three but there are many more. I count eight trucks and two tanks like that." He pointed to the Wolf Turbo.

"Armored cars," Jason said. "Is the dirt soft or hard?"

Hon tapped the earth. "Same there, same here."

Jason analyzed the threat. Based on the number of men Hon had counted and the eight trucks, he calculated they were facing approximately two hundred men. Besides the two armored cars, what else did they have? They had at least one mortar but were reluctant to use it. Did that mean they were short on mortar rounds? What about heavy machine guns or light artillery? He decided the heavy machine guns would be mounted on the armored cars and the soldiers would carry RPGs, rocket propelled grenades. He didn't like the numbers.

Neither did Leon. "We can shoot the bastards on foot, but what about the armored cars?"

"Who can handle dynamite?" Jason asked.

37

The Hague

Gus stared into the mirror in the holding cell and carefully adjusted his tie. He could see the worried look on Therese Derwent's face in the reflection. "I know you will be taking the witness stand before too long, maybe today," the psychiatrist said. The worry in her voice was obvious. "Du Milan will try to make you angry and say rash things. But remember, she is afraid of you."

Gus wasn't sure if the psychiatrist was being rational. "She is?"

"Trust me, she fears you deeply. When she tries to bait you, ask her why she's doing it."

"A witness can't get away with that in a court. A judge won't allow it."

"After all this time and you still don't realize you are not in an American courtroom. I must go and take my seat." She called for a guard and disappeared.

What does she know? Gus thought. He had to get to Hank. He got his chance ten minutes later when he stepped into the dock and Hank came over for a last minute conference. "Something's going down. Normally, prison guards escort me back and forth. This morning, the Dutch turned me over to two of the court's security cops and they brought me here. They've also got Derwent as part of the team escorting me."

Hank thought for a moment. "The Dutch know something, but what is it?" Then it came to him. "Oh. They expect Bouchard to rule on the Iraqi petition today, and are probably worried about a suicide attempt."

"Derwent should know me better than that," Gus said. His face turned rock hard. "Bouchard is doing a little softening up for the prosecution, weaken the opposition before the attack. So what? We knew the ruling on Iraq was coming. As far as I'm concerned, it's a non-event."

"I'll have to respond," Hank said. "Give me the high-sign if you're upset and need a break. I'll have a sudden case of diarrhea."

"That's logical, considering this is a shitty deal."

Hank was certain the pilot was going to be fine. "Let's do it. Just like we rehearsed." Aly motioned Hank back to the table in time for the judges' entrance.

Bouchard adjusted his glasses and looked at the audience, clearly savoring the moment. "The court has reviewed the Iraqi petition for transfer of the defendant to their custody to stand trial for a war crime committed prior to February 25, 1991. This request is unprecedented as the court has never been asked to transfer a person back to a member Party. Our jurisdiction is 'complementary' to national criminal jurisdictions, and as such, national courts have the 'first bit of the apple.' It is only after national courts relinquish their interest in a crime that the International Criminal Court has jurisdiction and a person is transferred to our custody. As the crime in question is not the one before the court, the court must defer to Iraq's primacy. Therefore, the defendant will be transferred to Iraqi jurisdiction upon completion of this trial if found not guilty, or upon completion of his sentence should he be found guilty."

For a moment, the courtroom was held in stunned silence. Then a woman gasped and started to cry as six reporters ran from the room. Gus sat in the dock, his gazed fixed calmly on Bouchard. Hank came to his feet. "Your Honor, I am stunned by this perversion of the court's principle of complementarity. Need I remind the court that Colonel Tyler is being held as a Panamanian citizen? Iraq should request his extradition from Panama."

"Your honor, if I may?" This from Denise. "The law is a two-way street. All member states must honor a warrant for arrest from the court. Therefore, the court must honor a warrant for arrest from any member state."

Hank humphed. "First bite of the apple and now two-way streets. Is justice a gastronomic endeavor or a problem in traffic control? The defense reserves the right of appeal."

"File your motion," Bouchard said, refusing to look at Gus.

"Indeed," Hank said.

"Please call your next witness."

"The defense calls Henri Scullanois to the stand."

Bouchard banged his gavel. "We've been over this ground before. Call your next witness."

"Where's Henri?" a woman called from the audience.

Gus held up his hand and mouthed the words "Thank you" to the woman. She returned his look, concern writ large on her face, as two guards escorted her out.

"The defense calls Colonel August Tyler to the stand."

"The defendant will remain in the dock," Bouchard ordered. Gus stood and the clerk administered the oath.

Hank turned to Gus. "Good morning, Colonel Tyler."

"Good morning," Gus replied, still standing.

"The defendant may sit down," Bouchard said.

"If it's all the same," Gus replied, "I prefer to stand."

"As the defendant wishes," Bouchard grumped.

Hank led Gus through the pro forma questions documenting Gus's background and training. The lawyer took his time establishing the pilot's credentials and spent over an hour taking the court through the countless technical details of planning a mission and a standard pre-mission briefing. Slowly, a consummate professional emerged and the image of a fighter pilot as a devil-may-care, irresponsible cowboy was put to rest. There was no doubt that Gus Tyler was a highly trained and proficient technician who flew, and fought, by the rules.

Satisfied that he had a solid base, Hank turned to the war in Iraq and established that Gus was acting under lawful orders, and attacking trucks and vehicles was standard practice consistent with the rules of engagement. When asked about attacking the Scud and bombing the bus in the desert, Gus answered, "I intended to do a visual recce, that's going to take a look, and report back. But when they shot at me, I was free to attack under the ROE."

Rather than belabor that incident, Hank came to the heart of the matter. "We're you ordered to fly a mission on the night of February 25, 1991?"

"Colonel Cannon asked me if I wanted it, and I volunteered."

"Did you visually acquire the target before attacking?"

Gus replied, "No. It was dark and they were running without lights. We first acquired them on radar and later through the forward looking infrared when we were closer in." Hank asked if they had seen anything, visually or electronically, that could be interpreted as a recognition signal? "They did launch two Gadflies at us. That's one awesome surface-to-air missile that can come down into the weeds to get you. I guess that a recognition of sorts but I wouldn't call it friendly." A titter of laughter echoed over the courtroom.

"Was this before you attacked?"

"Yes. We were still inbound, about ten miles out."

"At this time," Hank said, "I would like to show the court the airborne videotape from the mission that was recorded through your aircraft's heads-up-display."

"Objection," Denise called. "Defense has not established the validity of the videotape."

"How careless of me," Hank answered. He handed Gus a piece of paper and the videocassette. "Do you recognize this form and cassette?"

"The form is the certification I signed when I turned over the tape. This is the cassette and you can see the seal is still intact."

"Do you certify that this videotape is the complete and unaltered airborne video recorded during the mission in question?"

"I do," Gus replied.

"Your Honor," Denise protested. "This is ridiculous. The defendant could be lying."

"The court's technical staff can examine the cassette to determine if it has been altered," Hank replied. "Or the learned Prosecutor can produce witnesses or evidence to impeach the tape's validity." He paused and snapped his fingers. "Darn. I forgot. The witness lists are closed."

A man in the audience called, "Where's Henri?" Two security guards were on him and hustling him out the door.

Bouchard conferred with Della Sante and Richter. "The court recorder can verify the integrity of the seal." Hank handed the cassette to the recorder who quickly conformed the seal was in place and the cassette sealed. "The defense may present the videotape," Bouchard intoned. Denise started to object, but Bouchard motioned her to silence. "The Prosecutor may call additional witnesses as appropriate."

The room darkened and the screen descended from the ceiling. The greenish image of the infrared appeared surrounded by the

A Far Justice

lighted symbology of the HUD. Gus and Toby's voices were loud and clear over the noise of the engines. Gus slipped back in time as the video played and, for a few brief moments, he was there, condemned to relive it again.

February 25, 1991

"Check out Riyadh," Gus said as the F-15 Strike Eagle climbed out of the airbase at Al Kharj in Saudi Arabia. "Lit up like a Christmas tree."

"No can say Christmas in the land of Saud," Toby said with an Arabic accent.

"Don't they know there's a war going on," Gus replied.

"Allah's will be done."

Gus shook his head. "Right. And I suppose it's a good day to die."

"They do believe that," Toby said matter-of-factly.

Gus heard an unusual tone in his backseater's voice, almost as if he were reciting a basic truism of life. "For them, not for us," Gus said. There was no reply. "How's the Arabic coming? Still talking to the locals?"

"Every chance I get," Toby replied.

Their ground controller sent them over to the Airborne Command Post frequency. Gus checked in and they listened to the radio chatter. It was a very busy night in the air war. Then Toby saw it on his radar. "Got 'em." They were over sixty nautical miles away, still over the Gulf and abeam Kuwait City, but the Strike Eagle's synthetic aperture radar had reached out and found the convoy. The digitally enhanced screen showed an extremely narrow, very long, and very bright line snaking its way northward. Toby's left hand played with the hand controller, the joystick on his side console, while he punched numbers into the keyboard on the up-front controller with his right forefinger. The radar image cycled and became more distinct.

"Look at that," Toby said in a low voice. "They got to be puttin' out one humongous heat signature." He checked the FLIR, their forward-looking infrared, but they were still out of range.

Gus turned on their airborne videotape recorder that captured whatever he saw through the heads-up-display and heard through his headset. He keyed the transmit button and called the airborne command post. "Moonbeam, Driver One. Any word on my wingman?" Gus's wingman, Skid, had to switch aircraft for a maintenance problem and was late taking off. Gus was hoping he could catch up before they entered the target area.

"Negative, Driver One," Moonbeam replied.

"Rog," Gus acknowledged. He and Toby were going to attack the convoy alone.

Toby was all business as he worked the radar and described the target. "The main convoy is about two to three miles long, pretty well bunched up, moving at about fifteen miles an hour. Got some fast runners out front beating feet for home."

"Probably the high rollers in the Ferraris they stole from the Kuwaitis," Gus allowed.

Toby ignored him. "It looks like the head of the convoy is already across the border but there's a whole lot of slow pokes falling behind." He decreased the range on the radar and the long, bright string broke into a string of dots and dashes. "I'm breaking out the bigger stuff, probably trucks or tanks."

"Or mobile SAMs," Gus said. The Iraqis were reported to have Soviet-made SA-9 and SA-16 surface-to-air missiles, both highly dangerous to low-flying aircraft.

"No one said this would be easy," Toby replied.

"Never fly in the same cockpit with someone braver than yourself," Gus decided.

Toby moved the crosshairs on his display over a very bright return at the head of the main mass of vehicles. "That's our target."

"Fence check," Gus said as he descended into the cloud deck below them. Both men ran a checklist, readying the Strike Eagle for attack. Most of it was a double check to make sure all the switches were in the right position, but it was also a mental trigger, focusing them on the task at hand, which in this case was to destroy as many of vehicles and enemy soldiers as they could. Gus called up the armament display and selected bombs. "Ripple three Snakes," he told Toby.

"Sounds like a plan," Toby replied. The Mark-82 Snake Eyes they were carrying might have been 'dumb' but the two men and the Strike Eagle were not.

Gus dropped the big jet down to three hundred feet and flew up the Khwar 'Abd Allah, the estuary leading into the marshes of southern Iraq. "Moonbeam," he radioed when they were over the marsh, "Driver One feet dry."

"More or less," Toby quipped from the backseat.

"Roger, Driver One," Moonbeam replied. "You're cleared hot into the area." Gus nudged the throttle forward and the airspeed marker on his HUD touched 500 knots. Every second, they were three football fields closer to the fleeing convoy.

"Forty miles out," Toby said. Then, "Four minutes." The jet's TEWS, the tactical electronic warfare suite, came alive and shrieked, warning them that a hostile radar was tracking them. "It's a monopulse radar," Toby said tersely. "Probably a SA-11 Gadfly."

"Where the hell did that come from?" Gus wondered. The Gadfly was a very dangerous surface-to-air missile because of its guidance and tracking radar and ability to follow an aircraft down to fifty feet above the ground.

"A little lower would be nice."

"It is night out there," Gus muttered.

"The TFR is working fine," Toby said. The TFR was the terrain following radar. "And nothing is wrong with the FLIR."

It was true. The contrast on the forward-looking infrared display was unusually good. Gus squeaked the jet down to a hundred feet above the terrain. The TEWS protested louder. "Sweet Jesus," he said.

"He ain't gonna help," Toby said. "Just row the boat and I'll deliver the mail." Gus dropped to fifty feet and nudged the throttles forward until their airspeed was rooted on 540 knots. Now they were eating up the distance to the convoy at 911 feet a second. Toby updated the system, constantly refining the targeting solution. He hit the EMIS switch, putting the radar in standby and cutting off the electronic signature they were broadcasting. The TEWS shifted signals, warning them that a radar-guided SAM was locked on and coming their way. The TEWS automatically sent a burst of energy out to jam the hostile radar and dropped bundles of chaff in their wake. The missile flashed by their left wing, missing them by eighty feet. It exploded harmlessly behind them.

Gus scanned the sky, looking for a second missile. He found it at their four o'clock position just as its rocket motor burned out. He lost visual contact but he knew where it was. He turned into the missile, putting it at his two o'clock position and waited a fraction of a second for the missile to follow. He pulled up sharply, turned into the missile, and loaded the Strike Eagle with eight *G*s as he slammed the big jet back down to earth. Gus never saw the missile as it tried to turn with them and tumbled. He did see the flash as it detonated well above and behind them.

"One minute out," Toby said.

"I got 'em on the FLIR," Gus said, amazingly calm as the lead trucks materialized on his HUD. Bright red flashes from the convoy, tracers, drifted towards them and Gus jinked hard, loading the jet with little sharp and random turns. It worked and they bore down on the convoy. At the last moment, they flew straight and level for two seconds. It seemed an eternity but they had no choice if the weapons system was to do its magic. Three bombs rippled off and Gus jinked the Strike Eagle for all it was worth as tracers ripped past them.

The night exploded behind them as the Mark-82s walked across the lead trucks. The center bomb was a shack and hit the rear of the first truck. But the other two were not wasted as the fragmentation pattern of a Mark-82 reaches out over two thousand feet. The night erupted as three secondary explosions ripped the darkness apart. "Gas tanks," Toby said. A fourth explosion lit the sky. "Got something big." For a moment, only the sound of heavy breathing filled their headsets. "Let's nail the rear," Toby said.

"I've got a visual," Gus said as he repositioned the Strike Eagle. "Rip three."

"Got it," Toby said as he moved his crosshairs over the tail end of the convoy that was now stopped. Gus turned inbound and jinked. But this time the TEWS was quiet. A single stream of tracers reached out from the heart of the convoy but it was wide by a thousand feet. The run-in was a walk in the park. Again, the system worked as designed and the last three Mark-82s separated cleanly from the aircraft. The result was not as spectacular as the first time but it was every bit as accurate. They circled back. The flames from burning vehicles at both ends of the convoy lit the night and they had no trouble seeing the havoc they had caused.

"Moonbeam, Driver One," Gus radioed, his voice calm and measured, "the convoy is stopped on the highway. Both ends bottled up."

"Shit hot!" the controller aboard the orbiting C-130 yelled.

"What's he so happy about?" Toby asked over the intercom.

"Driver One," Moonbeam radioed, "Driver Two and Three are inbound, ten minutes out."

"Copy all, Moonbeam," Gus answered. Jim Cannon back at Al Kharj was starting to launch every Strike Eagle he could. "We've still got the CBUs," Gus told Toby.

"This is what we get paid for."

"One pass, haul ass," Gus said.

"Sounds like a plan."

Gus called up the weapons armament panel and selected the remaining stations to ripple the six canisters on one long pass. He circled back to the head of the convoy and flew a curvilinear approach onto the stalled vehicles. Neither man said a word as they flew down the length of the highway and the canisters separated one at a time, each spewing its deadly cargo. Gus honked back on the stick and climbed into the clouds. He never looked back.

"Radar's clear," Toby said, clearing them of any aircraft that might be in the clouds.

Skid's familiar voice came over the radio. "Moonbeam, Driver Two and Three. How copy?"

"Driver Two, I read you five-by," the controller answered. "Hold at angels fourteen while Driver One clears the area."

"Hope there's something left for us," Skid answered.

"Plenty to go around," the controller answered.

Gus nudged the transmit switch on the throttle quadrant. "Moonbeam, Driver One clear of area."

"Rog, Driver One. You're cleared RTB. Good work out there."

Gus answered with two clicks of the transmit switch as they climbed into the clear night sky.

The Present

The image on the screen abruptly ended and the lights in the courtroom came up. The audience sat in silence, stunned by the reality of combat. Hank's cool voice split the quiet as he brought them back to the moment. "Colonel Tyler, during the mission we have just witnessed, did you drop any bombs or CBUs off the highway?"

"No. You can see that on the video."

"At this time," Hank continued, "I would like to replay defense exhibit one, which is the complete and unedited video of the Highway of Death as documented by Harm de Rijn. Colonel Tyler, will you please point out for the court those destroyed vehicles that are on the highway or close to it. Just say 'stop' so we can mark the tape." Harm de Rijn's video came on the screen. But this time there was no sound and just the images. It played in complete silence. Finally, it was over. "Colonel Tyler, we have just seen 248 destroyed vehicles on the so-called Highway of Death. Yet you did not say stop once."

"None of them were on the highway."

"How do you explain that?"

"The highway had probably been cleared by the time this video was taken."

"But you freely admit that you bombed vehicles on the highway."

"I did. But I have no idea who bombed the ones we just saw."

Hank turned to the bench. "The defense enters the airborne videotape as defense exhibit ten."

Bouchard started to say something but thought better of it. He conferred with Della Sante and Richter. "The airborne video is so entered. As it is well past one in the afternoon and we have not recessed for lunch, court is adjourned until ten P.M. tomorrow morning."

* * * * *

Catherine was standing beside Marci when her director motioned they were transmitting live. "The court has just adjourned for the day and I have with me Catherine Sutherland. Catherine, what do you make of the court's ruling on transferring Colonel Tyler to Iraqi custody?"

"The ruling is unconscionable in the extreme. Not only that, but Bouchard timed his ruling to coincide with Gus taking the stand. It was an obvious attempt to put him under stress and weaken his testimony."

"That is a very serious accusation," Marci replied. "However, my Dutch colleagues were also stunned by the ruling."

"I'm not surprised. It's fair to ask what's going on? Why won't the court allow the defense to call Henri Scullanois to the stand?"

"Which is a very good question," Marci said, transitioning smoothly to the couple standing on her other side. "I also have with me the two spectators who were ejected from the courtroom for asking, 'Where's Henri?' She turned to the man. "Why did you say it?"

"I have been in the courtroom every day," he replied with a heavy Dutch accent. "It is obvious they don't want Scullanois on the stand. So I ask myself 'Why?' I think we should know, don't you?"

"And you?" Marci asked the woman.

She spoke with a French accent. "For the same reason. But there is something about Gus that tells me he is innocent. A woman knows these things."

"What do you think of the court's decision to turn Colonel Tyler over to the Iraqis?"

"This is not justice," the man replied.

"It's barbaric!" the woman cried. Catherine reached out and held the woman's hand.

"Mrs. Sutherland," Marci said, making sure the camera captured the two women holding hands, "as a lawyer, what do you see as the most damning evidence the prosecution has presented so far?"

"The deposition by the Reverend Tobias Person is the smoking gun the prosecutor needs to win a conviction."

"Which your husband has seriously questioned. Is there any chance the court will throw it out?"

"I seriously doubt it. The deposition was taken in accordance with the rules of the court and the judges aren't about to put the court itself on trial."

"How's Colonel Tyler doing on the stand?"

The woman answered. "*Magnifique!* He is the only man in the room."

* * * * *

Gus worked the problem. *So how do you play a shrink?* he thought. *What did Clare always say? "For a woman, intimacy is everything."* Then it came to him. *Talk.* He rehearsed the coming conversation and tried to gauge Derwent's reaction. He looked up when he saw her standing in the doorway, a concerned look on her face. "Thanks for coming." He held a chair for her at the small table and sat opposite her.

"How are you doing?" she asked.

He forced a sad look. "I knew it was coming, the Iraqi ruling. But I wasn't really ready for it. My stomach is in knots."

"I know," she whispered.

He reached across the table and enfolded her right hand with both of his. "I thought I was tough enough to take it. But I keep asking myself, are they right? Am I truly guilty?"

She placed her left hand on top of his hands. "No, you're not guilty. You are simply paying the price a sane man pays for the brutality of war." The lights blinked, telling them they had fifteen minutes to lights-out. She stood, lifted the phone receiver on the wall, and called the cellblock commander "This is Doctor Derwent. Please leave the lights and the heat on. I'm with my patient." She sat back down, certain they had turned a corner. Now she could help him.

"I don't know where to start," he said.

"It's all right," she murmured. "We have all night."

"It's hard to explain why I fought, but it wasn't courage. It was a need that I couldn't ignore."

"I know," she said. She listened as he talked, more his friend than counselor.

Southern Sudan

Leon passed the bottle of Napoleon brandy up to Hon who was sitting behind the wheel of the Wolf Turbo. Hon took a long pull, sighed, and passed it to Paride who was standing behind the machine gun in the rear. Paride sniffed at it and passed it to Jason, who was standing beside Leon, completing the circle. Jason finished it and held the bottle up for inspection in the moonlight. "*Un enfant mort pour la patrie*," he said.

"It's *un soldat français mort pour la patrie*," Leon corrected, referring to the tomb of the Unknown Soldier under the Arc de Triomphe. "You have been to Paris?"

"Oh yeah," Jason replied. "I went with my family when I was a teenager. I didn't want to go but my dad made me. We had a great time. I want to go back."

"But Americans don't like the French."

Jason thought about it. "We like to complain about them, but basically, we're family."

"I hope not," Leon scoffed.

The wail of Arabic music drifted across the runway and they could see shadowy figures dancing in the glow of campfires. Men started to shout and chant. "It looks like they're getting hyped up," Jason said.

"Opiates," Leon said. "I saw it when I was in the Legion." He listened to the sounds coming from the road. "They'll attack at first light."

"We've got some work to do," Jason said.

38

Southern Sudan

It was still dark when the Afrikaner scampered across the runway, reeling a wire out behind him. He piled into a DFP and keyed his hand-held radio. "Boss, we got the third string of dynamite in place." He quickly attached the wire to a clicker-type firing device and showed his buddy how to give it a half squeeze before removing the safety pin.

"Good work," Jason replied. The Afrikaners were manning the three center DFPs stretched along the runway, and, thanks to some last minute scrambling, each DFP was protected by a string of dynamite charges strung out along the far side of the runway. Jason tried to visualize the coming attack. If needed, he and Leon could man one of the end DFPs to hold a flank, and he still had Hon and Paride in the Wolf Turbo as a mobile reserve. Anyone making it across the minefield was in for a nasty surprise. He looked across the runway as the first light of the new day broke the far horizon.

"Boss!" one of the Afrikaners yelled over the radio. "They're coming. But the bastards are herding kaffirs in front of them, the poor buggers."

Jason stood on top of the Wolf Turbo and scanned the minefield with his binoculars. The coppery taste of bile flooded his mouth. Soldiers were pushing and prodding a large group of women and children into the minefield with bayonets. Two six-wheeled armored cars drove into place behind the soldiers and stopped, their engines at idle. "Leon, hand me the Remington." The Frenchman quickly unzipped the case holding a hunting rifle. He was careful not to jostle the telescopic sight when he handed the rifle up along with a box of .308-caliber ammunition. Jason quickly loaded the rifle and rested it across the heavy machine gun. He took aim and squeezed off a single round. Over three hundred meters away, a soldier collapsed to the ground. He squeezed off a second round.

Leon swept the field with binoculars. "You got one, Boss! Merde! You got a second one!" Now he could see the soldiers breaking ranks and running away. But a sergeant blocked their way and forced them back to herding the women and children into the minefield. Jason tried to shoot the sergeant but missed. The sergeant pointed in the general direction of the Wolf Turbo, obviously seeing it, and raised a radio to his lips.

"Scoot!" Jason ordered. Hon gunned the engine and raced for cover. They heard the distinctive whistle of an incoming mortar round as it arced over the minefield. But they were well clear when the mortar round impacted. The first of the mines exploded as the woman and children entered the mine field. Jason dropped the rifle, hating what was happening but unable to stop it. He felt sick to his stomach as more explosions filled the air. Suddenly, the explosions stopped only to be replaced with the crack of heavy machine-gun fire.

"Boss, look!" Paride shouted. "The people run away!" Jason raised his binoculars. The women and children were running out of the minefield and right into the muzzles of the machine guns mounted on the two armored cars. The gunners did not stop firing until the flow of humanity reversed and ran back into the minefield.

Jason's face froze as a pure hate swept through him. It had been a question of personal survival, but now it was something much more. Slowly, the explosions tapered off as the survivors cleared the minefield. Jason keyed his radio. "Let them through," he told his three teams in the DFPs. He froze as he scanned the minefield. "Were in hell did that come from?" An armored personnel carrier was clanking into position. It stopped, pivoted on its left track and pointed directly at the compound. The two armored cars motored into a 'V' formation behind it. Jason's eyes narrowed as he studied the new arrival with its center-mounted turret and stubby cannon. "It's a Russian BMP," he told Leon. "It carries a three-man crew and eight soldiers."

Leon studied the BMP. "The head sticking up in front of the turret, is that the driver? Why doesn't he button down?"

"I'm guessing his field of view is too restricted with the hatch closed," Jason said. He watched as foot soldiers moved into the 'V' for protection. The sound of a diesel engine revving carried across the still morning air. "Hon, hide the Wolf Turbo and don't let the BMP see you. He's got a 73mm cannon you don't want to mess with." He grabbed the hunting rifle and jumped down. "Go!" Hon gunned the engine and raced for the storage yard with its piles of drilling machinery and pipes.

Jason climbed onto the flat roof of a nearby cement-block shed and rolled into a prone shooting position. The vehicles and soldiers had reached the minefield and had slowed. Jason keyed his radio, calling the DFPs. "Hold your fire." A geyser of dirt mushroomed from the center of the formation quickly followed by a muffled explosion. "There's still some mines out there," Jason radioed. The formation kept moving. The armored car on the left flank disap- peared in a fireball and a sharp blast. A secondary explosion ripped it apart, sending a billowing cloud of smoke across the minefield. The mines were still taking their toll, but Jason had no illusions about their chances. He fully expected they would have to retreat into the swamp, which was a dead end. But they had a chance if they could inflict enough damage that the soldiers wouldn't pursue them. It was all they had.

Another mine detonated but the BMP was out of the minefield and less than fifty meters from the runway. Jason again keyed his radio. "Hold your fire, hold your fire." He waited as the remaining armored car cleared the minefield. Then, "Blow the bastards!" On cue, the three strings of dynamite erupted, raising a curtain of smoke, dirt, and death. The dust slowly cleared as soldiers still stumbled around in confusion. The remaining armored car was nose down in the dirt, its front end blown away, and the BMP was stopped. A small group of soldiers took cover behind the BMP and banged on the hatches. The commander's hatch next to the turret flipped open and a helmet poked up. Jason sighted the rifle, trying to lay the crosshairs on the helmet, but the hatch cover blocked his view. The driver's hatch popped open and a second head appeared. Jason shifted his aim as the BMP started to move.

Jason squeezed off a round and immediately keyed the radio. "Fire!" The top of the drivers head disappeared in a cloud of bloody mist as gunfire from the three DFPs swept across the runway, driving the soldiers to the ground. Driverless, the BMP jerked to the left and stalled. Jason was on the radio. "Pull back now! Pull back, pull back." He sighted again and squeezed off a second round. A soldier collapsed to the ground. "Oh shit!" he yelled. The BMP's turret was traversing towards him.

He rolled off the roof, leaving the rifle, his radio, and binoculars behind. He hit the ground running and bolted for the closest DFP. He dove in head first as the sharp retort of the BMP's cannon reached him. The shed vaporized in a loud explosion and debris rained down, burying Jason.

The Hague

Bouchard went through the opening routine and the court was back in session. Hank returned to the podium to continue Gus's testimony, but he could sense a difference in the audience. He looked at Catherine. Did she also feel it? She nodded and smiled telling him all he needed to know. Public sentiment was swinging in Gus's favor.

Bouchard called for a short recess and Hank turned on his percom to get Cassandra's reaction. "The media loves him," she said. "The military and aviation experts can't say enough good things about him."

"Any word on Jason and Toby?"

For a moment, Cassandra was silent. "NSA monitored a brief emergency distress signal from the compound Sunday night at 2304 hours, and there's no news on the helicopter. We should get satellite coverage of the compound later today."

"The distress signal was Sunday night, and we're just hearing about it thirty-six hours later? We're pretty low on the information totem pole."

The judges were back and Hank returned to the podium to resume questioning. "Mr. Tyler, did you review your personnel file that the prosecution submitted into evidence?"

"I did. It was complete and I don't think it had been altered. But I may have missed something."

"Moving on, did you find the testimony given by Ewe Reiss plausible?"

"Objection," Denise called. "By his own admission, the witness was not on the ground at the time. He was not in a position to judge one way or the other."

Della Sante tapped her microphone. "I would like to hear Signore Tyler's answer."

"And I," Richter added.

Gus looked the judges full in the face. "Ewe Reiss was there."

"Was it your bombs that injured him?"

"I assume so, but he was hit a second time by someone else."

"Mr. Tyler," Hank asked, "were you ever briefed on the international law of armed conflict?"

"At least twice that I can remember. It helped explain things."

"At any time in your career, were you ever trained in the use of weapons of mass destruction?"

Gus never hesitated. "Yes."

Hank left the podium and walked towards the dock. "Did you ever employ them?"

"Never had to."

Hank reached the dock. "Did you ever knowingly attack civilians?"

"No."

"Thank you. I have no further questions at this time." Bouchard checked the time and recessed for lunch.

Southern Sudan

Leon cleared the debris covering the DFP and snorted. "I thought you were dead."

Jason held his head and tried to focus through the pain and fog. "How long have I been out?"

"Maybe an hour," Leon replied. "I had a hard time finding you." He finished digging Jason out and examined the back of his head, still the medic. "Nasty cut." He snapped open his first aid kit and dressed the wound. "A few bumps and bruises, but you'll live. How's the head?"

"Hurts like hell."

"Concussion. But you've got a thick American skull." He handed Jason two pills. "Take these. You'll be wired for about six, eight hours." Finished, he brought Jason up to date. "They've regrouped at the runway and we've pulled back into the compound." He pointed to the three DFPs where the Afrikaners were dug in. "The Reverend's in the Wolf Turbo over there." He pointed to the storage yard. Both men flinched at the sharp crack of a rifle. "That's Paride sniping at them," Leon said. The BMP's cannon boomed in retaliation and the debris of the old radio shack fireballed. "Paride shoots, they answer back." He snorted. "The BMP is stalled and they can't get it started. Without it, they won't attack." He pressed the transmit button on his radio. "I found the Boss. He's okay." In the distance, they heard the cough of a diesel engine coming to life.

"Boss!" an Afrikaner yelled over the radio. "They got the BMP started."

Jason grabbed Leon's radio. "Paride! Get to the Wolf Turbo and help Hon."

"I go," the tall Dinka answered.

In the distance, they heard the clanking of tracks. "They're moving," Jason radioed. "How many soldiers?"

"Fifty, sixty," an Afrikaner answered." A loud explosion punctuated his transmission.

Leon grunted. "That was the last of the dynamite."

"But they don't know that," Jason replied. "It will slow them down."

Two soldiers burst into the compound, swinging their AK47s from the hip and firing wildly. Leon raised his M16 and fired a short burst. The two soldiers went down. Now they could see the BMP as it moved across the runway and reached the first building. Gunfire erupted from a DFP along with the sharp crack of Paride's hunting rifle. Three more soldiers fell but the BMP kept moving.

A Far Justice

"We've got to stop that bastard," Jason said. Leon dropped his M16 and bolted from the DFP. "What the fuck?" Jason shouted. He picked up the weapon and fired a short burst. More and more soldiers were streaming into the compound, taking cover behind the destroyed buildings. The two DFPs in the middle of the compound kept up a withering rate of fire, catching the soldiers in a deadly crossfire and driving them back.

A soldier broke from behind a pile of rubble and charged at Jason. Jason fired a short burst but covering fire drove him down into his DFP. He lifted the M16 above his head and fired blindly. He was rewarded with a scream of pain and pulled the M16 down to reload. A grenade tumbled in and rolled around at Jason's feet. He kicked at it but missed. He kicked again and it rolled into the deep shaft sunk in the bottom corner of the foxhole. Without thinking, he huddled in the far corner, wrapped his arms over his head, closed his eyes, and opened his mouth. The explosion was deafening but the shaft directed the blast upward and a geyser of dirt mushroomed over Jason. He coughed and sputtered as he fumbled with the M16, trying to reload.

He came to his feet, still a little dazed by the blast. Seven soldiers were coming at him. He fired as Leon skidded into the foxhole loaded with another M16 and six bandoleers of ammunition. "*J'en ai plein le cul!*" My ass is full of this! He stood and fired as the Wolf Turbo charged out from between two buildings, its heavy machine gun firing.

The BMP's turret traversed towards the Wolf Turbo as Paride fired, sending burst after burst of high-explosive fire into the side of the BMP. The stubby cannon fired as Hon twisted the wheel of the Wolf Turbo and darted out of its path. Now Paride raked the soldiers following behind the BMP. Most of them broke and ran as the Wolf Turbo raced for safety behind the stacks of pipes in the storage yard. The BMP's cannon fired again, but the round was far wide of the retreating Wolf Turbo.

Suddenly, it was quiet. The sound of crunching gears and a racing diesel engine echoed over them as the BMP reversed out of the compound and backed across the runway.

"They'll be back," Jason promised. "We've got to stop that fuckin' BMP."

Leon reached into his shirt and pulled out the brandy bottle they had emptied the night before. But now it was filled with gasoline. "We're not dead yet."

The Hague

The clerk called everyone to stand as the judges returned from lunch. Hank sat down and leaned into Aly. "Let's see if she bites."

Aly looked over Hank's shoulder directly at Denise. "She can't wait."

Denise stepped to the podium. "Monsieur Tyler," she began. "Why do you kill innocent civilians?"

"Objection," Hank called. "Madame Prosecutor's question assumes facts not in evidence."

"Overruled," Bouchard said.

"May we confer?" Richter asked. Della Sante and Richter leaned into Bouchard and they spoke quietly. Bouchard's face turned red and his head jerked once in acknowledgment. He turned to face the front. "Please continue, Madam Prosecutor."

"What happened?" Aly asked quietly.

"They disagreed with Bouchard's ruling," Hank explained. "There's going to be a lot of second guessing the next few days and they're engaging in damage control."

"Monsieur Tyler," Denise continued, "you testified that you 'volunteered' to fly the mission in question. Can the court assume that no order from your headquarters was ever given to fly the mission?"

"Then the court would be assuming wrong. The order to fly a combat mission is given through an Air Task Order, or ATO for short. It can come down to the wing by message or verbally. In this case, it came down from the Black Hole in Riyadh over the secure phone." Gus waited to see if she would ask what the Black Hole was. She didn't. "Once the wing receives an ATO, it's our job to carry it out. If Colonel Cannon had scheduled me to fly, I would have flown the mission. However, he asked and I volunteered."

"You said the briefings on the international law of armed conflict helped explain things. What are these things you referred to?"

"The Rules of Engagement, the ROE for short."

"And what does this ROE tell you?" Her words were laced with sarcasm.

"It tells us how to fight. For example, hospitals, mosques, religious shrines, and orphanages are prohibited targets. They're marked on our charts and we know where they are."

"What happens if you bomb one of these so-called prohibited targets?"

"It depends. If I hit one without first taking hostile fire, I wouldn't be here."

"Where would you be?"

"Most likely in Leavenworth Prison for violating the ROE."

Denise ticked off the next item on her legal pad. "You specifically admitted that you had been trained in the use of weapons of mass destruction. What were those weapons?"

"We were trained in the release and employment of nuclear weapons, much like all nuclear-armed forces in NATO. It's the same with the British RAF, and the French *l'Armée de l'Air*. If we had used them, you'd have known about it."

"Please only answer the question asked."

"Ah shucks, Ma'am . . ." He was rewarded with an appreciative guffaw from the audience.

Denise's head snapped up when she realized she was questioning Jim Cannon's clone. She looked at the assistant prosecutor. He shook his head, urging her to caution, and she gave him a look of utter contempt. He wasn't helping. "Monsieur Tyler, you have seen how your bombs killed at least one innocent civilian on Mutlah Ridge. Aren't you, by your own admission, guilty of willful murder?"

"I never knowingly bombed civilians."

"Monsieur, need I remind you that you bombed a bus without authorization."

"Only after we were shot at when we went to take a look. A pilot never loses the right of self-defense."

Denise swelled in indignation. "You are a mass murderer who killed innocent people! Nothing you say can relieve you of your guilt or your responsibility."

"There she goes again," Hank groaned loudly as he stood. "Objection! The chamber determines guilt, not the prosecutor." Bouchard huddled with Della Sante and Richter.

Gus fixed Denise with a level stare, his face a mask, as he took her measure. She returned his look, and suddenly she knew. He was a raptor, a bird of prey, and she felt the fear of the hunted.

"Sustained," Bouchard intoned. "The prosecutor's last statement will be disregarded."

"I have no further questions," Denise said.

Hank stood for redirect. "You said that prohibited targets were marked on your chart. Did you ever attack one of these targets?"

"Once. An Iraqi anti-aircraft artillery battery hiding in a religious shrine shot at us one night. We didn't react because it was a religious shrine and expected they'd be gone by morning. That was pretty typical, shoot and scoot. But for whatever reason, the Iraqis stayed and kept shooting at us. After three days, they brought in a surface-to-air missile battery. That's when we were ordered to take it down."

"Did you ever bomb one these prohibited targets by mistake?"

"No."

"So you followed the ROE."

"To the letter."

"I have no further questions." Hank waited to see if Denise was up for re-cross. She declined and Bouchard adjourned for the day.

* * * * *

Gus was in bed when the door lock clicked. "May I come in?" Therese Derwent asked. "I was wondering if you needed help sleeping."

Gus hesitated before switching on the light, hating to lie to her. "It would help." He hoped it sounded right. He switched on the light as she closed the door behind her. He sat up on his bunk as she drew a glass of water. She handed him the plastic cup and sat at the table. "My stomach is still in knots."

"I know."

He took a sip of water and swallowed the capsule. "May I ask a personal question?" She nodded. "You are very professional but how do you really feel about Americans?"

"I like most of the ones I have met, but not all."

"And me?"

"Gus, you are my patient but I do consider you a friend. I find you full of contradictions and while I know a great deal about you, I have much more to learn. For example, do you like the theater?"

"Shakespeare. 'O! withered is the garland of war, the soldiers' pole is fall'n; young boys and girls are level now with men; the odds is gone, and there is nothing left remarkable beneath the visiting moon.'"

"What a lovely refrain, 'and there is nothing left remarkable beneath the visiting moon.' So much better than there is nothing new under the sun."

Gus gave her a half smile. "'As You Like It.' Clare loves the Bard. She got me hooked on Old Will."

She returned his smile. "You do surprise me." They sat and talked about Shakespeare until he grew drowsy. "Until tomorrow." She switched off the light and left.

Southern Sudan

A flare arced high over the compound and drifted slowly down. The shrill whistle of incoming mortar rounds drove Jason and Leon deep into their foxhole. Both men covered their heads as the mortars walked across the compound, blasting what was left of the buildings. As quickly as it had begun, the barrage stopped and an uneasy silence came down. Jason's head bobbed up for a fraction of a second as he chanced a glance.

Every building had been hit and two were on fire, sending an eerie light flickering across the wreckage of what had been Westcot Five. His head bobbed up again. "Damn!" The mortar barrage had hit the storage yard where the Wolf Turbo had taken refuge.

"Hon!" Jason radioed. "Are you okay?" He was answered by another salvo of mortar rounds.

"They bastards are monitoring the radios," Leon said.

Paride's voice came over the radio, low and urgent. "Boss, mortar hit Wolf Turbo. Hon dead. I get Reverend out. We hide in last DFP next to swamp. But hole half-full of water."

"Stay there," Jason directed as more mortar rounds walked through the compound.

When the barrage stopped, only two of the other teams checked in. "Peit and Raul took a direct hit," an Afrikaner said.

Jason waited, expecting another round of mortar fire. But the night was quiet. "I guess they ran out of ammo," he said as Leon lit a cigarette and took a deep drag. "Those things will kill you."

Leon gave him a contemptuous look. "Not before morning."

39

Southern Sudan

The radio came alive as the sun broke the horizon. "The BMP's moving!" a voice yelled. Jason wasn't sure who it was. He chanced a quick look, and, as he suspected, the BMP was headed straight for his position. Gunfire erupted from the DFP nearest him, cutting into the soldiers trailing behind the armored personnel carrier. Amoeba-like, the soldiers clustered around the opposite side of the BMP bringing them into Jason and Leon's field of fire. Both men opened fire. The BMP's cannon fired and the round split the air directly over their heads.

"They can't depress the muzzle far enough," Jason shouted. He jammed another clip into his M16 and fired again. But the BMP kept coming at them. Suddenly it jerked to the left presenting its right side. The four firing ports on the side of the BMP flipped open and the muzzles of AK47s poked out. "Down!" Jason yelled as the gunners opened fire, raking the ground in front of the DFP. Leon raised his M16 over his head and fired blindly. The small 5.56 mm rounds pinged harmlessly off the side of the BMP. Suddenly, the BMP stopped firing. Jason bobbed his head up to see what was happening. The BMP was just sitting there, its engine idling. Behind it, he could see more soldiers surging across the runway, running to reinforce their comrades in the compound. "What the hell?"

It was the Golden B-B, that mystical bullet that combat veterans muse about in reflective moments at the bar, and the uninitiated chalk up to superstition. A single M16 round had entered a firing port and ricocheted around the crew compartment, grazing two soldiers before striking one in the head. The bullet tumbled in the soft brain tissue and blew off the back of the soldier's skull, adding to the panic and chaos. A top hatch flipped open and a soldier bailed out. Jason shot him before he reached the ground. More soldiers bailed out of the two hatches in the back. It was enough. Jason grabbed his walkie-talkie. "Everyone fall back to the swamp. Go! Go! Go!"

He grabbed two bandoleers, and jumped out of the foxhole, holding his M16 to his chest. He rolled into the shallow depression immediately behind and squeezed off a short burst. To his left, he saw the four Afrikaners running for cover as Leon climbed out of the DFP. Jason ran, crouched low, as bullets split the air around him. He skidded to cover behind a destroyed out-building and looked back for Leon. "No!" he shouted.

The Frenchman was charging the BMP, the gasoline-filled brandy bottle in his hand. The gas-soaked rag stuck in the bottle's neck was blazing, licking at Leon's hand. The turret on the BMP traversed, swinging onto Leon. The cannon fired as Leon heaved the Molotov cocktail. The 73 mm round blew through Leon, tearing him apart as the bottle smashed against the front of the BMP.

Jason was up and running, taking what cover he could as the air filled with gunfire, all coming from the charging soldiers. He was well clear of the compound when Paride's head popped up in front of him. "Here! Here!" Jason jumped into the DFP crowding Toby and Paride aside. Paride stood and fired. "Here they come, Boss."

Jason stood and emptied the M16's clip. Toby handed him a fresh magazine to reload. Jason looked to his left and saw two Afrikaners run for the tall grass and the swamp, abandoning their DFP. The all to-familiar clank of the BMP's track reached him. "Shit! Fuck! Hate!" he roared. He squeezed off a short burst as Paride stood beside him and fired. Jason thumbed the M16 to full fire and mashed the trigger, sending a long burst into the soldiers and the advancing BMP.

Toby handed him a fresh clip. "Two left," he said.

Again, Jason fired as the BMP came within twenty meters. He could clearly see the scorch marks left by Leon's Molotov cocktail. Suddenly, the BMP exploded and the fireball pillared high into the air as it kept exploding, shredding its armor and vaporizing the men inside. Then he saw it.

A small jet-powered, wedged-shaped aircraft, was sweeping in low. Two canisters separated cleanly from underneath its wings and opened like clamshells. What looked like a cloud of dust arced towards the ground. But it wasn't dust. It was a hail of golf ball-sized bomblets that started to explode before they reached the ground, ripping into the soldiers caught in the open. The aircraft pulled up and Gus wanted to wave at the pilot. But there was no cockpit. It was a UAV, an unmanned aerial vehicle.

A second UAV swept over the field, spreading the same blanket of destruction over the remaining soldiers. Twice more the UAVs returned, now working the runway and road. Moans and cries for help echoed over the battlefield as Jason and Paride climbed out of the DFP. A UAV swept over the field, this time low and slow, as it recorded the scene with a high-definition digital camera. It wagged its wings and pulled up.

"What's that?" Paride asked.

"The cavalry," Jason replied. They helped Toby out as a strange silence came down and Jason stood there, stunned by the carnage. He breathed deeply as relief surged through his weary body. Slowly, he raised his right fist in victory, his mouth compressed into a tight line.

Amsterdam

Max Westcot stood by the big window and puffed his cigar, sending wave after wave of smoke billowing across the penthouse suite of the Amstel Intercontinental. Outside, a winter storm beat at the window and obscured the low skyline of the city. He stubbed the cigar out when the elevator doors slid silently back and Hank and Catherine entered the suite. "Thanks for coming so quickly," he said. Hank nodded, not that he could avoid the summons. "Coffee? Some breakfast?" Westcot asked, always the genial host.

"Coffee would be lovely," Catherine said, sitting down next to the fireplace. A maid poured two cups of coffee and served them on a silver tray. Westcot waited until she withdrew to the pantry, well out of earshot.

"How's Gus doing?" Westcot asked.

Hank considered his answer. "Actually, better than me." It was the truth. The strain of the trial was taking a fearsome toll and the lawyer was having a hard time sleeping.

"Well," Westcot said, smiling, "there is some good news. We've got a plane overhead at Westcot Five and are in radio contact with Sergeant Tyler. Person is wounded but very much alive." Hank sank into his chair as relief flooded through him. He managed a weak smile and raised his right hand in gratitude. "We're not out of the woods yet," Westcot continued. "They fought off an attack by the Sudanese Army and the plane can't land until they get the runway cleared. But once that happens, it's two hours flying time to Addis Ababa where a commercial jet is waiting. Figure seven more hours to Schiphol. They should arrive here late tonight." He smiled and changed the subject. "Today's what? The seventeenth day of the trial? So how are things going?"

Hank suspected, rightly, that the financier knew exactly how things were going and this was the lead in to something he wanted. "Public opinion is swinging around to us and we've got momentum. I don't want to lose either." Westcot nodded, encouraging him to continue. "We hit two home runs with Cannon and Gus, now all I need to put the game away is to get Person on the stand."

"So Cassandra has said," Westcot added. "The good Reverend has the moral authority to offset Schumann and his testimony is relevant. So what's on the agenda today?"

Hank looked worried. "I can easily call a few witnesses and sprinkle a little legal dust around, but that would be redundant at this point. I'm also worried it will take the edge off Gus's testimony and cost us some momentum." He turned to Catherine. "How do you see it?"

"I agree. Right now, we've got the judges and the spectators sitting on the edge of their seats. We need to keep them there and let the anticipation build until we can get Person on the stand. We need to ratchet up the tension and delay at the same time."

Westcot paced the floor, signaling they had come to the reason for the meeting. "Call Henri Scullanois again."

Hank shook his head. "I've played that for all it is worth. Scullanois was a diversion to make it look like they're hiding some dark political agenda."

"Your instincts were right," Westcot said. "Scullanois is in this up to his eyeballs with Du Milan. We're talking conspiracy."

"Son of a bitch," Hank muttered.

"We need to get Scullanois in the news," Westcot continued. "Get in a legal brawl over Scullanois before Friday. Cassandra has a petition waiting at your office. It's pure bullshit, but get it out there."

Catherine caught it immediately. "Why is Friday so important?"

Westcot didn't answer. "I realize you need to get to court. My chauffeur will drive you." They were dismissed and the meeting was over.

Southern Sudan

The small group of men watched as the dark gray C-130 transport flew a short final and touched down on the runway. Dirt kicked up as the big tires on the tandem gear sank into the ground, but they had done their work well and the runway was clear of debris, spent shell casings, and bodies. The pilot slammed the four turboprop engines into reverse and dragged the big cargo plane to a halt with room to spare. The crew entrance door on the left side of the fuselage flopped down and Jim Cannon climbed out. He was wearing a desert-tan flight suit and combat boots. A 9mm Beretta hung in a shoulder holster under his left arm. He jammed a baseball hat on his short-cropped hair and marched up to Jason. "Jason Tyler, it has been a while." The two men shook hands. "Where's Toby? I need to howdy that gentleman."

"Over there," Jason replied. He led Cannon to where the four Afrikaners and Paride were clustered around a stretcher.

Cannon bent over and touched Toby's face. He was still running a fever. "We need to get you to a hospital." He stood and motioned for three of his crew to help with the litter. "Let's go," he said. They headed for the waiting C-130.

"What were those airplanes?" the youngest of the Afrikaners asked.

"Well, son," Cannon replied, "this is the way we kill the bad guys these days. Those airplanes you saw were unmanned drones that we control from the C-130 over there. We're down linked by satellite to a center in the United States where we're tied into about every reconnaissance platform and intelligence collection system known to man. And that includes some of the bad guys' as well. Under the right conditions, we can put ordnance about anywhere we want and service whatever is there. Doesn't matter where it is, bunker, cave, tank or auto, we can find it and kill it." He swept the area with a wave. "This was a piece of cake. The hardest part was finding you. Luckily, we monitored your emergency transmission and figured you were still alive and well."

The Hague

The assistant prosecutor stepped off the tram and walked briskly towards the court building. He was not happy as he contemplated his future at the ICC. The trial was going badly and he was certain Du Milan was going to shift the blame to him for the disaster bearing down on them. A man he had seen everyday among the spectators in court joined him and smiled in recognition. "May we talk for a moment?" he asked. The assistant prosecutor nodded. "You work for a very foolish woman." The look on the assistant prosecutor's face was ample proof that he had scored a bull's-eye. The man nodded at a nearby sedan and opened the rear door. "I have something that may be of some benefit to your, ah, continued success." The assistant prosecutor hesitated. "You do need some other options at this moment." The assistant prosecutor threw caution to the winds and got in.

The man crawled in behind him and closed the door. The sedan pulled into traffic and the man handed over a mini CD player. "Please listen to this. The Frenchman is Henri Scullanois and the other speaker is his counterpart in Beijing."

The assistant prosecutor did as requested and his eyes opened wide. "What are you suggesting?" "Nothing. It's yours to do with as you wish." The car stopped a block short of the court and he opened the door. "But my employer would be grateful if it should find its way to the American reporter Marci Lennox." He sensed a little more coxing was in order. "I assure you, he will be most grateful."

* * * * *

Hank studied Bouchard as the judge led Della Sante and Richter to their seats on the bench. The Belgian's face was flushed and swollen and he was unsteady on his feet. "He doesn't look well," Aly whispered.

Hank tapped the blue cover of the thick petition on the desk in front of him. "This isn't gonna help." The document was a book in itself and a masterpiece of legal murkiness, shadows, and misdirection. Bouchard asked if there was any business for the court to consider and Hank came to his feet.

"If it may please the court," he began, "we respectfully request the court reconsider its prior ruling on calling Henri Scullanois as a witness for the defense." Denise was on her feet, objecting and repeating the court's original rationale. Hank waited until she finished and handed the petition to the clerk who was surprised by its size.

Bouchard coughed and sipped at a glass of water. "I have repeatedly cautioned defense counsel not to waste the court's time on this matter. This court will not call a witness for you to engage in political debate. However, we will take your petition under advisement. Please call your next witness."

"Your Honor," Hank replied, "it was our intention to call Minister Scullanois and one more witness. Both witnesses are critical to the defense" – he paused before hurling the insult – "and both must be heard if the court is to reach a fair and unbiased verdict."

A loud and collective gasp escaped from the audience as Bouchard's face turned even a brighter red. Bouchard came out of his seat in a pure rage, and Hank feared he had gone too far. But Della Sante was beside Bouchard, guiding him back into his chair. Bouchard muttered a few words to Della Sante and Richter nodded in agreement. Della Sante picked up the gavel and held it in her hands. She glared at Hank and gave one hard rap. "Counsel is out of order," she said. "That is twice you have insulted this court with a baseless charge. Our patience is at an end. It is only because we are in the final stages of this trial that you are not summarily dismissed as defense counsel. Do not do it again. Call your next witness."

The two stared at each other locked in a contest of wills. "Your Honor, our other witness will not arrive until late this evening. We respectfully request the court adjourn and reconvene at this time tomorrow."

"I have no doubt," Della Sante said, "that counsel is prepared to call other witnesses to fill the rest of day." Hank slowly nodded, confirming her suspicions. "To what purpose these witnesses would serve totally escapes me." She glanced at Bouchard who was not recovering. "Rather than waste the court's time, we are adjourned until tomorrow as it will allow us time to review your latest petition in the depth it does not deserve." She fixed Hank with a hard look. "Would you be so kind to indulge the court with the name of your final witness?"

"The Reverend Tobias Person," Hank replied.

40

The Hague

Gus came to his feet when Jason and Hank entered the holding cell. "Toby's here," was all Jason said. Father and son reached out and clasped hands, neither saying a word. Hank stood by the door, not wanting to intrude. He did not consider himself a brave person, yet he was in the presence of two very courageous men who called him 'friend,' and he was part of the moment. He would remember it all his life.

"When can I see him?" Gus asked.

"After he's testified," Hank answered.

"He's in pretty bad shape," Jason said. "He took two bullets, one in his side and one in the leg. Infection set in. Hiding in a foxhole half full of swamp water didn't help."

"Does he know about his family?" Gus asked.

"I told him last night," Hank said. "I can't believe the strength of the man. He said he had heard the rumor and wasn't surprised. He blames himself for not being there."

Jason studied his father. "We talked about it, Dad. He's going back to rebuild. I want to get out of the Air Force and go with him."

Gus understood. "Have you talked to Aly?"

"We talked last night. She's all for it."

"I might be able to help with the Air Force," Hank said. "The State Department lodged a protest with the Pentagon about your going to the Sudan. It won't be pretty, but it is a lever to get you out."

"I hope you know how proud I am of you," Gus said. "Do it no matter what happens here, okay?"

Hank hated to interrupt. "It's time." He led Gus into the courtroom and waited while he entered the dock. "Everyone's on edge. Can you feel it?" Gus studied the audience for a moment and agreed. "Catherine is convinced something is in the wind," Hank continued. "She has good instincts, and no matter what, don't blow your cool."

"Got it," Gus assured him. Hank joined Aly at the defense table as day eighteen of the trial started.

Bouchard definitely looked better and was in his usual irascible mood as he reconvened the trial. "We have taken defense counsel's petition in the matter of Henri Scullanois under careful review. We find nothing of a compelling nature to warrant reversing our previous ruling. Petition denied." He peered over his glasses expecting a reaction from Hank.

"Thank you for your consideration," Hank replied as he came to his feet. A titter of laughter worked its way around the room at the shocked look on Bouchard's face and momentarily broke the rising tension. Bouchard coughed and told Hank to call his next witness. The lawyer turned to the audience and played the moment. "The defense calls the Reverend Tobias Person."

The side door swung open and Jason pushed in a wheelchair with Toby. He sat upright but his face was pale and drawn and his eyes watery and drowsy. A light bead of sweat over his upper lip caught the light and a lap robe covered his legs. Jason pushed him as far as the witness stand and then retreated to sit beside Catherine. Toby sat in the wheelchair and made no attempt to enter the witness stand. The clerk rose to administer the oath.

Denise was on her feet. "I must object. It is obvious this witness should be in hospital, and I seriously doubt he has the mental acuity to testify."

Hank was ready. "Reverend Person is under a doctor's care and the chamber can determine if he has the mental acuity to testify."

Denise's staff had done their homework and she scoffed. "Is the Reverend here with his doctor's approval?"

Hank knew better than to sidestep the issue. "Reverend Person decided to override the attending doctor's recommendation."

"May I remind the court," Denise said, "that this witness is here contrary to the ruling of the Witness and Victims' Protection

Unit, which specifically directed the court not to transport the witness for his own safety. Defense counsel deliberately ignored this ruling, and the court can see at what cost." She raised her head in indignation, claiming the TV cameras. "The court's duty is to protect the weak and innocent who cannot protect themselves. We cannot let anyone, prosecutor or defense counsel, ride roughshod over this basic principle. To do so would make us all derelict in our duty."

Hank shot her a look of contempt. "Is procedure more important than the truth? Is the prosecutor afraid to hear what Reverend Person might say now that he is here?"

"Must I repeat myself?" Denise countered. "The witness is not in a fit state to testify. Further, given the nature of his wounds and resultant high fever, the court must assume he has suffered permanent cognitive damage, making any testimony questionable."

"It is the court's duty to determine if the witness is capable of taking the stand and evaluating his testimony, not the prosecutor's."

Bouchard was at the end of his patience. He held up his hand, commanding Hank to silence. "Monsieur Person, are you here contrary to your doctor's orders?"

"Your Honor," Toby answered, "a doctor did recommend that I not testify." His voice was weak and reedy, barely audible. "But I am a doctor and know I am capable of taking the stand."

Denise was ready. "The court has determined by other means the relevancy of the witness's testimony."

Hank faced the three judges. "I am appalled by the prosecutor's argument. Every defendant has the right to examine, in court, the evidence and witnesses against him. In this case, the evidence in question is an alleged statement by the Reverend Person that was presented to the court by 'other means.' These 'other means' have been called into question. Reverend Person is now present in court and ready to testify. Further, the Reverend Person has in his possession his copy of the electronic recording of his original statement."

"Your Honors," Denise protested, "first we are asked to hear the testimony of an obviously sick man. Now we are presented with 'his copy of the electronic recording of his original statement.' How can the court be expected to verify the authenticity of this recording? There is no established chain of custody and the recording, by nature of its timing and the way it reached this court, must be considered suspect."

"And the honorable Watban Horan's testimony is not?" Hank asked.

Bouchard had heard enough. "We will recess to consider the prosecutor's objection to the witness." He stood and marched out of the room as Della Sante and Richter followed.

Aly rushed over to Toby and knelt beside the wheelchair. Hank was right behind her. "So this is what Gus has been going through," Toby said. He turned to his old friend and raised his hand in greeting. Gus stood and nodded in acknowledgement. They waited in silence for a few moments until the red light on the clerk's desk flashed. The court was back in session.

Bouchard adjusted his glasses and started to read. "We have taken the prosecutor's objection to the witness under consideration and find that she is correct. The Reverend Person will not be allowed to testify, and hence his recording of his statement will not be allowed into evidence." A loud rumble of disapproval swept through the audience. Bouchard banged his gavel until he could be heard. "If there is another outburst, I will order the courtroom cleared." The audience calmed. "Further, I will remind defense counsel that this chamber is fully capable of evaluating all evidence against the accused. We are not a panel of untrained and inexperienced jurors. You may call your next witness."

"Look at Gus," Aly whispered. Hank turned towards the dock. Gus's face was frozen, his eyes hard, his body tensed and poised. For the first time, Hank saw the warrior. This was a man, who, under the right circumstances, would kill without hesitation or guilt.

Hank came to his feet shaking his head. "Your Honor, you leave me at a total loss for words. We request a brief recess to confer with Colonel Tyler."

Bouchard banged his gavel, using it like a weapon. "We have addressed the issue of proper titles in the past. Do not try this

A Far Justice

court's patience further or you will be removed as defense counsel. The court is in recess for fifteen minutes." He stood and marched out leaving a stunned Della Sante and Richter behind.

* * * * *

Gus stood in the center of the holding cell, his arms folded across his chest, his feet apart as Hank and Aly rushed in. "Close the door," he ordered. "Hank, I need to speak to Cassandra." The lawyer opened his percom and handed it to Gus. "Cassandra, are we being bugged?" Gus asked.

The image cocked her head at Gus, and, for a moment, didn't answer. "Yes, you are."

"Jam the living hell out of 'em. Whatever you can do, do it."

"I'll need a power source. Place your percom next to any electrical outlet or fixture in your cell and I'll do what I can." The image smiled. "Oh my, this is going to be exciting."

Gus turned to Hank. "Fuck those bastards. End it. The sooner the better."

Hank started to protest but the look on Gus's face convinced him that any argument would be fruitless, if not dangerous. "Done."

"I need to speak to Aly," Gus said, motioning Hank out the door. The door closed and she was in his arms, crying. He felt her heart beating against his chest and he slowly relaxed. "It's going to be okay. Trust me." Her tears slowly quieted. "Do you still have that business card I gave you?" She nodded, her face still against his chest. He whispered in her ear, telling her exactly what he wanted.

* * * * *

They were back in session and Hank stood at the podium. "If it may please the court, the defense rests." He sat down.

For once, Bouchard did not have to confer with the other two judges. "I hereby declare the submission of evidence is closed. At this time, we invite the prosecutor and defense to make closing statements. In accordance with Rule 141, defense will have the opportunity to speak last. Madam Prosecutor, do you wish to make a closing statement?"

Denise came to her feet, still stunned by the rapid turn of events. "Thank you, your Honor, we do. If it pleases the court, the prosecution would like to prepare over the weekend and present our closing statement on Monday."

Bouchard made a note. "Does defense wish to make a closing statement?"

"Indeed we do, your Honor. How about today?"

Bouchard arched an eyebrow. "Does the defense relinquish the opportunity to speak last?"

"No, we do not. However, it is the defendant's wish to end this trial as soon as possible and we see no need for further delay at this point. If I may quote your Honor, 'this chamber is fully capable of evaluating all evidence against the accused.' You are, indeed, a panel of experienced and learned justices who do not require direction or explanation." He almost added "from mere mortals" but thought better of it.

Bouchard stared at Hank, not quite certain if he was being sarcastic. He made a decision. "We are adjourned and will reconvene tomorrow, Friday, at ten o'clock in the morning to receive closing statements."

* * * * *

Therese Derwent sat beside Gus in the corner of her office and handed him a demitasse. She waited while he sipped. "In court today," she began, "when Justice Bouchard would not allow Person to testify, I have never seen you so angry."

Gus set the small cup down and tried to look forlorn. "That was the whole ballgame right there." He drew in a deep breath and gave a little shudder. *Don't overdo it*, he thought. "The court will never hear the truth and Horan's testimony will convict me."

"Have you spoken with your wife recently?" she asked, desperate to move him away from the despair she believed would drive him to suicide. She reached into her handbag and handed him her cell phone. "Please. It's late morning in Minnesota." She retreated to her desk to give him as much privacy as she could.

Gus punched in the number and Clare answered. His spirits soared. "How are you, love?" he asked.

"I'm sitting by the window and reading. The sun is out and Michelle is doing volunteer work at the boys' school. We're all doing fine."

"You sound great. How about turning the camera on so I can see you?"

"No way!" she laughed. It was the same laugh that had enchanted him so many years ago, and, for a moment, he was young again. "They've got me on a new medication and my hair is falling out. It's not chemo but I am having a reaction to it. Don't worry, I'm much better."

The psychiatrist tried not to listen as they talked, but she couldn't help herself. Gus was intelligent, loyal, and warm with charm and consideration. He was exactly what she valued in any human being. When they were finished, she rejoined him. "Are you going to be okay?"

"Yeah, I think so."

"I have an engagement tonight in Amsterdam and won't be here. If you need help sleeping, I can have the prison's doctor bring you a sedative."

"Thanks. I'll need it."

41

The Hague

Gus sat down in the dock and glanced at the audience. His rooting section was there and had grown. *Now that's encouraging,* he thought. He stood when the judges entered. Bouchard sat and peered over his glasses as he went through the opening formalities. He nodded to Denise. "The prosecutor may present her closing statement."

Denise walked slowly to the podium as commentators in the media booth talked about her regal beauty. Her hair was pulled into a bundle on the nape of her neck and she was wearing new glasses. She methodically uncapped her OMAS pen. "War is a terrible thing that we must end."

You're preaching to the choir, Gus thought. *Convince the other guys.* He listened as the prosecutor spoke, and, after seventy minutes, doubted if she would say anything new. He hid his disgust when she said, "We must discard our emotions and evaluate the horror of Mutlah Ridge for what it was, a senseless exercise in killing. The Iraqis were an army in disarray and retreat. There was no need to attack them."

Gus shook his head. *The Kuwaitis might have a few words to say about that.* Again, he listened. After another hour, he was beginning to wonder if she would ever finish.

"The evidence has shown that the criminal Tyler knew civilians were present, and he attacked with this knowledge.

Yeah. Right.

"When every soldier understands that killing defenseless civilians is prohibited and will be punished, humankind will have taken a significant step in ending war."

There are some things still worth fighting for. Again, he listened as she ticked off her points, wielding the pen like a wand of indictment. Twice she sipped at the glass of water by her side, and twice she used the pause for effect. It was a well-rehearsed performance that built to a climax.

"By his own admission, the defendant employed prohibited weapons that are specifically prohibited under Article 8. Further, the coward Tyler employed them from the safety of a supersonic jet at a safe altitude."

Two hundred feet isn't high and 540 knots isn't supersonic.

"Following orders is not justification for murdering innocent civilians as finding an enemy spread over a large area does not excuse employing unjust means for attacking that enemy. Our common sense tells us all these things. We have before us the rare opportunity to bring a small justice to a far land, and in the name of humanity, I charge you to do your duty. Do not let this cold-blooded murderer escape the consequences of his actions." She sat down to a burst of applause from the audience.

Do I get a vote?

Bouchard checked the time. "As the hour is approaching one o'clock, we are in recess until three this afternoon. He tapped his gavel as the commentators in the booth assured their audiences that Denise Du Milan had driven the last nail into Gus Tyler's coffin.

* * * * *

Marci Lennox followed her cameraman as he cleared a path through the mass of people marching down the broad boulevard leading to the palace of the International Criminal Court. She keyed her microphone. "The police estimate that over ten thousand people have poured into this quiet seaside city. Ahead of us, you can see the Dutch police lining the sidewalk and sealing off the palace from the demonstrators." The cameraman panned the area and focused on Ewe Reiss holding his sign proclaiming

HIGHWAY OF DEATH

A Far Justice

in front of the police line. Another demonstrator stood beside him holding a sign proclaiming

NOT GUILTY

It was an image made to order for TV.

"These two demonstrators are a microcosm of what we are experiencing here on this cold and clear day where the demonstrators appear evenly split as to the guilt of Gus Tyler." She continued to walk. "This is a very orderly and somber demonstration, but you can feel the tension building underneath, awaiting the spark to set it off." She was off the air.

"That's a good one, Marci," her director in New York said. "Now get the hell out of there."

"Do you know something I don't?"

"I know a powder keg when I see one."

* * * * *

Hank stood and slowly scanned the room, letting the moment build. *You're spinning your wheels,* Gus thought. *The verdict was in before I was arrested.*

"If it may please the court," Hank began. "August Tyler is a warrior who does not run from the truth. He is a fighting man who has willingly risked his life fighting for the freedom of others. And for this, he stands before this court accused of war crimes. August Tyler is a pilot, a master of his aircraft with the heart of a hunter. He is that rare breed of aviator called a fighter pilot. He blends skill and ability with intelligence and dedication that few pilots can match. He follows the rules of his profession diligently and with honor. And for this, he is accused of the willful killing of civilians, and employing prohibited weapons.

"But this is an honorable court, as Alex Melwin and Marie Doorn proved at the price of their own lives. It is entirely proper and fitting that we should hold to account any individual who falls within the jurisdiction of this court, and has committed crimes within the court's purview, for we are an honorable court."

Bouchard's face flushed and he raised his gavel, glaring at Hank. Hank mouthed the words "go ahead." For a moment, they silently locked wills. "May I continue?" Hank asked. Bouchard lowered his gavel. "August Tyler freely acknowledges he participated in the Gulf War. He was one of the many who helped free over two million people from the grinding oppression of a ruthless dictator who invaded their country. Can there ever be a more just war? And for this, this court would take his freedom from him. But no one in this room that I know of can wear a similar badge of courage.

"Did anyone in this courtroom watch August Tyler's face when he had to relive the hell he created on Mutlah Ridge? That is the price an honorable and decent man pays for war. He never denied that he employed cluster bomb units on the fleeing Iraqis. And for this, he is being prosecuted as a war criminal. Supposedly, he is before the court as a Panamanian citizen, a country that did not participate in the Gulf War. Yet, he is a citizen of the United States, born of United States citizens. He is not a citizen of Panama. The prosecutor relies on the concept of 'universal jurisdiction' as a basis for prosecuting August Tyler. But there is no chain of jurisdiction, universal or temporal, binding him to this court."

Gus studied Denise's reactions as Hank went through the evidence, tearing it apart. *She's a cool one.*

"You have before you August Tyler's personnel record," Hank continued. "It would have been easy to portray Natividad Gomez as a spy who betrayed the trust of her fellow countrymen. But really, she is only a woman in love who was badly used by her lover. Further, there is nothing in his record to be rationalized away or explained. It offers you a snapshot of his career, a career marked by dedication and professionalism. We welcome it into evidence. Then there is the testimony of Davis Armiston, a politically ambitious man deficient in flying skills. His motivation speaks for itself.

"With the exception of Hassan Ghamby, a truck driver who was transporting goods stolen from the Kuwaitis, the prosecution has failed to directly link August Tyler's attack on the convoy to a single civilian death." Hank pointed at the pile of evidence stacked on the clerk's desk. "Yet the only evidence of Ghamby's death is the word of one witness, a scarred and politically motivated man, and an identification bracelet taken off a body by a doctor. Given the turmoil and chaos of war, it is reasonable to assume that body was Hassan Ghamby. But given the looting and pillaging that was rampant among the Iraqis, it is only an assumption, and not a proven fact.

"Ultimately, the prosecutor's case rests on the tainted deposition submitted by Watban Horan. Yet the one witness who could substantiate or refute the deposition entered into evidence against August Tyler was not allowed to testify because defense counsel did not adhere to court procedures. Such is the game of justice."

Denise shot a sharp look at Bouchard who picked up his gavel. *Touched a nerve there,* Gus thought. Hank held up his hand and Bouchard laid the gavel down.

Hank continued to review the witnesses and evidence. "In the end, it comes down to a very simple question. What law applies? Is it the Rome Statute creating the International Criminal Court, which came into force some eleven years after Mutlah Ridge, or is it the international law of armed conflict? Need I remind the court that under the law of armed conflict, Gus Tyler has committed no crime?"

He turned to Denise. "The prosecutor appealed to our humanity and sense of justice when she said 'We have before us the rare opportunity to bring a small justice to a far land.' But how can we bring justice to a far land without first establishing justice in this court, in this land? A far justice begins here."

He sat down as applause erupted from Gus's rooting section and spread across the room. Bouchard banged his gavel and slowly regained control of his court.

Gus checked his watch. *Thirty-one minutes. Not bad.*

Bouchard mustered as much dignity as he could. "The chamber will now retire to consider a verdict. The court stands adjourned."

The clerk popped to his feet. "Please stand as the judges retire."

The clock is running, Gus thought, feeling sure and confident for the first time in months. He looked at Aly who nodded back.

* * * * *

Hank paced the carpet in front of his desk. "I blew it."

Catherine exhaled in frustration. "You knew the odds when you went in. Be honest, it's an ego thing. You hate to lose."

Hank slumped in his chair. "I know."

She leaned over him, her cheek next to his. "No one could have done better. Now let's go to dinner."

Aly ran into the office. She grabbed the remote control and cycled the channel to CNC-TV. Marci Lennox was seated in a studio with a bearded young man. "With us is Hans Gerhardt who is considered the world's leading expert on electronic voice authentication." She listened attentively as Gerhardt confirmed the voice they had just heard on the CD was Henri Scullanois. "Can you determine when the conversation took place?" Gerhardt said he could not, but the recording was authentic.

The screen cycled and Liz Gordon, the channel's premier anchor in New York, appeared. "Marci, I have with me the Netherlands' ambassador to the United Nations, Doctor Peter Rohr. Dr. Rohr, while we cannot reveal the source of this recording, I can assure you the source is unimpeachable. How will your government respond?"

The ambassador cleared his throat. "Well, I must confer with my government. However, if what you say is true, there does appear to be compelling evidence that the French minister of foreign affairs was in collaboration with officials in Beijing to use the International Criminal Court to bring undue influence to bear on the United States and turn it to political advantage not only in the United Nations but within the European community."

"Dr. Rohr, the political alliance between Scullanois and the prosecutor's husband, Chrestien Du Milan, is well known. What are the implications, not only for the trial of Colonel Tyler, but for the United Nations?"

"I cannot speculate on that. But as you are well aware, there is a growing dissatisfaction among my countrymen with the trial of Colonel Tyler, and the exact role of the prosecutor, Denise Du Milan, in all this must be determined."

The screen cycled back to a split image of Gordon and Marci Lennox in the Netherlands. "Marci, what has been the reaction in Europe?"

"It's far too early to tell," Marci answered. "But a high Dutch official I spoke to minutes ago said, and this is a direct quote, 'It certainly raises the specter of a Doctor Strangelove prosecutor.' What effect this will have on the three judges who have entered deliberations remains to be seen." The newscast broke for a commercial.

Hank connected the dots. "So that's what Westcot was up to."

"Let's go talk to Gus," Catherine said.

* * * * *

Without a word, Hank opened his percom to jam the bugs in Gus's cell. Cassandra announced that they were secure and called the Mayo in the States. Hank stepped outside to give Gus some privacy. Michelle answered on the first ring. Her voice matched the concern on her face. "The news is so confused over here," she told him.

"It's confused over here too," Gus replied. "Don't give up hope."

"We won't," she said. "Here's Mom." Michelle swung the phone's camera around as Clare walked across the room pushing a walker. She was wearing a stylish exercise outfit and moved with surprising confidence.

"Hello darling," Clare said. They talked for a few moments and she reassured him she would be walking unaided in a few more days. "I'm making amazing progress. Now, what's happening over there?"

"I'm not sure what's going to happen now." He lowered his voice so Hank couldn't hear. "I don't know when I can call again."

She understood. "Do what you have to do. We'll be here."

"I love you, Hon."

"We all love you," Clare said.

Gus broke the connection and opened the door for the lawyer. They talked for a few moments before Hank left. Gus stretched out and pretended to read and ignored the TV that he suspected was again monitoring his every move and word. He turned on the shower, peeled off his shirt, and absentmindedly threw it over the TV. He quickly shed the rest of his clothes, but rather than get in the shower, he unwound the roll of paper towels where he had hidden the sleeping pill. He placed it in his pants pocket and jumped in the shower just before the automatic valve turned off the water. When he retrieved his shirt, the monitor recorded his wet head of hair.

An hour later, Therese Derwent knocked on his open door. "May I come in?" She held up two carrier bags with dinner. He motioned her in and she unpacked a dinner. They carried on a light conversation until they were almost finished. Slowly, he ratcheted up the tension, venting his anger and despair.

"You really dislike Bouchard," she said. "Does he remind you of anyone?"

"You mean like my father? No, not at all." They continued to talk as Gus cleared the table. He poured the wine in plastic cups and handed her one. She sipped as she listened to him talk and slowly unwind. The lights blinked, warning them they had fifteen minutes to lights out.

"I do have to go," she said.

"I'm enjoying the conversation," he said.

She nodded and reached for the phone. "I'm with my patient. We require privacy, and leave the door unlocked."

"They'll think you're spending the night," Gus told her.

"It doesn't matter what they think," she replied. "You are my patient." She gave him a beautiful smile. "And a friend."

Gus hated what he had to do as he paced their conversation. He walked to the kitchenette and refilled their cups. He dropped the sleeping pill he had hoarded into her wine and padded back to the table as the lights dimmed. She took the cup.

* * * * *

A Far Justice

Gus was worried. Therese was curled up on his bunk, not moving. The pill had worked much faster than he had expected and he was afraid that it might have been too strong for someone her size. He checked his watch. It was 1:20 and she had been asleep for over three hours. Her breathing seemed normal and he covered her with a second blanket. He rummaged through her handbag and found her ID card. He stepped to the door and depressed the latch. The guards had left it unlocked for her as she had ordered.

He stepped into the corridor, surprised to find it was in half-light. *The frugal Dutch*, he reasoned. He moved down the corridor towards the gated entry point. *Be asleep.* He swiped her ID card through the lock and heard it click open. He walked through and looked into the control room. The guard's head was slumped forward. Gus ghosted down the corridor and into Therese's office near the main entrance. Once inside, he took a deep breath and sat down. His knees were weak. He switched on the light and found the psychiatrist's handbag. He rummaged through it and found her regular badge. His mouth was dry and he filled a glass with water. He guzzled half of it. He took another drink and held it in his mouth, letting it trickle down his throat.

He wasn't sure what to do next. Rather than return to the main corridor, he tested the rear door to her office. It was locked. But there was no groove in the lock to swipe the ID card. He held her regular badge against the lock and was rewarded with the familiar click. He cracked the door and glanced outside. *A service corridor.* He looked for a video monitor but couldn't find one. He stepped into the dimly lit passageway and closed the door behind him. Again, he searched for a monitor. He found it mounted directly above his head, rotating back and forth. *Damn.* He watched it sweep back and forth, timing how long he had to reach the end of the narrow hall and get through the next door.

The camera rotated past his position and he ran for the door. The lock was different and neither the ID card nor the badge worked. The camera was swinging back toward his end of the passageway. Desperate, he ran the edge of the ID card down the door jamb finding the lock bolt. He pressed and the bolt slipped back. He darted through the door, hoping he had made it in time. Much to his surprise, he was standing in the center hall of the business offices. *I'm inside the administration block. That explains the regular lock to the service corridor.* He walked quickly to the heavy gate at the entry control point. Again, the ID card worked and he stepped into the lighted main entrance hall. *Ah shit!*

A guard was sitting behind the console, his back to Gus and facing a bank of monitors. Gus's inner Klaxon was in full alarm. He was out of time and ideas. *When in doubt do something, even if it's wrong.* It was a suicidal fallback position and he knew it. He marched up to the guard's console as if he owned the place. He studied the monitors over the guard's shoulder. The guard wheezed and snored lightly. *Complacency: the price of constant vigilance.*

He studied the control panel, trying to figure out the switchology. It was simple; the control button for each gate was directly under that gate's monitor. The guard snored again. Gus walked around to the front of the console, reached over, and pressed the button under the monitor for the main gate. He heard a faint click and the heavy door slid back. He walked into the entry rotunda and the gate slid closed behind him.

He walked straight ahead, certain a guard was drawing down on him. He pushed through a heavy glass door and stepped into the street. *Okay Aly, where are you?* He trotted down the steps and turned left. A blue Mercedes drove up and stopped. The window rolled down. "Get in," a voice said.

42

Amsterdam

The phone rang at 5:13 Saturday morning. Hank fumbled for it. "Yeah." He sat up in bed. "When?" He listened for a moment. "We'll get there as soon as we can." He nudged Catherine awake. "Gus escaped last night. That's all I know." He jumped out of bed and turned on his percom. "Cassandra, are you there?" There was no answer. "Must be out of juice." He leaned the percom against an electric outlet to recharge while he dressed. Four minutes later he picked it up, but it was still dead. Catherine was ready and they ran for the elevator.

Maarn, the Netherlands

Gus sat back in his chair and cradled the hot cup of coffee in his hands as a young man cleared away the remains of an exquisite breakfast. He gazed out the window of the sunroom of the old manor house where he had taken refuge. He wasn't surprised when Max Westcot walked in. Gus came out of his seat and they shook hands, still two old friends. "I can't thank you enough for helping Clare and now all this." He waved at his surroundings. "I can never repay you."

"Actually, you have," Westcot replied. "It isn't often we make a medical breakthrough like that and Clare was the key. There's a lot more to it than we told you, and part of it was very painful at times. As for the ICC, I was more than happy to get involved when the President asked."

"By the way, where are we and how safe is this place?"

"We're less than fifty miles from The Hague, but I don't think the Dutch are too interested in finding you. Not after yesterday." He laughed. "You really had us jumping through the hoops when Aly called Suzanne. You had no way of knowing that we were going to spring you. It was all in the works for when the Dutch transported you to a more secure prison."

"And if they turned me over to the Iraqis?"

"We would have intercepted the jet taking you there. Walking out on your own made things a lot easier. You'll have to stay here for a few days while we arrange to transport you to Morocco, which is not a member of the ICC. From there, it's a piece of cake to get you to the States."

Gus thought for a few moments. "I need to take care of some business first."

"This had better be important."

"It's something I have to do." Gus leaned forward, savoring the idea. "But I need a little help."

The Hague

The forecourt to the palace was awash with TV crews, reporters, and spectators when Hank and Catherine drove past. The cab driver drove around to the rear of the building and let them off at the staff entrance. But they were immediately surrounded by a crush of reporters. Marci Lennox's burly bodyguard bulldozed his way through the crowd, clearing a path for Marci. "Hank," she called, "do you have a statement?"

"Sorry," he called, "I'm still under the court's gag order."

"Is the United States behind his escape?" she shouted.

"At this point, you know more than I do." He pushed his way through the gauntlet with Catherine right behind him.

Aly was alone in the office, waiting for them. "Any news?" Hank asked. She shook her head and Hank looked at Catherine.

"You need to speak to Max Westcot," she advised.

Aly punched at the phone while Hank tried to call Cassandra on his percom. But it was still dead. The phone buzzed and Hank answered. Winslow James, the deputy charge of mission, was on the line and demanded his immediate presence at the Embassy.

* * * * *

Winslow James was icy politeness when Hank and Catherine arrived at the Embassy. "The ambassador is in teleconference with the Secretary of State. The Dutch government is demanding an explanation that we cannot provide."

"I'm in the dark as much as you are," Hank replied. He hoped it wouldn't become a permanent condition.

James didn't answer and buzzed the ambassador, telling him that Hank and Catherine had arrived. "The ambassador will see you immediately." He led the way into the ambassador's office and introduced them.

"That will be all, Winslow," the ambassador said. James nodded coldly and left.

"That's why he's so frosted," Catherine murmured as they sat down. "He's out of the loop."

"Well," the ambassador said, "your Colonel Tyler has certainly embarrassed our Dutch hosts. Apparently, he simply walked out of the prison last night and disappeared. There was a woman involved, the prison psychiatrist. She was found in his cell this morning. He had drugged her with one of the sleeping pills she had given him and he then used her ID card to open the gates." The ambassador tried to play it straight, but he was obviously enjoying the moment. "The guards were asleep at the switch, so to speak." He gave up any pretenses and laughed heartily. "By the way, you wouldn't happen to know where he is?"

"I have no idea," Hank admitted.

"As I assured the Secretary of State." There was no doubt that the ambassador was pleased with the turn of events. "The Colonel's escape solved a major problem for the Dutch, especially after the revelations about the French connection with the Chinese. It's becoming increasingly clear that the trial is a gross miscarriage of justice, but the Dutch are caught on the fence. They can't afford to anger the EU and the United States at the same time. They are more relieved than upset, and I don't think they will press the search too hard." He paused to let it register. "It would be in everyone's best interests," he added, "if you were not available for comment to the press, and then returned to the States as soon as possible. I fully expect the Senate will investigate and that you'll be called to testify in the very near future."

Hank bristled. "I'm not going to be the Senate's whipping boy on this."

"Credible denial will be essential when you're testifying before a committee," the ambassador said. "You've done your part in this. It's time to step aside." He was all charm as he stood. "Counselor, Mrs. Sutherland, thank you so much for coming."

Hank held Catherine's arm as they walked out. He waited until they were safely in an embassy staff car and headed back to the ICC before he vented. "What the hell is going on? I'm feeling more and more like the proverbial mushroom."

"The ambassador was very candid," Catherine replied. "Think about it."

He did. "That was the carrot to step aside."

"And the threat of a Senate investigation is the stick," she added. "The ambassador was right, let it go. You've done all you can." Catherine's cell phone buzzed with a message from Aly. She glanced at it and hesitated before punching it off. "Bouchard's called the court into a special session Monday morning."

"Well," Hank said, "we're not going home quite yet."

* * * * *

Denise stood at the big window of her fourth-floor office. Her arms were clasped tightly and her head was lowered as she studied the demonstrators swirling down the street below her. Even without her glasses, she could easily read the signs that proclaimed

DR STRANGELOVE LIVES HERE

An arrowhead of other demonstrators cut into the first group chanting "Guilty! Guilty!" Then as rapidly as it had started the two groups separated, going in opposite directions. She willed Chrestien to return her call, but the phone remained silent.

Denise returned to her desk and sat down. She picked up the remote control and switched on the DVD to replay the last day in court while she followed along on the printed transcript. She uncapped her OMAS and underlined Hank's key arguments. She circled the phrase 'Ultimately, the Prosecutor's case rests on the tainted evidence submitted by Watban Horan.'

The office intercom buzzed at her. She checked the name on the readout. It was the assistant prosecutor and, suddenly, she knew. "You asshole," she muttered in English. There was no doubt that he was the 'unimpeachable source' of the intercepted telephone conversations between Scullanois and Beijing. But how did he come by it? Her anger flared. In her world, he was a piss ant of a man, not worth the time of day. She ignored the call. Yet a voice deep inside held her to account. She had been more than ready to condemn an innocent man because he happened to be an American and it suited the politics of the moment. She was very much part of the very system that was collapsing around her.

She closed her eyes and took a deep breath. "Damn you!" she cried, including herself in all those she indicted. Tears streamed down her face. She dropped the OMAS to the floor.

43

The Hague

Catherine was frightened as the taxi nudged through the crowd surrounding the Palace. A protestor banged his sign off the roof and yelled an obscenity in German. "Where are the police?" the Dutch driver said in English. "There are times when I'm ashamed of my country."

"I have the same problem," Hank grumbled. The driver stopped at the security barrier to the rear entrance where four very troubled guards refused to wave the cab through. "Looks like they're better at keeping people out than in." Hank got out and partially closed the door. "Cathy, all things considered, it's time to get the hell out of Dodge. I think you'd be safer at home, in the States."

She pushed the door open and got out. "I wouldn't miss this for the world." She glared at the guards who split apart and let them enter.

As usual, Aly was waiting in the office with the morning newspapers and coffee. "You'd think Gus is the most dangerous man on the face of the earth," she said, dumping the newspapers in front of Hank. He glanced at the headlines. "Isn't your government going to do anything?"

"Aly, I just don't know." He glanced at the clock. "Time to go."

The courtroom went silent as Hank and Aly took their places at the defense table. "Good morning, Madame Prosecutor," Hank said. Denise ignored him and looked straight ahead. The spectators buzzed in anticipation but quieted as the clerk announced the judges entrance. Hank studied Richter and Della

Sante, trying to read them as Bouchard went through the opening ritual.

Bouchard cleared his throat and looked at Hank over the top of his reading glasses. "As you may know, this chamber met over the weekend in its efforts to achieve a verdict. We are nearing that goal. However, the escape of the defendant at this point creates an unprecedented situation that the framers of the Rome Statute did not anticipate and therefore must be clarified. Madam Prosecutor, do you wish to address the court before we continue?"

A very subdued Denise stood. "The prosecutor only wishes to remind the court that flight by the defendant presupposes the assumption of guilt by the defendant." She sat down and Bouchard nodded at Hank.

Hank stepped to the podium. "If it may please the court . . ."

Bouchard interrupted him. "It does not." Applause swept through the audience.

Hank handed a blue-covered petition to the clerk. "Article Sixty-three of the Rome Statute requires the accused to be present during the trial. Without the defendant's presence, we cannot continue here." He sat down.

Bouchard allowed a little smile. "The court has anticipated your petition and is ready to rule." He started to read. "The absence of the accused by virtue of his escape, after testimony by witnesses, evidence presented, and final arguments made, does not preclude the trial chamber from rendering a verdict in his absence. In fact, to not do so would be a lapse of our judicial duty." He glanced at Denise before continuing. "However, the court cannot impose a sentence as long as the defendant remains *in absentia*."

The side door burst open and one of the court's security guards scurried up to the clerk's table. He whispered in the clerk's ear as his eyes kept darting at the three judges. For a moment, the clerk stared at him, not fully comprehending what he was hearing. The massive double doors at the rear swung open and every head pivoted.

Gus walked in wearing his uniform.

His medals and service ribbons were carefully in place under his pilot's wings, his shoes buffed to a bright shine, and his hair cut short in a military style. There was no doubt a warrior was in the courtroom. Jason followed close behind with three of his fellow security policemen. The four men were not in uniform but dressed in dark suits with carefully knotted red ties. Jason closed the doors behind them and the four men stood easily by, guarding the door.

Gus took six steps and halted when he reached Toby Person. He threw his old comrade-in-arms a sharp salute before continuing down the aisle. Every eye followed him but instead of stepping into the dock, he joined Hank and Aly at the defense table. Gus nodded at the bench. "Your Honors, I apologize for being late." He sat down.

The clerk hit the panic button under his table and the side door burst open as six of the court's security force charged through. They headed straight for Gus. "Halt!" Jason ordered. The six men skidded to a stop and looked at each other. "We're not armed," Jason reassured them, opening his coat. While the guards carried Mace and radios, the court did not allow them weapons. Jason jerked his head at the side door, his face hard. It was an unspoken command to leave. They quickly retreated, not willing to challenge the Americans. The first security guard, who was still standing beside the clerk, looked at Bouchard whose face had gone deathly pale. The guard glanced over his shoulder as his six companions disappeared out the door. He hurried to join them.

"Please continue," Gus said, his voice full of command.

Bouchard's mouth opened but no words came out. Saliva dribbled out the corner of his mouth and he slumped forward. Della Sante was at his side immediately. "Call the medics!" she ordered.

"I'm a doctor," Toby said. He was out of his seat and hobbled to the bench where he leaned over the comatose Bouchard. "He's suffering a stroke." He started CPR as pandemonium broke out among the spectators.

* * * * *

Marci was on the TV, splitting the screen with Liz Gordon in New York. "I have never witnessed anything so electrifying in my entire career. Gus Tyler's entrance was a moment timed to perfection and a challenge to the court's authority. Yet at the same time, he was yielding to the court, but on his own terms."

"Where is he and what is happening right now?" Gordon asked.

"Colonel Tyler is in the defense counsel's offices with Hank Sutherland and four bodyguards led by his son. The Reverend Person is reported also to be with them. Justice Bouchard is in the hospital and the latest report indicates he suffered both a heart attack and a stroke. He is in critical condition and not expected to survive. The Dutch police refuse to enter the palace and claim it is beyond their jurisdiction. However, the court's own security guards, who are not allowed to carry weapons, want nothing to do with Colonel Tyler's son and his bodyguards. I might add that all four are huge men and Jason Tyler is an overpowering force in himself. These are men no one wants to trifle with."

"So is this a standoff of some type?" Gordon asked.

"I'm not sure. The two judges, Della Sante and Richter, have met with the presidency of the court and are now closeted with President Relieu. We can only assume they are going ahead and are still considering a verdict."

"I think it is safe to say that there is definitely more to come," Gordon said.

"Indeed there is, Liz. This is Marci Lennox standing by in The Hague." They were off the air.

"Marci," Gordon said, still maintaining the downlink, "good work. We're out in front on this one and swamping CNN, Fox, and the other networks. An interview with Person will bury them." She checked her watch. "Make it happen in ninety minutes and it will lead the news tonight. We're talking a ratings blow out."

"I can do that," Marci said.

* * * * *

Aly was back from the canteen pushing a cart laden with sandwiches, salads, and drinks. "Lunch," she sang. She maneuvered through the crowded office passing out the food. She stopped beside Toby. "How are you feeling? I have some hot soup if you would prefer that."

"My fever broke over the weekend and I'm weak as a kitten but feeling much better. Soup would be fine." She handed him a bowl.

"Did you hear anything at the canteen?" Catherine asked.

"No one really knows anything but everyone has an opinion. I did hear that Della Sante asked for the verdict guidelines, but I don't know what that means."

"It means," Hank replied, "that they've reached a decision." He paced the floor and stopped at the window overlooking the forecourt. "Look at that. It's deserted."

"Everyone is holding their breath," Gus said.

"Gus," Hank said, "whose idea was it that you come back?"

"All mine," Gus answered. "I wanted to show the bastards that I wasn't afraid of them and make it clear that I'm not some common criminal."

"Then you always intended to go back?" Catherine asked.

"No. But Max brought me up to speed on what was going down, and I had a quick change of plans."

The phone buzzed and Aly picked it up. She listened for a few moments and hung up. "The court will reconvene at nine o'clock tomorrow morning."

"That was fast," Jason said.

The phone rang again and Aly answered. "Hank, she said, "please turn on your percom." She dropped the phone into its cradle. "In private."

"Was that Cassandra?" Hank asked.

"It was a woman with an American accent. I didn't recognize the voice and the screen was blank."

Hank beckoned for Catherine to follow him into his inner office. She closed the door behind them and moved out of the percom's field of view. Hank opened the cover and a woman's image came on the screen. But it was not the computer generated Cassandra. This was a very plain, very dowdy, middle-aged woman with salt and pepper streaked hair. "Cassandra?" he asked.

"This is the real me. Is Catherine with you?" Hank motioned his wife to join him. "There's nothing more we can do to help

363

which is why Mr. Westcot cut us off. But there are a few things you probably should know. Our ambassador to the UN submitted a resolution for the Security Council to censure France. It's a dead issue and isn't going anywhere, but it was enough to force the issue into the open and upset France's applecart. The EU is making ominous noises and France is running for cover. The foreign minister, Henri Scullanois, along with his buddy, Chrestien Du Milan, are taking the fall on this one. The UN is actually showing some backbone and China is looking for a compromise."

"What's happening with the court?" Hank asked. "I don't have a feel for it."

"Our sense of the situation," Cassandra said, "indicates they are cutting their losses and want to be rid of Gus, and you, the quicker the better."

"Cassandra," Catherine asked, "does Max Westcot know you're talking to us?"

Cassandra shook her head. "I didn't want to go without saying good-by." The screen went blank.

"Why did she do that?" Hank wondered. "Westcot will probably fire her when he finds out."

"Because she's a woman," Catherine answered. She wanted to tell him that Cassandra loved him, but she was certain he would not understand. They rejoined the others in the outer office. "Where's Toby and Jason?" Catherine asked.

Aly looked up from her desk. "Toby's down in the main courtroom doing a live interview with Marci Lennox. Jason went with him."

"No harm in that," Hank said.

* * * * *

Marci took her cue and looked directly into the camera. "I'm in the main courtroom of the International Criminal Court in the Hague with the Reverend Tobias Person." The camera panned backed to include Toby sitting in his wheelchair with the judges' bench in the background. "Reverend Person," she began.

"Please call me Toby."

Marci nodded. "Thank you, Toby, for talking to me. First, please let me extend my condolences, and those of my friends and colleagues for the recent loss of your wife and family. I know it must have come as a great shock when you learned your mission had been destroyed."

Toby nodded. "Thank you, but it wasn't a shock."

Marci blinked, temporarily at a loss for words. "I don't understand."

"I live and work in a very dangerous part of the world, Marci. Everyone at Mission Awana knew the hazards and the dangers. We live with that knowledge everyday of our lives."

"I know many of our viewers are wondering why you didn't take your wife and family to safety when you could."

Toby never hesitated. "Because that was their home, their world. D'Na, my wife, dedicated her life to making it a better place for her children. It was my privilege to be a part of that."

"But it was only by chance that you were spared."

Toby smiled gently. "I was spared because there is still work for me to do."

"I noticed you did not say 'The Lord's work.'"

Again the smile. "I do believe that."

"You must find it extremely disappointing that you came here for nothing."

The camera zoomed in on Toby's face as he fixed Marci with calm gaze that astounded her. "I believe there's a lesson here for the world. If ever there was an innocent man, it is Gus Tyler. He fought a war that needs no justification. The facts speak for themselves, and fighting that war was simply the right thing to do."

Above all, Marci was a journalist, not afraid to ask the hard questions, to follow the trail wherever it led. "But by defending Colonel Tyler, aren't you justifying your participation in that war?"

"Marci, we were fighting to correct a terrible wrong when there was no other remedy. Yes, I killed the enemy. And yes, in doing that I killed innocent people who were simply caught up in the way of war. I carry that burden with me every day of my life, as I carry the burden of my family's death. But we accomplished our mission." He gestured at the bench of justice with its three empty chairs. "There is no justice here, only a sad collection of people hiding behind a thin veneer of civilization, merely spectators to all the wrongs of the world. So in a pitiful attempt to soothe their consciences, and in the mistaken belief that war can be civilized, they judge those who were in the arena, fighting a war they could not."

"But mistakes were made," Marci said. "Shouldn't someone be held accountable? Isn't that what justice is all about?"

"Marci, in the midst of war terrible forces are set in motion. We stumble, we make mistakes, we go forward, and we fight to end it, the quicker the better. That is the way of war. All we can do is pick up the pieces afterwards and try to make a better peace. Because of Gus Tyler and many others like him, I think we did that. However, we all know there are evil men in the world who do terrible things and should be brought to justice. But Gus Tyler isn't one of them. This court failed because it couldn't make that distinction."

"So you are condemning the court?"

"There was only politics here, Marci, not justice. The court did not make the world a safer place."

"That is a hard verdict. Perhaps we should leave it there. But Toby, what are you going to do now?"

"Go back and rebuild."

"But why?"

"For D'Na and my children. I don't want their legacy to die with them."

Marci turned to the camera, her eyes moist with tears. She paused. "This is Marci Lennox from the Hague." She bowed her head and lowered her microphone.

44

The Hague

The glass double doors to her offices were locked and the lights were out when Denise arrived Tuesday morning. She fumbled with her ID card and finally managed to unlock the doors and turn on the lights. She looked around and not seeing anyone, walked into her private office.

The morning edition of Le Monde was on her desk where someone had laid it. "Ah, my loyal staff," she said to herself in French. The headline screamed

TRAÎTRESSE!

Without sitting down, she quickly scanned the lead article that labeled her as a Dr. Strangelove who had betrayed France and perverted the course of justice in what was being called 'The China Affair.' Standing immediately behind her, but not quite as guilty, was Henri Scullanois who had submitted his resignation and gone into seclusion.

The whereabouts of Chrestien Du Milan was unknown and he could not be reached for a comment, but his lawyer said he was filing for a divorce. Another headline proclaimed, in English,

MAKE THE WORLD SAFER!

She didn't have to read the story to know where that came from. Marci Lennox's interview with Toby Person had captured the news and had ignited an explosion, pitting the staunch defenders of the court against its critics and Gus's defenders.

Denise walked to the window and studied the huge crowd filling the street below. "Vultures," she said aloud. As if by magic, the crowd parted as an ambulance nudged its way to the court. "Person," she muttered. Denise donned her black robe and adjusted the white dickey. She glanced in a full-length mirror hating the image before her. She quickly shook out her hair and let it fall to her shoulders in massive disarray. She needed something to carry into court and picked up an elegant leather folder. Her eyes found the OMAS pen that was still lying on the floor. She stepped on it and slowly pivoted. It cracked and black ink stained the carpet as she walked away. She stood by the window, the folder clasped to her breast as she waited.

* * * * *

Aly gasped when she switched on the lights in the office. Gus, Jason, and his three fellow security policemen were sprawled out around the office, still asleep. It was an assault on Aly's Dutch sensibilities and she glared at Jason. "Clean it up before Hank and Catherine arrive." Jason tried to explain that things were going to get messy when five men had to camp out overnight but she wasn't having any of it. "I'm going to the canteen and when I get back, this had better be spotless." She dropped a clean uniform shirt for Gus and Jason's shaving kit on her desk. "You all need to shave," she ordered. She jerked her head in the direction of the restroom and walked out.

"Now that is one tough lady," one of the security cops said.

"Tell me," Jason muttered as they dressed and went to work. They were still cycling in and out of the restroom when Hank and Catherine wheeled Toby in.

"How's it going?" Gus asked. The two men talked for a few minutes and it was clear that Toby was still weak but well on the road to recovery. "We saw your interview with Marci Lennox last night," Gus said.

"It's all over the TV," Catherine added.

Hank smiled. "You blew 'em out of the water, Toby. If that doesn't get a few folks to thinking, nothing ever will. One thing's for damn sure, Marci got max play with this one." He humphed. "She'll probably get an Emmy out of it."

Gus sat beside Toby. "I don't think there's any way I can thank you enough." Toby arched an eyebrow, not understanding. Gus tried to find the right words. "I feel responsible for what happened at the mission, by sending Jason there."

"Jason just happened to be in the wrong place at the wrong time," Toby said. "Stop blaming yourself."

Jason shot Aly a knowing look and she answered with a little nod. "When are you going back?" Jason asked.

"As soon as possible," Toby replied.

"You totally astound me," Gus said.

A gentle look spread across Toby's face. "Do you remember what you said after Mutlah Ridge when I asked you why we do what we do? You said, 'There is an obligation to serve that we must honor.' It was true then, it's true now."

"Yeah, but we don't talk about it. Doesn't go with the image."

"Time to go to court," Aly said.

* * * * *

Catherine leaned across the bar and spoke in a low voice when Denise entered the courtroom. "How can anyone look so beautiful and so devastated? She's Marie Antoinette going to the guillotine." As one, Gus, Aly, and Hank twisted around to see.

"Or Mary Queen of Scots," Hank said.

"I'm voting for Anne Boleyn," Gus added.

"Stop it," Aly commanded.

The door behind the bench opened. Relieu, wearing a blue robe, led Della Sante and Richter to their seats. Relieu sat down in Bouchard's seat as the clerk called the court to order. He opened a folder and read. "It is with sadness and regret that we must announce Justice Gaston Bouchard cannot continue because of ill health and must withdraw from this court. In accordance with Article Seventy-four of the Rome Statute, the presidency must replace a member of a trial chamber if a member is unable to continue. After due deliberation, I was appointed to fill the vacancy.

"Further, Article Seventy-four states 'The judges shall attempt to achieve unanimity in their decision, failing which the decision shall be taken by a majority of the judges.' However, given the late stage of the current proceedings, my participation in any deliberations would require rehearing the entire trial."

"Which means Toby takes the stand," Hank whispered to Gus. "Which is the last thing they want." He couldn't help himself and asked in loud voice, "Where's Henri?"

Relieu ignored him. "As it is still possible to achieve a majority verdict without a third vote, the presidency of the court has ruled that Justices Della Sante and Richter must continue and try to reach a verdict without my participation in the deliberations. They have done so. Unfortunately, they have not been able to unanimously agree."

"For shame!" a man shouted from the rear. Two court security guards escorted the man out as the audience buzzed with anticipation.

Catherine leaned forward. "You hung the court."

"Thanks to Gus," Hank said.

Relieu rapped for order. "When the court is not unanimous in its verdict, the trial chamber is required to state the views of the minority, which, in this case, is twofold."

A loud murmur swept through the spectators and Richter tapped his microphone until it was quiet. "The question of the defendant's guilt is not in question." He recapped the elements of each charge and the evidence that proved Gus's guilt. He droned on, summarizing the legal logic that justified a guilty verdict. He finally reached the end. "In view of the above and after careful deliberation, I find the defendant, August Tyler, guilty as charged." Loud applause surged through the spectators and Relieu let it ride and build. Finally, the spectators quieted.

Now it was Della Sante's turn. "The question of Colonel Tyler's guilt . . ." She was interrupted by a collective gasp for using Gus's proper title. She scowled at the spectators. "August Tyler earned his rank with honorable service to his country and should be so acknowledged. As I was saying, the question of Colonel Tyler's guilt is overshadowed by two erroneous interpretations of the Rome Statue. First, Colonel Tyler is not subject to the court's jurisdiction as he is a citizen of the United States, which was not, nor is now, a signatory to the Rome Statute, and hence, not a member of the court. While I personally believe that the court can reach back in time and prosecute crimes against humanity, this capability must be exercised with extreme care and diligence, applies only to members of the court, and can only proceed at the behest of the member party.

"Second, at the time he employed the weapons in question, the Statute's Elements of Crimes did not prohibit them for the simple fact that the Rome Statute and the court did not exist. A fundamental principle of criminal law forbids prosecution of acts that were not identified as crimes at the time they were committed. This standard is so basic that to violate it strikes at the very legitimacy of this court." She swept the audience with a stern look. "This court must be governed by the law and be above political influence.

"In the matter of the first count of willful murder, there is enough evidence to suggest that Colonel Tyler was responsible for the death of at least one civilian. However, this was not proven beyond a reasonable doubt. Therefore, I find the defendant, Colonel August Tyler, not guilty." She jerked her head, signifying she was finished.

A smattering of applause worked its way around the courtroom. Relieu waited for it to subside. "In view of the above," Relieu said, "this case is returned to the prosecutor for her consideration and the defendant is returned to the custodial State. This chamber has completed its task and stands adjourned." He stood and marched out of the courtroom with Della Sante and Richter close behind. Jason and his three companions immediately marched down the aisle and formed a human wall around Gus.

"Does that mean I go back to jail?" Gus asked.

Hank stood. "Well, the Dutch don't have jurisdiction in the palace and they aren't about to come in to get you. So that means court security has to transport you to Dutch jurisdiction."

"Which ain't gonna happen," Jason announced.

Gus took charge. "It looks like we've got a classic standoff going. Let's go back to the office and see what it takes to get out of here. Toby, you want to come with us? It might get a bit pushy." Toby readily agreed and Gus turned to leave but Therese Derwent was standing a few feet away, blocking the way, her face serious.

She nodded at him. "August Tyler, I will never understand you but I will always count you as a friend." A half smile played at her lips and she made a zooming motion with her right hand, down and away, the classic gesture of a fighter pilot peeling off and diving. Gus saluted in acknowledgement. She stepped aside as Hank pushed Toby in his wheelchair, leading a V formation out of the courtroom with Gus safely in the middle. Aly closed the huge double doors and vowed never to enter them again.

They all crowded into the elevator for the short ride to the second floor, and marched down the deserted corridor to their office suite where Max Westcot was waiting with Winslow James, the deputy charge of mission from the embassy. "What the hell is going on?" Gus demanded.

"The Dutch have released Colonel Tyler and declared him persona non grata," James said. He checked his watch. "We have twelve hours to get you out of the country."

"How did that happen?" Hank asked.

Westcot was obviously pleased with himself. "Let's just say the Dutch want nothing to do with you. Winslow here . . ."

Gus exploded and turned his anger on James. "You worthless toad!"

Westcot held up a hand. ". . . has arranged for a helicopter." He checked his watch. "It should be here any time and the Navy has a cruiser waiting off shore. Go easy on Winslow, Gus. He can make things happen. Besides, as long as he's here, no one is going to touch you."

James drew himself up to his full five feet three inches. "Colonel Tyler, I am not a brave man. However, I know my duty."

The phone rang and Aly answered. She listened and then hung up. "The court is typing up an order transferring Gus to the Iraqis. It should be signed and served within the hour."

"Some poor bastard is gonna get it shoved up his ass," Jason promised.

"Please, be calm," James urged. "The court can issue arrest warrants or transfer orders until they run out of paper. But it has no enforcement authority in itself and must rely on its members to act in its behalf. And right now, there is too high a political price to pay for the Dutch to touch you."

Hank understood and turned to James. "Thank you."

"We had to put some quid pro quos in play," James admitted, "and the Dutch realize it is in their best interests to disengage in this matter."

"I had to shut Cassandra down," Westcot added. "I don't know what got into her but she was playing havoc jamming communications. The Dutch were mightily upset so I turned her off."

"You know she did talk to me afterwards," Hank said. Westcot nodded. "Please don't fire her."

"Not to worry," Westcot said.

The phone rang again and Aly answered. Without a word, she turned on the TV. Marci Lennox was broadcasting in front of the ICC. "We've just learned that the prosecutor, Denise Du Milan, has submitted her resignation effectively immediately." The TV camera

A Far Justice

panned the crowd that was surging back and forth, pounding at the police line. "The situation is very confused here and I can only tell you that this is a very angry crowd on the verge of becoming an uncontrollable mob." The police line broke and people rushed through, coming directly at the reporter. The camera was still on and gyrating wildly as Marci and her crew ran for safety.

Overhead, a US Navy helicopter hovered into view and landed on the roof.

"That's for you," Westcot told Gus. "Let's go."

Winslow James led the way and held eight court guards at bay when they crossed the fly bridge connecting the two towers. Halfway across they stopped and took in the scene. The palace was completely surrounded by demonstrators as a black sedan pulled out of the staff entrance. The mob rocked the sedan and forced it to stop. A demonstrator broke a rear window and wrenched the door open. Even from seven floors, they could see Denise's distinctive mane of auburn hair as two men and a woman dragged her out of the car. "They've got Du Milan!" Catherine shouted.

"They'll kill her," Hank said, remembering the killing lust that had captured the mob on the Bay Bridge. "I don't see any police."

"Go get her," Toby said quietly.

Gus sighed loudly. "Gimme a break, Toby."

"It's what we do, Gus," Toby replied.

For a moment, no one moved. "Let's go," Gus ordered. He ran for the elevator with Hank, Jason, and the three security cops right behind him.

Westcot hesitated. "I can't believe I'm doing this." He ran after them and piled into the elevator. Aly and Catherine joined Toby and James at the window to watch and wait.

Far below, the seven men erupted from the building in a tight V formation, and headed straight for the sedan. Jason was on the point as they ripped into the crowd. For a brief moment, a knot of demonstrators stopped them. Jason's right hand punched at the man in front of him, his fingers curled into a hard karate fist. He drove his knuckles into the man's Adam Apple, shouting obscenities at the top of his lungs. The man went down and they pushed over his twisting body. A jolt of pure fear shot through the people caught between the charging Americans and Denise. They scrambled to get out of the way, only to be caught between the demonstrators surging forward.

But the Americans couldn't be stopped. They bulldozed a path, driving whoever couldn't get out of the way to the ground and stepping on them. They finally reached the car where a snarling woman had Denise by the hair and was throwing her around like a rag doll. Jason kicked at the woman's left knee and she collapsed, falling over Denise and dragging her head across a broken bottle lying on the ground. The jagged glass cut into her scalp, peeling it away. Gus pushed the prostrate woman aside and carefully laid Denise's bloody scalp back in place. He scooped her up in his arms, and with one hand pressed against her wound, retraced his steps, heading for safety.

A burley, wild-eyed young man made the mistake of trying to cut him off and one of the security cops came at him. The cop feinted and then drove a fist into the man's sternum, collapsing his lungs. His mouth came open as he tried to breath. But nothing happened. "Someone give him mouth-to-mouth," Jason shouted. He grabbed the man's shirt and threw him into the arms of a man and pushed them both back, clearing a path. Then they were in the palace.

"Where's the infirmary?" Gus yelled at the court's security guards who closed and barred the door. One pointed down a hall and Gus strode quickly in that direction, leaving a trail of Denise's blood on the floor. Jason and the three cops were right behind him.

Westcot bent over, his hands on his knees, and breathed deeply. He looked up at Hank. "Damn. This is more fun than owning a football team."

Gus tried to push through the double doors leading into the infirmary but they were locked. Without a word, Jason stepped around Gus and kicked the doors open. He charged through and quickly found an examination room. "Put her in here," he told his father. Gus laid Denise on the table. "Keep pressure on her scalp," Jason said as he rifled through the cabinets, finding the supplies he needed.

Denise was fully conscious, her eyes locked on Gus' face. "Why are you doing this?" she whispered.

"It's what we do," Gus answered. "Not that you would understand."

Jason pushed Gus aside and pulled on a pair of surgical gloves. "Time to stitch you up." He went to work, quickly cutting away her heavy hair and dosing the wound with Betodine. The smell of the antiseptic filled the small room. He ripped open a suture kit.

"You've done this before?" Gus asked.

"I've been getting a lot of practice lately," Jason replied.

"Are you going to use an anesthetic?"

"Hell, no. She needs to remember this. Besides, it will give her something to complain about later." He quickly tied the first stitch, talking as he worked. "You've lost a lot of blood and will probably need a transfusion." She flinched as Jason stitched her scalp closed and stopped the bleeding.

Denise reached out and touched Gus's hand. "*Merci*," she whispered. She was crying, but not from the pain. "I do under- stand."

Aly was standing in the doorway. "Gus, you've got to go. Now." She held the door for her future father-in-law and followed him out. Suddenly, Aly turned and gave Denise a contemptuous look. "You owe them." Without waiting for an answer, she spun around and hurried after Gus, leaving Denise alone.

* * * * *

Winslow James led the way onto the roof where the helicopter was waiting. Aly hugged Gus and wouldn't let go as tears streamed down her cheeks. "Did Jason tell you?" she asked.

"About you two going with Toby?" Gus replied. She nodded, her cheek cradled against his chest. "I'm so proud of you," he said. She let go and he turned to Hank. "I don't know what to say. But thank you."

"It was my pleasure," the lawyer replied. Then the old Hank was back. "Besides, it beats the hell out of teaching at Berkeley." They shook hands.

Catherine gave him a quick kiss on the cheek and stepped back as Max Westcot waved at him. "See you in the States."

"Go!" Toby said. Gus threw him a quick salute and climbed on board the helicopter. James followed him in and a crewman closed the door.

The small group clustered together and watched the helicopter as it headed out to sea. "I'm freezing," Aly said as Jason pushed Toby towards the elevator. "Before you go back to Africa, will you marry us?" "I'd be honored," Toby said. "But shouldn't your minister do it?"

"You are our minister," Jason replied. "We want to join you, as soon as I can get out of the Air Force."

Toby's eyes were still fixed on the helicopter. "Why?"

"It's something we have to do," Jason replied.

Toby understood. "You sound just like your father."

Epilogue

Riverview, Maryland

Clare got out of the car and took in the colonial-style home overlooking the Potomac River. "It's lovely," she said, "absolutely lovely. I must see the garden."

"This is where Hank first met Max," Gus told her. He rang the doorbell. "He says the garden is a thing of beauty."

Catherine Sutherland opened the door and ushered them into the sunroom with its magnificent views of the Potomac and Mount Vernon. Hank was standing next to the window with Suzanne Westcot while Max occupied the couch, smoking a cigar. "How is the family?" Catherine asked.

"We got a Christmas card from Jason and Aly last week," Gus replied. "They've got problems but they're still in the Sudan, building a new mission with Toby. Aly's expecting next month. You won't believe this, but Denise Du Milan showed up. She's affiliated with a children's program sponsored by the EU and wants to help."

"The woman's a survivor," Hank muttered.

"She seems to like Toby," Gus said.

"Poor Toby," Catherine murmured.

Westcot humphed. "The good Reverend can take care of himself. I wish he worked for me."

Clare walked over to Westcot and took his hand. It was the first time they had met, and she bent over, kissing him on the cheek. "Thank you for saving my husband."

"He saved himself," Westcot told her.

"You've done so much for us, I just don't know what to say."

"You can always say 'yes.'"

Clare smiled. "Yes to what?"

"We want Gus to run for the Senate."

Clare considered it. "Where could we live? Our daughter and her sons live with us, you know."

"We're still raising a family," Gus added.

"You can live here," Westcot replied. "This place could stand some life."

"I haven't got a clue about politics," Gus admitted.

It was Suzanne's turn. "But you have great instincts and you'll be a breath of fresh air."

Hank waved his hand. "If you need help, I'm a volunteer."

"Financing the campaign will not be a problem," Westcot promised.

Hank gave him a studied look. "It's tempting Max, and an honor. But please forgive me, I know how you work and there would be too many strings attached."

Westcot thought about it for a moment. "Other than not messing with the oil depletion allowance, there wouldn't be any."

"And if I did mess with it?"

Westcot puffed on his cigar and considered his answer. "I wouldn't be happy, but I could live with it. The offer is still open, think about it."

"We will," Gus promised.

"Would you look at that," Suzanne said, still standing at the window. "It's broad daylight and you can see the moon. I've never seen it so big."

Gus looked at his wife as he slipped back in time. The memories flooded back, and, for a moment, they were young again. "And there is nothing left remarkable beneath the visiting moon," he said.

Hank disagreed. "Nothing except courage and honor."

THE END

AFTERWORD

For those who would argue that I have misrepresented the International Criminal Court in *A Far Justice*, I urge them to read the Rome Statute, the treaty creating the ICC. While the goals of the ICC, as set forth in the preamble to the Rome Statute, are laudatory, there are several basic objections to the court's protection of individual rights and liberties. and ultimately, its ability to render just decisions.

First, the Rome Statute specifically limits the ICC's jurisdiction to states that are parties to the Statute, and to crimes that were committed after the ICC came into existence in 2002. However, many jurists and supporters of the ICC claim that the concept of universal jurisdiction, which is not embodied in the Rome Statute, extends the court's jurisdiction to states that are not parties to the court, and that the court can reach back in time to prosecute crimes that were committed before it was created.

Structurally, in the ICC there is no trial by jury, defendants do not have the unqualified right to confront the witnesses against them in court, and there is double jeopardy. Trial by jury, a defendant's right to confront witnesses in court, and freedom from double jeopardy, are individual rights guaranteed by the Constitution of the United States. While the Rome Statute incorporates an appeals process, the court itself rules on an appeal to its judgments, which, in my view, is an internal review. In short, there is no higher authority to the court's jurisdiction. It rules and then rules on its own rulings.

Finally, it comes down to a question of sovereignty, the supreme power or authority. The ICC has jurisdiction over all war crimes and crimes against humanity. In short, the ICC trumps any national legal system in these cases.

To say that I find all this troubling is an understatement, and if I have provoked the reader into a closer examination of the ICC, so much the better. But in the end, *A Far Justice* is a story of people first, and how they are caught up in the turmoil of the modern world and doing their best to survive.

ACKNOWLEDGMENTS

Writing is a lonely business and I am indebted to a small group of people who helped in the making of this book. *A Far Justice* is dedicated to the memory of Janice Hayes Perkinson, a wonderful friend and incomparable Superior Court Judge who explained the world of law in a way I could understand. John Lescroart started me on the journey and encouraged me to delve into the International Criminal Court. John Perkinson provided the legal mechanisms for this scenario that are actually coming into play. As always, William P. Wood was there at critical junctures, offering advice and saving me from many errors. Three friends helped immeasurably; Don and Judy Person with their sage advice, and Mel Marvel who took a final look at the manuscript and provided yeoman labor keeping it all in perspective. Finally, my agent, Peter Rubie, proved again he is a superb editor. To all, many thanks for the help and, as always, the errors are mine alone.

While the battle of Mutlah Ridge, the "Highway of Death," that occurred during the Gulf War of 1991, is an historical fact, the version in this story is fictitious. Nothing can detract from the courage of the men who actually engaged the enemy, and their story remains to be told.

Printed in Great Britain
by Amazon